SON OF NO MAN SERIES

TRAITOR

BOOK 6

SON OF NO MAN SERIES

TRAITOR

BOOK 6

D. LAMBERT

Traitor
Son of No Man Series Book 6
Copyright © 2023-2024 D. Lambert. All rights reserved.

4 Horsemen
Publications, Inc.

Published By: 4 Horsemen Publications, Inc.

4 Horsemen Publications, Inc.
PO Box 417
Sylva, NC 28779
4horsemenpublications.com
info@4horsemenpublications.com

Cover and Typesetting by Valerie Willis
Editor Laura Mita

Library of Congress Control Number: 2023934410

Paperback ISBN: 978-1-64450-918-0
Hardcover ISBN: 978-1-64450-919-7
Audio ISBN: 978-1-64450-921-0
E-Book ISBN: 978-1-64450-920-3

TO THOSE WHO SHARED MY JOURNEY INTO ESPAR.
I APPRECIATE YOU ALL.

Table of Contents

Prologue 1
Chapter 1 8
Chapter 2 20
Chapter 3 40
Chapter 4 57
Chapter 5 69
Chapter 6 76
Chapter 7 89
Chapter 8 104
Chapter 9 121
Chapter 10 137
Chapter 11 152
Chapter 12 160
Chapter 13 172
Chapter 14 185
Chapter 15 201
Chapter 16 213
Chapter 17 226
Chapter 18 241
Chapter 19 257
Chapter 20 272
Chapter 21 284
Chapter 22 296
Sneak Peek of A Tale of Espar His Last Name 323
Chapter 1 325
Glossary 329
Author Bio 335
Book Club Questions 337

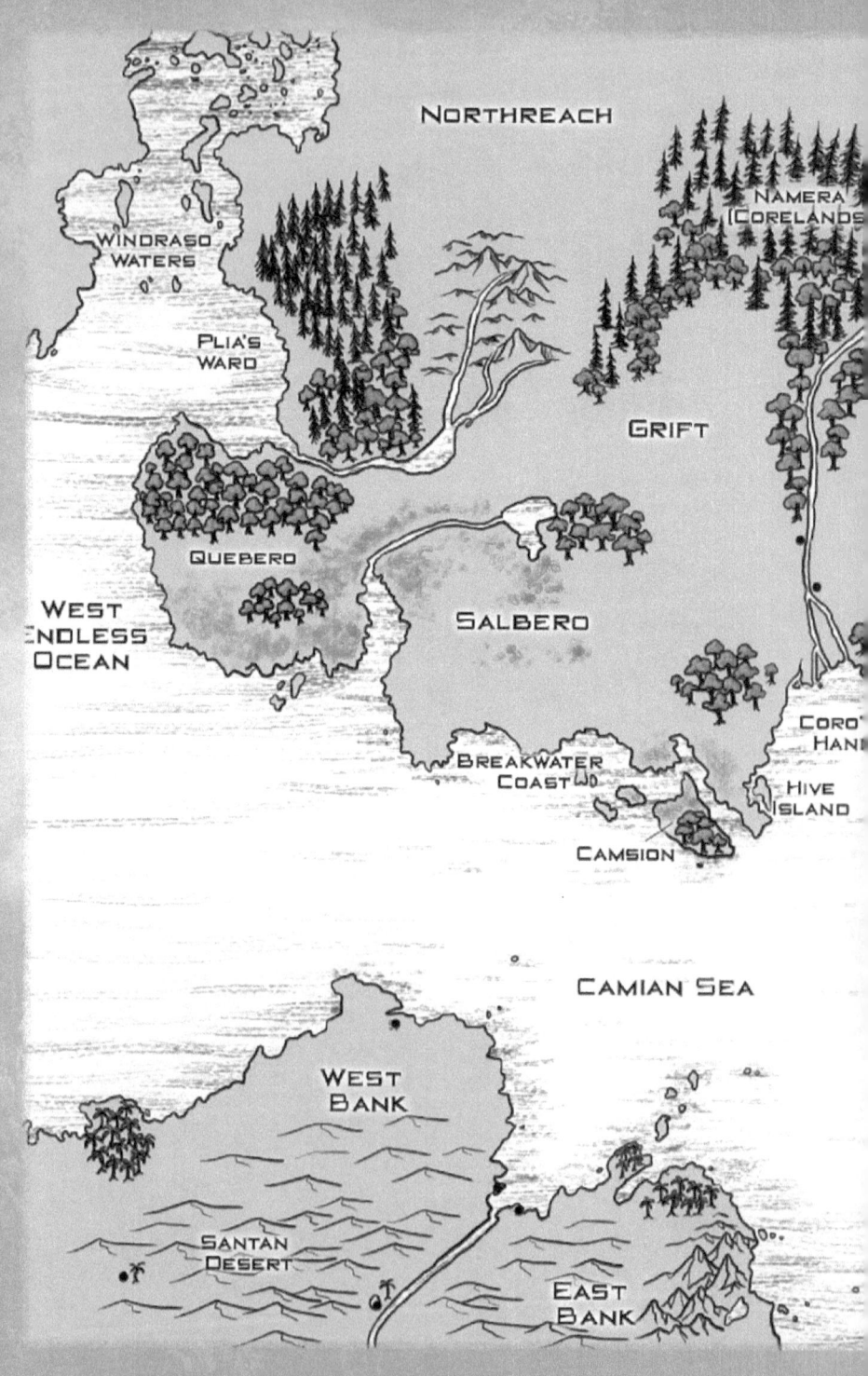

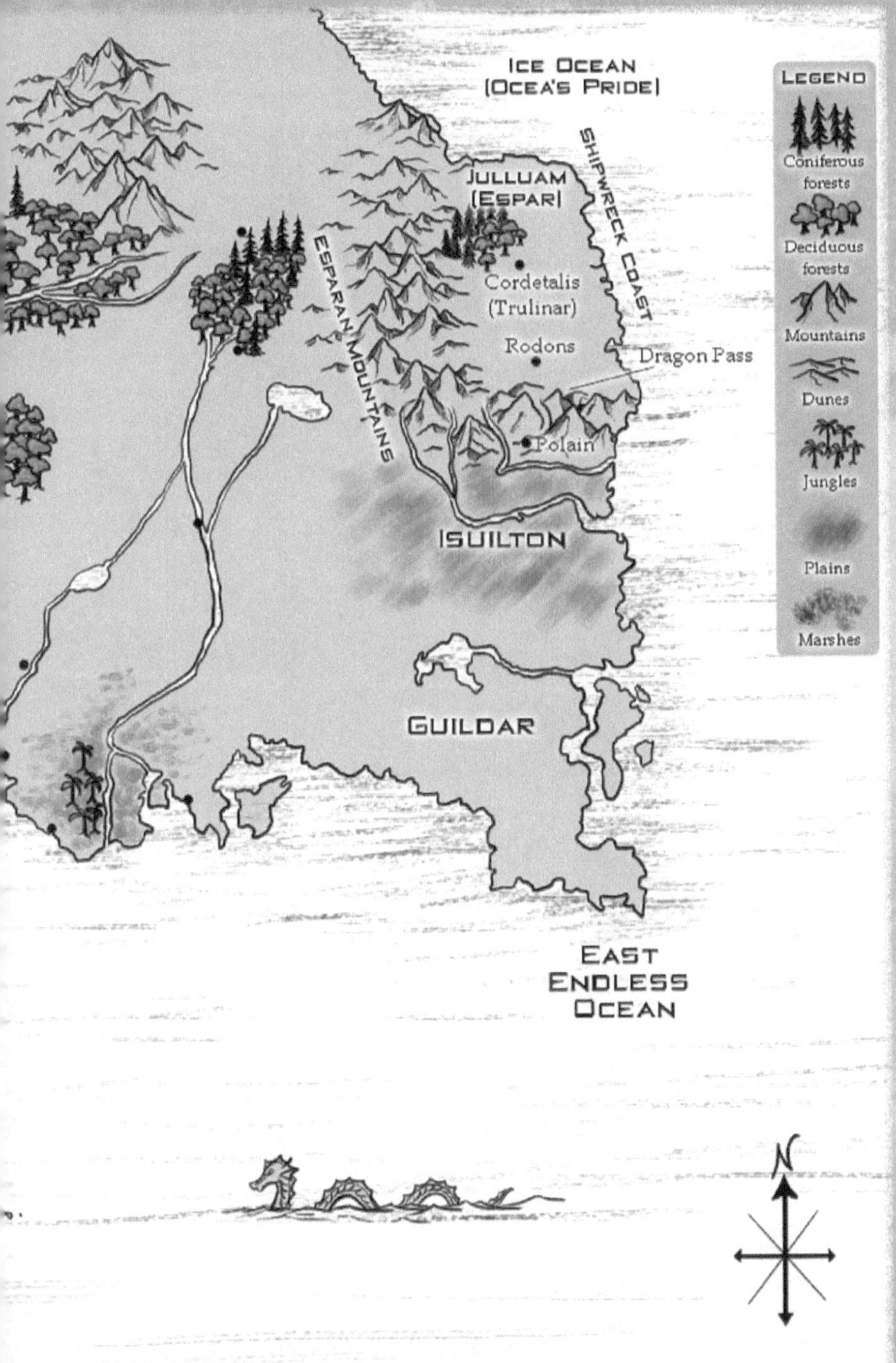

Ice Ocean
(Ocea's Pride)
Julluam
(Espar)
Shipwreck Coast
Esparan Mountains
Cordetalis
(Trulinar)
Rodons
Dragon Pass
Polain
Isuilton
Guildar
East
Endless
Ocean
N
Legend
Coniferous forests
Deciduous forests
Mountains
Dunes
Jungles
Plains
Marshes

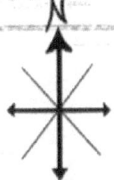

"WE WILL CLEANSE THE WORLD OF
THE TAINTED BLOOD IT STOLE."

- GANNON, SEAT OF THOUGHT
IN THE WATCHING CIRCLE

Prologue

"You called for me, Father?" Valia asked from the library doorway. Folding her hands, she put her eyes meekly on the woven rug within the room. Now posed like a suitable child, she waited for the admittance that would force her to stop avoiding the confrontation. Her father, Prince Dorakon of Gaidol, sat among the bookcases, looking dour, his beard stretched by his long frown. High Guardsman Bosul sat across from him in a wide chair, a drink in hand. He wore no uniform, although she still recognized him. His sword was unmistakable on his hip.

Valia's feelings of misgiving grew. The servant summoning her had suggested she wear shoes, not her slippers. It sounded like a warning.

"Valia," the prince called, gesturing her forward. She complacently found her place on the short stool by his feet. The tradition had not changed over her entire living memory, no matter her coming of age, and she did not expect it to until her father finally forced her to marry. Then she'd be sitting at someone else's feet, no doubt.

"What do you know of the situation with Galanth?" he asked.

Valia pared her knowledge down to an acceptable level, unwilling to reveal her interest in the war that crept toward them. "Prince Tohmas has declared dominance over Espar and named himself 'king,'" she said, keeping her voice flat as if the fact was irrelevant to her. "He is officially opposed by Trulin, Gaidol, Nothor, and Damoria, although Polthian may yet be another enemy to him. Why do you ask, Father?"

"Trulin has fallen," the high guardsman said, his voice gravelly. He leaned back in his seat, his lounging position making Valia worry. No one was on good enough terms with Prince Dorakon to be that calm in his presence, not usually.

One of her ladies had told her about Trulin's fall two nights before, but she knew her father preferred to think he controlled what she did and did not know.

She mocked surprise. "So soon?"

"The Prince of Trulin is dead, and his heir surrendered. King Tohmas marches to our borders," her father said.

He was omitting how her father's Gaidolon forces had already crossed that border a quartercycle ago to tangle with Tohmas and his men. They had expected to attack Prince Tohmas from the south while Trulin held the north, but Trulin had folded too soon.

Valia nodded gravely. If Prince Tohmas was crossing the border, Gaidol's forces must have already retreated to their territory.

"I will ride to join up with our armies," her father declared, and Valia again nodded, hoping her gesture looked full of duty and understanding. She saw the real reason for his decision; Trulin was not the only princedom to fold. Nothor, led by Valia's uncle, had also withdrawn from Gaidol's army. Rumors said the reason was holy visions, but she had yet to hear a first-hand account of the event and was not sure she believed it.

With Trulin conquered and Nothor pulling out, the forces of Gaidol were alone. If their prince came to lead them, he could rekindle their morale. Without his presence, they would bleed out deserters.

"High Guardsman Bosul will be taking command here in SwordWood," Prince Dorakon said next. "You will marry him."

The two statements were delivered in the same voice, but the first was inconsequential, and the second hit Valia like a kick to her stomach.

Despite herself, she shot off the stool. "I do not wish to be married!"

She regretted her outburst as her father stood. Even straightening to her full height, Valia's head only reached his shoulder. She was forever left staring at the crest on his chest, the blue with the white shark central.

"I did not ask you," Prince Dorakon said, every word an anchor on her heart.

Valia dropped her stare to the floor, fighting back tears. She bit off further retorts. Challenging him directly was fated to fail and doing so in front of a witness was a form of suicide. She knew better.

"That's more like it," the prince said. He put a hand on her head, patting her like the child he seemed to think she was. "Now go."

Dismissed, Valia bowed to her father and left.

She finally understood the servant's suggested shoes; slippers were unsuitable for running. But there was nowhere to go and no one to turn to. The city would never let her escape.

All of SwordWood knew about her wedding by nightfall, and she retreated to her room to avoid the collective excitement of the capital. Friends wished her well while distant caretakers tried to involve her in plans and gossip. Her heart aching, Valia sat by the window in her room, looking over the city to the western horizon.

He was still out there. While the giddy girls who followed her around wondered if High Guardsman Lance Carraway was even alive, Valia was certain the man she loved was still waiting for her. Despite the spin her father had put on Lance's departure, Valia had always known her favorite high guardsman had left to join Prince Tohmas in his war against the Northlanders. Was it any wonder he remained with the Prince of Galanth now that Tohmas had turned his eyes to the conquest of Espar?

Lance now stood on the wrong side of the war. He was her enemy.

Her father knew of Lance's affection, so he kept them apart. In the last year, Lance had visited SwordWood only three times and, even then, only for a few candles of time. On his most recent visit, there had only been time for ten words.

Her heart skipped as she remembered those words and the forbidden kiss they had shared. She knew he was alive because she could still hear his voice whispering, *When I come back, I swear I will marry you.*

The knock on her bedroom door woke her from her dreams of Lance. She turned to see her ladies admitting a different high guardsman: Calus Bosul. Waving from the high guardsman chased the ladies out until only Valia remained.

She faced her window and ignored the intrusion.

Lance had been young to his post; he was thirty-five this year. Calus Bosul was an average high guardsman and nearly three times

her eighteen years. He had married before, but his wife had died four years prior in childbirth, and the single child was being cared for by the high guardsman's sister. Valia knew little else about him, but what she knew was not bad. He had been an integral part of the fighting in the north, which Lance had mostly avoided by being a guardsman in SwordWood at the time. Now that they were of equal title, Calus' position in SwordWood technically outranked Lance's in Varidee because SwordWood was the greater responsibility. It had always been clear that Dorakon held Calus in high esteem, and no one had ever said any unpleasant things about him, not even in gossip.

Step by step, Calus crossed the bedroom, stopping behind her to look out over her shoulder. His breath smelled of pipe smoke and wine; her father was indeed spoiling him now. Valia had seen it before. Prince Dorakon lacked the means to inspire people, counting instead on lavish gifts and money to buy loyalty.

"Is it so terrible?" he said softly. "I have a good house, a daughter. Your father has named me defender of the capital in his absence. We will stay here."

His words made sense. Even if Lance was alive, he had betrayed Gaidol and could never return. Valia had expected to be married off to an important person at some point. What was wrong with Calus?

She tried to put Calus in Lance's place for a moment, but it took only a blink for her to shake her head.

"I do not love you." Her heart belonged to Lance, tied to him with the band of pearls he had gifted to her and now carried with him in his travels. She could never replace him.

As the hand of her father's chosen suitor touched down on Valia's shoulder, she shivered.

"You are the daughter of a Prince of Espar. Why would you expect to be married for love?"

His touch was cold. Her skin prickled with gooseflesh.

"Just..." she said, releasing the word as a sigh into the window, "just something someone said once."

Just something Lance once said, her heart finished.

Staring into the sunset, Valia felt she could almost see Lance in the garden below, his mustache bent and his eyes shining. For years, he had walked in her shadow as her defender. She had come to trust and depend

on him. When a midnight assassin attacked, she spent a candle with only Lance while the other defenders took the attacker away. He had let her cry without criticism. He had been with her when her mother died and was still there when her sister followed. In every memory Valia had of hard times, her guardsman was there, stroking her hair and holding her as she wept, whispering promises of daylight and a new beginning.

No matter how awful things were, there was always hope. The sun always rose again, and he would stay with her until it did.

She did not know when it had changed from friendship to love, but after his promotion to high guardsman, the thought of him going away made her realize how much she wanted him to stay forever.

"Whoever said it was a fool," High Guardsman Bosul said. "I will give you a good home. That is enough."

Calus turned her to face him even as she shook her head. A finger interrupted her motion, lifting her chin from where she had dropped it. He leaned down.

Terrified, she dared not move as his lips pressed against hers. Tears welled in her eyes at the memory of her only other kiss. Lance had been desperate then, his hold tight, but his kiss had been sweet, unlike Calus' lifeless embrace. She searched but found no emotion.

He released her, and she pulled back as far as the windowsill would allow.

"Hardly appropriate," she said, turning to hide her tears.

He caught her arms and turned her to him. With his hand on each of her shoulders, she could not move.

"We are engaged. I can do what I want," he told her.

He planted another kiss, and it was rougher. Valia's tears fell, but he did not seem to notice as he untangled her lacing and ran fingers over her skin from her neck to her waist.

"You would take from me the right to wear white on my wedding day?" she choked out, her voice a whisper.

He was not listening, and he was not stopping. The cold hand reached her waist and held Valia fast.

Realization struck. Calus would not touch her without her father's permission.

Her father knew Lance held her heart. Her marriage to Calus would be one victory against the high guardsman who had betrayed

them, and this was the other. Regardless of what happened, she would never have her proper wedding night. Even if Lance came to rescue her on the morrow, he would be too late.

Her broken heart let the last piece fall with her tears. Closing her eyes, she clung to her first kiss and the winsome smile of her guardsman. When the stranger touched her, she hugged Lance tighter in her mind until she could feel him stroking her hair and hear him whispering how it would be all right come morning. Everything always looked better come morning. She just had to make it to daylight.

She felt nothing, hidden away where only Lance could find her.

When she finally stirred to burned out candles and moonlight, Calus slept, and she was free to move.

Her dress lay scattered across the bedposts. Her underclothes were stained by blood and tears. Her legs and breasts hurt, a fire burning below her navel where the blood still trickled.

Feeling colder than ever in the weak wind of the summer night, she moved back to her window. It was hard to see the stars as the sunrise lit the sky behind the manor, but the moon shone brightly over the city. Her window looked west, which kept the dawn from being visible for candles more.

Will he want me now? When Lance returned, would he still love the woman who could not wear white to her wedding? What would he think?

Ashamed, her tears were renewed, and Valia fell against the casement.

But in the wind ruffling her hair, she felt her beloved's hand once more stroking her head. The dawn was coming. It would be light soon, and the sun would chase away these demons. It was a new day. Anything was possible.

The wind whispered his voice: *When I come back, I swear I will marry you.*

As her eyes rose to examine the fast-fading moon, the wind dried the last of her tears.

So there was going to be a wedding. Valia had always known that. Her father thought it would be to High Guardsman Calus Bosul, but he was wrong. The only man Valia would see standing at her side in front of a Celebrant of Ocea was Lance. She had to make it happen.

If Lance were with King Tohmas, who was now waging war against Gaidol, they would come to SwordWood. So long as this new conqueror of Espar survived, Tohmas would bring her love to her. And she would be here waiting at the hand of the man in charge of the capital of Gaidol.

She would help Lance. She could make the marriage her father had thrust upon her work to her advantage.

There would have to be a delay, but who could deny her that? If she were to be a bride, she would be a proper one. A dress, flowers, and temple decorations were all requirements that would take time. Or the feast itself; who needed to be invited and given time to arrive? There were a thousand things to do before she could say vows correctly.

And while the coming wedding kept the city busy, she would be in the position to pass on information to Lance.

She would have her revenge.

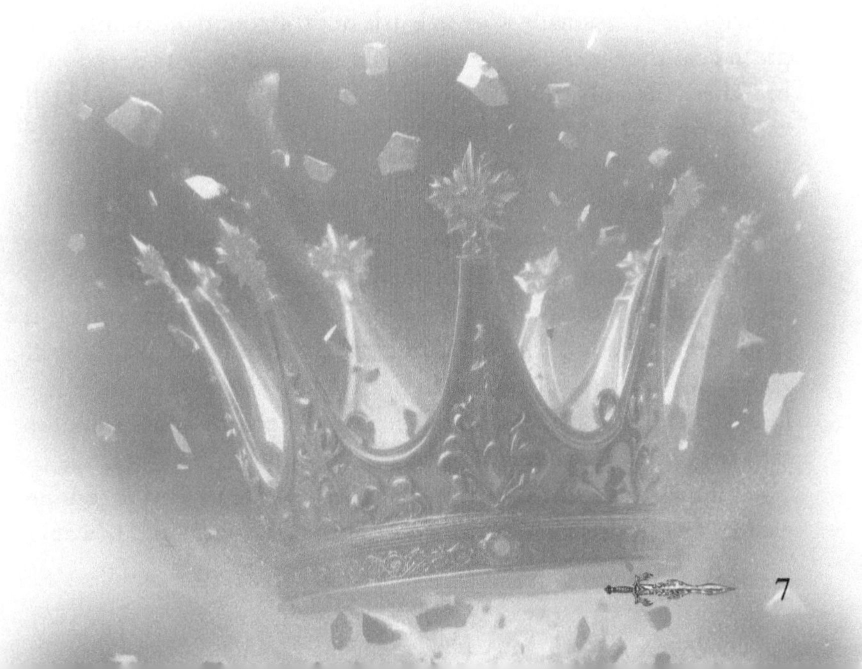

Chapter 1

The days passed as a blur in the rundown city of LandWater. Tohmas understood nearly nothing of the proceedings, but the people around him seemed to know what they were doing. By Esparan tradition, he was forbidden from seeing Arnika the day of the wedding and instead retreated to the forested hill outside the encamped army to wait out the morning.

They had dressed him in the Galanth chain and leather armor combination he occasionally wore in battle but still found unfamiliar. The green coat they presented was new and matched to fresh deep forest breeches. The only thing he managed to keep, as far as he could tell, was his sword. No one could take SoulBurner from him; the enchanted sword remained on his belt or within reach at all times now.

With his horsehair bracelet made from Schlavarai's tail hairs, he waited for full dawn to cover the camp. Scouts reported no movement from Gaidol's army, and Kitable had promised to keep a magic eye on it on this important day, but the threat of the south was still vivid in his mind. Gaidol's forces had not moved since Prince Neillan had withdrawn his support. Tohmas suspected they were waiting for Prince Dorakon to join them, but whether the older prince would leave the safety of his capital remained to be seen.

Tohmas was ready to defend LandWater if he needed to, but he wanted to take to the field, which meant marching soon. He would

engage Gaidol. Trulin was now his land to defend, and they were trespassing.

In some ways, he was victorious and thought he should be content. He had kept his word to avoid further killing in his conquest of Trulin, and Celebrant Corolys had offered her blessing, which seemed to be expected of the groom before a wedding. He had won the final loyalty and, perhaps forgiveness, from all four celebrants and was again in favor with the gods. That was a good thing.

But it did not feel any different. Even if he married Arnika Trulin, he could not touch her without her permission. Besides being allowed to sleep in his tent again (although how they would sleep on a double cot without touching, he could not figure out), nothing had changed.

Prince Tandar, the new Prince of Trulin, giving an oath as kingsman would make the difference. With Tandar came the rest of Trulin. Although this increased his forces only barely back up to where he had started, Tohmas was satisfied. One enemy was vanquished. Now he had to turn his attention to the Princedom of Gaidol. From there, Damoria was next and last.

He should have been nervous about facing Prince Dorakon of Gaidol, but Tohmas again felt indifferent. They would defeat him, and all of Espar would be his. He had to believe.

Lance came and got him, moving surprisingly well, a new splint from Celebrant Darak supporting his limp left leg. He wasn't quite up to riding yet, but given time, Lance promised he and his warhorse Bolt would re-establish their glory. He planned to rejoin the morning spars to retrain himself. With the splint holding his otherwise immobile leg, he had to relearn everything about fighting.

Once back in LandWater, Carsh joined them, having been inspecting the cleared wedding area. A bookkeeper was trying to convince the Rydan to wear something other than his breeches, bracelets, and baldrics, but the man gave up as Carsh silently went on with his duty of protecting Tohmas. Rydans did not have marriage ceremonies, and the thought of dressing up for a celebration was laughable.

Of all the Esparan soldiers and servants around Tohmas, only Lance seemed to realize that Tohmas, despite being an Esparan of a royal line, had never attended an Esparan wedding. He had the decency to pretend he was explaining to Carsh but kept Tohmas one step ahead of the

traditions as they manifested through the morning. He saw no point to them although he felt like every formality was designed to prevent him from reaching his bride.

Tohmas wished he could follow Rydan tradition, grab Arnika, and simply kill anyone who argued over his claim. But he was Esparan, at least by blood. He had to play the part.

He put up with blessings from each celebrant, a period of silent prayer, receiving gifts from his mother and from Arnika's cousin Tandar, as well as a ceremonial washing of his hands. Finally, Tohmas reached the small round table where he was to be married. Four candles stood before him, each decorated with seashells and Ocea's teardrop symbol.

With a deep breath, feeling ill-prepared, he faced the observers.

Who exactly was attending, Tohmas had left to his mother and bride-to-be. Although he had feared they would end up having to move half of the army to make sufficient space, Arnika's lack of relatives or Lady Fayela's pragmatism resulted in a small crowd. Every protector, however, had been put on duty. In their smart green tabards and green rank ropes, they formed a layer three men thick around the area.

Wisavi Kitable, Master Wizard of Galanth, stood off to one side with his enchanted stare following various things among and far beyond the guests. Tohmas couldn't determine if he was there as a dignitary or another defender but settled on it being both.

Prince Tandar, the newest Prince of Espar and Tohmas' soon-to-be kingsman, had been allowed to bring whomever he chose. Since he was the local prince, he had about the same number of ranking officers as Tohmas did, plus a row of what appeared to be official bodyguards in a rank at the back of the seats. All seemed quiet.

"We begin," the soft voice of Celebrant Corolys called, and Tohmas faced her. From the first day he had met her, Celebrant Corolys had always been regally dressed, but today she wore a fortune of sapphires on her robes, including three that made the mark of the tear drop down her cheek. A silver double wave symbol of Ocea glittered silver from her brow.

The other celebrants stood behind her, silent observers for now. Their individual attire was similarly elegant. Celebrant Loni wore the gold dress she had donned at Prince Dragal's funeral but seemed to be wearing enough gold in her hair and arms to make Tohmas wonder

where the dress stopped and the jewelry began. Her counterpart in worship to the Goddess Inac, Celebrant Sedgan, must have helped with her attire; the dress was remarkably modest for the usually scandalous woman. Calanor and Sedgan had silver or gold in their robes—formal robes, Tohmas assumed—although no one had managed to find something suitable for the Celebrant of Pari, Darak Degree. He wore his robes and cutter tools plainly and looked like he had rolled out of bed fully clothed and rushed to be on time.

He might have.

No matter their silver and gold, none of them were as glorious as Arnika in Tohmas' eyes. When his wife-to-be was called from the east, Tohmas lost his breath.

The white and silver dress the seamstresses had so quickly put together made the bride glisten more than a silver dragon, and she walked with the grace of a thousand dancers. A flurry of white wildflowers fell down her back in a long veil as if replacing her shorn locks.

There were words, but Tohmas hardly heard them. Someone welcomed the people and asked for the gods' blessing, but he did not care. He could not take his eyes off the beautiful young woman standing at his side in front of the table.

Someone cried out suddenly, breaking Tohmas' joyful haze. Carsh moved up, a second knife in hand already. Rydan instincts kicked in.

Tohmas dared not reach for SoulBurner—the anti-magic aura would cripple Kitable—so instead, Tohmas ducked, grabbed the nearest table leg, and spun the defense around. In place of the candles he had toppled, the table surface sprouted arrows.

Someone was attacking.

Carsh's knives had already taken down two enemies, and how Kitable was waving his hands seemed to imply magical aid, but Tohmas still had to throw the table wide to his right to stop another barrage of arrows shot from the line of Tandar's bodyguards. His makeshift shield blocked both of the arrows that got through before Kitable finished what he was doing; subsequent arrows hit a barrier a stride in front of Tohmas, protecting him while he kept the table out to protect Arnika.

Carsh rushed in to fight but was blocked by the invisible magical barrier. The attackers were using their own form of magic it seemed, for

the ranks of protectors were unable to get through. They grew more frustrated by the moment.

"Charger Granton, stop this at once!" Arnika shouted.

Tohmas' jaw dropped. Sweet, cautious, shy Anika was flushed and furious. He wanted to pull her back when she pushed aside the table-shield, but he had sworn not the touch her, and that oath still stood.

Evidently recognizing someone from the line of archers at the back of the area, she stared down a man with a plume of black.

"The invader must die! Prince Kelland died keeping this monster out of Trulin!" the man said from behind the ducking crowd. By the plume, he was a charger and one of the highest-ranked men in Trulin.

Tohmas had never seen the daughter of Prince Kelland so incensed. He prayed he would never have to again.

"My father," Arnika shouted over the charger, "set his conditions under different circumstances! Things have changed. I am helping Trulin! How dare you try to shoot me!"

Interrupting her wedding was acceptable, but shooting at her was apparently not, Tohmas mused.

"Your—" was as far as Granton got. Prince Tandar joined in, jumping onto a bench, sword in hand. For the first time Tohmas had heard, Tandar made his voice sound like it belonged to a prince.

"Charger! Stand down! Prince Kelland is dead. Get used to it!"

There was silence from the far end of the clearing for a long moment. Tohmas quietly put down the table, thinking about SoulBurner, but Kitable was still too close.

As the pause drew out, Tandar looked up at Tohmas. "Let me have them. It's a misunderstanding."

Tohmas strenuously smiled. "Justice in Trulin is your right as kingsman, Tandar. They are yours unless you want rid of them. Then they become my problem."

Tandar turned back to the attackers. "Put away your weapons," he commanded. "We will sort this out. We are all loyal to Trulin after all."

It took another dozen heartbeats before there was movement, but when the men stood at the back, it was with weapons extended or sheathed. Tandar left his place at the front to talk to the strangers, and Kitable dropped his wall to let him go.

CHAPTER 1

The way Carsh flinched made it clear another spell had gone up as soon as the first one had been dropped. Tohmas did not feel any more vulnerable.

Soon the rest of the spells either expired or were extinguished, and the protectors moved in. Tohmas relayed his command to let Tandar deal with the attackers, then waited for them to sort themselves out. At length, Tandar came forward once more. Him retaking his seat seemed to signal the end of the ordeal. The angry Trullers left, and the rest of the guests returned.

"Tandar," Tohmas asked before the celebrant could say anything, "could you invite Charger Granton to dinner?"

The prince, soon-to-be kingsman, cocked an eyebrow at him. "Not enough excitement for one day?"

"From a whimsical point of view, I would like him to get a chance to talk to the guardians and kingsmen and see if they can change his mind. From a practical point of view, I would rather he doesn't show up somewhere I don't expect him."

Tandar nodded in agreement, and Tohmas went back to getting married.

There had been little Sedgan could do about the intrusion on the wedding, but his best contribution was keeping Loni from throwing herself at the Trullers who had interrupted her champion's wedding. It was hard to say if the trained soldiers or the celebrant would have emerged from a confrontation, but Sedgan did not want to know the answer. Loni could be a respectable force, but when she was enraged, she was impossible to reason with. Having her slaughter the Trullers would not do well for the peace King Tohmas was founding.

Once Prince Tandar settled the matter, the celebrants returned to overseeing the wedding.

Loni sneered, scoffing as the bride and groom swapped bracelets. "Who told him to do that anyway?" she grumbled.

"The exchange of bracelets is tradition, Celebrant. It used to be a sign of trust. In older days, black magic could be used on the hair of the bracelets, but now—"

"Not that!" she snapped with a pout. "Fall in love! Who told him to fall in love? Most inconsiderate!"

Sedgan could only roll his eyes. Lust was the Goddess Inac's domain, but love belonged to Ocea. As a Celebrant of Inac, he had no use for love, but he understood it was common.

"Most people don't control when they fall in love or to whom. Does that make them lucky or unlucky, I wonder?" he mused.

She frowned with her arms crossed. "Well, I did not give him permission!"

"He doesn't need your permission," Sedgan pointed out.

Loni fixed him with one of her grins, which was gaining notoriety through the camp. It sent a thick shiver down his spine. "Yes, he does," she hissed, each word heavy.

When she left, Sedgan dared not follow. It was unlikely that her departure went unnoticed, but he hated to think what the sudden departure of both Celebrants to Inac would do for rumors. Praying she would not get into too much trouble while his back was turned, he instead focused on the wedding and pretended nothing was amiss about her storming off.

For some reason, her final words lingered with him, and he promised himself he would keep a closer eye on her. He had lost track of her before, only to find her suspiciously close to the king's tent. Still, Wisavi Kitable confirmed that she had never been with the king, which was a comfort. But Loni was a prostitute of impressive skill. Sedgan would not have been surprised if Tohmas himself had enjoyed her company.

Tohmas has a wife now, Sedgan thought. *Let Arnika Trulin deal with the king's needs.* How could Loni sneak past that?

A troubling thought followed. How would Inac? Ocea, Inac's milder sister, was now showing power. Like Loni, Sedgan found the prospect a little unsettling. Tohmas had always been a proud follower of Inac before. He was now divided.

The thought stayed with him like a bad omen as the ceremony completed, and they were declared husband and wife. Kingsman Tandar came up to take his oath next, which Sedgan officiated over.

Every word was correct. It was done.

CHAPTER 1

After the newest kingsman gave his oath, Carsh was delighted to find out there was a party. It sounded much like a Rydan victory celebration, making Carsh feel a bit more at home. Esparans had rules about mistakes during oaths, but neither Tohmas nor the Truller made any errors, and everyone seemed happy when the two men knocked fists. Finally, they could have some fun.

Lance had warned them that, according to tradition, no further drink would be served after the groom drank his cup to the bottom. As a result, every man at the table did their utmost to see that the king's cup was never empty. Even Tohmas must have been starting to feel the drink by the time night fell.

The women sat at a table apart from their men, swapping stories in place of drinks. At Tohmas' new wife's insistence, Shimmer Weaver had been invited, which meant a caster was present. Even Wisavi Kitable had said he trusted the dancer from Fixer City, and that was enough to make Carsh relax a little. Besides, the wisavi seemed to be keeping an eye on her, and Carsh knew he could trust Kitable to keep unwanted casters in their place.

The women left just after nightfall, and Tohmas watched them go with hunger in his eyes. The men worked to give the women a head start, managing to keep the king with them for another candle before he finally grabbed his cup and swallowed every last drop in a single gulp. Like those who spotted it, Carsh made a point of refilling his cup as Tohmas drank. The moment Tohmas' empty cup hit the table, servants removed the pitchers and jugs.

Wearing his new bracelet, Tohmas rose and went out. Carsh, still aware of his duty as prime protector and, more importantly, Tohmas' friend and brother, followed.

The bracelet, Carsh had to admit, looked familiar on Tohmas' wrist because Tohmas had once worn the grass bracelets of the Outlands. Still, the thinner braid was not quite big enough or noisy enough to properly replace the symbols he had left behind. Now, Carsh wondered if his blood brother would ever take the grass bracelets back up. No Esparans knew of his upbringing as Rydan. It would seem odd to them.

After a short walk, Tohmas stopped at his tent's entrance and examined the plank of wood he had erected outside it. During the wedding preparations, someone had painted the wood with the green and silver

tree crest of Galanth. The silver tree seemed to catch Tohmas' attention as he passed it in the moonlight.

Although they often could tell precisely what the other was thinking, Carsh felt left behind. For once, the Rydan could not even be certain his brother knew he was still there, but Carsh decided that was because he was superfluous. He took it as a sign to leave.

Darcina would be asleep by now, but she was used to his arrival at night. If she thought no one else was awake, she might not even bother putting up a fight. Most nights, that would have disappointed him, but tonight he hoped she would be calm, maybe even loving. It had been almost three years since he had requested that Chief Tamv spare her, and Tohmas' marriage had reminded Carsh of his anniversary. He wanted to spend the night with Darcina to celebrate.

As he moved along the moonlight toward the Rydan side of camp, Tohmas finally decided not to bother knocking on the plank and entered his tent.

Gannon sat forward and rubbed his eyes. The Scry in front of him kept perfect shape despite his distraction. He could sleep and hold the spell, but who would watch what it saw if he slept? And it wouldn't do for the Watching Circle to catch him sleeping on the job.

He had to remind himself that being a part of the Watching Circle, one of only two Circles in all of Wanter, was a great honor. However, days of sitting and watching had removed much of the luster from the otherwise prestigious post.

The Tainted Circle was broken and had been since the spring before. Unlike the Circles of Wanter, the Tainted Circle did not appoint members; they seemed to hope for one to stumble into their gathering blindly. Years, if not decades, could pass between new members. A completed Circle was, as a result, rare. It might be another century before it reformed.

And he, with the rest of the Watching Circle, would sit and watch for it, just in case.

And he would be bored for every moment of the long and useless chore.

"Might be faster just to kill them all," Gannon grumbled into the empty cavern. The other six members were already home in Wanter. With no Tainted Circle complete, they took turns keeping the Scry open. Of course, that meant the lowest rank had to watch the most. As far as Gannon knew, Rean, the Voice of the Circle, was not even taking a turn.

But the danger of being caught not paying attention to the Scry kept Gannon honest. Here, an old woman in bird feathers. There, a man with a long beard and a white pelt over his shoulder. There, a thin man with a hooked nose and a hat of hawk feathers...

Six impossible disruptions to magic, somehow mixing their magic with Wanter's.

He was still staring at the Scry, moving it from Circle member to Circle member, when Yonny arrived through the portal from Wanter.

Like Gannon, Yonny had a focus gem set in his forehead and wore the ribbon robes of the Circle. They would earn another ribbon for every year they served. As the youngest, Gannon's robe had the fewest and thickest ribbons.

To allow Yonny to take over, Gannon anchored the Scry to a spot on the ground outside of his defenses. Letting go of the Scry was like finally closing his eyes after staring at the sun. The buzz of magic did not leave him—his spells were a constant comfort—but releasing the Scry at least allowed him to turn his gaze away and blink without feeling guilty.

Yonny took a seat on the cavern's rough ground with a self-satisfied grin, adjusting the cushion he had brought. Usually, the Seat of Divination in the Circle never wasted an opportunity to mock Gannon. *Has he not found a reason yet, or...*

Yonny's grin grew with each passing moment, and Gannon's curiosity would not allow him to leave without finding out why.

"Why exactly are you so pleased?"

Yonny would have to keep watch for twenty days now without rest. It was shorter than Gannon's twenty-five days, but it should not have been met with such enthusiasm.

"Can't read my mind?" Yonny replied.

With no patience remaining after his long vigil and having little when dealing with Yonny, even under good circumstances, Gannon narrowed his eyes on the divination master. Most focus gems would change

colors depending on the user's thoughts—a strange side effect no one understood—but Gannon was the Seat of Thought in the Circle, and he could control what thoughts the gem accessed. In this case, the gem stayed pure, brilliant blue, not showing his annoyance.

"Could if I wanted to," Gannon replied, his voice tense. "Of course, Rean might be mad if I yank your smug thoughts through your nostrils."

Yonny's smile vanished. Gannon felt more than one spell pulse nearby like the flexing of muscles.

But Yonny did not lash out. Instead, proving he was in a far better mood than Gannon had expected, Yonny's lip twitched only once as he turned back to the Scry. "You crude Shantanese," he grumbled. "Always about brute force. No finesse."

There was no point in trying to prove Yonny wrong. Thought magic, Gannon's strength by far, was all about finesse, but it could be used roughly to great effect, just like any element or domain of magic.

Feeling his question about Yonny's sanguine mood would go unanswered and was not worth the headache to chase, Gannon headed for the portal, only to pause at the sound of Yonny's laughter.

He refused to turn around but paused long enough to hear Yonny say, "My divinations say the time is coming. We will have to act before my watch is over. I alone will be witness to..."

Knowing every word was an attempt at goading his temper, Gannon forced his feet to carry him forward. The moment he was through the portal, Yonny's voice was too far away to be heard.

Gannon paused in the portal room on the other side, taking a moment to lean against one wall. If Yonny was right, which he usually was when it came to divinations, then the Tainted Circle would reform soon. The Watching Circle would be needed once more.

They could not allow the contaminated blood of the World of the Tainted to stain their magic. Any who touched the powers had to be killed.

Would slaying one suffice? It had not taken long for the Tainting Circle to replace its missing member. Gannon thought he would push for the death of all Tainted Circle members should the situation arise. He had no desire to go tromping back to the World of the Tainted unnecessarily.

CHAPTER 1

He decided to find somewhere to rest. He would need his energy for when the Watching Circle called him again.

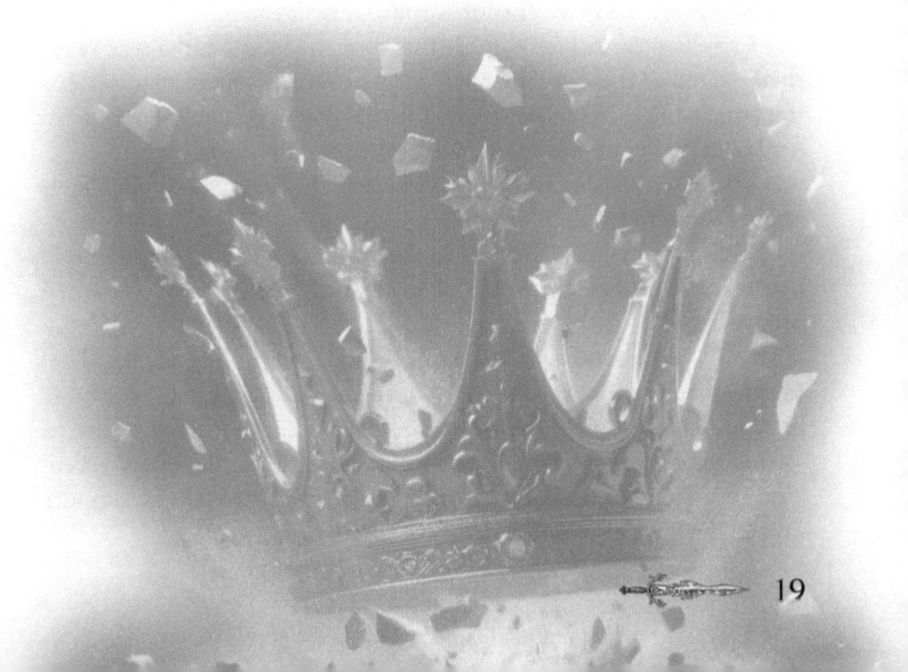

Chapter 2

The attending women changed Arnika out of the dress, bathed her, perfumed her, and dressed her in finely woven bedclothes. The tent felt foreign for the first time since Arnika had settled into it. When it was time for the women to go, Arnika huddled on the cot with the blankets pulled over her knees, trying to stop shuddering.

There had been a dozen women helping, primarily friendly faces from Trulin, but the one face that seemed to most recognize Arnika's unease was the Lady Mother of Arnika's now-husband.

Lady Fayela shooed out all the women once Arnika was ready, then paused at the exit. She made half-movements more than once as if having something more to say. Her delay was just long enough for Arnika to gather up the courage and whisper, "I'm scared."

Like a herding dog listening for the whistle, Fayela was immediately at the foot of her bed.

"Thank the gods!" she said as she came to sit at Arnika's feet. "I had feared you had forgotten all emotion! You said not a word! I was worried!"

Lady Fayela gently rubbed Arnika's ankle, reminding Arnika of her mother who had also done that to soothe her after nightmares or heartbreaks. Arnika, not for the first time, wished her mother was alive to see the wedding and be the one to comfort her. It was strange to accept kindness from her husband's mother, but Arnika needed the support. Any loving mother would do.

CHAPTER 2

"I should never have agreed to this," Arnika confessed. "I don't know what I'm doing! I don't know how to be a wife. What if he is mean? What if I make a mistake?"

"Easy, child," the mother said. "Do not think you are the only woman to face marriage with uncertainty."

"You know him best. Will he—?"

Lady Fayela put up her hand gently, and Arnika's words dropped off. As she pulled a blanket over Arnika's knees, Lady Fayela's gentle smile faded to a thin line. "I do not know him well at all, dear child."

Arnika's heart skipped with confusion. "But you are his mother!"

"I have learned more about him these last cycles than in all the years before." Her stare was distant for a long moment, her expression becoming grim. At length, she shook her head lightly and again tucked in the blanket around Arnika's hip. "What matters is that he needs me, and he needs you. We will temper the fire in him and forge a leader for Espar unlike any in history. I am here for that, my child. I cannot even say I knew who he was before. But I know him now. You will come to know him as well." Her smile was slow in returning. "Do not fear. None of us know what we are doing, especially not in the bedroom. A man might think he knows, but I assure you, he will be as lost as you! All the rules change when you have a new lover."

Lover, Arnika thought. He had promised not to touch her without permission and thus far had striven to hold to that oath. But would he even ask? She couldn't stop him if he chose not to abide by it.

"Be assured, you are in good hands," Fayela added. "He loves you. That will take care of you." Fayela sighed wistfully. "He will either be just as confused as you, or more likely, he will be too terrified to step a toe out of place."

Arnika nodded, her chin pressed to her knees, and she closed her eyes as she received a final kiss on her forehead. When Arnika opened her eyes, the Lady Mother had left, and Arnika was alone in the lamplight.

She nearly cried. The man she had dealt with thus far had been very different from the one she had believed was invading Trulin. Which was real? What if the one she had accepted had been a lie? The thought petrified her.

When Tohmas Galanth, King of Espar, finally arrived, Arnika's tears had still not fallen. Clinging to what Fayela had said about love,

she forced herself to stand. She didn't love him, but she'd seen glimmers of what she assumed was his love in their interactions. Tonight, she would learn if it was real.

He kept his eyes down and moved softly. Without a word, he took to pulling off his chain and leather armor. Seeing the arrangement of the clasps was the same as Trulin armor, Arnika moved to assist.

In the shadows of Inac's lamp on the altar, King Tohmas flinched away from her. His voice was soft when he said, "You don't have to do that."

Arnika's voice was a whisper. "I am your wife now. I am trying to act like one."

As he faced the altar, Arnika could not see his smile, but she heard it in his voice. "Most princes' wives don't know anything about armor anymore," he teased.

She reached for the next tie, and he remained still, allowing her to remove his shoulder guard.

"My father used to punish my brother by taking away his servants so he could not go out and play his war games," she said. "So Anga taught his little sister how to assist with armor."

As Arnika pulled the leather chest plate clear, the king seemed sad. A moment of silence lingered between them.

"I am sorry for the pain I caused you, my lady," he finally said.

For the last quartercycle, she had been "fair lady." At last, she was "my lady." If he kept his oath, she would be his only lady too.

He was not apologizing for Anga's death, as even Arnika could see why her brother had died, but Tohmas seemed to regret it genuinely. Strange as it seemed, it all felt years old although she knew it had been only a mooncycle. Too much had happened for the grief to be fresh, and she thought she understood the circumstances well enough now to appreciate that Tohmas had tried to spare Anga for as long as possible.

Did he mean it, his regret? She couldn't tell if he was lying and could not decide if that was because he had never lied to her or because he was very good at it.

"It was war, and Anga was stupid about it. We are moving on now," Arnika told him. Her new mother-in-law's words replayed in her mind: *He needs you. We will temper the fire in him.*

Placing the armor to dry overnight with the rest of his belongings, she reached for his belt.

He retreated a step, his hands raised in surrender. "I swore I would not touch you."

Shocking herself, Arnika answered swiftly. "And I swore to carry your heir. We cannot both hold to our oaths." It was her wedding night, after all. "I..." was the only thing she could say at first, but closing her eyes and taking a few breaths let her finish, "I permit you. Just..." It was her turn to be shy, and she lowered her head. "Just please be gentle."

For a man who held a sword like it had been grown in his palm, the touch of his hand on her chin was remarkably soft. He lifted her chin gently. As she wondered what she was supposed to do next, he leaned forward and kissed her.

Warm lips pressed against her mouth, sending a shudder down her spine. Tears formed in her eyes, but no longer tears of fear. The sensation of his lips, slightly parted, against hers made every muscle in her chest shiver. New feelings rose from a place behind her navel but had little chance to build before he pulled away, although he held a finger under her chin.

"I would never harm you," he whispered. The hand under the chin moved to trace the lines of her face, then fell away content.

Her lips still moist from the kiss, her voice trembled. "Kiss me again like that?"

He grinned, a spark flashing in his eyes. He placed a kiss, like a tease, on her cheek before gliding his hand down her neck and spine, stopping at the small of her back.

"I can do better than that," he said. Heeding her request, he kissed Arnika softly before leading her to the cot they were to share.

After the wedding celebration, Darknim DoomDragon, Kingsman of Tanble and leader of the Northlander people, went home. He was not as drunk as most of the men he left behind, partially because he found drinking upset his innards recently and partially because he was too old to carry on like a pup without regretting it the day after. Besides,

he convinced himself, Tiki had been left with Layla all day; the new mother would need rest.

His tent was of the traditional kind, whalebones and seal pelts, but it was the only one. Most of the Northlanders had happily accepted Tohmas' new cotton and wood posts tents as they were easier to carry and repair. They had even started traditionally personalizing the tents, only now decorated with dyes instead of beads and bark.

It was one of many things the Northlanders had embraced: swords instead of spears, helmets instead of hoods, wood carvings instead of bone... the list was extensive. Although the Northlanders did not wholly forget the traditional ways, Darknim's people were adaptable and would not refuse things just because they were new. This was especially true if the new ways proved to be better. It was, and always had been, a matter of survival.

Even in the limited moonlight, it was clear that a group of people was waiting for him when he arrived home. The moonlight would not have been enough to recognize the people, but DoomDragon's sight naturally revealed magic. The softly-glowing shapes of a wolf and an owl were among the people gathered. Sure enough, he easily made out how Ela's shroud of owl feathers ruffled when she shifted her weight, and the presence of the wolfskin draped over Tril's shoulders despite the warm evening.

"Elder Ela and Elder Tril," he said, bowing in Esparan fashion, thinking it ironic, "I am honored." To Tril, he added, "You have returned rapidly." Elder Ela led the Circle of the Raven, but Darknim knew well that Tril had gone north to seek another Circle member, as the Circle of the Raven had lost a member to a wizard's attack. The other lost Aspects had been rediscovered in his absence, new animal spirits fusing with their powerful counterparts. Elder Cark had continued the Northlander trend of accepting the new southern things by taking a horse as an Aspect. However, finding another Northlander capable of Aspecting was a different matter. As a Circle could remain incomplete for decades, if not centuries, no one had been expecting much from Elder Tril in his quest north.

But Tril did not seem to have returned alone. Darknim was hopeful.

CHAPTER 2

Two women and two boys were with the elders. It was not until DoomDragon guessed the boys' ages that he paused. The Circle and its Aspects dropped from his head completely.

"You found them," he breathed with a smile, trying to make out their faces in the shadows. The remaining visitors were two mothers and their sons. One had a hand on the shoulder of a boy about eight, and the other stood behind her six-year-old.

"May I present your sons?" Elder Tril said. "The younger is Tek, and the elder is Dant."

It was hard to make out the details of any of the four before him now, but he had seen just enough to recognize the women. He could not stop himself from smiling at the memories of warm affection beneath the pelts in the latest years of conquest and war.

Addressing them formally, knowing they had been years apart, he asked, "Do these two have fathers who have taken them in?"

His older lover, Calia, replied, "We knew them to be sons of the Dragon. No other would do. They have no fathers."

"And would you have me take them?" A family was about loyalty and love. If these two women were tired of him, he would not blame them. Was he a good father? Had he ever been? All of his other sons had died at young ages. Was this a punishment that would be forced on the two children because of him? Would they believe him cursed? He was getting too old for child-rearing.

"We would be honored to have you named their father, DoomDragon," Bea answered this time from her place behind Tek, and he quickly remembered her voice. She had been known for singing like a nightingale. It was a sound he would be happy to hear again.

"Would you have me take them, knowing I am no longer the DoomDragon?" he pressed. "The Circle is broken. There is no..."

Elder Tril suddenly shook on his feet until the only thing keeping him up was his hold on a new walking stick. The faint orange wolf whimpered and looked on like a friend unable to help. The motion made Darknim turn and what he saw made him look twice.

Sitting on a nearby water trough was a firedrake, the small, swift cousin of the larger dragons. As only red and black dragons had blood that boiled hot enough to tempt the ice of the north, DoomDragon

had glimpsed only the dangerous full dragons before. Seeing the thin silhouette of the dog-sized firedrake startled him.

The curious beast perched along the thin edge of the trough with its tail floating in the water. He was confident there were plenty of streams and ponds in the area, and he did not know why a wild animal would come so close to people for a drink.

Without thought, Darknim moved toward the trough, surprised when the firedrake calmly awaited his approach. Once he was within reach, Darknim placed a hand under the beast's chin, and the creature sighed.

He caught the collapsing body as it toppled from the water trough, but there was no life in it. He caught it, holding the limp body across his arms.

"I have..." he stuttered in confusion.

"He is with you now, DoomDragon," Tril explained in a shaking voice that matched his quivering body. As he turned, Darknim understood further.

His eyesight was different. Where once the moon's shadows had been difficult to penetrate, every hint of light was amplified to a brilliant white. A new part of his mind was waking and interpreting the vision by filling in the grey with shapes, and soon Darknim could see clear lines to Tril's face and each feather in Elder Ela's coat. He could even see the expressions of surprise on his sons' faces.

The contrast was clearer by a hundredfold, and that was not the only change.

He felt lighter and faster, and his heart beat more quickly. He was cold suddenly, and the furs around him were not enough in the warm night. Even his skin tickled strangely.

"Complete again," Elder Ela said into her shawl of feathers, her voice like a hoot. "For how long, I wonder."

Again, Tril shuttered, and Darknim saw the colorful shades of visions darting to and from the divination master of the Circle.

"Long enough," Tril answered. "Claim your sons, DoomDragon that is once more," the elder insisted. "Then join us at the Circle. You are the final elder we sought."

Darknim DoomDragon, who had once been nothing more than a hunter in the vast stretches of the Northlands, felt the body in his arms

go heavy as the last of the spirit passed into his consciousness. Like a bird, the firedrake seemed to perch in a corner of Darknim's mind to make a nest, chirping to him amicably. It was a welcoming, familiar sound, and one Darknim at once felt he had been missing all his life. He had been seeking family, and now he had it.

Taking in the two boys and their mothers, he swore to be a good father and give the boys all they needed, then took them to meet their half-sister and adopted brother within. Among friends and family, the little firedrake sharing Darknim's mind curled up contently and sighed in relief. He had come a long way, Darknim knew, and was tired. Now, he could rest. Now, at last, he had found his flock.

Once the children were sleeping and the women were weaving together and exchanging stories about him, Darknim found his way to the Circle's hut. The frozen pool waited for him when he ducked into the structure and left his axe at the door, for the first time a participant instead of an observer.

Gannon came out of the portal from Wanter unsteadily. Someone had conjured the portal a step higher in the World of the Tainted, dropping his foot unexpectedly down by a hand's breadth. He stumbled against a pillar of stone, where the ribbons of his robes turned up a cloud of dust to make him sneeze.

It was not the kind of entrance a member of the Watching Circle wanted to make, but the others were busy around the pool, and either did not notice him or ignored him.

He took a moment to brush off his robes before joining them. Yonny had been right; he cursed as he made his way over to them and the steaming pool. If he was being summoned, the Tainted Circle had reformed.

As he took his place at the southwest edge, Gannon became keenly aware of his age. He had passed his fortieth year and had none of Rean or Gilan's wrinkles. Likewise, he had no children like Fantorn or Yonny; though, none would have expected him to for a hundred years more. That he had earned his ribbons just out of school was an impressive feat, but among these elders, he often was made to feel the fool. Still, every

Circle had to have a new graduate among them. Without them, the continuity of the two Circles of Wanter would be interrupted. That meant the Watching Circle was stuck with him.

There was no Linking today, which was a relief. Linking allowed them all, with a thought, to point out all the things he was overlooking and why a young man such as him could never understand what was going on as well as they could. The fact that they each had twenty-five or more years spent among the Circle did not seem to humble them at all.

"The Tainted Circle has been completed again," he was informed by Yonny's deep bass voice, often a surprise to hear from the thin man. Yonny had been in Gannon's place twenty-five years before, making him the youngest of the others, but he seemed determined to pass along the same disregard and disrespect he had endured.

"Stop gloating," Gannon replied. Pre-empting the rest of Yonny's boasting, he added, "I take it you saw it?"

"You left your shift but three days ago," Fantorn snidely commented from Gannon's left. "Of course, he saw it." The woman had a permanent scowl, which had added years to her face despite her attempts to streak her hair in a younger style. Her personality matched her element well; as the Seat of Force, she was blunt and aggressive. The gems beside her eyes flashed a dark red in her mood. Even focus gems as small as hers magnified powers, but they came with a cost; emotions were easily revealed. Gannon assumed his was flashing an orange-yellow, showing his irritation. He'd made no effort to hide it.

Gannon took his place at the mark of thought element and adjusted his robes once more. "I meant," he pressed, "what was seen? Did you have Spell Sight active? Are we any closer to understanding this strange mix of magic?"

From Fantorn's left, Yonny rolled his eyes dramatically. "I practice divination above all else, and you wonder if *I* had Spell Sight up?"

"Nothing was seen," Rean said, interrupting the feud from the north seat of the circle. The older woman turned her scowl on each of the younger members, making them hold their tongues by the force of her glare. "The taking of an animal's life force is an example of their Tainted magic. It is not visible to us. We must break their Circle again."

That much was a given. The Watching Circle's only purpose on the World of the Tainted was to monitor and control the use of magic,

magic once inherited from forbidden bloodlines. The presence of a Circle, much like the two in Wanter, had been a curiosity until they recognized that this Circle, despite being composed of precisely the same combination of elements and domains as the Watching Circle, was profoundly different.

Nothing could explain or duplicate the animal spirits that were tied without magical bindings to the Circle members here. Their efforts to understand this phenomenon had revealed the presence of what they now called "Tainted magic."

When channeled in isolation, Tainted magic could destroy all wizard powers. That in itself had initially made them consider abandoning the research. Still, when Tainted Circle revealed itself to be a fusion of both powers, Wanter had commanded the Watching Circle remain. They would not let the pilfered powers be perverted.

"Shall we call on that Tainted man again? The one in the north? He can attack them without revealing us."

Gannon could not even remember the man's name as their interaction had been so insignificant. Thanks to his skill with thought magic, Gannon had been included in all their dealings, but both visits with the stranger had been short. They had given him a spell to help him break the Circle. Because he had already been plotting the demise of the Tainted Circle, they had needed nothing more.

"He has inconvenienced us by dying," Fantorn said. The gems by her eyes flickered mischievously. "Killed by Kitable."

The name sounded distantly familiar to Gannon, but the way Fantorn watched Rean for a reaction made him think this was another caster from the Tainted world the Circle had dealt with before.

"Then why not get this Kitable to break the Tainted Circle for us?" Gannon asked when no one else spoke. The rest, by their pensive frowns, seemed to know the character in question, but Gannon's service on the Circle was barely four years old, and he did not recognize "Kitable," except that he suspected someone had mentioned the name once.

A binding reached out to him. He deliberately forced down his defensive shields. Ironically, it was a thought spell, and he could have tied it into knots or obliterated it easily. Instead, knowing he was among allies, he accepted sharing his mind for the moment.

The binding was from Gilan, the eldest of the group but had served the Circle for less time than his lover, Rean. The two often worked together, and Gannon suspected Gilan was explaining on Rean's behalf. The man standing on Rean's left had a calm blue gem set in his forehead, although it was nearly lost under the creases of his brow. At least the blue meant he was calm and kind.

Kitable, Gilan explained in a thought, *was observed some years ago. He had developed a new form of casting, which was assessed and rejected by Wanter. We approached him because of his skill, but he chased off messengers.*

A Tainted caster chased off a member of the Watching Circle? Gannon thought back with emphasis for effect. *They are not even real wizards!*

He was highly suspicious of all contact, Gilan calmly replied, *and we decided he was not valuable enough to pursue.*

So he had put up a small fight, and the Circle had gotten bored of it, Gannon translated. Still, to have argued effectively with the Watching Circle was interesting.

The full Linking came through, and Gannon again pulled aside his defenses to allow it. Things would move faster now, as they could share thoughts evenly and not waste time speaking aloud.

In a blink, Gannon understood that Kitable had allied himself with the Tainted Circle. From Yonny, Gannon saw the first breaking off the Circle and the injuries Kitable had suffered trying to prevent the death of the Tainted Circle's members. That was where he had heard the name: the other tainted caster had mentioned him. Kitable had wounded their previous agent. Another flash of divination showed one of the Circle members, a man wearing a wolf pelt, sitting with Kitable, sharing a cup of tea, further solidifying their relationship.

His immediate thought, seen by all the Circle, was to wonder how a wizard could be friends with someone who channeled Tainted power. His second was wondering if Kitable even knew.

The universal answer was "no," but there were no visions to prove it. It felt as though the Watching Circle had all assumed the Tainted caster would not know because they thought him too stupid to notice.

The thoughts moved to their new purpose. They had to break the Tainted Circle, and it would be easiest to do it soon. They would attack three Tainted at once in hopes of capturing or killing at least one. Two

Watching Circle members would go against each of the three targets. The first target was the newest member, the man bound to a firedrake, as he would be the most unfamiliar with his powers and, thus, the easiest to kill. The confidence of that determination offended Gannon mildly. The second target was the feather-dressed leader of the Tainted Circle because they knew the leadership would be more difficult to replace. Following that, they targeted the man they had come to believe was the leader's replacement: the man with the wolf pelt.

Gannon was to go after the current leader of the Tainted Circle, for the woman's element was thought; Gannon had to keep her powers at bay. While pure Tainted magic was a threat in all its forms, all previous observations had indicated that the Tainted Circle did not know how to separate their magic or manifest it well. The Watching Circle contained the most proficient casters of the domains and elements. It would be simple.

The image that entered Gannon's mind made Gannon laugh aloud. His adversary, surely, was older than even Gilan! Her bent frame was covered with pelts and feather coats, but it was easy to see she was frail. He was tempted to let her go, figuring she would be dead before the end of the year regardless of what he did.

She is indeed ill, came Yonny's specific thought, *but she is getting aid.* In demonstration, Yonny showed Gannon the vision of a red-haired man in colorful clothes handing the woman herbs. *You can track her down that way.*

Their plans set, the Linking dropped. Gannon pulled his defenses back into place.

"Be quick," Rean insisted as the one who would be monitoring them all. "If we can take them to Wanter, we will do so. If we must slay them, so be it."

There was the hope, Gannon knew from the residual thoughts of the Circle, that not killing a member would prevent them from being replaced, and they were all looking forward to having one of the hybrids to investigate. There was much about their way of casting they did not understand.

Paired with Gilan's fire magic, Gannon left the Circle to kill Elder Ela.

After watching the army pass through the town of Newar, Anrive retook his place in the square. His mind was buzzing as he tried to focus on splitting the stones brought down from the mountain. He was meant to be a quarryman by trade, but paying attention to his supposed job was impossible after witnessing the second army passing through Newar.

The Gaidolon forces had moved north earlier without their prince a mooncycle ago, crossing the bridge in long formations. It was no secret they had marched north to aid Trulin in defeating the renegade Prince Tohmas, who was rumored to be attempting to conquer all of Espar. But this morning he'd seen both Prince Dorakon and men wearing red and blue, the colors of the Princedom of Damoria, also march across the bridge. That surprised and shook Anrive. How dire was it that Prince Dorakon was needed with his soldiers? And he had brought Damorians with him. This was unprecedented; Damoria and Gaidol had never been allies before. All the unconquered princedoms had rallied against Prince Tohmas, and now that included Damoria too.

Includes everyone except for Nothor, Anrive reminded himself. Nothor, Gaidol's traditional ally, had retreated south across the bridge a quartercycle earlier. The bridge leading into Trulin was wearing thin from all the feet crossing it.

He would have to tell the family. His father needed to know as soon as...

"If you don't like it, you can tell the prince yourself," a voice said, catching Anrive's attention. He knew the voice: High Guardsman Craddock. The crooked-nosed man had been transferred into Newar a year prior, coinciding with when Prince Tohmas had passed through on his way north to fight Northlanders. Anrive had theories about how the two events were connected. Now, it fell to Craddock to defend all of Gaidol; this would be the route in.

"I'm just saying it can't be done easily," the bookkeeper objected.

Anrive invented a chore to fetch water and quickly made to follow the two.

"You mean it'll be expensive," the guardsman replied. "Price does not matter. This is the security of the princedom. You'll get it done."

CHAPTER 2

Anrive assumed that meant the bookkeeper and his workers would not be paid, but he had to wonder if the bookkeeper knew as much. Working for princes was unreliable these days. All too often, the pay was poor or non-existent, and there was no way for the workers to object. There was no higher court than the prince. If he decided to call it a civic duty, they would never see a single coin, and there was no recourse.

"The main pier column is the weakest point," the bookkeeper said. Like many of his kind, he reviewed his memory as he walked. The book-keepers were renowned for their memories; what he saw in his mind would be as clear as if he was reading it in the present. "We could rig it, but it'll have to be properly done. One mistake and the entire bridge comes down too early."

"Then don't make any mistakes," the burly guardsman replied. He reminded Anrive of a training partner he had had in his youth. For some reason, big men seemed to think threatening people made them better workers.

Anrive stopped at the well, running out of excuses. If he followed now, it would be obvious he was eavesdropping, and his father would not forgive him for getting caught.

The bookkeeper grumbled as he moved out of earshot.

That afternoon, Anrive volunteered for the job of modifying the bridge. It was not hard to get in because enough people knew the pay was not guaranteed. He ensured he wasn't the first volunteer, careful not to look too eager. But they were happy to have him as a quarryman on the job.

That night, he stole a horse and rode out of town.

It was nigh-on midnight by the time he dismounted, knowing the trail into the mountains nearest Broken Falls Lake was treacherous for a horse who did not know it well. He could hardly return the horse in the morning without question if it were lame. It would be hard enough to clean off the sweat from the coat and the road dust from its hooves.

Once on the rise over the lakeside, coming down from the east, Anrive paused.

"I assume someone's on watch," he said to the empty hillside, squinting into the quarter moon's light. "It's me, Anrive." Shortly, he heard rustling, and a small figure appeared from the hide beside the road. "You sent on the signal?" he asked.

"Course, Uncle," the shy boy replied, Hanni by the tone of his voice. The boy was only eleven this year, barely old enough to be allowed to be a lookout.

"Traded shifts, did you?" Anrive asked. The shift rotation should not have allowed a youngster like Hanni to watch overnight. Boys of that age tended to fall asleep on duty.

In the shadows, Hanni nodded his head reluctantly.

"Did that myself a lot," Anrive said. "But don't tell your grandfather I said that. Just remember that if you're going to take this shift, you'd better stay alert. The gods themselves won't save you if grandfather catches you sleeping on lookout duty!"

"I'd never!" Hanni declared, his chin lifted defiantly.

"Good. I'll be back this way later, so I'll check on that."

Anrive led the horse on. He planned to head back by the lakeside trail but knew the threat would keep Hanni awake all night.

Tethering his horse by the barn's trough, Anrive followed the dim light of a lamp into the barn, and there, he waited.

The family entered in trickles. Each group brought a lamp with them, illuminating the barn as if it was midday, not midnight. Mothers brought their children if they were older than ten and hustled them into perches on the hay bales or in the loft. Every last person hugged Anrive on their way in. From his brothers, he got a pat on the back or a warm squeeze on his shoulder. No one spoke except for the eldest of his brothers, Brandin, who said, "Must be important."

Anrive nodded. Brandin took his place on the main floor with his brothers, the far end of the line as the eldest. They were all needed.

Anrive tried not to grin, but seeing the family responding to his presence was strangely exciting. He was the youngest, considered "the baby" at twenty-five years old. Hells, some days he still got his hair tussled by his closest brothers. The only mother he'd known was his older brothers' wives, who continued to dote on him even though he had a trade and a life of his own. Now here, they were to hear what "the baby" had to say.

His pride left when Hiron Carraway, hunched over his cane, entered the barn. The family's patron did not limp, but he deliberately placed his unsteady feet as he entered the barn, the only place large enough to fit the whole family.

A single chair lived in the barn, and two of Anrive's nieces brought it out to the center of the barn for Hiron as Anrive scrambled to join the line of his brothers. He left a gap to his right, acknowledging where his missing brother should have stood.

Silence swept over the barn in anticipation.

Anrive's father cleared his throat. "We are here. Anrive, you have the floor."

Anrive cleared his throat, acutely aware of the number of eyes watching him. They had, as children, done reports as their training, but he'd never been called upon to do a formal one. He came to his father's side.

They are just family, he reminded himself.

"As you all know, the Gaidolon army passed through Newar on the 25th of the last cycle," Anrive said in a clear, calm voice he'd learned from his father. It seemed appropriate although it lacked Hiron's authority. He had never figured out how his father could add such strength to mere words. "His ranks number just short of six thousand. They took, and held, Galvay as he entered Trulin's land. Nothor's forces were with them then but have since retreated in full. However, today, Dorakon himself crossed the bridge into Trulin. He brought with him a thousand soldiers from Damoria."

Anrive paused, waiting for his father, but Hiron did not speak. He rarely did anymore. Although none of them admitted it aloud, they knew it was their father's way of preparing them to take over governing the family.

Hiron looked out into the crowd and found Cardeth, Anrive's third eldest brother, and prompted him with a stare.

Cardeth's voice had authority like Hiron's when he spoke into the hush of the listening family. "He goes to support the morale now that Nothor has withdrawn. Any news of Trulin? What do they think of the loss of Galvay, I wonder."

Hiron looked to Anrive for the reply. The youngest son filled in: "The guardsmen retreating said Trulin and Gaidol were allies against Tohmas, but that is my other news: rumors came yesterday that Trulin has been defeated." A gasp, sounding like the final breath of a dead man, whispered through the barn. "Prince Tohmas Galanth has married Lady

Arnika Trulin. Her cousin Tandar Oranon now claims to be a kingsman under the conqueror."

Hiron looked out once more, and he caught the stare of Brandin, his eldest living son. Brandin smoothly continued, "So King Tohmas' army will come south. What plans has Prince Dorakon set, little brother?"

Any gaps in his information gathering would disappoint his father. But this one, Anrive could proudly answer. "They have a plan to injure the attacking army before they retreat although I do not know the details of that attack. The main defense will be in Gaidol where they can control the terrain," Anrive replied. "I have also learned that they plan to collapse the bridge at Newar behind them."

He felt the stares of his family, which he had initially considered exciting, gain weight. He was beginning to feel it was nicer to be ignored.

"He would destroy the only bridge across the river?" Hiron said, his voice as clear as a summer's day. "Short-sighted of him. He is afraid." There were dozens of smaller footbridges, but the rocky, steep banks of the BrokenFall River were not easily joined. Only the narrowing at Newar allowed a solid bridge for waggons, horses, and carts. Destroying it would cut Gaidol off from their usual enemy, Trulin. More immediately relevant, it would force Prince Tohmas' invading army to go around the lake, risking the treacherous mountain trails and waterfalls.

Brandin was prompted to continue the thought. "It might save Dorakon from this so-called king," Brandin said, spitting, "but it'll cut off all trade north. It's not like Gaidol can walk through Solta these days either. Losing the bridge will hurt Gaidol and its allies like Nothor."

"Nothor is out of this. Prince Neillen claims the gods appeared to his emissary. He has retreated," Anrive reminded them.

"So Dorakon has bought allies from Damoria as a replacement," Cardeth said. "Those alliances will be fragile. He will have to attack Tohmas' forces soon."

All eyes went to Hiron for the reply. Anrive's father sat posed, his jaw set and his stare hard. For a long moment, there was silence.

No one had mentioned Lance. The second youngest member of the family marched with Prince Tohmas. Lance had left Gaidol under the pretense of being on loan to Prince Tohmas, but he had broken his oath when Gaidol had declared their opposition to Galanth, and Lance had refused to be recalled. Now he was meant to be their enemy.

CHAPTER 2

The Carraway family personally had no qualms with Tohmas. In some ways, it could be the opposite if they decided to throw aside their loyalty to Dorakon.

Loyalty to Dorakon had been their only option; without it, they all knew their lives were forfeit. Lance had embodied that the most of any of them, and yet he had left them. Was that a sign of things to come? Anrive hadn't been involved in any of the decisions about Lance. He still didn't know if the family sanctioned his brother's opposition to Dorakon or not. He knew it had resulted in the family's withdrawal into hiding.

The blood that united the family alienated them from Dorakon. The prince knew the sons of Minette Vont could dispute his right to rule. He had been ready to act on it, wipe them out, and defend his position. For decades, Hiron had given him no excuse. Despite ten sons—almost an army by himself—Hiron had kept himself or his sons from ever looking like a threat. When Baran, the eldest, had opposed Dorakon's rule, the family confronted it. Baran lay dead because of Lance, a desperate act to protect the family from Dorakon's distrust.

"I want the bridge." Their father's voice cut through the silence. A stir of uncertainty trickled in its wake.

Dorakon's plan would hurt the people of Gaidol, and Hiron, in honor of his wife, would not allow that. Their ultimate loyalty was to Gaidol, not to her prince.

"What are his plans for the bridge?" Hiron asked, his stare on Anrive.

"Rig the main footing," Anrive replied. He took another moment to gather his thoughts. This was not going how he had expected. "They've got a bookkeeper who claims they'll set pulleys to yank it out and drop the bridge. They aim to have some of the enemy cross first, pull it after."

Hiron looked at Granth, and another of Anrive's brothers picked up the discussion.

"He's hoping to isolate those who crossed the bridge for an easy kill," Granth agreed. "And anyone on the bridge is as good as gone. Once in the water, there's no way to get them out." The cliffs around Newar were steep. Old ladders hung on either side of the bridge as a final hope of reaching someone who fell, but the current was swift and broken by stones. To Anrive's knowledge, no one who had fallen in had ever been

retrieved. "Father," Granth asked openly, finally voicing the question they needed answered, "are we to oppose Dorakon now?"

They waited again, watching their father. Many of them were guardsmen in Dorakon's army or had been until they had been summoned away by their father. All of them had been told a thousand times that they were to be loyal to Gaidol. They could not let their mother's heritage show.

"It sounds like we're giving Dorakon the reason he needs to wipe us out," Anrive added cautiously. He would abide by whatever decision his father made, but he was tired of living in the shadows of a name that could damn him. The family should not be divided. He missed his closest brother and wanted Lance home.

Hiron sat in silence for a long time, and no one, not even the youngsters in the rafters, dared fidget. This decision would commit the family to war. If they chose the wrong side, they would be hunted down.

At length, Hiron raised his bearded chin. "I will not allow Dorakon to threaten my family. Lance is coming home. Let us open the path for him."

Anrive let out a yip of joy.

"Let us begin," Hiron said, a stern glare on Anrive for his outburst. "Let us, for once, plot our freedom. Brandin, take the floor."

The eldest strode forward to address the brothers closely, but they spoke loud enough to include the entire family.

"Anrive, what forces are there in Newar?"

"High Guardsman Craddock and his guard. That's six hundred men in the city."

"We don't need that many to hold the bridge," Brandin said. "He plans to let some of them cross. That means the guardsman will focus on keeping the Galanth forces on the bridge. They won't be defending the Trulin side."

He checked over his shoulder. Hiron nodded approval at the reasoning.

"One team to stop the pier from going down," Brandin said. "The other takes the bridge and keeps it open. All over the age of fifteen joins."

Butterflies filled Anrive's gut, but he stood proudly among his brothers and tried not to let his nervousness show. Others were trained as guardsmen. Others had been in battle before. Anrive knew a sword

well, but he had never expected to use one against a Gaidolon. And now he would lead a team of his nieces or nephews. It seemed mad.

He kept thinking about Lance. He would get to see his brother again if they survived this. That was cause enough.

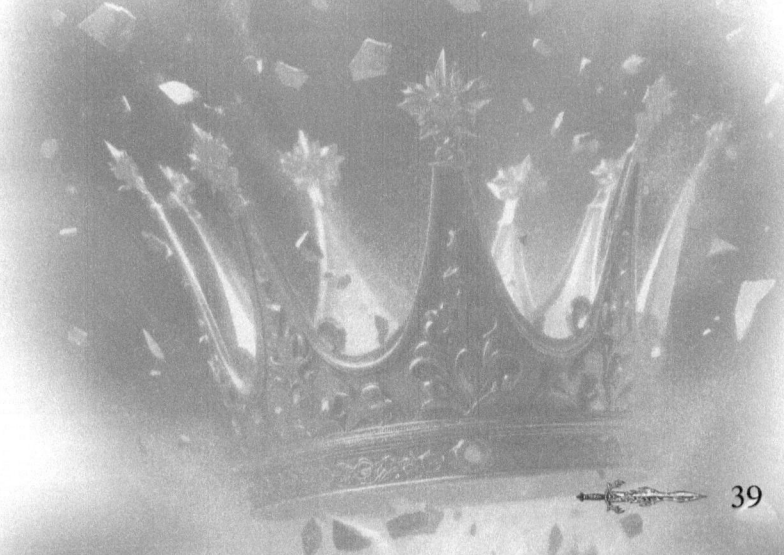

Chapter 3

Arnika stirred when Tohmas pulled away from her side but had not fully awoken by the time she heard the armor moving. Dragging her head out of the wool of sleep, she still had her eyes shut when she grumbled into the dawn light, "How can you be awake? You were up half the night!"

Half rolled over and ready to bury her head in a pillow in denial of the dawn, Arnika heard someone laugh.

"Haf a nite?" the Rydan's voice said, startling her into sitting bolt upright. "Tohmas," the prime protector said with a tsk, "I been tinkin' ya go ahl nite."

Now wide awake and flushed in embarrassment, Arnika clung to the pillow as she spotted the sarcastic Rydan standing inside the tent entrance. Tohmas wore half-leather armor, but SoulBurner was already on his belt, and he was smiling into the slight light.

She had not even managed to form a sentence before Tohmas touched her cheek and planted a light kiss on her forehead.

"Anything you can say to me," he said in recognition of her reddening face, "you can say in front of Carsh. Don't worry."

He had finished putting on his boots by the time she found her voice. Determined not to be dismissed, she said, "It was my stamina. The first times are tender. I'm sure I'll keep up better tonight."

Both men laughed. "Spunky!" the prime protector said with an approving nod to the king. "I be lykin'!"

The king smiled again at her, his eyes mischievous but private. "I look forward to it."

Now dressed in his leather with green and silver overcoat and sword, he rolled his shoulders and added, "For now, I need to get going. I want this army out of Trulin in four days, which means marching today. With Gaidol on the way, there's plenty to organize. Your cousin also apparently has a few things he wants to go over, so I have a busy day. Take as much time as you want, my lady. They can always catch up."

She nodded, unable to say anything, and watched him leave. The Rydan sent her another grin before following the king out.

She was dressed before the servants even dared to stick their heads through the entrance. Her bleeding had started unexpectedly, but she had all her belongings at hand to deal with it. Unwilling to slow him, she oversaw the striking of the tent and had them ready to go before dawn.

How the protectors always knew where he was remained a mystery, but when she asked Protector Ganth, who was watching over her, to take her to her husband, the man obeyed immediately.

While the army broke camp and started marching, the kingsmen met with the king in the new planning tent. They paused when she appeared in the doorway, and several of them scowled openly. Still, their position around the table with the maps was close enough to a CampCircle to give her confidence and request a stool. Tohmas himself brought it forward.

Dressed in her brown and white deliberately, she took her place at their CampCircle.

Tohmas carried on the conversation for only two sentences before the eldest of the sons of Zayban, Kingman Sol of Solta, interrupted.

"Is it wise to go over this now, Tohmas?"

The conversation was about Gaidol's known position and scouting patterns. They expected a confrontation with Trulin's southern neighbor shortly. It was up to the kingsmen to be ready for it.

"I would rather not discuss it after Gaidol engages us," the king replied with a raised eyebrow. "Is there a problem, Sol?"

It was evident to Arnika that the grizzled kingsman was looking at her when the king asked the question, and the look should have been the answer. Instead, Sol shook his head and looked away. "Naw," he said in an almost Rydan tone.

They moved on but had just started discussing more complicated combinations of horn calls when Sol paused again to stare at Arnika. She pointedly ignored him and instead watched the map. The areas they were moving through were familiar to her, but Tohmas' people seemed to know the land as well as she did. Someone had been scouting well.

When Kingsman Barnon asked his brother a question, the rest of the group realized Sol was not listening.

"Sol!" came Tohmas' un-ignorable voice.

The kingsman snapped free of his thoughts to reply, "She's a Truller!"

Tandar had headed home to Caint that morning after speaking with Tohmas, and she would not see him again for many mooncycles. Her cousin Altana had found a place among Lady Fayela's women until they set up a private abode for Arnika closer to the marital tent. Tohmas was surrounded by only his older friends: the two sons of Zayban, the now-kingsman of Clandac, the prime protector Rydan, and one guardian, who seemed to have done the scouting between Gaidol and Trulin. Arnika was an obvious outsider.

Tohmas raised an eyebrow at his uncle again. "Trulin is now an ally."

"A recent ally," the kingsman argued. "I don't like discussing anything that might be—"

"She is my wife, Sol," Tohmas interrupted. "If she wishes to stay, I welcome it."

The ugly looks from the rest of the room made Arnika acutely aware that she was without other allies. The one exception seemed to be the guardian, who took advantage of the pause to sit back on another stool. She recognized him then as Guardian Carraway, for he wore a splint down the length of his left leg. At least he seemed content with her, but she doubted he would leap to her defense.

"Tohmas," Kingsman Barnon pleaded, "without any insult meant to the lady, she is still a stranger to us. We want to be careful."

It was Tohmas' turn to stare at her, and she feared he would ask her to leave.

"Among my people," Arnika insisted, "the closest female relative of the prince must always be present at CampCircle. This is my place."

With a sigh, the king turned to his prime protector. "Carsh, you will hold any oath I make for me?" he inquired.

The prime protector snorted. "'Course," he replied.

"Good." Tohmas pulled his knife from his belt and offered it to Arnika. Hesitantly, she took the jeweled piece, then watched in shock as he knelt before her.

"I absolve you, for the next candle, of all crimes. Nothing you do will be held against you. Carsh will see that oath through. That being done, I beg you, if you now or ever will plot against me or wish me ill, cut my throat. I would much rather be dead than believe you disapprove of me."

"Toh—" was as far as Sol got. Carsh's lithe form was immediately between the concerned kingsman and the kneeling king, blocking Sol's advance.

Undeterred, Tohmas went on: "Cut on one side or the other..." He pointed to where she knew blood ran. "...not the middle. I swear by the Flame, I will not move."

When Altana had returned to the Esparan camp, she had carried two knives to help them do precisely what Tohmas was now offering. Then, Arnika had been too terrified even to try harm the giant of a man, knowing well his skill with blades and his constant vigilance would likely see the blade turned against her. With him now at her feet, she briefly considered the option.

He had sworn by the Flame, but it was hard to believe he would let her cut his throat.

She turned the blade over and extended the hilt back to him. "I have no desire to see you slain," she said as firmly as she could.

He raised his hand to refuse the blade as he rose. "Keep it," he told her. He turned to the rest of the stunned room. "You have all witnessed. From now on, an insult to her is an insult to me. I trust her. That is all there is to be said on the matter."

With the threat in the statement, no one argued.

They went back to their discussions, and Arnika did not move from her seat on the stool, the knife on her lap. Every now and then, a head turned to cast an uneasy glance her way, but there were no more objections. When they left the tent, they bowed to her in due respect. Having men who had once been princes bow to her was such a strange experience, she remained on her stool for long moments more as servants loaded the table. When it came time to drop the tent, Arnika finally made her way into the daylight.

Horses had been readied, and she was ushered to where Tohmas was overseeing the last of the camp from Schlavarai's back. The dappled mare gave Arnika a welcoming nuzzle before the new wife could mount her horse, Emerald Glory. She had to give one of the protectors the knife to get into her saddle.

"I'll have a belt and sheath made for you if you wish to carry it," her husband offered as she settled into position on horseback. "Most women I know carry knives."

At first, she thought the statement untrue. Celebrant Loni had been seen with a blade, but His Lady Mother certainly was without. What other women did he associate with?

Leaving as they were, near the end of the train, Arnika found her sights filled with them. Riding in front of their husbands, the Rydan women brought up the rear of the army leaving LandWater. True to Tohmas' word, every last one of the women had a short knife on their hip or leg.

"I am unfamiliar with it," she admitted, leaving it in the protector's hand. When they arrived at their destination, she could store it in the tent as a gift, but she had little other use for it.

"Would you like to learn?" he surprised her by asking.

Arnika shrugged. "I could, I guess."

Her answer seemed to please him; he grinned as he gave an unseen signal to Schlavarai to trot. "I'll have someone teach you." He glanced back, checking that she was following. Emerald had not needed any sign from Arnika to trot after the man. "I fear I may not be around often enough. Come on; we need to catch the center of the march."

She spent the first day marching at his side and never once wished for a waggon.

They marched the length of the day, following Lance's route toward his homeland. Although he heard of skirmishes between his scouts and the vanguard of the enemy's forces, Tohmas did not even glimpse the primary column by the time evening fell.

They set camp in an abandoned field. Tohmas missed the rise of the foothills, which would have given him a lookout point. The sky here was more like the Outlands: wide and open.

Ironic, he thought. He had once argued that the vantage point was not required in combat; leading from within the fighters was best. Now he had to wonder if setting up a platform was better for the sanity of the commander when the horns were silent.

To his relief, he spotted DoomDragon winding his way through the tents. He needed to stop thinking about Gaidol's movements; Kitable had been assigned that task. Guessing what the wizard would see was a waste of Tohmas' time.

"You didn't come out this morning," Tohmas accused in a shout once his friend was within earshot. Nearby protectors let the Northlander pass between them with a wry smile. "I was almost offended."

"A meeting with the Circle," Darknim replied in a similar shout. "In other words, none of your business!"

Once Darknim was within a dozen paces, Tohmas noticed something profoundly different about his kingsman. On a mundane level, DoomDragon had found another dragon, albeit a small one, to add to his scale armor and horned helm, but the thing that alarmed Tohmas most was the change to the Northlander's eyes. Carsh sidled away, muttering as he sought a good luck trinket to fend off the strangeness.

Less bothered, Tohmas looked Darknim in his yellow, slit-pupil eyes and asked, "What happened to you?"

The man, proving that the change was only superficial, smiled broadly under his beard and laughed. "The Circle is again complete. DoomDragon has returned."

Skeptically, Tohmas asked, "I knew you when you were DoomDragon before, Darknim, and your eyes were never so reptilian. Care to—"

"*I* completed the Circle. For the first time, the DoomDragon is now an elder as well. And a kingsman!" the Northlander said. "This could be tricky to balance, but for now..."

"Ah," Carsh said, coming forward. He lifted the head of the skinned dragon draping Darknim's shoulders, then let it drop. "Naw magic?"

Darknim opened his mouth, then closed it, his brow creased in thought. "Might be," he said. "I can't say I understand much of it."

Sniffing like a dog, Carsh circled Darknim, making the Northlander chuckle. Carsh ended by wrinkling his nose. "Naw," he said. With that decided, he returned to his place behind Tohmas.

"The Circle has been reformed?" Tohmas asked.

Darknim straightened, matching Tohmas' imposing height and bulk. His voice took on a formal tone. "I have come to pledge the Circle's aid once more. Although the powers we control are limited to Scrys and divination, we are at your service, King Tohmas." The Northlander even bowed like an Esparan.

"I am glad to hear it," Tohmas said. "And I think Kitable will be glad too." Kitable had been managing all the defenses and the reconnaissance so far. He could let go of at least some responsibilities; the Circle of the Raven was particularly apt at scrying and could probably learn more about his enemies than Kitable. They were not as powerful as Kitable when it came to manifesting magic and doing damage, but their illusions could be potent if needed.

"When you have time," Darknim added with a broader grin that revealed slight sharpening of the teeth to resemble those of the firedrake around his shoulders, "I invite you to come meet my sons, Tohmas. I have finally gathered my family around me. My life is full: three wives and four children!"

This time, Tohmas cracked a smile. "I would be honored."

"After we take Gaidol?" Darknim suggested, to which Tohmas nodded.

"Agreed. Take care of them until then!"

Darknim was already on his way. With all the titles the man carried, Tohmas expected him to be tired, but the Northlander trotted back to his tent as if he was twenty years old once more, full of enthusiasm. *Just like any man with three waiting women would,* Tohmas thought with a chuckle.

Tohmas ducked inside the planning tent, eager to return to Arnika but knowing she had not settled into the tent yet. He had time to plot the attack on Gaidol and reconsider retaliations and options. Dorakon's forces were in retreat, but Tohmas did not wholly trust that.

He located his tokens used to arrange the various fyrds, but he was interrupted by Kitable entering the tent. Without preamble, the wizard found a seat at the large table.

It was evident that Carsh knew what was about to be said, but a blink was all it took for Tohmas to measure Kitable's guilty look.

"Did they pay you well?" he asked as Carsh handed the wizard wine and tossed Tohmas a waterskin of wildwater. After one of the smaller swigs he had ever swallowed, Tohmas threw the skin back. They were getting low on the drink, and he did not want to deprive his brother of it. He, unlike Carsh, did not mind balancing the Rydan drink with Galanth wine, Clandac ale, or Northlander tea.

"Not a coin," the wizard insisted with an offended look that proved the man recognized the jest. "Plenty of flattery, though. 'You are the only person he will listen to. You alone can make him see' and all that."

The way Carsh perched on the back of the chair across from Tohmas identified his brother as another willing party to the confrontation.

"Both of you?"

"I be you greatest defense!" Carsh mimicked the kingsmen's pleas. "I be havin' to speak reason."

"Regardless," Kitable interrupted, "they are right, Tohmas. You must realize that you have a blind spot over Lady Arnika. She is Truller. You are responsible for the death of her brother and father both. She cannot be trusted!"

For Tohmas, the argument was simple. "She is my wife." He loved hearing that word.

"That does not mean we can trust her," Kitable answered.

Tohmas knew they were confused by his immediate faith in the little woman who now shared his tent, but they were both missing the overwhelmingly simple explanation. He tried elaborating; "She has thrown her lot in with us, Kitable. My success is her success, just as my failure would be her failure. Carsh, you, of all people, should understand. She is my wife. I can trust her."

Looking like an indignant rooster on the back of the chair, Carsh made a face. "I naw be trustin' Darcina!" he objected.

"You sleep next to her most nights," Tohmas replied. "You sleep next to a woman who carries a *shanye* and knows how to use it well. Is that not trust?"

"Tohmas, this is not—" Realization suddenly appeared on the wisavi's face as the sentence fell off. Spinning in his seat, he stared at Carsh. "You are married?!"

Tohmas could not stop himself from laughing. "Has been for nearly three years now," he informed the wisavi. "Just like Arnika, Darcina could not hope to be in a better position. She will not betray that."

For several flickers, the wizard seemed to debate whether he should confirm his discovery with the Rydan or continue the conversation they had evidently agreed to have with Tohmas. Purpose won out, but the look the wisavi gave to the Rydan insisted that he would have to come back to this later.

Having been challenged, Carsh was reconsidering his position, leaving only Kitable to confront Tohmas on the believed indiscretions.

"The fact remains that she is a stranger to our company. Gaidol will be seeking a means to disrupt you. She could be dangerous," Kitable insisted.

The answer did not change. "She is my wife."

The wizard rubbed the brow of his nose as he considered the assertion. When he again looked up, he stated the obvious. "You are in love with her."

Tohmas laughed again. "She is my wife!" he repeated. If he had married her, then he loved her.

Carsh shot to his feet like he had been kicked. "I naw be lovin' Darcina!" he pre-emptively insisted.

"Arguing that with you would just annoy you. The point is," Tohmas said with a nod to the wizard, "yes, I love her. She is my wife."

Kitable put his head back into his hand and closed his eyes. "We cannot win this." Now lacking an ally in the Rydan, the wizard stood and straightened his robes. "I cannot argue that. You love her, fine. I hope Ocea is kind to us, my king, for you will not let yourself even entertain the thought of her betrayal. I cannot defend you from that."

Tohmas stood to see the man out, not knowing what to say. He knew Arnika would not betray him, and he could not see why they failed to recognize that fact.

"I truly hope," he told his wisavi, "you understand someday."

Kitable dejectedly shook his head. There was no one that Kitable trusted that deeply, and it was obvious. "I doubt it, my king," the wizard replied. Straightening once more in the entrance, he added, "I did as you requested, scrying. Dorakon is directing the Gaidolon army himself. They look ready to run."

"Thank you, Kitable," Tohmas replied. "You're faster than any scout I have."

Kitable shrugged. "Let me know if there's something more you want me to do."

Tohmas shook his head. "Defend us, but don't go hunting them unless you detect magic getting involved. If I am to have Espar under a single banner, it must be won through unity, not magic."

"As much as I hate waiting, I understand. Good luck" was the last thing the wizard said on his way out.

Turning back around, Tohmas found Carsh's wagging finger under his nose.

"I naw be lovin' Darcina!" the Rydan protested again, and Tohmas smiled.

"Then why do you tolerate her disobedience, Carsh? You should have killed her by now."

"Sha be fun," Carsh declared happily. It was true that the Rydan seemed to enjoy the fiery rejection from the woman he had claimed, but Tohmas believed his brother had the logic backward.

"She is only fun," Tohmas said, "because you love her spirit. If she were anyone else, you would have knifed her a dozen times by now."

The way his brother wrinkled his nose before following Tohmas out into the night made it clear he was as of yet unconvinced.

They parted ways at Tohmas', which again included his altar. Arnika awaited him shyly.

Taking off his shoes for prayer, he said, "We can have another tent if you would rather sleep alone, my lady."

Her immediate reply warmed him. "Do you tire of me so quickly?"

Unable to stop himself, his arms reached around her and pulled her close so he could kiss her neck.

"Never. Never will I tire of you, my lady," he promised, knowing it to be an oath. He should be praying, but he knew he was losing the argument with himself when she cautiously touched her lips to his chin.

It was a kind of respect to the Goddess Inac, was it not? Inac was known as the Lady of Lust too.

He took her to bed without another thought.

Love. Damn it. Of all the times to be playing with love, Kitable could not think of a worse one. Tohmas had known Arnika for just over a halfcycle. How had a meeting become love?

There was nothing Kitable could do. Magic could not touch the soul; Kitable was powerless in the face of love. He had never expected Tohmas, who dealt with people practically, to fall for a pretty face, but he could not stop the king from sabotaging himself.

Upon Kitable's arrival back to his waggon, three celebrants were waiting for him to begin their evening discussions.

Calanor was untouchable, the perfect antithesis of magic, but the more time they spent talking, the more in common they seemed to have. Of the two untouchables Kitable knew, the other being the unpredictable Celebrant Loni, only Calanor had started manifesting his powers, and what Kitable saw made him want to study it more.

Calanor could target someone, and he could cast a Scry. He could create, destroy, alter, or summon things, but he had yet to succeed in summoning something by defining it. It could have been the celebrant's inexperience, but anything he affected seemed to have to be visible to be changed, and that made his creation and summoning far more limited than Kitable's.

But Calanor created spells with his thoughts alone, and that was an advantage Kitable wanted to understand better. It was a shame he was missing his tongue. Requiring a translator for his projected magical speech, in the form of his wife Celebrant Corolys, slowed down their discussions markedly.

Today, Celebrant Darak attended with the other two celebrants.

"Just a moment of your time," the Celebrant of Pari requested. The bearded man hefted a contraption of wood and hinges. "I was wondering if you could enchant a splint to help support the leg. See, limp limbs hang, and the blood pools in them, and to get the blood back..."

Kitable pushed Tohmas' infatuation to one side of his mind and focused on the task.

He had finished with the splint and moved on to another debate about Calanor's ability to view dreams, something no wizard had ever accomplished, when they were interrupted by an approaching conversation.

"You dare lay another hand on me," a woman's voice shouted, "and I'll blast you straight to BellRoost!"

Kitable had last seen Shimmer Weaver at the wedding. Before that, the last time he had "seen" Miss Weaver, he had been under a spell, and his vision of her had tried to kill him. That experience reinforced his determination to avoid the dancer from Fixer City at all costs. She was an evident danger to him, and he, unlike his king, was unwilling to expose himself to such hazards.

That meant he did not want to see her and her bright clothing any time soon.

Behind the red-haired dancer came Sabian. Proudly a Follower of Carsh, the Esparan boy had taken up the Rydan's style and wore only trousers and his baldric wherever he went. He had no knife out for once, but that seemed to be because he was trying to catch the elusive dancer.

"You could try!" came the retort as the boy chased after Shimmer, then around her to stand in her path. "I'm responsible for Seria's death, remember? She was more powerful than you!"

Instead of moving around, Shimmer met the boy's threat with her glare firm and her hands on her hips.

"It's not about amount of power," Shimmer replied. "It's about how you apply the power. I'll—"

The sight of her reminded Kitable too much of the Heart's Desire spell he had narrowly escaped. Rising to his feet and making his voice as imposing as possible, Kitable demanded, "What, by the hells, is going on here?"

Sabian looked like someone had grabbed his shoulders from behind and shouted "boo"; he leaped around defensively and stood beside the smug dancer before recognizing Kitable. He immediately lost most of the color in his face.

"Nothing, Wisavi," he said.

Beside him, Shimmer Weaver smirked further and tossed her head.

"Then go do 'nothing' somewhere else! I have better things to do than listen to you two bicker!" Kitable replied.

"Of course, Wisavi," Shimmer said with a nod. She was around the corner of the next vardo before Sabian had even gathered his senses enough to realize he had been told off. He went after her in a blink, and Kitable sat back down.

Celebrant Corolys rose to her feet, her long blue robes trailing. The crow's feet on her eyes made the sparkling teardrops on her temples crease when she smiled apologetically.

"I think I should speak to that girl," she said. "Timon should be able to cover translation for a bit." With a pat to the young acolyte between them, who sat so silently that Kitable often forgot he was present, she followed the two intruders out. Celebrant Darak was also gone, but Kitable did not bother to wonder why. With silence again presiding, he tried to forget about the red-haired woman and continued the conversation that had been interrupted.

"Do you ever dream, Celebrant?"

Shimmer refused to run away, but she walked with long, proud strides. The moment they were out of reasonable earshot, Sabian caught her arm again despite Shimmer's attempts to twist it free. His voice was softer, but he kept to his resolve. "The Rydans still see you as a threat," he warned her. "I can protect you. They cannot object if they know I have—"

"Have what?" Shimmer spun to face him, her heart skipping several beats to hear what she thought was a threat. "Have claimed me? Is that it? Claim me, Sabian? You have no right to touch me!"

She had thought they had come to an understanding, but the way he held her arm made it clear that he had either forgotten or never understood in the first place.

She was not strong enough physically to shake his grip, but she had other means of protecting herself. A whispered word activated a Heat Shield, which responded to the intrusion and seared the inside of his hand.

"I have every—" By the time the pain overruled his determination, his hand was blistered red.

A Rydan curse, proof he had been following Carsh for too long, escaped him

"Then why did you stop?" she demanded. "Why did you tell the wisavi it was nothing? Why deny it if you think you are in the right?"

With his good hand holding the wrist of the wounded hand, Sabian paused, his eyes suddenly aware.

She had, at last, dragged reason back into his thick head. "Because you knew," she told him, moving forward and forcing him to step back in the heat, "that Esparans don't do what you are trying to do. And whether you like it or not, you are Esparan." With a final toss of her head, she stormed off. Cold or water spells could help his hand, but she did not even give them passing consideration. He deserved the burn.

"Kitable doesn't understand!" Sabian shouted, not moving to follow her.

For the best. The next spell would be more aggressive.

"You're the one who doesn't get it!" she shot back.

Although she let the Heat Shield drop, her fury at the encounter persisted as she strode on, walking right into the Celebrant of Ocea, Celebrant Corolys.

The older woman was clearly waiting for Shimmer and smiled in a motherly fashion that annoyed the dancer. Most of the time, she could barely convince herself to tolerate celebrants, but today was not promising to be easy.

"Don't waste your breath," Shimmer insisted the moment the woman opened her mouth to speak. "I have neither the time nor the patience for gods."

The smile would not be upset; instead, Celebrant Corolys cocked her head. "How about a concerned mother? Do you want to talk about it?"

"About what? About Sabian?" Shimmer forced herself to laugh. "Do you think that was the first time someone tried pushing me around? I only tried to be gentle with him because we used to get along so well. I don't know what has gotten into him, but I don't think it's my problem! Good riddance!"

Her stomping feet tossed her colorful skirts about her as she sauntered a few more steps.

Celebrant Corolys's voice reached out like an offered embrace. "Do you want to talk about what happened to you?"

Shimmer stopped just as cold as Sabian had, and her throat tightened. It was fast becoming common knowledge that Celebrant Calanor was both hearing and speaking thoughts, but Shimmer had not expected it from the man's wife. Further, she was sure she would have noticed any

such intrusion, if only because the magic he used was untouchable and it would have dispelled her current defenses and hovering spells.

"About what?" Shimmer tried instead, forcing every bit of her acting skills to camouflage how much the comment had distressed her. There was no way the celebrant saw through it, yet the concerned smile remained.

"Shimmer," the woman gently said, placing a loving hand on her shoulder, "you are a beautiful young woman who has her pick of any partner in camp and yet accepts none. You are not looking either. You tease them madly, then walk away. Did you want to talk about the reason for that?"

Shimmer had never explained the reasons to her father, and she certainly would not discuss it with a stranger.

"Nothing to discuss. Tell your goddess you tried, but I'm too far fallen to be saved by kind words. I know too much to believe."

Leaving both assaults behind, she rushed for the sanctuary of her home vardo and shop, Match and Mixer. Still, the memories Celebrant Corolys had brought to the surface lingered, and it took until the dancing was done that night to finally banish them. If the woman had been trying to help, she had failed.

Some things were better left buried.

As soon as the colorful dress vanished around the corner, Sabian cursed. She was right. He hated even to think the words, but she was right. Esparans did not accept the Rydan way. They were wrong, but...

A wisavi was a respected advisor to great leaders, and Sabian knew no better leader than Tohmas. Wisavi Kitable had to be wise then, so why did he side with the Esparans? The world was about taking what one wanted and dealing with more influential people to get the rest.

Did Kitable not understand how the world worked? It was easy to see!

Sabian wanted the fiery beauty of Shimmer Weaver, but he had failed to take her. Did that make her and her fire magic stronger?

"What was I thinking?!" he finally shouted, stomping his foot. As much as he wanted to hit something, his burned hand did not allow it.

"Same thing every man thinks when he looks at her," came the voice of the Celebrant of Pari from where he was leaning against a waggon. Celebrant Darak stared after the place Shimmer had vanished. "Gods, she's gorgeous. How can I get under her skirts?" The celebrant chuckled with a flash of a smile and a pair of suggestively raised eyebrows. "I'm just as guilty as any, of course, but at least I have the sense to be quiet about it."

Sabian dropped his wounded hand instinctually as if facing a Rydan and wanting to keep the injury secret, but the celebrant was already lifting a hand to him.

"Let me see it. I can fix it up for you."

Both cultures asked him to obey the celebrant. Rydans feared and respected the rare celebrants that made rounds of their lands and did displays on holy days, and all Esparans honored the celebrants of their area. Celebrant Darak was sworn to Tohmas, and that had Sabian complacently extending his hand.

"I don't need your help," he informed the man.

The celebrant shrugged as he examined the blistered skin. "Of course, you don't," he said. "I offered the aid. You can take it or leave it."

The celebrant kept hold of Sabian's wrist with his right hand as he searched for something in his many pockets with his left. The plant he pulled out from one of the hidden corners of the robes was cactus-like, but smearing it on the deepest part of the burn was cool and not painful.

Certain something was expected of him, Sabian pressed, "I'm not a follower of Pari."

"I don't care," replied the celebrant. When he glanced at the boy over the hand, he kept an eye on the wound. "Do you think it matters to Pari? Do you think he spends his days counting my flock? You could worship the demon creators for all I care. You could do with some healing. I do healing. That's all I need."

The next thing to be pulled from the endless pockets was a bandage, which he wrapped around the hand expertly.

Finally, Sabian understood. "Did Lance put you up to this?"

The bandaging paused, and the celebrant again peered up at his patient. This time, he lifted one eyebrow. "Why would Guardian Carraway have anything to do with this?"

Pulling his hand free and taking to wrapping the injury himself, Sabian snorted. "He's been trying to convince me that the world is about giving and sharing and all that nonsense. He said he would prove it."

He had gotten the bandage in place, but tying the tiny knot on the end proved difficult with one hand. Seeing the celebrant extend his hands again, Sabian let him add the final touches.

"Silly thing to be trying to prove," the celebrant agreed, and Sabian felt vindicated.

"I keep telling him—"

"Course it's true," the celebrant added as his thick hands tied the knot to the perfect tightness, "but impossible to prove."

"True? How can it be true? Do you walk about with your eyes closed? Just look around! Look at—"

The celebrant started laughing, and Sabian stopped at once. He was relatively certain the laughter was *at* him, and he did not like the sound.

"I am looking," Celebrant Darak said. "Now *you* look." He pointed toward the encamped army. "Do you think life would end if I missed a temple service? Do you think Pari would stop this year's crops if someone forgot to light an incense stick? Would the oceans dry up if we said the wrong prayers to Ocea?" There was little point in answering any of the obvious questions, which gave the celebrant the silence he needed to continue. "These gifts around us have nothing to do with what we have given the gods, Sabian. There is your giving right there!"

"People are always giving gifts to the gods to buy favor," Sabian replied. "How is that generous?"

"Those people," the celebrant said, snorting in turn, "are doing things backward, which is why I said it would be impossible to prove. We give to the gods in thanks, not to buy favor! What possible difference does a coin, or a candle, or a prayer make to a *god*, Sabian? We give it because we want to show gratitude, or at least we should."

"You are just as bad as he is!" Sabian said, hearing Lance's voice in the celebrant's words. "You are optimistic idiots!"

At this, the celebrant's laughter sounded once more. "Better than a pessimistic sage," he retorted.

Chapter 4

T he sound of his children playing had Darknim smiling wistfully as he settled after supper. The Circle had left him alone for the moment, content that their purpose was now to await the king's commands. The firedrake within him watched the boys play their beads and string game with fascination, but Darknim was happy to sit on the skins and finally begin work on his family's puzzle box.

It was an old tradition to build a puzzle box to pass to one's children, but Darknim had never made one. In part, he had feared beginning the box would jinx his children, who had never lived long enough to receive it. But now that he was confident of their survival, he struggled. His father had built one, but it had been smashed during a raid.

Now, guided by the women and the memories of the Northlander Circle, he felt ready to build his box and pass the legacy to his children.

While Layla, easily the more adventurous of the two infants, investigated Ciala's wiggling fingers with concentration, her adopted twin Degan slept in Bea's arms, rocked with the gentle humming of the substitute mother. Both infants had been fed recently, and the food inspired Layla to activity while simultaneously putting Degan to sleep.

Now seeing the boy at rest, Darknim had to consider how lucky he was to have the child. When the Celebrant of Ocea had brought Degan to Darknim initially, he had thought it unwise, as Tiki's illness had made her milk thin and shallow. Still, he had surrendered once the celebrant had pointed out the vast array of women DoomDragon had already

brought to feed his daughter in the absence of her mother's milk. Both children were sustained on the milk of no less than three mothers, and both rapidly got fat in the plenty.

With the addition of Ciala and Bea, Tiki was able to rest more as well.

While Darknim watched Layla, Tek lost the game to his older half-brother, and Darknim saw the boy storm toward the door. In a glance, Darknim realized that his new axe, freshly delivered from the weapon-smith, was propped beside the entrance.

Although he had initially been unconvinced, he was confident his firedrake was giving him greater speed, for he arrived at the axe and put a hand on it by the time the boy reached for the handle. It was a new great axe, sharp and dangerous.

"Not a plaything, Tek," Darknim corrected, hefting the blade away.

"You should keep that somewhere harder to reach," Ciala softly said.

Darknim shook his head. "Until the two little ones are old enough to crawl, the axes will stay at hand." He followed Tek as the boy went to join his brother, wary of the stranger who was now his father. "These two should know better. They will have to learn. They are Northlanders. I will not coddle them."

Introducing weapons and responsibility to the child was paramount to a Northlander's life. Darknim had been Tek's age when he had first thrown spears in hunting, and it was something he looked forward to teaching both of his sons. They had to learn to be careful with weapons.

He was still watching the two boys to judge their thoughts on the matter when his vision filled with half-light flickering through several colors. While the colors varied, the overall structure of the spell was statically crystalline, but he did not know what that meant besides being magic.

Regardless, the firedrake in him panicked, and he knew whatever was coming could not be good. Kitable was not prone to magicking himself around, and no other caster he could think of would dare intrude on DoomDragon in such a manner.

A feeling of dread stabbed into his gut. He had lost fifteen sons already. He would not allow anyone to harm those he had only recently discovered.

"Out!" Darknim shouted. "Everyone, out!"

CHAPTER 4

When he moved forward to put himself between the light and his gathered children, who had retreated to their mothers, he was stopped by a cloudy green spell.

Two people appeared in the multi-colored spell, both dressed in strange robes of colored ribbons that hung from their shoulders to their ankles. One was a tall woman with blond and black streaked hair who wore glittering blue gems on her cheeks and knuckles. The other was a man about half Darknim's age with long blond hair tied into a tail with another colored ribbon. Both faced DoomDragon, and neither looked friendly.

Having the strangers between him and his flock drove the firedrake into a fury. Darknim answered by swinging his axe, like the snapping bite of a dragon, into the green wall blocking him.

The spell cracked, then shattered. DoomDragon rushed through the gap with the speed of his Aspect, charging the enemy.

The strange man turned to the family escaping under the seal skin flaps while the intruding woman continued to regard Darknim passively. She lifted her hands when he broke her wall and sent a crashing line of green light into him, knocking him sideways. Her hands had gems embedded on each knuckle, flickering in the green light.

Agility from the firedrake kept Darknim's footing firm despite a crash into the tent wall that pulled down the wall and broke a whalebone post. He held tight to his axe in the tumble but found himself buried in heavy pelts.

Magic swept over the area, lifting high the pelts and revealing Darknim. While the woman still had her hand raised to direct her spell, Darknim launched himself, bringing the axe down upon her but was pulled aside by a long tendril of smooth magic. The line wrapped around his axe, bending the shaft.

And the male attacker reached for Ciala.

Darknim instantly changed targets; releasing the enchanted axe, he punched the man's face. The man's nose broke under Darknim's knuckles. It was unfortunate, DoomDragon reflected as he kicked out, that it had been with his off-hand. Had he delivered the blow with his stronger right hand, he would have shoved the broken bones deep enough to kill. The kick knocked the stranger aside.

A new spell, a green, cloudy wall, surrounded DoomDragon. The woman muttered something, tightening the green magic around him until he was held, his arms at his sides.

They spoke in another language, and the man nodded with one hand still over his bleeding nose. Ciala had failed to get clear, the last to escape as the eldest woman waiting her turn to let the others flee with the infants. The strange man caught the Northlander woman by her shoulder and dragged her back.

Darknim's vision shifted. In a blink, he saw both strangers as red silhouettes against a grey and black background. The firedrake in him screeched, and Darknim, infuriated, slammed his knee against the spell.

It cracked.

Ciala had never been a weak woman, and she had just had her son threatened. She spun, closing the distance between her and the attacker with one confident stride. Again, the caster seemed caught off guard by the physical assault. She punched him in the shoulder, scratching her nails across the ribboned robes and coming away bloody.

Her next swing was aimed at his face. He backed up to shelter his fractured nose, only to find himself the target of a well-placed kick that took him between his legs. He crumpled as his female companion rolled her eyes.

Darknim slammed his knee against the magic wall surrounding him for a second time. The woman glanced at him, concern flickering over her features. Or was that disbelief?

"Hold still!" the strange woman shouted, surprisingly, in Esparan. "I'll make this far more—"

His kick broke the spell. Snatching up his axe, he swung over her raised arm to cut down into her shoulder. The spell around her stopped the blade, but nothing stopped the force he applied. He knocked her to her knees.

Fury-filled, the firedrake's spirit reared up and lunged. It burst out of Darknim, taking form as a flash of yellow light. It joined him the next instant, scratching and screeching at the fallen woman to keep her down. Darknim's axe smashed into her again. The shield broke.

When the axe cut into her arm just below the elbow, the woman shrieked to match the firedrake.

Whatever she shouted next was not in any language Darknim knew and seemed to be directed to the other man, who called back from where Ciala was still kicking at him. In a moment, the multi-colored crystal aura returned, and despite another hearty swing after them, Darknim's target vanished.

"Serves them right!" declared Ciala. "Think you can intrude on DoomDragon's household and get away with it?" she shouted at the empty tent, looking up to the heavens and waving a fist at the invisible enemy they had vanquished. "Never!"

With the casters gone, the spell holding the tent upright dropped, and the pelts collapsed around them both in the middle of Ciala's cursing.

Once Darknim had shaken the tent from his shoulders, he sought the family. Finding them safe, he dispersed them into the Northlander camp to other relatives until a new home could be made.

He then went to Elder Ela, seeking answers.

When Gannon stumbled through the portal, his steps were unsteady with Gilan's weight on his shoulder. The portal, thankfully, was perfect and had him stepping evenly into the cavern.

He cursed his luck when his first sight was Yonny. The Seat of Divination was sneering at him immediately.

"One old woman too much for you to—"

Gannon had no idea if Yonny dropped the sentence because he finally noticed Gilan's state or if Rean had chastised the caster via the thought spell he detected. Ignoring them, Gannon lowered Gilan onto the floor. For a rare moment, Yonny was utterly unimportant and could be dismissed. Gilan was in danger still.

Rolling Gilan over, Gannon placed a hand on either side of the older man's head and launched his thought magic in search.

The assaulting thought magic tangled through every corner of Gilan's mind. Somehow, within a breath that had not even spoken words, the Tainted woman had scrambled Gilan's mind into dehiscence. Gannon's magic had protected him from the effect, but Gilan's weaker defenses had been obliterated.

Gannon sorted through the leftovers, trying to make sense of them. It did not feel like destructive magic, just alteration, which was a relief. All the pieces were still present; he just had to put them back together.

It took him over a hundred minor spells to reassemble the disaster of Gilan's mind. When he finally leaned back and breathed, a hand supported him briefly, and he realized that Nanmi, the best alterationist in Wanter, had been assisting quietly. Feeling his head swimming despite the aid, Gannon was grateful. His focus gem felt heavy and dull at the center of his forehead, entirely used up.

Gilan was stirring by the time Gannon focused on the cavern the Watching Circle had created. He found five Circle members staring at him. Rean, the only one not to leave the cavern this night, spoke.

"What happened?"

As tempted as he was to tell her to ask Yonny, for surely the man was already viewing the ordeal through his divination, Gannon could tell by Rean's tone that snide remarks were ill-advised.

"She was too fast," he confessed. "I swear, she did not use a single word, and I had my Translation up just in case! There was nothing! She would blink and cast! My spells protected me, but she could both defend and attack at once. Gilan never had a chance."

The Seat of Fire rolled over and slowly got to his feet, but the man had a glazed look that confirmed the repair was still taking some getting used to.

Gannon watched closely, seeking mistakes he needed to readdress. So far, Gilan was moving well. "I think I fixed it, but I have never seen anyone cast like that!" He lost control of his voice and exclaimed, "It was alteration! Not creation, not destruction. There was even an occasion summoning spell. Even I cannot cast those!"

As much as he did not want to look weak, Gannon dared not conceal his failure. And he did not feel ashamed that he had been bested. Gilan, the next in line for inheriting the leadership of the Watching Circle, had been crippled in the encounter. It was not that they had been feeble; the other caster had been too strong.

Now standing and regarding them each in turn, he was pleased to see each Watching Circle member nodding in understanding. They knew summoning thought magic was something very few casters in the entire history of Wanter had achieved, and none of them had ever

mastered it. That the Tainted woman could summon thoughts was a true indication of the danger he had faced.

His count of the members came up short. Fantorn, Seat of Force, was missing.

"Did we get any of them?" Gannon asked.

Namni grimaced and shook his head, his stone as pale and empty as Gannon felt his was. "Like you," Namni explained, "we found our target more dangerous than expected. He broke Fantorn's force magic more than once, and we cannot determine if he used his Tainted powers to do it or did it by physical force. He was a warrior, not a caster. Fantorn has been wounded. She is back in Wanter to be treated. She will return shortly."

None of the Watching Circle were healers; Namni was their closest approximation. Still, the man's mastery of alteration powers to repair flesh was mediocre at best.

"But we got the one we were sent after!" Yonny called victoriously. "At least *we* succeeded!"

A gesture brought Gannon's attention to a kneeling captive behind the casters. Sure enough, the man's white wolf pelt was wrapped around his shoulders, his semi-feral eyes watching them in wide wonder. The Tainted caster shook either from cold or fear.

"He did not give you trouble?" Gannon asked, seeing the wild eyes of the fur-clad man. He had learned that the Tainted caster's pelts represented the animal they had bound. From what he understood, a wolf was a dangerous animal to trap.

"He is a diviner." Yonny scoffed. "What exactly do you think he could do?"

Finally smiling, Gannon stood straight. "I often wonder what diviners do myself!" he said, winning a few chuckles from the rest of the Circle when Yonny failed to recognize the insult.

As one, the Watching Circle surrounded their prisoner.

At first, the Tainted spoke in a strange language, but as Yonny started to put up a Translation spell for the cavern, the stranger swapped to a language Gannon understood.

"I don't belong here, Wanters. Let me go before it is too late."

As the eyes of the Circle turned to him, Gannon groaned.

Of the seven, only Gannon had come from the southern United Provinces of Shantan, and it was a fact he tried to avoid drawing attention to. Shantan had been the hot seat for multiple wars over centuries, but it was most known for being the original home of Derelict Leugan, who was to be blamed for the Watching Circle's presence in the World of the Tainted.

When the rest of the World of Wanter had refused to get involved, Leugan had disobeyed every authority to come the World of the Tainted and aid them against the invading demons. Because of Leugan, wizard powers had left Wanter. Now, those powers were being corrupted by the local Tainted magic.

And their prisoner, who had without a doubt never been to Wanter, spoke Shantanese.

Rean seemed to read his reaction. "Leugan probably taught his descendants his language. We knew that was a possibility," she said in the commonly-used Gavorian.

With a shiver, the prisoner ducked his head again. "Not wise, not wise," he muttered as the Translation spell took effect. The spell delivered the words into his head so quickly Gannon could not be sure if the prisoner was still using Shantanese or not. Gannon always heard translations in his native language.

"What is not wise?" Yonny asked the Tainted.

Proving the spell was now affecting the prisoner, the Tainted man again raised his head, tilting it like a dog. "My presence," he said. "Keep me here, and you will die, Master Yonny."

The Seat of Divination narrowed his eyes menacingly. "How do you know my name?"

Silly question! Gannon thought. They already knew this man was the Seat of Divination of the Tainted Circle. He had probably divined it!

Gannon reconsidered. They had gone to great lengths to shield the Watching Circle from divinations. Had their defenses failed?

"You told me it," the wolf-man grumbled. "Or rather... no... you have not told me it yet." The Tainted caster squinted at them, then paused. "Would you like to introduce yourself?"

A few chuckles escaped the other members, but they sounded nervous.

"How do you know about Wanter?" Gannon asked, thinking the others may not have heard the brief reference to their world when the man had been speaking Shantanese.

The bestial eyes turned to Gannon. When there was a smile under the beard, Gannon spotted enlarged canines.

"You want to take me there," the man said. "To do so will ruin your world." The man shivered again and ducked his head.

A Spell Share reached out from the Watching Circle. The moment it touched Gannon, he saw with Spell Sight. The aura of the divination spells around their prisoner became evident. For a long moment, Gannon doubted the vision. The Tainted caster had not been casting—they would not have allowed it!—but it was hard to deny the flickering of the man's eyes. He was divining, and what he saw alternated between confusing and annoying him.

"Why would that ruin anything?" Namni asked.

The smile became a snarl, and the magic they could see flaring around the man intensified. Under the weight of the powers, the Tainted caster slumped.

"Read his thoughts on the matter," Rean commanded Gannon. "We must know what he sees."

"Certainly," Gannon answered.

While the stranger mumbled into his pelt, Gannon rearranged his magic defenses and initiated a Thought Scan. It was a simple, superficial Scan and easily managed.

As he entered the mind, Gannon saw the prisoner standing in a vast darkness, with ghost-like colors of magic hovering around him. Some tried to approach him, only to be chased back by the man, who hefted a spear and charged the divinations away as if scattering birds, and by a white wolf.

The man paused in the darkness and looked directly at Gannon, confirming that the prisoner knew his mind had been intruded upon.

Do you want to see? the Shantanese-speaking voice inquired into Gannon's mind. Want to see what I see?

The man lowered his spear and, with a silent whistle, called off his wolf.

The visions once kept at bay flooded in, overwhelming them all.

TRAITOR

With part of his mind tied to the Tainted caster, Gannon saw every vision. It was a flurry of images, complete and fragmented, future and past, kind and cruel, and it came with such intensity it stunned him out of consciousness.

Thankfully, being knocked out meant losing the Scan, which meant losing a reason to be unconscious. He woke lying on the ground. Namni stood over him, looking mildly curious but unconcerned.

Gannon did not censure his curses as he pushed himself up.

The images echoed in his mind like spells off Force Walls. Even now that he had a constant selection of the images, he could not make out many of the details. Sometimes they involved him or the Watching Circle, and he thought he saw the towers of Gavain, perhaps even the Fields of Shantan's wasteland, but he could not be certain.

The prisoner, Gannon saw as he rose, was equally unconscious, lying on his back with his eyes moving behind closed lids.

"Like the woman we fought," Gannon explained to the Circle, "he doesn't cast. Instead of calling powers to him, he has to keep them out. He just failed to do so."

"But what did you see?" Yonny demanded.

Gannon shook his head to clear the remnants out of his mind. An army camp? A man with a glowing sword? A tunnel? Wolves, owls, bears, dragons... something else?

"His visions are random," Gannon answered. Sneering at Yonny as he contemplated the collapsed Tainted, Gannon added, "You could always take a look yourself."

There was little doubt that the Seat of Divination was interested in trying, for he was better trained to understand the mess of images, but if the strength of the visions had disrupted Gannon's thought magic, then there was no hope Yonny would hold.

"Only one will ever return from Wanter," the Tainted caster suddenly said, although the man looked no more conscious than before, "and it will not be you, Kitable. If you go, you will die."

"Kitable?" Gannon echoed.

"He is seeing visions again," Yonny pointed out, waving a hand dismissively. "He doesn't know where he is or what he's saying."

CHAPTER 4

The nod shared around the Circle was weak. The power demonstrated by these Tainted casters was spooking them all. Not knowing what they were dealing with kept them from deciding how to approach it.

Assigning Yonny to watch the prisoner for now, as he would be the best suited to decipher the mutterings, the Circle dispersed to other tasks as they waited for Fantorn's return.

Gannon went to Rean.

"I want to seek out Kitable," he told her.

Rean's wrinkles deepened with her frown. "He is not an ally," she replied. "You did not deal with him. He kills even his own kind. He—"

"He is a Tainted wizard," Gannon interrupted. "If he's close to the Tainted Circle, then he might know more about them. And he should be told about Tainted powers. We are his ancestors, are we not? We are his family more than they are."

Rean's face crunched further together until even the slit of her eyes seemed to be nothing but another wrinkle. "Shantanese thinking," she warned. "You speak almost with pride."

Gannon felt himself flush and was thankful none of the other members were near enough to be eavesdropping. "Leugan was an idiot," Gannon said. "Everyone knows that. Yes, I'm ashamed I have any connection to him, even by living on the same spit of land as he did. I am not trying to repeat any of that. I think Kitable might become an ally if we explained what the Tainted Circle is. They are our common enemy."

Rean let out a long breath, and Gannon cut off the rest of his arguments. It sounded like he had reached the end of her patience. He dared not push it.

But as he pressed his lips together in thought, she gave a second sigh and nodded. "Go," she said. "There may be merit in finding out what he knows about the Tainted Circle. You may explore. Do not be found."

Gannon grinned wide. "They won't remember seeing me," he promised, turning from her to set a portal. Their cavern was far south of where most people lived in this part of the world. He would need a portal to reach them and return.

When he saw Gilan stagger slightly, Gannon reminded himself to be cautious. The Tainted were proving to be more taxing than expected. Even this Kitable had once been enough of a hassle to chase off the Watching Circle. He would have to make an oblique approach.

Valia visited the temples daily, silently giving her prayers to each god in turn.

May Dorakon never return to SwordWood.

During the daylight, Valia planned her wedding. She ordered the flowers then arranged for them to be lost on their way from the coast. She attended fittings for her dress and declared it was too tight, this time across the hips. And that loosened bodice was now too loose. More corrections were required.

Hearing of a meeting between Bosul and the remaining defenders of SwordWood, Valia arranged to bring the men their midday meal. She arrived earlier than usually would be expected to ensure they did not disperse, then eavesdropped while setting the table and directing the servants and their food trays.

Personally, she handed High Guardsman Bosul his drink.

He smiled at her, and she received various nods of approval for her proper behavior. Since the night Calus had come to her room, Valia had played the part of the perfect wife. For the last four days, as far as they knew, she had settled into her place in the manor.

But as she was serving them, she listened to every detail. She knew where the siege weapons were going to be placed. She knew the number of guards at each gate. She knew when the messengers were expected from Dorakon to report on the battles in the field. She knew precisely where Tohmas was and how long it would take for him to reach Gaidol, if he got that far.

Most importantly, she knew they had decided to change the horn signals. Lance had sided with Tohmas; the horn patterns were known. Training would take place from now until Dorakon's return.

Once she could no longer delay her departure with cleaning up the meal and dishes, she finally had to leave. Immediately, Valia wrote down all she had heard, and that night, once her husband-to-be had been tempted into taking her to his room and satisfied by her clumsy affections, she copied his list of horn calls onto her letter. At dawn, one of the women purchasing pearls for her new dress design left the city and went north.

A woman's war did not involve swords.

Chapter 5

Gaidol retreated. Besides a few engagements with rear guards and scouts, they avoided combat. Kitable watched them from a distance, wondering about casters, his paranoia worsening. Prince Dorakon joined the forces from the south, bringing more of his guardsmen. Having the prince with the army seemed to give them purpose but little courage. Day by day, they marched back toward their lands, Tohmas' forces on their heel.

The news that the Circle of the Raven had been reformed reached Kitable after the news that it had been broken. The advantage of having another set of casters to defend Tohmas' army was lost as soon as it was realized. The Circle's greatest strength was only achieved with a complete Circle. Tril, the most able to work without the Circle, was missing. Unable to find Tril despite their efforts, Elder Ela came to Kitable, making him the first to know of the attack.

Kitable had not seen the wolf-elder for some time, as Tril's quest to remake the Circle had taken him north for quartercycles. On the last check, Tril had been managing his innate divination, which was threatening to spiral out of control, reasonably well, thanks to the spells Kitable had taught him.

But the more the *visaln* was used, the stronger it became. The magic had no upper limit; at some point, it would destroy him.

The account of the attacks that had failed to take either Ela or the newest Circle member, the imposing DoomDragon himself, made

Kitable fear for Tril's life. *At least there was no body,* he considered. But if attackers had gotten into the camp without Kitable's knowledge, they were all in trouble.

Kitable's searches came up just as empty as the Northlanders' had, increasing his dread.

Ela had a solution, but it meant leaving the camp and traveling far north.

The farther Gaidol fled, the more certain Tohmas became in the conferences Kitable overheard.

"He's not running fast enough. He's setting us up."

But no matter how many spies they called upon or how many Scrys Kitable ran over the Gaidolon army, they could not see what the Gaidolons were planning.

Promising to keep an eye on them from a distance, Kitable headed far north with Elder Ela in the Northlands, which required him to source a two-person Relocation spell to replace his one-person version. In retrospect, he figured he could have written it in less time than it took to find it, but at least by using a published form, he could be sure there would be no errors.

One by one, Ela directed Kitable to each Northlander village as Gaidol continually retreated, day by day, south. Everywhere they went, they had to stay for food and drink, as Ela's snowy owl clothing identified her as a respected member of the Circle of the Raven. She told stories through the meals, and Kitable was prodded by endless questions until they left. He had prepared for the environment by setting up a constant a Translation spell as well as a Heat Shield as part of his Moulded Shield.

Ela's request for the man "Kohd" in the third village was answered by multiple nodding heads. With one eye on the Scry observing Tohmas' army, Kitable waited for them to bring the man forward.

When Ela had suggested searching out someone who had been showing talent to rival that of the missing Elder Tril, the magic had translated the Northlander word as "Tril's relative." Seeing the child come forward with a protective mother in his shadow, Kitable wondered if he was looking at Tril's son.

No, there was a father now joining the pair along with an older boy. Ela waved, and the mother nudged the youngest child forward.

CHAPTER 5

The elder smiled under the feathers and called Kitable. Ever at the ready, the Translation spell he had put up that morning made his words into Northlander for the onlookers.

"This is the one Elder Tril identified as a diviner?"

The elder nodded, and the crowd, except for the family, took several steps back. The audience's utterings translated into words like "southerner" and "naked," but Kitable dismissed them. The Northlanders were layered in warm furs and skins against the cold. With his magic protecting him, Kitable wore only his customary robes and looked profoundly out of place.

Kitable knelt before the boy and triggered the general Thought Scan spell he had pre-casted for this moment.

Although it was possible to focus the spell, it was an area spell initially, and that meant he saw the thoughts of every person around him for a moment. Thankfully, the Translation spell only translated the spoken word, leaving many of the thoughts as gibberish. But the associated images flooded in, briefly confounding him. The most potent image was the snowy owl, presumably from Elder Ela. There was a spattering of faces, places, and emotions to sort through before finding the boy's thoughts.

For a moment, Kitable saw himself through the eyes of the child. Indeed, he had never seen such robes before, and he was wondering how Kitable would survive in the cold. He was equally wondering how Kitable spoke such wonderful Northlander when he was so clearly foreign. Because of his association with Ela, there was instant reverence, but it combined with fear.

Now locked onto the boy's thoughts, Kitable said, "I hear you are good at finding things." Ready, Kitable followed the mixture of emotion, words, and images that were triggered.

The boy briefly wondered if he should check with his mother for guidance but then decided that Kitable was a friend of the elders and, thus, an influential leader. He would try to help.

"My mother hides shells sometimes," Kohd said, and Kitable saw the memories of the game flash through his mind. "I find them all every time."

There was more to that. Not only did the boy find all the shells in the hut, he never made mistakes, knowing exactly where they had been placed.

Kohd was having visions. The child had seen divinations about his mother hiding the shells.

"My uncle says I must practice it lots."

Kitable stopped himself from insisting "not too much," having shared Tril's cascading visions. Practicing was good, but how much could a boy take?

The reference to "uncle" brought Tril's wrinkled, smiling face to the boy's mind. There were plenty of memories of him, but the strongest one by far was the vision of Tril kneeling outside the huts with a white wolf lying in his lap. From the child's memories, Kitable knew the family had seen Tril reclaim the Aspect Kitable had once stolen from him.

"Your uncle," Kitable prompted, "is missing."

The strongest emotion, echoed by the peripheral thoughts of the onlookers, was sadness. They all knew Tril by name and face. Many of them were relatives; one was a brother, and none wanted anything to happen to the youngest Circle member.

A view of Tril went through the young mind. Again, Tril was kneeling, but he slouched in the manner Kitable had learned to associate with uncontrolled visions. His staff, a recent acquisition, lay at his knees, and the background was dark. There seemed to be stone and possibly someone present, but the image was gone too quickly to be certain.

Kitable tried again.

"I want you to find him, Kohd. I want you to tell me where to find him so I can help him."

The following image was in the mountains overlooking a long drop to a river. Tril was there, and Kitable stood next to him in front of a cliff face although Kitable could not tell why.

"You will find him," Kohd said, his voice full of certainty.

"Where?" Kitable asked.

The image repeated itself, and Kitable tried to memorize it. He needed something definable to make an anchor. The river valley looked steep, but he did not know the mountains well enough to know how many rivers cut through them. He searched up but found only sky. It

would be midday, partially cloudy, when they met. North or south? It was impossible to...

The boy's thoughts went to a face, and Kitable's spell obligingly followed. She was a woman with dyed, streaked hair, dressed in strange robes made of ribbons that seemed to shift colors in the sunlight. Her eyes glowed in shades to match, allowing Kitable to recognize her as a caster. She matched the description Darknim had given of the female who had attacked him.

But there would be at least four of the casters, probably six, as all three assaults had been simultaneous and paired. She was undoubtedly just the beginning of the problem.

Atop a boulder beside the woman was a twisted, broken tree scorched by lightning. How many such trees existed in the mountains? There could not be many.

He had a target.

Pulling his thoughts back then dropping the spell, Kitable stood and faced Ela. "Got it," he informed her.

"Knew you would." She chuckled at her joke.

"You will find him," Kohd insisted, to which Kitable nodded.

"I know where I will find him."

The mother moved up as Kitable turned away and had a protective hand on her son's shoulder when Kitable glanced back. Kitable's earlier Scrys had defined Tril perfectly, which meant there had been no reason for his Scrys to have failed. The group of casters had to be defending themselves from Scrys, but then how had the child gotten around it?

He would have to investigate, Kitable decided. There was plenty he did not know about the Circle of the Raven already, and he had just added another big piece. There was never enough time.

They still had to stay for dinner, and Ela told stories until dusk while Kitable watched Tohmas set up a short distance from where Gaidol had camped. They were a day from the border of Trulin although Kitable had doubts that Prince Dorakon was aiming for his capital. But if he was not, then where was he going and why?

Kitable slept in his own bed that night as Ela was happy to leave once the village slept. He promised to find the tree he had identified and renew the search for Tril come morning.

From a place hidden among the waggons, Gannon watched Kitable return to his vardo. He had eliminated his spells to prevent Kitable from detecting him. It had surprised him to learn that Kitable had already mastered a skill pupils in Wanter spent two years learning: to sense the presence of magic. Who had possibly taught the man to do that, and did he see, smell, hear, or feel it? Or, Gannon mused, was he one of the very rare who tasted magic from a distance? That, he considered, would be amusing to explain to the Watching Circle.

With the focus gem requiring charging, Gannon had removed it and now could pass as Esparan. He had traded his robes for local clothing bought from a man who thought he had been swindling Gannon. At least the man was happy, and Gannon had fine-cut clothing in a local style to call his own.

Within only a few moments of watching Kitable's waggon, Gannon determined he was not alone in his stalking. The other observer was a Tainted woman, beautiful and persistent. She was blond as Fantorn had been before she had streaked her hair with Falbeast blood and stained it black. Unlike Fantorn's straight figure, the woman had curves to match her curls and seemed to draw attention to those fine features as she moved among the Tainted people, distracting them from her true purpose, which seemed to be to watch Kitable.

Feeling he may have found an unexpected ally, Gannon allowed her to see him, and she, bolder than him, confronted him.

"You are a new face around here, stranger," the woman said in Shantanese with a sultry voice that oddly slurred some words. "Where are you from?"

There were very few advantages to being from Shantan, but the ability to use a local language without needing magic was one of them when he stood so close to someone who would take note of spells.

"West," he replied, pushing off the vardo wall where he had been lounging and checking her over. "From the mountains." It was a half-truth, spoken by habit. Even lie-detecting magic would not have sensed it although this woman had no magic on her.

"Not with that accent you're not." She surprised him by scoffing playfully. Her knowing glance looked up at him from under long lashes.

"So where do you think I'm from based on *that* accent?" he replied, turning the question back to her.

She pursed her lips in thought but then smiled gently. "Can't place it," she admitted. "Nowhere around here."

He laughed and made a Shantanese gesture of confession and concession, which he knew she would not understand or appreciate. "You're right, dear girl. I am from very far away. I'm here to watch."

The word "watch" had multiple meanings in Shantanese, but she seemed only to understand the simplest of them when she raised her eyebrow.

"You and I are watching the same person: Wisavi Kitable."

He paused to hear the strange word. "Wisavi?" he echoed. "What, do tell, is a wisavi?"

She leaned against the waggon with her arms loosely crossed and her shawl slipping off her shoulders. "A Rydan word," she explained. "It means an advisor to a great leader, apparently. In our case, it also means magic, but you knew Kitable was a wizard."

It was easy to make up his mind about the woman. He could stand and watch Kitable more, which had been painfully useless so far, or he could utilize a local information source. With thought magic at his easy disposal, he could get anything he wanted out of her and leave her without so much as a memory of the encounter. Based on what she had gleaned thus far, he had already decided to purge her mind. If he was going to go through that effort, he justified, he should at least make it worthwhile.

His head was getting sunburned anyway. Time to take a break.

"If I wished to ask you some more questions about Kitable," he asked her, "in the most polite way possible, how would I do it?"

She batted her eyelashes at him charmingly. "Tell me your name," she said with a smile, hooking his arm with hers, "and buy me a drink."

"Gannon," he introduced, letting her lead him away from the useless waggon clearing. "And you?"

"Maybel," she whispered back.

Chapter 6

W hispers outside Shimmer's waggon woke her. She was outside in the next blink. Maybel, to her surprise, was slowly easing into her roll by the campfire and lifted her head, bleary-eyed, at the intrusion. A strange man knelt at her side.

He was off in several ways. Smooth-headed, he wore a mix of clothing as if he had robbed three separate clotheslines to make his outfit. A courtier's shirt, thick work trousers, luxurious riding boots, and a belt that looked like it belonged to a cutter...

"Maybel? Everything all right?" Shimmer called, tentatively coming down the steps of Match and Mixer. The hairs on her arms stood on end as if a thunderstorm approached. Logically, the level of magic present seemed important, yet Shimmer felt strangely apathetic about it. It made her wonder but did not concern her.

"Just fine," Maybel answered, her voice languorous as she nestled deeper in the roll. "None of your business, Shimmer." Her long blonde hair swept around her like a fall of autumn leaves; she seemed to instantly fall asleep.

The man attending her gently tucked the roll over her shoulders, then stood tall. "Shimmer, is it?" he said as he faced her. He examined her from top to bottom, wrinkles spreading over his bald head when he narrowed his eyes. "Yes, I appreciate what he sees in you."

CHAPTER 6

Shimmer withdrew a step. The man sounded strange like he was from nowhere, or perhaps everywhere, in Espar. Her stomach knotted while her body froze.

"Who?" she asked, her voice catching on the word.

"Kitable, of course," the man said. He smiled, his teeth a perfect row of white. "I heard some fascinating news about him. He's got a soft spot for you."

Shimmer tried to shake her head but couldn't move. The feeling of static in the area rose, a strike of lightning seemingly looming around the campfire. There was magic active, and she knew that should worry her. No, more than that...

She wanted to trust her defenses, but something about the stranger felt so profoundly wrong she didn't know what to think. She feared her usual defenses were insufficient here although the thought did not worry her either. Her mind was fuzzy.

"You are mistaken," she replied. Where was Dust? He would hear the conversation, and he'd sense the magic. She needed his help. Or did she?

The stranger stepped forward, and Shimmer tried to move away. The magic around her tightened, powerful beyond any she had sensed before. She knew with a jolt it had permeated her defenses: the warm powers turned in her mind, sorting through her thoughts effortlessly. She was aware at last that she was being held through her thoughts. That, she knew, should terrify her, yet it was as if the fear could not build enough to be felt.

"Don't lie to me, dear girl," the man snidely said. "I'll know."

An image snapped through Shimmer's mind: the stranger walked through a portal of blue and green, a large colored gem mounted on his forehead. A robe of ribbons replaced his boring attire. The land on the other side of the portal was black and grey, the landscape sparse.

"Who are you?" Shimmer choked out the words, the pressure making it difficult to draw breath. Or perhaps she'd forgotten how to breathe, her mind too occupied by churning thoughts that refused to coalesce. She knew she was frightened—she had to be—but no emotions rose. Only logic made its way through, one thought at a time.

This was wrong.

This man was dangerous.

"It doesn't matter," the man replied, sweeping one hand through the air. "I can tell you I am known as Gannon, but you won't remember that. You won't remember any of this."

The haze in her mind crept in, muffling her thoughts further. It became difficult to see.

"Why?" It was her voice, but she didn't know how she had spoken. She didn't remember where she was anymore. She was standing outside, but why?

A man's voice answered: "Taking one member is enough to break the Circle, but I want more than that. I want them gone, every last one. If we cannot do it, we will help others do it for us. That is the way of the Watching Circle. All I had to do was break Kitable's alarms. Now the enemy is among you, and my job is done."

Silence lingered, the heat of magic slowly fading.

Shimmer blinked, vision returning. She was outside in her sleeping clothes, a drab blanket over her shoulders. The fire was low; although, it would burn with enchantments until morning. Maybel stirred briefly in her bed beside the embers.

A wave of old magic rolled over Shimmer. "Gods," she said. "What have you been doing, Maybel? You positively glow with magic!"

"Entertaining, if you must know," the blond woman grumbled before rolling over. "Was that worth waking me over?"

No, was the obvious answer, and the thought reminded Shimmer that she had no reason for waking anyone yet. Still, something felt so profoundly wrong this night. She'd come outside for a reason, although she couldn't remember what the reason was.

She cast Dark Sight to allow her to see in the shadows. People were moving around in the main army camp, but that was all it revealed.

She modified her spell to see as a dragon did in the dark, and the people glowed red in her vision. Now she could also see the many people sleeping in the tents.

Tohmas' forces could not be doing both, not at that number.

The last time, the attack had hit Fixer City too, and Shimmer was unwilling to let her neighbors be targets again. She rushed to wake them.

Maybel rolled over and went back to sleep.

CHAPTER 6

The moment he woke, Tohmas knew something was wrong. Although he had not yet seen the threat, he knew it was there. Tohmas' first concern was for Arnika lying curled against his front.

He held Arnika against him as he rolled out of the way. His right hand found his knife, kept under the pillow, and cut the cot from under them. When he rolled back, they fell through the material and onto the ground.

By the time he hit the earth, Tohmas had fully registered the people in his tent. He was under attack.

But he never left himself that vulnerable. SoulBurner was not far. As his left arm pressed Arnika, who was awake but muted by shock, to the head of the bed to protect her, he kicked at the set of legs he saw beside the bed.

The man jumped back with a half-laugh at some comment his companion made, but Tohmas dismissed them. The man on Arnika's side of the bed was the only one who recognized Tohmas' goal.

"The chair!"

Tohmas' kick had already hooked the chair legs and toppled it. The man who had dodged his kick lunged forward, but before he could stop it, it leaned low enough to put SoulBurner, slung in its scabbard over the back of the seat, within Tohmas' reach.

Red light ignited the moment Tohmas' hand touched the grip.

Tohmas turned onto his back and grabbed the cot frame above him. With SoulBurner in the wrong hold, his only defense was to snap the wood of the cot frame into the attack that arched down on him, aimed no doubt by the red light glowing from his hand. He caught the enemy's sword in the broken wood of the cot and tossed the entire bundle—man, sword, and cot—back with a shove. It gave him the room he needed to come to his feet.

Now standing in the red light of his sword, he had a clear view of the room. There were four enemies, with two more joining in answer to the commotion, and all were wearing Gaidol's colors. Swords were the predominant weapons, but one soldier making their way into the tent carried a long spear.

None of them worried him in the slightest.

Based on their hesitation, Tohmas guessed he had tangled the leader in the cot, but their delay was his advantage. He flipped the sword to his left hand, the knife to his right, and attacked.

The man with the chair was the first to die, but he was rapidly followed by one of the other initial intruders, as neither of them moved nearly fast enough to keep both sword and knife at bay, even with their shields. The next to go was the sword-bearing arrival, who Tohmas handily knocked into his spear-wielding companion and saw him, if not killed, disabled.

Arnika finally rose, covered in a blanket and looking sheepish. Tohmas did not immediately fear for her; the enemy's attention appeared to be on him alone.

The cot-trapped man roared out from under the material and called for allies to join him. Despite the man's white and blue uniform, Tohmas recognized first the voice, then the man's red-shadowed face.

It was Warrah Damoria. The son of the Prince of Damoria had been at Narsol during the treaty's declaration. Tohmas had not expected to see the man who had stormed out from the discussion again until the march was much farther south and closer to Damoria's borders. Damoria had never had allies so far north.

Warrah lunged with his blade, forcing Tohmas back a step as he reassessed. Fast as he was, Warrah managed to turn his attacks instead of allowing Tohmas to block them, seeming to know that his sword would break against SoulBurner. His skill was apparent: this was no mere soldier but the trained son of a prince.

A flicker of uncertainty found Tohmas as two more enemies rushed into the tent. Had the shouts not been heard by the protectors?

While at war, he usually wore armor, but having a new wife had changed that habit. Now, he sorely regretted not having been more cautious. Outnumbered by adversaries far more proficient than he had expected, Tohmas decided this was not a fight he could win.

His whistle was two-fold. The first was a call to Carsh, given with a silent prayer that the attackers had somehow driven Carsh off and not done him injury. He assumed the nearest protectors would answer as well; they knew the sound. His second whistle, louder than the other, was for Schlavarai.

CHAPTER 6

Tohmas finally managed to block Warrah's strike, breaking the fine sword against SoulBurner's edge. He twisted into the gap to dodge a spear. More people were arriving through his unguarded entrance, each wearing the enemy's colors.

He put his back to the wall to limit the number of attackers, but the tent's cloth provided no real protection. He heard movement and voices on the far side. These were not his protectors. He steeled himself in readiness.

He was surrounded.

Catching the spear as it attacked, he yanked the tip past him and into the wall at his back, where it sank into flesh. The cloth, pinned, tore and exposed Tohmas further.

Unfortunate time to be right, he thought. A crowd of at least a dozen had come around behind the tent. Each wore Gaidol's dark blue and white, and each was armed.

As he recognized the danger, a sword snuck through his defenses and added a new scar to his left leg; Warrah had rearmed himself with a new sword and shield. Tohmas ducked under another swing, kicked the attacker off balance, and swung the blade into one of the man's companions. SoulBurner killed one more.

He had to keep moving; the moment he stopped, he died. But he saw no end to their reinforcements. Tohmas was trapped from all angles.

He dodged, and Warrah hacked into one of the tent's wood supports instead of Tohmas' neck where he had been aiming. Inspired, Tohmas finished the cut with SoulBurner, chopping the pole in half and felling it. He ended his pivot by sinking his knife into an exposed face, although it wasn't Warrah's. When the blade stuck, he let it go.

"Kill him!" Warrah's voice rose above the clatter in his southern accent. "A hundred gold wheels to whoever kills him!"

Tohmas pushed a spear thrust into the ground with enough force to see the wielder ram himself into the haft. The man knocked another attacker prone, which in turn toppled the spearman and gave Tohmas an opening. As he escaped the circle of foes, he knocked out the other tent post.

Half of the tent went down behind Tohmas, landing on Warrah and his attackers as they moved to pursue.

Tohmas snatched up the clothing he had left on the ground, charged Arnika, and scooped her up with his left arm. He had reached the altar by the time a Gaidolon broke from the tangled material Tohmas left behind. Tohmas snatched Arnika's knife from the altar, took instant aim, and threw it. His only regret was that it was only a Gaidolon solder he slew, the knife piercing the throat.

With a final yank to the cloth behind him, Tohmas brought the entire tent down and released his hold on SoulBurner.

The area fell into darkness, the collapsed tent smothering the altar's light too. From behind the altar, Tohmas held Arnika beneath him and pressed a hand to her mouth to keep her quiet.

"Spread out!" It was Warrah's voice. "Find him! He cannot escape!"

"Gone!" someone nearer to Tohmas' hiding place grumbled. "Demon-cursed ghost! Just like—"

"If I hear another word on that line—"

"Prime protector vanished too!" the second voice insisted. "They knew we were—"

"Demon shit," Warrah insisted. "He was out, that's all. Now start searching. Spread out! He's under the cloth!"

Tohmas was still listening when a hoof landed beside his head. A soft snort sounded directly above his hidden, prone body.

He let himself breathe a tiny sigh of relief at the familiar grunt. "Schlavarai," he whispered as quietly as he could, "*lyh doh.*"

"What's that horse doing?" one idle voice said as the Rydan mare knelt, then lay beside Tohmas' place.

Warrah's voice squeaked when he snapped, "What horse? Where!?"

Snatching up his sword and clothes in the hand still wrapped around Arnika's waist, Tohmas launched out of cover. Tossing aside the green tent cloth, he was instantly on the mare's back, Arnika held in front of him.

"*Rann!*"

Schlavarai lurched to her feet. Digging in hard, she took off at a gallop.

"Shoot! Shoot him down!"

If there were arrows, Tohmas did not see them. Schlavarai dashed into the darkness faster than any arrow could follow.

Arnika clung to Schlavarai's neck as the horse sprinted. With her stomach already tossing from the bloodshed in the tent, Arnika felt sick with the horse's movement. Her grip on the horse unrelenting, she willed herself back to the unfamiliar cot and the man she had only recently allowed to touch her, wishing all the while that the entire ordeal witnessed in the light of the enchanted sword was a nightmare. She tried to block out the sound of the shouting, but it kept echoing in her ear.

As Tohmas pulled the horse up with a whisper, Arnika had to open her eyes, and reality was still there. Although she initially held on to the steed, the man she had married gently pried her from her seat and stood her before him.

"Are you injured?" he asked. She tried to say "No," but all she could do was shake her head.

The moonlight illuminated Tohmas' injuries bleeding long shadows down his leg. He was hurt, although he worked not to show it.

Apparently satisfied, he pulled on his breeches quickly, then slid yesterday's tunic over Arnika's head. It covered her to her knees but sagged around her shoulders and left her legs entirely bare. Stealing a piece of rope from a nearby tent, he made her a belt. His was wrapped around SoulBurner's blade, which allowed him to hold the sword without touching the hilt that would set off the light. It also made the weapon useless if there was combat, but at least it was not advertising their position.

"Gaidol has gotten through the defenses, somehow, and isolated, distracted, or killed the protectors. It sounds like they didn't see Carsh, which means he was probably with Darcina and will be in the Rydan camp, so that's good. I need a horn," Tohmas said, all without checking if she was following his commentary. "That means getting a guardian or a far crier. Wait here."

She grabbed his arm. "You are not leaving me!"

She was embarrassed for her childish outburst, but the thought of being left in the darkness where dozens of Gaidolons roamed terrified her. If she met more of the enemy now, she feared for her life, especially if she met them while dressed in only her husband's Galanth tunic!

He seemed to want to argue, but either the tone of her voice or her grip on his arm stopped him. With a nod, he let her hold on to him as he ducked into the nearest tent.

A group of companions was dozing within. One step in, Tohmas was within easy reach of all four beds.

"Up," he commanded in an intense whisper. "Now, all of you. Up, companions."

They were awake at once, but it took them another dozen blinks to figure out who was crouched amidst them. All it took was a single whisper:

"King..."

They were on their feet and scampering out into the moonlight, trying to get their clothes on, in the next flicker. Thankfully, none of them seemed to notice Arnika still holding her husband's hand.

"What's your fyrd?" he demanded as they shuffled to get their things together from under the tent's fly.

The squad leader answered promptly, "Fyrd of Rest, my king."

Their night vision, she had to admit, was pretty good. One of them had noticed that Tohmas was without a shirt and offered theirs to him, but he shook his head. The leather would not have fit him anyway.

"Any far criers among you?"

"None, my king," the prime companion replied.

"Nearest guardian?" Tohmas pressed without pausing.

"Guardian Faron."

"Alright, you three," Tohmas indicated those who had not spoken yet, "are going to wake as many people as you can and get them together." He pointed at the speaker. "You will take me to—"

The whistle that echoed through the night was painfully distant, but Tohmas froze at once, his words forgotten. His voice changed, tight fear coming through. All other plans were discarded. "Get to the nearest far crier and have him sound the all up and out! Go!" he called. If she had not been attached to his arm, Arnika suspected Tohmas would have left her behind, so quickly did he rush to Schlavarai. With Arnika ahead of him, he swung into his seat and was off like an arrow before she could ask about the whistle.

CHAPTER 6

The pounding of Schlavarai under them was relentless, and the wind seemed to gain volume as they rushed blindly through the night.

Tohmas whistled again, but it was different from any other call he had made. Usually, his whistle was sharp, demanding. This one sounded forlorn.

When he got an answer, however, it was abrupt and insistent. He guided Schlavarai toward the sound.

On the rise ahead was a faint light, torches on the ground sputtering in dirt and mud. Bare-skinned fighters were surrounded by light, a host of white and blue-clad enemy soldiers moving in. Arnika was not optimistic about the predicament.

Tohmas did not slow his horse, but she felt him shifting behind her. Leaning forward, his mouth was by her ear when he said, "Stay with Schlavarai." Then, he was gone.

There was shouting, sounds that blended into one cacophony. Many of the cornered people shouted in joy while the attackers gave cries of both surprise and anger as the horse slammed into them from behind. Her husband was the loudest of them all, who gave a battle cry as he launched himself off the galloping horse.

The horse rammed into the people and made a hole in the circle of enemies cornering what Arnika could now see were Rydans. To her surprise, there was only one man among them: Prime Protector Carsh and his dancing knives. The rest of the people, dressed in various animal skins and bones, were women wielding short bone knives. The only thing that seemed to save them was the enemy's disbelief that these beauties were fighting them.

But the women were not victims. They were at the disadvantage because of their short weapons, but they attacked together, making their little knives into deadly claws that killed everything in their path.

Neither Tohmas nor Carsh wore any armor or carried shields, but Carsh was draped in baldrics of knives, and Tohmas had SoulBurner. Schlavarai and Bashuran, Carsh's great black stallion, evened the odds; both Rydan horses enthusiastically threw themselves into the fray. They were trampling, kicking, and biting as fast as Tohmas swung his blade. Arnika could only duck and cling to the horse.

She had ridden spooked horses and helped break green yearlings, but this was different. The horses were moving deliberately, not

frantically, and their every blow was effective. With each potent attack, they worked with their owners to beat the enemy back.

Tohmas had picked up a knife from Carsh somewhere along the line, for the next time Arnika saw her husband clearly, he wielded a blade with each hand once more. The women had closed around the pair of men, but the circle they temporarily made rotated and changed with every step. The ring became a clearing, and the clearing grew to encompass the two raging horses.

A horn sounded, but Arnika did not know what it meant until the camp started answering. She would have to, she promised herself, learn the horn calls soon. It was frustrating to be so blind.

There were lights across the camp within moments, and voices reached her ears. She had to guess that the soldiers Tohmas had woken had gotten to their far crier.

Rapidly, green-dressed men were rushing toward the fiery light of SoulBurner, weapons in hand.

With the help of another score of soldiers, Schlavarai soon stopped her kicking and switched to prancing.

Breathing heavier than the horse under her, Arnika looked up again to see the last of the Gaidolons fall. Now only Galanth soldiers in their green tabards surrounded them.

"What the hell! How'd they get here?" one of them asked. His voice had a Gaidolon accent. It took another moment for Arnika to recognize Guardian Carraway with a crutch under his arm, lacking his leg brace.

"*Ovarun*," Tohmas answered. The king corrected himself quickly, switching to Esparan, "We have Gaidolons and Damorians in every corner of the camp, Lance. Get your horn and sound a rally. If we stay divided, this ends here."

Lance limped into the light, but at least he was holding a horn. To Arnika's surprise, it was a shell horn, not the usual cow's horn.

Tohmas must have indicated his curiosity because the Guardian of Arrow's fyrd lifted it and said, "Normal one got smashed. They planned this well, Tohmas."

He blew a combination of pitches before turning back and adding, "I happen to have a spare."

Tohmas nodded, but his face darkened. If others were awake now, it might take them some time to rise, and more importantly, other horns

might have been sabotaged. The guardians were going to need time to figure out alternatives. There were plenty of far criers, but a complete reorganization would take too much time.

Already, their brief peace had run out. Another crowd of Gaidolons rushed the assembled Galanth. *Gaidolons*, Arnika assumed. But some could be Damorian.

The Rydans had reorganized themselves, and the women were returning to their own camp at a run. A single woman stayed. Although she had initially had only the one bone knife, the woman now wielded a pair of blades.

Schlavarai went to Tohmas, and Arnika, still on the horse's back, went with her. The Galanth soldiers, having shaken off every hint of sleep, expertly arranged themselves and locked shields to stop the incoming Gaidolons.

The Rydan woman gave a warning shout. They turned to see another run of Gaidolons coming in from behind.

"That's a lot of idiots," Lance remarked, his voice even. "Horn gave you away, I fear." Although the guardian carried a weapon, his crutch made it evident that his lot tonight was to direct others. He called three squads to cover the back and assigned one of the two squads to Tohmas' close defense to cover the gap.

"Not the horn," Tohmas corrected. "SoulBurner's light. They don't know what the horns mean." In a leap, Tohmas was again behind Arnika on the horse. "I can lead them off and let you rally. Repeat the call as often as you need. Get people together!"

"Tohmas!" Guardian Carraway snapped as the clash around them began. Carsh leaped onto his black steed, and two knives helped keep Lance's back safe by taking out the two Gaidolons who broke through behind them. "The kingsmen will have my head if I let you—"

"Lance," came Tohmas' calm response once he had his arms around Arnika, "as much as I like you, shut up and do what you're told!"

If there was going to be an argument, it came too late. The last thing Arnika saw of the group was the angry, if worried, stare of the Rydan woman. Unable to reach his belt to return the knife properly, she quickly tucked her borrowed knife through the leg of Carsh's breeches. She watched them leave with frustration evident in her green eyes.

Carsh on their tail, Tohmas turned Schlavarai back the way they had come and goaded her on. He held the red-glowing sword high as another horn sounded behind them. The eyes of the attackers followed them.

Thanks to the warhorses' furious hooves, they broke free through the crash of Gaidolons. Arrows chased them, but none could get through the red light of the goddess' blessed sword. They were soon making their mad rush back through the camp, Arnika praying every step along the way.

Chapter 7

C arsh hated using the whistle to call for Tohmas, but it had saved him more than once, and he had to appreciate it for that. How Tohmas had gotten Schlavarai so quickly, or why his wife was wearing one of his tunics and nothing else, were two mysteries he did not expect ever to solve, but the mere presence of his brother was enough. Together, they broke the enemy around them and earned a moment of peace.

Once Tohmas and his guardian had sorted things, and the Rydan women had returned to camp, it was time to start their run. Freed from his corner, he was ready to fight. With his brother in stride with him, they were unstoppable.

The enemy followed the light of the magic blade as it raced through camp. Horns sounded all over now, most reporting an attack and giving fyrd identification, but Lance's horn rang out the commands of coordination over them all. They would listen to him despite the light of SoulBurner being elsewhere. The enemy, on the other hand, did not know any better.

Carsh and Tohmas ran the length of the camp and found themselves coming out the other side just as the arrows following them unified into a proper, coordinated volley. After a pause only barely long enough to glance back and gauge the army he had attracted, Tohmas turned Schlavarai and made his way out through his defenses.

The farther the enemy was from the Galanth men who were organizing, the better. They had to keep going.

Not surprisingly, however, Tohmas soon guided Schlavarai to the right. As much as they wanted to give the Galanth time, they needed to stay close to their friends and Followers.

Just as they passed a corps of trees, arrows hit from the front and were reduced to ashes by the magic light of the sword. The arrowheads steamed in the mud ahead of them, singeing the grasses.

They stopped again.

The horses snorted, stomping angrily. There were enemies behind, to their right, and now ahead.

Tohmas, somehow, put out the light of his sword, and they moved to the left in the sudden dark to take refuge in the trees.

Despite the clear night, it was impossible to determine the exact numbers facing them, but Carsh still considered his assessment disappointing. Carsh would never have dared try this fight with Bashuran alone. Having Tohmas and Schlavarai with him, he was slightly more optimistic, but he still hesitated. There were too many, and they were well organized now. It would be hard to get behind their shields, and until they did, they would both be the target of arrows and spears. It was not the kind of battle he wanted to fight.

"The river," Tohmas' wife said from Schlavarai's back where Carsh had forgotten she was. Why Tohmas had not left her behind with Lance was another mystery to Carsh, for the woman only served to tire Schlavarai. Darcina at least could wield a knife!

"What river?" Tohmas complacently replied from the shadows. The enemy advanced, and Carsh was trying to decide if going forward would be better than going through the woods. They were on the forest's edge, but how much undergrowth was there? If they tried to pass through and got stuck, then what? It seemed better to risk rushing the enemy or attempting to circumvent them before they surrounded them too closely, but Tohmas had yet to make a decision, and the time was fast passing.

"Bankwatch river," the girl said. "We washed the clothing there this afternoon. It runs behind that cabin," and Carsh thought he saw her point. It took another few moments for him to sort out the shape of the house with the willow by the door. It was only a short run from the woods.

"How wide?" Tohmas asked.

"Too wide for a crossing," she admitted in the dark, "but I thought maybe it would do well to have something at your backs, so you cannot—"

She was interrupted when Schlavarai surged forward. Even blinded by Tohmas' touch switching to SoulBurner, Carsh followed on Bashuran. The area lit, Carsh saw the four rows of men between him and the white-painted house in the distance well enough to put knives into two men before they could lift their spears.

Into the gap, the horses trampled. Hooves and blades struck the Gaidolons down, breaking through the line.

Carsh and Tohmas did not wait to see the effect of the hit. Without looking back, they ran for the cottage.

Carsh wondered if Tohmas was going to use the building as a fortress, but the first son of Tamv turned Schlavarai away from the door to the cottage before the thought was fully formed in Carsh's mind. One did not fortify without expecting some relief. They needed open land to make their run.

Sure enough, the river flowed just behind the house through the field. There was no hope for cover; the surrounding foliage had been cut to make room for crops. SoulBurner's light protected Carsh from more arrows, but that was their only defense.

Giving up on arrows, the enemy charged down the bank with spears lowered.

"Can you swim, my lady?" Tohmas asked. Carsh did not hear the reply as he sent knives into what he thought were the highest-ranking men attacking them, then the nastiest-looking ones, but he guessed the answer had been negative because Tohmas' question was followed by, "Then hold tight to Schalvarai. Whatever happens, do not let her fall out of reach. I will be with you, I swear."

By the time Tohmas finished his sentence, the Gaidolons were among them, and Carsh and Tohmas were forced to drop from their horses and fight back to back. This allowed the horses to clear the space between them and the river. Soon, it was a bloody mess.

Carsh let Tohmas decide how long they stayed there killing Gaidolons, for he knew his brother would fade before he would. But Tohmas seemed in good form this night, and they managed many killing blows. Instead, it was Carsh who slowed first, feeling unexpectedly winded.

Tohmas responded to his faltering at once, heading for the water. Carsh already knew what his brother had planned. To the shout of "Widma!" for the horses, calling them after him, they all plunged into the water and let the currents sweep them away.

The red light went out, and they dropped into cold, wet blackness.

After his days of travel, Kitable had been looking forward to his bed and a night of solid sleep. The sound of a horn destroyed it.

He knew the first horn ordered everyone to rise and get ready. The second was a rallying call, which seemed strange until Kitable stepped outside. He heard the next series of horns claim attacks were underway.

Late night, or very early morning, depending on which way one approached the time, was a dangerous time for casters. All of his hovering spells had twenty-five candle durations, meaning the assortment from the day before was still active, but there was always the threat of an overnight dispel. There was no logic as to when a wizard could become dispelled overnight, and it had not happened in years, but it was a danger.

A quick check confirmed that nightmare had not materialized. Kitable had not been ready for fighting, but he could rise to the occasion if he had to.

"Wisavi?" a woman called, and he nodded to acknowledge the girl at the bottom of his steps. She was one of Lady Fayela's. Since Kitable had promised to look into her son's past, the Lady Mother had consistently set her waggon close to his.

"Have your lady stay in her vardo," he directed as he searched the darkness with magical vision. "I will erect a one-way force shield to prevent anyone from getting in. She will be able to leave, but no one can enter after it is cast. Am I clear?"

The girl nodded and rushed off. He waited for her to enter her mistress' waggon, then placed the spell over the waggon before the lady could object. Content that she would wait until things cleared up before venturing out, he looked to the camp again.

He tried to find Tohmas, but the red light that he could see with his eyes when he looked out over the camp was invisible to his Scrys, being

untouchable magic. The damned sword was becoming a problem. With its magic, Tohmas was hidden from Kitable's powers.

The repetition of the rallying call continued to nag him until he finally saw the light of the king's sword vanish. With a curse, he obeyed the horn's command. Activating a Relocation, he appeared next to the horn-caller.

Tohmas was not there. He ended up next to Lance Carraway.

"Where's the king?" Kitable asked.

"He will make his way back to us," Lance promised, although his expression was worried. A kingsman arrived, Kingsman Talbit Darmac, as Lance added, "He went to pull them off. Had to. We'll never get people together otherwise!"

Rows of Galanth fighters were finally making their way into the torch lights, battered and beaten. Most of the Gaidolons' attention was heading west at a run, giving them the opening.

Kitable had seen similar raids before; they had been efficient and deadly. So long as the attackers kept their enemy scattered, the defenders would perish.

Barnon and Sol appeared to be trapped, but the fyrds nearby answered Lance's call. Kingsman Talbit took control, reassigning the soldiers as they arrived. Encounters were being reported both by horns and runners in every corner of the camp. Talbit acted as the central post for directions.

Kitable didn't have words to curse with, feeling there was no time. But there should not have been any chance of such a large-scale attack. Kitable had alarms rigged around the camp's perimeter; activity like this should have triggered them and alerted him. He regretted the loss of the Circle of the Raven in the next thought. They would have been able to hide the army as it moved. And they would have seen even concealed forces approaching.

All too soon, a mass of Gaidolons assembled at the base of the rise Lance had used as his rallying position. Had they killed Tohmas or just given up on him? Kitable wondered. Or were there sufficient enemies to both harry the king and attack his supporters?

But time was too short to waste on bemoaning Elder Tril's absence. Whispers were haphazardly counting the dead, and it was evident some areas had lost as much as half their forces to the raid. Tohmas' absence

did not help the dwindling morale; Kitable overheard the fearful suppositions. If they did not act, the army would fall apart. But he had few spells available for this kind of fighting. He had not expected it.

"We need time," Talbit said softly. Although he was the highest-ranked Esparan present, he was new to his post. He had been an ambassador between princedoms before becoming the son-in-law of a prince and then inheriting the princedom and the loyalty to Tohmas. Kitable had expected the man to be flustered by the fighting, but the kingsman exuded calm and acceptance. His voice was matter-of-fact.

"Any ideas, Wisavi?" Lance asked.

In reply, Kitable lit illusionary fires along the enemy's front lines and watched the Gaidolons skitter back like cockroaches fleeing lamplight. It was a weak illusion made of light only, but it made them reconsider. To make his point, he added a Fire Blast where he figured someone important might be positioned.

There was silence for a moment, broken by a horn from the enemy. Kingsman Talbit squinted into the distance as if seeking the sound, no doubt missing his eyeglasses. *Left beside the cot,* Kitable thought.

"They're holding," Lance said.

The kingsman rotated to face Lance. "You know their signals?" His narrowed eyes had gone wide.

Lance shrugged, his crutch making the gesture stilted. "I am Gaidolon, technically." Giving Kitable a sidelong glance, Guardian Carraway added, "I think you may have hit something."

Kingsman Talbit cracked a wide grin, nearly laughing out loud.

"My aim is pretty good," Kitable replied.

It was easy to keep the illusion of fire up with minimal concentration as they unanimously decided to wait. He added heat in patches, causing confusion and making some of the illusions capable of injuring people. There were still plenty of Galanth and Galanth-sympathizers trickling in, and the longer they waited, the more would come. Kitable cast new spells, trying quickly to come up with some that might be useful and putting them into hovering positions, ready for activation.

They were still organizing their ranks when a Gaidolon horn sounded.

Lance winced. "Arrow volley," he explained. Putting his shell to his mouth, he ordered the Galanth to lift their shields. Not all of the stragglers had them. They were vulnerable.

Casting quickly, Kitable finished a spell and threw his arms wide.

Those behind shields didn't see, but many more witnessed the arrows slow, then stop. For a long moment, they hung suspended in the air in the darkness, the leading edge only visible thanks to torch and lamp light. Once he was confident all arrows had been trapped, Kitable brought his hands together, then drew back as if shooting an invisible bow.

In the sky, the arrows turned around. With Kitable's release, the volley flew back toward the enemy.

A horn sounded from the other side. Kitable hoped it was too late.

Lance laughed, making the people nearest them flinch. "Yeah, your aim is very good." A weak cheer trickled through the Galanth forces. It was still more than Kitable had expected for the trapped fighters.

Kitable dropped his voice, not wanting to ruin their brief boost to morale. "I think I overshot slightly. Hit men at the back. I like it better when they trip on themselves. Life is easier when they cannot charge."

Memories of defending Galanth in his youth with Tohmas' father Habal echoed in his mind. He would never have been able to perform the Slingshot then, and he certainly would not have been able to maintain an illusion while full casting! Further, he reflected, he would not have recognized that the simple illusion was the more effective of the two spells. The fire illusion was preventing the main attack.

He would, however, need to know what was going on in the darkness before he could continue terrorizing the enemy. Fed up, he reached for another spell.

"*Ecina*!" he called, followed by "*Extein*." He had only one light spell available, and given the circumstance, he could think of nothing better to do with it. The Lie Light appeared between the two forces, hovering over them like a new moon. The extension spell tripled its size. White light fell over the entire camp.

He regretted the spell in the next breath.

The blue and white tabards stretched back through the tents to the very edge of the light, which was detecting lies and truths at a pace that had it swirling. With so many Galanth missing or dead, there was no doubt they were outnumbered severely.

"I think I just halved our morale," Kitable said.

"Nonsense. Just gave us a better view," Kingsman Talbit corrected. "We have Arrow's fyrd here, and most of the fyrd of Rest came through. Boro and Flystead are hurting but accounted for. Hmmm... Fixer City seems awake but unchallenged, which is considerate of Dorakon. West side was Solta and Rabarch..." *It would be easier if they had Sol or Barnon now*, Kitable thought. Those two knew battle. With an unproven kingsman at the head, authority might not be as easily maintained.

Lance suddenly cursed, and Kitable checked him. He was looking north.

Kitable's stomach dropped. Rydans were coming up fast, their horses making use of the flat area around the river at the hills' back. They assembled, one group breaking off to head up to where Kitable stood. If any Rydan identified Kitable as a caster, they'd try to kill him. But if Kitable dropped the fire that seemed to be keeping the enemy at bay, they were all dead.

Kingsman Talbit's words fell off. He'd not dealt with Rydans, Kitable realized. Few Esparans could convince a Rydan to take them seriously at the best of times, and it seemed unlikely the kingsman, barely thirty and half blind without his glasses, would be the exception.

"I got it," Lance said, hobbling up to the crest and then tossing his crutch aside to a friend. He stood firm, masking the wounded leg as best he could as he called over the Rydans in their own language. He performed a salute, hand to palm. It drew the riders to him.

Burlotak was the lead rider, arriving on his massive grey horse and towering over Lance. He shouted incomprehensibly although one word caught Kitable's attention: "*Flya.*" That was a word he knew; it meant "wizard."

Demons, was all Kitable could think. The forces below were starting to test the fires. If he dropped the illusion, the hill would be swarmed.

But Lance didn't flinch. Surprisingly fluent in Rydan, he replied, then argued with Burlotak. Kitable did not dare put up a Translation spell, fearing Burlotak would know. Something was decided, and after a saluting fist punched to his left shoulder, the Rydans left back the way they had come.

"Wha...?" Kingsman Talbit choked out.

Lance took back his crutch and shrugged. "He was alarmed by the flyer magic and wants to kill it. I told him Carsh and Tohmas were

somewhere out there, and we agreed he would get half of the spoils of the battle if he covered our east flank. He only agreed, I presume, because he was in a hurry."

Another horn rang out. All eyes went to Lance.

"That was a forward call. They're advancing," he interpreted.

As the kingsman left to join his fyrd, Lance leaned on his crutch, staring impassively at the ranks Kitable's Lie Light had made plain. "I think we're almost outnumbered two to one," Lance commented as the lines of Gaidolons moved forward steadily, walking through the fires. They'd figured out the illusion. Giving up, Kitable dropped the spell.

Lance sighed, then shouted over his shoulder: "Form and hold!"

The ranks behind him tightened in preparation. Horns sounded warnings, then repeated the call to hold. The expanse of Gaidolons wrapped around three sides of the hill, covering the east and pushing to the west, eliminating hope for escape. Kitable was surprised; he'd never thought the Gaidolon forces so numerous.

The Rydans were shouting, but they were facing long spears. Planted well, they would be a real danger.

Lance checked over his shoulder. "Kitable? You any good at making bridges?"

Kitable followed his gaze. A river ran at the base of the hill beyond the Rydans. The trees had already been cut from the banks, exposing the wide and slow-flowing waters. It probably flooded this area in the winter.

"I can make something if we need it. It's our only way out. It—"

A shout went up from the Rydans. As Kitable watched, a red aura emerged out of the river. Two horses followed.

"Lance?" Kitable called, pulling the guardian's attention back to their escape route.

Lance's voice was suddenly bright. "Ha! That demon! About bloody time!"

The cheers started from the Rydans, but with SoulBurner's light announcing Tohmas' arrival, it grew through the ranks like thunder. The cornered forces were *cheering*.

What impression will this give the Gaidolons? Kitable mused.

Habal had told Kitable more than once that battles were not won by force of arms. They were won by the spirits of the people fighting.

These spirits were now flying on the wings of dragons.

Riding Schlavarai, Tohmas arrived at the brow of the hill as the Gaidolons swapped into a full charge. Laughing, Lance caught Tohmas' wife as he handed her off. There was time for a wink and nothing else. The king was down the other side of the rise at a gallop, his Rydan prime protector on his tail. He blared out a hold command from Lance's seashell horn as he took his place at the front of his army, red light blazing from his sword.

Knowing Habal had been right, Kitable used an alteration spell to change the Lie Light's color to red. The final touch was modifying the shape to that of a chariot of gold pulled by two small dragons.

The Champion of Inac had entered the fray, Inac's chariot above him like an omen from the goddess herself.

Chaos followed.

With Tohmas leading the charge and Kitable providing support, the Gaidolon's attack turned against them. The Galanth and their allies surged forward, and Dorakon's forces folded under the religious and magical onslaught, retreating into the darkness south. Tohmas drove the attack on, rescuing the cornered Trullers while the fyrd of Rest went to free Rabarch from its fortified pocket of tents and waggons. Three other fyrds sounded their intention to pursue the enemy, and Tohmas let them go. If they thought they could drive home the counter attack he wanted them to do it.

After a quartercandle, the horns reported all three fyrds were returning. The enemy had escaped.

With Arrow's fyrd, the least affected by the raid due to its position close to the Rydans, guarding against retribution, Tohmas pulled back. Soon, he had an assortment of kingsmen, guardians, and runners following him. Seeing Schlavarai snort at them aggressively, he quickly checked her and released her to get food and water. No one dared get in her path as she and Bashuran trotted back to the river.

Tohmas led the way to his collapsed tent on foot, needing the belongings in the fallen shelter to make plans. "Horns were sabotaged in every kingsman's tent," Kingsman Talbit informed him candidly. He sounded flustered.

"What of the protectors?" Tohmas asked, receiving a mob of shaking heads.

"Carsh is the only one I've seen," Kingsman Sol replied. "We'll get to the bottom of this," he added, eyeing Talbit pointedly.

"Find those who broke the horns," Tohmas commanded, "and get to organizing the fyrds; I need to know who we lost. Sol, give Guardian Faron a hand getting your brother out from his corner. The rest of you, see to your fighters. Talbit, check in with Fixer City. Everyone report back quickly and keep your eyes out. I want to know how they did this."

"I'll give you all a hand with that," Kitable offered from behind him. Tohmas nodded approval.

Tohmas sought the nearest protectors' tents.

He let the light of SoulBurner show the way when he ducked inside. Instead of the expected slaughter, he was surprised to find all four occupants lay unharmed yet thoroughly dead in their cots.

"Get the cutters!" Tohmas shouted. A runner left.

A dozen healers seemed to be there in the next blink. Celebrant Darak was first among them, probably waiting at Tohmas' tent after the battle in anticipation of Tohmas being injured. Tohmas' cuts took second place. The celebrant expertly examined the closest dead man, who had a dark shade to his skin.

"Check the others," Darak ordered his flock, and like busy ants, the cutters and acolytes rushed out to search.

Meanwhile, Stitches, Darak's old hound, barked. Darak translated in a formal voice unlike his usual snide responses. Was he finally cognizant of the need for appearances in public?

"Poison, my king," he said, "at least three kinds in this tent. The dark-hued man probably got a heavy dose of bellanon. I'm not sure about the others; dark root? Fanont's dust? Or sufferweed maybe…"

The acolytes and cutters reported back swiftly. A handful of protectors were found alive, but the majority lay dead.

With the healing waggons certainly overrun by this time, Tohmas helped replace the poles of his tent and used it as a shelter to sort the protectors. In the end, a hundred and three of the one hundred and forty-four protectors of Galanth were pronounced dead.

The fact hit Tohmas hard. Although they had not been Followers according to Rydan tradition, Tohmas had fought with these men and

had come to trust them. He knew their names, every last one. They had died only a dozen paces from his tent.

The poisoners had used everything from food to wounds to administer their deadly mixes. Like the horns, it had been coordinated. Some survivors had been elsewhere. Others had seemed merely lucky to have been spared a lethal dose. They remained in care, too sick to rise.

Once he had finished reassigning surviving protectors and the guardians to assist the various injured in the camp, Tohmas finally sat down on the steps of a waggon.

The failure overwhelmed him. Hundreds lay dead, the protectors, those closest to him, among them. The army built over the years was now fractured and demoralized. Everything he had accomplished since stepping foot into Espar felt undone. Defeat crushed down onto him.

Darak returned, his hands covered in thick leather gloves to protect him as he handled the poisoned dead. His face was drawn, his mouth a thin line. With so much weight on the man, there seemed no room for humor; the light in his eyes was gone.

"I had them clear a tent for you and your wife," Darak said solemnly. "You need rest."

His words brought Tohmas' attention to Arnika, who had stood in his shadow silently since the end of the fighting. She was still dressed in only his tunic and a piece of rope as a belt.

He looked up at her standing mutely by him, not knowing what to do or say. Nothing had prepared him for failure.

She reached out and took his hand. With gentle pressure, she pulled him to his feet and led him to the quiet tent Darak indicated. It was no grand poled tent but a simple army shelter. He could not stand straight within, but kneeling on the sleeping furs on the ground seemed fitting.

As the flap closed behind Arnika, the full scope of the defeat dawned upon him. Arnika, his most precious treasure, had nearly been taken from him.

Catching her in his arms, he held her against him with his face buried in her hair. "Gods, I have never been so terrified. I thought I would lose you."

War did not frighten him. Waking to see enemies had surprised him, but it had not scared him. The death of his protectors angered him more

than anything. But this night, those swords in the dark had nearly taken her from him, and that thought horrified him.

When she squirmed, he released and saw her tear-filled eyes looking back at him in shock. She shook in his arms now that the worst was over, and it was clearly permissible to collapse slightly. Apparently unable to speak, she sank against him again, and he held her to stop the shaking.

"I will not let anyone hurt you," he promised, kissing the top of her head. "I swear."

They were still huddled together when the kingsmen returned to give their report. The dawn light had come, and the day had to be addressed. They wanted vengeance, and they expected Tohmas to lead them in it.

Feeling like a hunting dog being recalled, Valia had to take a moment to compose herself before meeting with High Guardsman Bosul. Usually, he called for her when in his room, but tonight he requested her presence in the music room. She ensured she was presentable then adjusted her blouse's collar down again to be a bit more distracting.

When she entered the room, she found Calus seated by the fireplace, his feet on another chair, toying with an old fiddle. He did not, by the way he held it, seem to know anything about playing it.

Valia was used to being met with anticipation, but Calus' face was stern as he rose from his seat. Had he tired of her so quickly?

"Sit," he invited, pointing to the chair he had so recently been using as a footrest. Pretending not to notice the mild insult, Valia obediently sat, folding her hand properly and straightening her back, aiming to have her bust displayed.

It worked; he took another few moments to remember his reason for calling her. The fiddle, which he laid onto the nearby table, tipped from his hand and clattered noisily to a stop.

He placed the bow deliberately beside it, making certain it made no sound.

"I heard a strange rumor today," he said.

"I was always told rumors were the work of idle and devious minds," Valia replied, keeping her eyes low and her voice soft.

"There is sometimes truth to be found in rumors," he justified but his voice tensed and she heeded the warning; something had put him on edge.

She fell completely into the perfect woman she was pretending to be. "Wise words," she said. "What did the rumor say?"

He cleared his throat and found his seat, taking up a mug. Sadly, someone else had prepared the drink tonight. "You knew High Guardsman Carraway," he said.

Valia forbade any emotion from reaching her face, no matter how much her heart skipped, then sped, upon hearing Lance's name. To keep from smiling, she thought of all the things they would do to Lance if they caught him. The terror of that kept her face somber.

"He was a guardsman of mine years ago," she confirmed, certain Calus must know as much. It was not worth denying.

"Some say you were fond of him."

Was that jealousy? Calus was gripping his mug tightly enough to be using it as a weapon.

"He was a guardsman," she said with a shrug. Shyly, she dared to meet Calus' eyes but quickly looked away. "There were many I dreamed about as a child. A girl is allowed to dream about a romance with a successful soldier, a guardsman, or high guardsman, no? And if her dreams become true..." She met his stare again and timidly smiled before looking away.

He dragged his chair forward and sat up to put a hand on her knee. His grip was firm. She had to remind herself not to flinch or pull away.

"Do you miss him?"

Why the music room? she wondered. Was there something here he expected to give her away? She knew wizards could detect lies and, if a wizard could, an enchanted item could to. He was trying to corner her into confession, she was certain. Was he hoping for a lie?

She carefully formed her next sentence.

"Lance Carraway betrayed his princedom by forsaking his oath to my father. How could you think I would entertain any thoughts about him at all?"

Burying her disgust as far down as she could, Valia unfolded her hands and placed one on Calus' knee in mirror. She made her touch gentle.

"I know my place," she said in a whisper she hoped sounded enticing. *Standing beside your grave, laughing,* she finished the thought.

Calus straightened with a contemplative frown, but nodded. "It did seem strange," he said. "Well, you will be pleased to know your father has moved against the invaders. Lance Carraway is likely dead by now. With Damoria's support, Prince Tohmas' army is ended." His smile was victorious.

But Valia did not believe him. His words were bluster, as irrelevant as a spring breeze.

Valia let drop her hand and adjusted her collar just enough to draw his attention to the pendant hanging low over her breasts. She made the gesture absently as if she was nothing but a preening girl.

"I am pleased our lands are safe," she said. "No doubt my father will return soon, his duty finished."

"Tonight," Calus declared, retrieving the fiddle, "your duty is to me."

She lowered her head to hide her frown and hoped it looked like a nod of approval or at least acceptance. "I will attend."

She couldn't bring herself to say "happily." The only joy she knew was in keeping her secret, ready to drive it through his heart the moment she could.

Chapter 8

When Arnika woke, she was alone in the bed.

There were no fancy double cots here. The tiny tent was hot from her body heat, the furs soft under her chin. But her husband was missing. Since his clothing and sword were also gone, she did not worry but rose into the late morning. As she tried to sort out how to find an actual dress, her cousin Altana stuck her head into the tent and, seeing her awake, shuffled in to pass her a gown and cloak.

Altana, usually brimming with questions and thoughts to share, was silent. They struggled to dress her in the tight quarters, the tent too short to allow her to stand. Rolling around on her back to get her feet through the dress surely was unladylike, but it was the best she could do.

"Are you all right?" Arnika asked her cousin. Altana looked as pristine as ever, her hair neatly pleated and tied back, her dress pressed and proper. She usually wore a charm given to her by a protector, but the necklace was missing this morning.

"How could I be?" Altana replied. "Were you so far from the fighting that you didn't hear the screams? How about the smell of it? Barbaric! What kind of monster attacks at night? How could they get in? Or kill so many? Did you not hear? The protectors were slain, nearly to a man, Nika! Protectors! They are supposed to protect you, and they failed, didn't they?" Instead of rising, Altana's voice slowly grew softer, as if strangling the words before they left her mouth. "This is madness,

having a woman out in this war, right in the path of danger! This is his fault, you know. King Tohmas should have—"

Arnika put her hand over her cousin's mouth, eliciting a squawk from Altana. She wasn't exactly sure where Altana's tirade was going, but the tent's walls would not protect them well enough from listening ears. Although she doubted Tohmas himself meant her harm, the people nearest him already distrusted her. Having her cousin spouting discontent would not do.

"He defended me, Tana," Arnika insisted, her words soft but firm. "Mind your words." She released her grip and finished lacing her bodice, feeling it pinch against her hips as she knelt under the low ceiling. It would have to be adjusted outside where she could stand, but it was a fine sight better than a man's tunic and a piece of rope as a belt.

Altana pressed her lips and said nothing as she followed Arnika out.

Protector Linco stood outside, his drawn sword in hand. His beard had been partly shaved, exposing a stitched wound, the edges of it puckered and purple. He still smiled at her.

"Where is my husband?" she asked.

"Planning tent," Linco replied, his "t" sound muted as he worked not to pinch the wound. "This way, my lady."

He led the way without sheathing his sword, his shield over his back.

She'd typically have two protectors, she realized. This was the toll the raids had taken. It made her heart sad.

The memories of the night before trickled through as they walked— memories of riding blind through the darkness, the grip around her waist, Tohmas' calm voice reaching her through the chaos. All the panic and fear rose again, but it fell off as she remembered his warm face pressed against her neck and the words she knew he would never speak to another.

Gods, I have never been so terrified.

Tohmas Galanth did not show fear. For as long as she had known him, his control had been absolute. But he had broken down for her, only for her.

As she approached the command tent, Arnika became aware of the smoke in the air. It was wood smoke, she was certain, but a powerful perfume lingered in the air with it.

"What burns?" she asked Linco.

The protector pursed his lips, stretching his stitches. "Celebrant Loni has insisted the dead are heroes worthy of the fires. The pyres will burn for days at this rate, my lady."

She recognized the scent: whitebroom flower. It was used to mask the smell of death during funerals. She wondered where they had found enough of the seedpods.

Darknim DoomDragon's voice boomed from the tent as she approached, "I wish it weren't so, but without the Circle, the people's faith is broken. We have no unity without the Dragon of the North. Perhaps this raid was a sign from the gods; the Circle of the Raven must be complete to wage war. It is our way."

Arnika entered in, finding herself behind Darknim himself. The Northlander looked smaller than usual, his trademark dragon scale armor missing. Only pelts covered him now, his smaller axes on his belt.

The kingsmen were present, although they also included the Guardian of StoneTop's fyrd and Guardian Carraway. It made sense; Guardian Vantin was Kingsman Loritat's representative, and the Fyrd of Arrow had no kingsman. They seemed to answer to Tohmas directly and would continue to do so until a kingsman was named for Gaidol, as that was their origin. Until then, Lance led.

Tohmas leaned over the table at the far end with the kingsmen, Sol, Barnon, Talbit, around him. Barnon still favored his right side, an older injury that the fighting had aggravated. Sol moved stiffly, but Arnika spotted no wounds on him; his wounds seemed to be a more general ache. Talbit did not seem to have rested or changed, his polished glasses high on his nose as he stared down at the map and tokens on the table, his expression dark. The spirit and humor had left him. She doubted even a good rest would bring it back.

Pyres and prayers had filled the night. Counting the dead had left her numb as well. She imagined her expression matched his.

"This is bigger than traditions! You know that, Darknim!" Kingsman Barnon replied.

"It does not matter what I think. It is the way of my people. The Circle is broken without Elder Tril or a replacement. We failed, Barnon. We did not see the attack. We could not protect our people. We cannot do war without a Circle. It is not our way." Each word was simple and short, a grandfather lecturing an obstinate child.

"Give us time to get Elder Tril back," Tohmas requested softly. He glanced up but did not hold the Northlander's stare.

"That is not up to me. I will try." The Northlander turned and left. Arnika had moved to the side. She doubted he even saw her.

Protector Linco came up behind Arnika, offering her a stool. When she nodded, he placed it reverently against the wall, the elegant table before her. The normality of joining the CampCircle grounded her.

Kingsman Sol faced Tohmas, leaning heavily towards him, his hands wide on the table. "We've got hundreds gone, half of Trulin's forces missing, and far too few protectors left."

"Trulin?" Arnika involuntarily said, the word a squawk. She'd seen nothing of her brown and white in the fighting the night before, not that she remembered anyway.

"Your Charger Granton headed out, apparently," Tohmas said softly. "He's headed west, away from the fighting. But it was unexpected."

"We need blood, Tohmas," Sol interrupted, his voice sharp.

"You can't charge after Gaidol," Guardian Lance Carraway protested. He was the only person left on the opposite edge of the table near the door. She interpreted it as sides; he opposed what the other kingsmen wanted.

Arnika checked the map, registering the tokens. They would be guessing the location of the Gaidolon army unless Kitable had managed to find them. But their position on the map was just north of the border to Gaidol, still in Trulin territory. *BrokenFall River*, she recognized. And she knew that land well enough to know Lance was right.

"If we harry them now...." Kingsman Sol said, moving a stack of tokens onto the map.

"You'll get your men killed," Lance interrupted. His eyes were on Tohmas, who refused to lift his stare from the map, leaving the two to argue. "The approach from the north is singular, but the south is shored up with a hundred hiding places along the hills. And once you reach BrokenFall River, you have only one bridge across. They can hold you there for cycles."

"We can't go around," Kingsman Talbit said, his voice tired. "Going around the lake will cost too much time and resources."

"Then give me another alternative!" Sol snapped, his tone making Arnika jump in her seat.

"There isn't one," Lance admitted. "We're too few. Maybe once some have recovered, or we call in other forces. What about Lour? Can they spare more than just the one fyrd? Or perhaps Clandac..."

"Kingsman Courion is rearranging the borders of a princedom, if you recall. He's busy enough!" Kingsman Talbit insisted.

"Lour has been more than generous. Perhaps the Northlander is right, and the gods oppose you now," Guardian Vantin said coarsely, bristling from where he had withdrawn to the side opposite Arnika. Physically, he stood half way between Tohmas and Sol. *In between the two,* Arnika thought. He's siding with neither now.

Tohmas' voice cut through. "We have to go forward. Otherwise, we lose momentum." He was not wrong; the forces were fragile. Tohmas' purpose had overruled old animosity between princedoms, but it would not take much to bring them back. She'd heard about the march to the north, when the ill-fated Prince Marfaie had worked to divide the forces. She thought it ironic that, for all his efforts, he had been less effective than time had been.

"Good!" Sol said, slamming a fist down.

"It will not work," Lance insisted. "I know these lands, Tohmas. I have come through here. This is suicide."

Arnika's voice surprised even her. "He's right," she timidly said.

At last, Tohmas lifted his head and met her eyes. She felt her face flush powerfully, embarrassment filling her. She didn't like the attention, but the words had to be said. This was her duty.

He held her stare as the kingsmen around her protested, their voices blurring into one.

"If we give Gaidol more time to mobilize the others, we could face twice the number of enemies!" Sol insisted.

"If we have time to reach for Lour, he has time to woo Polthian. Besides, we still have those loyal to Trulin among us; what if they swap back? How many others are on the fence, waiting for the winning side to become obvious? Don't think Lour won't change sides if Dorakon has the bigger need for his resources. He'll..." Guardian Vantin's infuriated voice cut into the ruckus as he protested the accusation.

But Tohmas wasn't listening to them. Arnika let the voices of the kingsmen fade out of her attention too. His eyes were on her as if they were alone in the tent, and only her voice could reach his ears.

The realization shook her. It seemed wrong that she held such a place of focus for him.

At length, he blinked, and his expression lightened.

"Trulin and Gaidol agreeing," he said, and the tent went quiet to hear him out. "I think I must heed this sign. When ancient enemies stand together, I have to believe them."

The silence lingered. Lance looked content, but even he did not have enough energy to smile.

"Then, what do we do?" Kingsman Talbit ventured.

Tohmas reached over the map and pulled the pile of enemy tokens in half. "Damoria and Gaidol are not friends. We divide them. We can face Gaidol if it stands alone."

"How can we divide them?" Kingsman Barnon asked. He rubbed at his forearm as if trying to soothe a tight muscle. "Damoria hates Galanth and has for generations. Warrah will come for your head, Tohmas."

"But I am not as important as his territory is," Tohmas pointed out.

The kingsmen moved up around the map, tracing the lines of the borders. Damoria was not on this map at all, being too far west.

"We cannot get to them," Sol declared. "As Talbit said, our supplies need replenishing. Crossing the mountains was hard enough. We can't go back that way, and the villages around BrokenFall Lake are too small to offer any resupply, even if they wanted to."

"We have an ally in the south. We send them in," Tohmas said, nodding with great confidence now. "Runnah!" The runner came in slowly. He was limping but presented himself sharply. "I need Kitable and Sabian in here. *Geddit*." The runner left at a hobbling trot.

Tohmas swept his gaze through the tent, taking the measure of each of the leaders with him. "Hold your fyrds. We will give the Rydans time. When Damoria breaks from their alliance, then we advance." His eyes found Arnika. "Our unity makes us strong. We will use it. Gaidol will be ours, or it will burn."

Satisfied, he dismissed the kingsmen.

Once the others had left, Arnika asked Tohmas about Trulin's forces once more, the implications of Charger Granton's desertion still weighing on her.

He shrugged. "I have a new commander for the remnants. None of them are talking about Granton or where he went, and I don't have

the people right now to hunt him down. There'll be hell to pay once I do though. One whore from Fixer City claims she heard him making a deal with someone with an accent she couldn't recognize the night before, only she never saw anyone go in or out of the tent. Then he was last seen riding west with his soldiers during the raid. They'll hit the mountains in that direction and are unlikely to bother us again. If he shows himself, he'll face a starvation post. I just wish I could figure out who he had been talking to."

She nodded, lost in thoughts, then ventured, "Can we ask Kitable to check into it?"

He glanced at her, surprised. "A fine idea," he said, his eyes distant for a moment in thought. "Thank you."

Kitable arrived as he spoke, Sabian on his heels. All business at first, Tohmas sent Sabian to the Outlands with Kitable's help. Carsh's Follower was to contact the Rydans and set them against Damoria from the south.

Sending in the Rydans into the unguarded south of Damoria was turning a wolf loose with penned sheep, Arnika was certain. But with the recent casualties, the pyres of which were still darkening the skies with smoke and filling her nose with the stench of whitebroom, Arnika felt it appropriate.

But once Sabian was on his way, Tohmas held Kitable back and asked about Granton and his departure.

Kitable frowned deeply; his beard looked longer whenever he did. "Yes, I needed to talk about the situation from a magic perspective," he said tentatively. "I reviewed the raid extensively and caught a few glimmers of magical involvement. I suspect whoever attacked the Circle of the Raven was involved. Considering what the Circle said about them, they could be the strange accent. However, what they would want with a Trulin Charger I cannot guess."

Kitable scowled at the wall in thought for a while, his eyes strangely distant, but this time Arnika wondered if the wizard was actually seeing something, not just lost in thought as her husband had been. At length, he said, "We need the Circle of the Raven to look into it. I need to find Elder Tril."

The pause lingered in the tent like an unwanted visitor. With neither of them speaking, it fell to Arnika to ask, "So how do we find him?"

Kitable started and stared at her as if having forgotten she was present. He smiled at her, and she struggled not to find it patronizing.

"I have some clues to follow but I have to leave to chase them. I just wanted to know what timeframe I am looking at."

Tohmas glanced at the map. "With Sabian in the south, I've set the Rydans into Damoria. When the Damorian yellow and red leave the Gaidolon camp, Dorakon will run for SwordWood. I want to be on his tail. He needs the bridge. If I'm on him, I can take it. "

"Not much time then," the wisavi reflected after a pause. "Rydans ride fast."

"Two days," Tohmas agreed, "for them to get into Damoria and to start harassing the locals. It'll be a few more days while Wevan decides if he needs his additional forces. Then a few more while the messengers ride through Gaidol to get to the men here. I'd say you have six to ten days before Damoria's men pull out."

Kitable sighed loudly, staring at the map as Tohmas did and seeming to forget about Arnika again. "I hope to be gone only a short while, but as far as we can tell, pairs of wizards attacked three Circle members simultaneously, meaning there are at least six casters. I do not yet know why they attacked the others and kidnapped Tril, or why they meddled with my defenses or if they were involved with Charger Granton, so I cannot even begin to guess how difficult it will be to get Tril out. I wish I knew more, but..."

"The Northlanders are making plans to break off," Tohmas warned. "We have only a day or two left before they go. Only Elder Tril will stop them. The longer we leave Tril, the less likely it is you will find him alive. I want the Circle of the Raven back. Besides, we need to know who those casters are. If you think this is the best way to deal with them, get to it quickly."

Kitable nodded absently. "There is a chance I will not return in time to pursue Gaidol."

Tohmas shrugged. "You keep those casters out of this, and we will take out the soldiers." He made it sound so simply, but Arnika had her doubts.

"Then I will go and see what I can find. I hope to return before the day is out, but it remains to be seen. Otherwise, good luck."

Tohmas smiled. "You too. I know Tril was a friend. I hope he is well."

It warmed her to hear the genuine care in Tohmas' voice when he passed on his well-wishes. These were his people, and it was evident he thought highly of them. While it was obvious the Circle of the Raven had many strategic uses, there was also the simple fact that Tril was a friend of Kitable's, and Tohmas wanted him to be happy.

Kitable bowed awkwardly to Arnika and left, his green and silver robes billowing around him. Arnika pursed her lips.

"Should he go alone?" she asked.

"I would suggest another caster assists him, but he won't do it. He considers people a liability. The more people he has to defend, the worse off he is."

That sounded sad.

"Then his solitude is voluntary?" Arnika asked.

"Very much so," Tohmas replied, offering her an arm off the stool. She gratefully took it; like him, her legs were stiff from immobility. It took several steps to push the tingle out of them.

"But is it what he wants?" she asked.

Her husband paused and blinked several time down at her before speaking. She thought perhaps she had offended him, but the expression that eventually took over his face was surprise. "I don't know, my lady. And I probably never will."

Sabian knew magic was not the terror the Rydans believed it was. He had seen Shimmer's shows and had witnessed Master Kitable's marvels. Magic was a tool. Like any weapon, it could be used for good or evil purposes.

And yet when the feeling of magic washed over him, he cringed. It felt cold on his skin, like falling into a river. It took effort to hold still as Kitable had instructed.

The Esparan camp in Trulin vanished in a blink, replaced instantly by grasslands. Sabian's stomach lurched into his throat and tried to turn itself inside out; he swallowed hard and focused on not throwing up. He took a moment to check his surroundings and found it clear of Rydans, then crouched and closed his eyes, waiting for the feeling of illness to pass.

After a dozen breaths, his innards settled, and Sabian took a closer look at his surroundings. Master Kitable had set him as close as he dared to Tohmas' greeting post on Polthian's border. Should a Rydan see Sabian's appearance, no amount of explanations would save him. While very few of the grassland people shared Carsh's ability to detect magic passively, they all hated magic with a similar vehemence. If it were obvious magic, Sabian would be seen as a flyer and immediately killed. It was bad enough that he was Esparan.

Rydans would instinctually distrust an Esparan, no matter how well he spoke Rydan or acted like them. But a Rydan would never permit the use of magic, and there was no other way of getting a message passed to Gaidol's border. Sabian was the only person who could both speak to the Rydans and tolerate Kitable's magic.

Sabian struck out north. He slung his pack loosely over his shoulder, two waterskins swinging off it. It had been five cycles since he had been stabbed through his left shoulder. In his efforts to avoid weakness, he had made the left side stronger than the right, perfect for carrying weight. It left his slightly more deft right hand for drawing knives if required although he had worked tirelessly to make his left just as fast. Carsh was ambidextrous, and Sabian strived to be the same. The baldrics, in Rydan style, crossed his chest for use for either hand.

After one day of walking, Sabian spotted signs that he was being stalked. The grassland birds gave the predator away; where it passed, they went still, while farther out, they gave chittering warnings.

It would be a Rydan or a hill cat. Either way, his best chance was a confrontation.

Sabian turned around and, setting himself into a ready stance, tracked down the beast following him.

There was nowhere to hide in the field, and running would reveal them for a thrown knife. When Sabian came upon his position, the young Rydan chose to hold his ground, a *stafnye* in hand. Once he had assessed his opponent, the Rydan rotated his *stafnye* to be leveled at Sabian, a sneer of dismissal on his face as he lunged.

The boy had misjudged his opponent.

Sabian knocked the *stafnye*'s attack wide with his left hand. Coming through from the block, he used his powerful left fist to punch, and the boy twisted out of the way.

Sabian palmed the knife in his right hand, allowing him to grab the boy's arm as he moved passed, too focused on the attack to recognize how fast Sabian could move. Once he had the boy's arm, he pulled him over, hooking his leg over the *stafnye*'s base and keeping it pinned as the boy went down.

He paused, rotating his grip to bring his knife back into his palm. His knee now holding the right arm and chest to the ground, Sabian had his knife on the Rydan's throat.

It struck him then that what he considered a boy was, in fact, his age. He was disappointed he had been so little of a challenge.

"I am a messenger from the Arm," Sabian said in Rydan. "My Leader said no bloodshed unless for my life. My words are for Chief Tamv only."

Sabian pulled back, not feeling he had to warn the boy off more. It was clear any further exchange would be deadly.

Reorienting himself, Sabian returned to his travel. The Rydan had no throwing knives or spears. The only tool he wore would do poorly as a throwing knife. For the boy to attack again, which would be folly, he would have to chase Sabian down. Sabian was ready for it.

As expected, the boy waited for Sabian to be a safe distance away. When he rose, he did so slowly, his eyes on Sabian for any sign of disapproval. Sabian gave him none, allowing the Rydan to shadow him at a respectful distance. If Sabian looked his way, the boy stopped, with a cock of his head asking permission to continue. When Sabian trekked on, the boy followed again.

After a candle, the boy cautiously approached again. Sabian was grateful; he had not dared rest while being followed and was happy to have an excuse to pause for a drink. The sun was hot in the late summer so far south. He had become accustomed to the cooler wind in the north.

Keeping one knife in hand, he twisted the blade over his knuckles deftly.

At a dozen paces from him, the Rydan paused and asked, "Messenger from Carsh?"

Sabian nodded his head once.

The boy straightened proudly, thumping his *stafnye* into the dirt. "I will clear the path," he declared. Darting off in a Rydan's loping run, the boy dashed ahead of Sabian. By going forward, ostensibly to tell others

to allow Sabian through, the boy silently offered to guide Sabian to the camp by the most direct route.

Sabian decided to take the boy at his word and followed.

The boy led him to the *Greet Po*, Tohmas' bloody handprint marker still standing proudly in the tall grasses. Rydans had built a miniature city beyond it, keeping to the Outlands but dangerously close to the Polthian border. Sabian could even see the short stone wall that marked the princedom on the horizon, flags hanging limply in the stagnant air. The occasional glint of metal hinted that soldiers manned the wall.

Sabian lost sight of his escort as he arrived among the short domed homes of the Rydans. Knowing the chief's house was the *shella*, the only proper building, he made his way into the village. He held his first knife, always, in his strongest right hand in readiness. Trying to quell his nerves, he did not draw his second blade yet.

He had spotted the *shella* among the hovels by the time a Rydan blocked his path. The rest of the Rydans, women and children included, had stood by and watched him pass through their village. Sabian had assumed the boy had told them to stay clear, and they lacked sufficient rank or gumption to confront him. In seeing his escort cringing behind the Rydan who blocked his path, Sabian assumed this person had decided the boy was wrong.

The Rydan was an elder, but his muscles were still strong. His skin was dark as oak from the sun and looked as thick as leather. His weapon choice was *rawpnyes*, curved blades best used to slash open abdomens or sever tendons. He had a tattoo on his chest, but it was faded; it could have been a wild cat or wolf. Had Sabian been part of the Clan, he would have known the man's name by his tattoo, but he was a stranger and asking would insult the man by making known his lack of notoriety.

Carsh had said no bloodshed.

Sabian took a strong stance before the man. "My words are for Chief Tamv," he declared in Rydan. He made the three salutes; first right hand into left palm as a salute to Tohmas, then right hand to the left forearm to indicate Carsh. Lastly, he acknowledged Tamv's supremacy over them by placing his right fist on his left collarbone, right over the scar under his shirt.

The Rydan wrinkled his nose, assessing Sabian. He knew this custom. If he assessed too fast, they were dismissing him as weak. A

long assessment meant they thought him formidable enough to be cautious before interacting with them. Too long though, and they may be considering challenging him to clarify the ranks.

Sabian assessed the Rydan for a respectful time, then said, "I do not know this clan," to prompt the stranger.

"Takar," the man said, introducing himself. He gave no Leader name, meaning he was a Leader himself. At least, he was not a Follower of Tamv or his sons, freeing Sabian from the concern that he might offend someone who far outranked him.

"Sabian, Follower of Carsh," Sabian replied, saluting the Arm once more.

He felt the tension around him rise. Esparans may have gasped or whispered to their neighbors, but Rydans became all the more still when surprised. That stillness tightened the air physically, making the tone heavy. While they had not gathered around him, Sabian was well aware that every eye of the village was set on him.

"Esparan," the man replied.

With one insulting word, Takar had refused Sabian's claim.

"My Leader said no bloodshed unless for my life," Sabian replied, his hand on his second knife in readiness, "but I must give my message to the Shoulder."

The man glanced behind himself, then quickly back at Sabian. Sabian allowed his eyes to do the same, ready for a threat but heeding the man's attention.

A Rydan stood at the entrance of the *shella*, observing the confrontation. In place of the typical grass bracelets, he wore red stained grasses, the bones in his bracelets outnumbering the blades of grass. The tattoo prominently displayed on the man's chest was a dragon, distinctive and recognizable, albeit faded.

The chief was watching.

Sabian waited, knowing the chief would direct them now. Either Takar would be called off, or he would be given leave to test Sabian's claim. After all, Carsh would never have accepted a weak Follower. If he claimed to be Carsh's Follower, Sabian had to be able to defend himself. If he died, then he was an imposter.

The challenge had been issued; Sabian did not take his eyes off Takar. When the chief did not call off the Rydan, Takar drew his *rawpnyes*

and stalked forward. Tethered knives, the *rawpnyes* could be thrown and reeled in, spun, or used in hand. They were unusual weapons that required skill to master. Sabian was used to throwing a knife once only, retrieving the blades once the opponent was dead.

Throwing a knife in for a kill would not serve here. Tamv needed the final say as to who lived or died; one of them had to be defeated first. That meant allowing closer combat to declare the victor.

Drawing a second knife, Sabian dropped his bag in readiness, knowing his life was at stake. Takar would aim to kill, and no one would think ill of him. Sabian was just an Esparan, after all. But Sabian had to disarm or defeat his opponent, preferably without permanently crippling the older, more experienced man.

Unlike the boy from before, Takar had assessed Sabian well. He kept his weapons close, knowing Sabian's knives allowed for short strikes and speed. He was ready for them.

Settling his heartbeat, ready to move in any direction, Sabian let Takar approach. He even let the man strike first.

As he had expected, Takar went for a fatal blow; he feigned left and then sliced right, aiming to eviscerate Sabian. Going for the core meant Sabian would have to move his entire body to dodge, slowing him. Instead, Sabian blocked the strike, using the edge of his blade. Takar's shale *rawpnye* chipped against the iron edge of the Esparan dagger. The knife caught slightly, delaying Takar when he tried to withdraw.

Sabian was already reaching out with his right hand. In a flicker, he sliced through the tether holding Takar's *rawpnye* to his wrist, all without breaking the skin.

Takar skipped past, slicing at Sabian's inner leg. Sabian dodged back and did not immediately retaliate. He waited, letting the people see the severed tether and realize what it meant.

He could have slit his opponent's wrist with that blow.

The silence deepened.

Takar again went for the core, slicing at Sabian's face and tossing his tethered knife to give it reach. He probably expected the Esparan to lean back reflexively, but Sabian turned instead. He kicked quickly at one leg, then at the other when Takar pulled his left leg back. Takar stumbled, his knife falling over Sabian's shoulder.

Sabian went in faster than the knife that swung down at him. He struck the hilt of his blade against the man's hip bone where there was no muscle coverage. He danced back two steps, pausing to give the man time to straighten. Then he looked to the *shella* for permission.

Any knife fighter could tell this battle could have ended twice. Had he used the edge of his blades correctly, Sabian would have dealt two lethal blows.

The chief met Sabian's stare and nodded, telling him to leave the man alive. While grateful for that, Sabian was unsure how to proceed. He could not kill the man, and any blow that hurt could be deadly with a touch of bad luck.

The Rydan did not give him time to think; Takar lunged with his *rawpnyes*, having brought his tethered blade to his hand. The man was skilled, using only the barest energy required for each strike, but Sabian was faster, and his blades were stronger.

They had been unimpressed by the speed of the kill. Perhaps the chief wanted to see extent of his skills.

While defending against Takar, Sabian started tossing his knives in and out of the combat. In addition to switching hands, he threw his blade over his shoulder or around his back. While he rarely made an attack, the display contrasted the precise motions of the Rydan he faced, and he never failed to have a knife exactly where he needed to keep him safe.

Takar started smiling. Around them, Sabian heard more than one Rydan chuckle.

Sabian pushed it farther, adding a third knife to his display. Takar's attacks slowed, the Rydan losing focus as he laughed. The delays gave Sabian enough time to make even more outrageous displays, juggling two or three knives over his knuckles or under a leg.

When the Rydan paused completely, staring in amusement, Sabian darted in and snatched the man's *rawpnye* from his hand. He chose the one cut earlier, disarming the man.

But before the Rydan could panic, Sabian added the *rawpnye* to his other three and juggled it as if he was in the camp once more, entertaining children. One by one, he caught his knives and put them away, ending by holding out the *rawpnye* to Takar, hilt out. He had no blades

out except Takar's, but he kept his hand near another of his own in case he needed it.

He checked again with the chief, but Tamv did not look impressed. He did not seem angry either, leaving Sabian unsure.

Takar laughed openly, returning his *rawpnyes* to his belt.

"Trained by the Arm," Takar declared.

Sabian bowed his head in agreement.

Takar turned and faced the *shella*. He dropped into a ready position, one knee bent but not quite touching down. Saluting the Shoulder, fist on his left shoulder, he called, "Will you hear his words, Chief?"

The chief nodded pensively, then returned into the *shella*.

Takar went to Sabian and guided him forward. "You are a foolish man," Takar told Sabian, "but a dangerous fool. I wish you well."

None of the Rydans gave Sabian another look. The excitement was over.

He entered cautiously, reviewing what Carsh had said about showing respect. He saluted the Shoulder and kept his head down. He took a ready stance before the chief, kneeling in the dust of the cleared earth as the chief sat above him, just as Takar had done.

Delivering the message was simple, and the chief decided then and there to begin. Unlike Esparans, the Rydans did not have to pack equipment or tents. They threw belongings into a sack over their horses' packs and were ready to ride. Wives stayed behind in the village, minding the children and taking over the hunting without hesitation. The men were prepared for war by morning.

Sabian traveled with them, surprised that an Esparan was given leave to stay with them. Within days, they arrived in Damoria.

At the Chief's command, Sabian went on ahead. He played the part of the panicked local, relaying the approach of the Rydans to give the non-combatants time to hide and those who would fight time to assemble. It had been Tohmas' suggestion, but the chief liked how the tactic brought the armed men together for a swift death and prompted the women and children to get out of the way. Sabian was silently pleased it spared the villagers who might otherwise have ended up unwillingly in a Rydan's path. He wondered if Tohmas had planned for that as well.

In between raids, Sabian shared a fire with the Rydans. Although he was never allowed to speak to the chief again, Takar and his Followers

paid homage to the Arm and ensured Sabian had whatever he required. The raids brought them great spoils to share.

By the fourth village, Sabian gave up on pretending. Once he arrived in the town, he told them the Rydans were coming and suggested they call for help from Prince Wevan.

Some men called him a traitor to his people. Women cursed him. One guardsman tried to stop him from leaving.

Sabian laughed at the attempt and left the man with a knife in his throat.

He joined the raids from thereon.

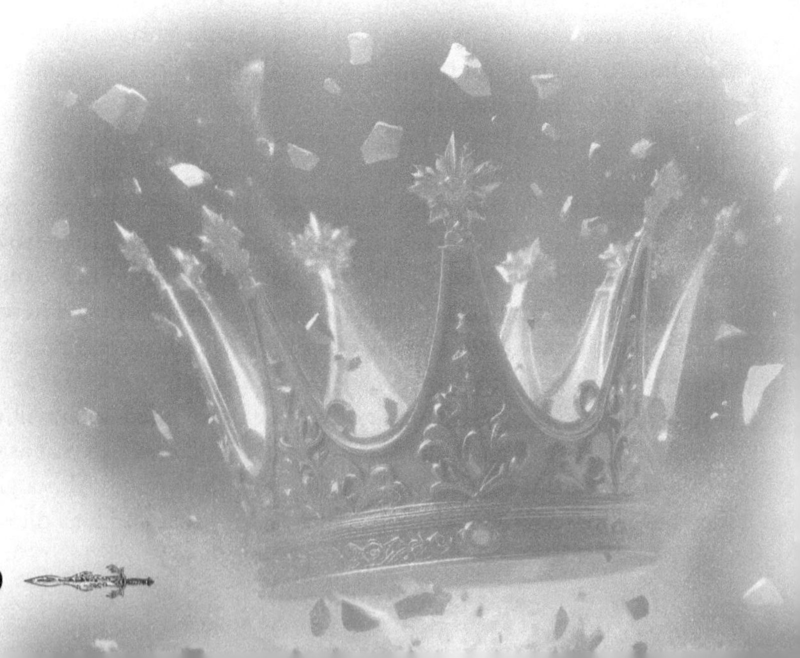

Chapter 9

With Fantorn freshly returned, all six other Circle members were in the cave when Gannon walked in. The way they were all facing the portal he had created made it clear Yonny had warned them of his impending arrival.

Gannon was brought to a halt by their accusatory glares, and he caught himself mentally going over his activities during the last few Tainted days. After leaving Maybel and disrupting the Tainted forces' defenses, he'd recharged his focus gem, nothing more. No call had come from the Circle. He had assumed they had been working with their prisoner and would notify him if they needed him.

"Where have you been?" Yonny's deep voice demanded.

Gannon raised an eyebrow. "Oh great diviner, why do you ask? Do you not already know?"

The scowl he received was venom. "You have been talking with Tainted soldiers and fraternizing with a Tainted women!" Yonny accused, jabbing his finger as if he was a father who would soon wag the finger in disapproval.

That, Gannon realized, would be why the others were staring at him. Yonny had told them he had been talking to the Tainted. Considering his origins, that would be sufficient to make them nervous. It had taken over a hundred years for the United Provinces of Shantan to be considered for Circle work, and only a handful of applicants had been accepted through the rigorous selection process. To those outside the

United Provinces, everyone from Shantan seemed to look exactly like the Derelict.

"I was laying down backup plans and asking her about your mysterious Kitable," he confessed with an easy shrug. He had done nothing wrong and felt no need to defend himself. Luring a disgruntled soldier away from his fellows had been minor in the grand scheme of things. He was prouder of helping one army raid although Yonny hadn't mentioned that yet. Did he know? Or was he just too interested in how Gannon had interrogated Maybel?

"Have you any concept of the word 'privacy,' Yonny?" Gannon said with a sneer.

"You are of the Watching Circle," Namni replied. "There is no such thing."

Feeling more assaulted by Namni's comment than all of Yonny's yammering, Gannon straightened himself and answered the charge. "In that case, you might as well all know that I merely spoke to the woman because she revealed that she knew Kitable. I spoke with her at length and learned a great deal about Kitable and the Tainted world. I then replaced her memories of the event. I ran into another Tainted woman and spoke to her briefly, but she was not helpful. Neither will even remember having met me." He eyed Yonny as he finished, "Tainted do not interest me in the slightest."

"But Kitable does," Rean said, her croaking voice calm, almost encouraging. By her expression, he had to presume he was not the only one who found the Tainted caster intriguing.

"Absolutely fascinating," Gannon admitted. "Did you know the man is only thirty-two years old? I know that they age faster than we do, but how can one even learn so much in such a short time? Oh, and he has been studying Tainted magic as we have, only they call it 'untouchable' magic and believe it comes from greater beings called 'gods' that oversee everything they do. They think there are four greater beings, but the Tainted were vague about this. They used many words I could not translate. One said I should talk to a 'celebrant,' but only the ancestors know what that means, I am sure!"

His talking broke down their suspicions. He pressed on happily.

"Apparently, there is a kind of pure Tainted magic user, and two travel with your Kitable. He studies them, researching their powers. He was

also friends with the Tainted Circle, which they call the 'Northlander Circle' because it consists of people called 'Northlanders.' None of them realize that these 'Northlanders' channel the same 'untouchable' magic that the others do!"

He knew he was using too many new words but did not care enough to slow down.

"As for Kitable, he is a pure caster, certainly a descendent of Leugan, and he cannot handle any of the Tainted magic. He is a defender of some leader, but the woman I spoke to revealed that she was his enemy. She claims to have found a weakness in the man in the form of a 'Heart's Desire Spell,' which sounds like a Desire spell attached to light illusions. And I met her, the woman that Kitable desires! My contact is in position to use that advantage. We are merely waiting for the opportunity, assuming the attack I gently facilitated didn't kill them all in the last few days."

There was a brief pause that warned that he may have lost them. If they were confused and he understood, then that spoke well of him and poorly of them.

And he did feel he understood the Tainted world better. The people here knew about pure Tainted magic but did not understand where it came from or how to summon it. The true magic of Wanter was also within reach for these people but usually kept apart. The Northlanders were a mystery even the locals had yet to sort out.

At length, Rean cleared her throat and said, "You have done well. We will certainly have more dealings with this Kitable as time goes on."

Reminded, Gannon pointed out, "Might be sooner than we expect. Kitable is looking for our prisoner. At the request of the Northlanders, he has been searching."

Yonny scoffed, tossing his hands to throw ribbons about grandly. "We are protected from divination, and no Scrys can penetrate our walls. How will he find us?"

"I have no idea," Fantorn said, the tension in her voice poignant enough to draw their attention. She was staring. "But he did."

To avoid fussing with light spells, they had opened one cavern wall to the outside then sealed it with a transparent wall. The opening looked over a ledge and down into a deep river valley, giving them a view much like the Grand Mountain Islands of Wanter. When they looked now,

however, their attention was solely on the man in green robes standing on the ledge just beyond their barrier.

The changes to the wall had been complex and included an illusion on the outside. Kitable, despite his proximity, would be facing a normal-looking rock face. As surprising as it was to see the Tainted caster there, Gannon thought it convenient; now he didn't need to answer questions about any of his other dealings.

"How!?" Yonny exclaimed, which the others *shushed*. It was unlikely that Kitable would hear him, but they dared not risk it.

Protected by the wall, they turned to the prisoner for an explanation.

His world was one incomprehensible, uncontrollable image. Tril tried to put up the shield Kitable had taught him, but his captors intercepted him every time. Without that protection, he was at the mercy of his *visaln*.

He walked in the blackness outside his mind on the fringes of dreams. He could see the giant spiral of light in the distance, its many colors matched the auras of every domain and element of wizard magic. A cloud of magic followed him, gifting him with visions that formed with every thought.

He saw every possibility. When a stray thought went to his friends, he saw the thousands of paths of their lives. Some of the older lives were ending soon, and he saw Elder Ela breathe her last. Despite what must have been days of staring at the flashing images, he could not say who, if anyone, would replace the Voice of the Raven in the Circle.

Darknim was often in the visions, as a kingsman, as the Dragon of the North, and as an elder, and Tril was pleased by those visions. Unlike many of them, the Dragon would leave behind a fine legacy. One could hope for nothing more in life.

Tril's legacy was weak. His family would miss him if he did not return, which seemed a real possibility, but they would not grieve for long. Even his wife would remarry within the year, for his absence was more common than his presence even now. He had not realized how far he had drifted from his brother or the son and nephew he had once spoiled.

CHAPTER 9

For Tohmas and his ambitious march, the future was dark. Rydans seemed to dominate the visions, and the images alternated between earning the Rydans' respect and their hatred. More than one vision saw Tohmas slain by hooked knives or spears, with one showing the Pack Runner being the murderer. Carsh either fell with the king or barely survived; though, in one shocking vision, the trusted prime protector was the king's killer. True to his reputation, the single blow hit the heart. The king died instantly.

The fact that such possibilities even existed terrified Tril.

Tril was lost, and he knew it, but there was little he could do. Through concentration, he kept the visions from sweeping him away, but he could not push them back far enough to let him return to his mind. In some ways, he was grateful for the reprieve as he felt certain (and the visions confirmed it) that if he had been more present in the cave, he would have been a greater source of interest to his captors. That could have meant a visit to Wanter, and he had to avoid that at all costs.

Their world, which he could see in his visions, looked very much like Espar. There were snow-capped mountains like the Dragontail Mountains, grasslands like the Outlands, and tundra like the Northlands. There were fields of food growing in small batches, but the one thing Tril did not see was wild forest. There were more rocks as if the entire world had been built on the foothills of mountains, and the spaces between gardens and fields were nothing but grey-brown stone that baked red in the sun and made the air shimmer in the heat.

The buildings were strange and spectacular but impractical and foreign, and the people were the same. Although he could see men and women he thought looked Esparan, he never saw anyone with the muscular build of a Northlander or the lithe form of a Rydan, and their customs made even those that looked familiar seem wrong. Despite a language he could understand as a thick Esparan, he found their world strange. Magic coursed through everything in the visions until every building, person, and living thing was nothing but an illusion in his eyes.

The light blinded him, forcing him back to the blackness once more.

The spiral in the distance, Tril recognized, was Wanter. The spiral of magic that the wizards drew upon, that Tril formed into visions unwittingly, was the wizarding world itself. Wizard power was the power of Wanter.

TRAITOR

Tril followed the history of the United Provinces of Shantan from its colony days to its current semi-power position. He found himself living the life of Shantan's most notorious enemy, Derelict Leugan, who had defied all authority to come to Tril's world to help fight off the invading demons. He followed the man as dragons drove off the monsters. Leugan fell in love and married.

Tril saw Leugan's children grow up in a world where raiders were pushed back by sword and wand. Slowly, the people came together, and the children had children of their own. The blood thinned. It mixed with those able to channel the power of the gods. The untouchable magic blended with Wanter's, rendering the powers inert. In rare individuals, it could still be manifested but only if the natural dreamer powers of the caster were distanced.

Tril saw the shame of the United Provinces at their connection to the corruption of Wanter's powers by the unwanted—the tainted—magic. That embarrassment was what Gannon fought so determinedly and would die to overcome.

His life had been long, but Gannon was still young in many ways. Three decades he had spent at schools, specializing in a single element. While most casters were broad and varied, those who showed talent in a given element or domain could be groomed in their chosen constituent. From this group, the Circle drew its members.

Gannon was proud of his place in the Watching Circle and of his skill with thought magic, but he hated embarrassment, and Ela had embarrassed him by handily thwarting him in his preferred element. That frustration was not to be long-lived. Gannon would have to move on to other things soon enough.

He would take his revenge, Tril could see, but not on Ela. Gannon would take his revenge for another slight, something that had yet to happen, but Tril could not quite see what it was or how the retaliation would manifest.

A death, a death Tril had already predicted and tried to avoid, but one that would be happening soon.

In the black of the world between dream and magic spiral, Tril frowned. Very soon. Something was happening, the images told him, and he started seeing himself in the visions. Previous thoughts about

escaping had been met with visions of his death, but one promising future was forming.

That course still had an uncertain ending.

He would need his knife. He had not opposed his capture, knowing it was futile, and they had thus not searched him for weapons. His knife was still folded under his pelts.

One man stood between him and escape. The knife could help him overcome that.

He needed to concentrate, and that meant keeping the visions back. Thankfully, his time nearest the spiral of magic in the darkness had let him rest. His wolf, ever at his side in the dark world between worlds, seemed to nod in agreement.

She would keep the weaker images back and let him see only the powerful, likely ones. With her guarding him, he could return to consciousness.

The moment for his success came closer, and he watched it unfold as if living it a dozen times. Soon, he had it memorized and was ready.

Leaving the wolf to chase the visions back, which she did with her teeth gleaming in the shadowless light, Tril rushed back to consciousness. Before he was even fully present, his hand found his hunting knife, and he pushed himself to his feet.

The cavern came into focus after he was up. He could make out the silhouettes of his keepers against the light of the wall he now knew was not solid. The closest man, and the only one who could stop him, was the young one who had captured him initially. He was physically weak, Tril knew.

Tril rushed for the wall, and Yonny lunged after him as the vision had warned. The knife was already positioned to deflect the grab. Before the other six could act, Tril crashed into the false wall.

The Watching Circle had replaced the wall with a conjured, breakable material. The illusion on the outside would keep Kitable from seeing through it, but there was not enough force in the spell to keep Tril from smashing a hole.

Rolling clear, Tril was on his feet in time to see Kitable reacting. Recognizing Tril at once, Kitable turned his shimmering gaze to the opening in the wall and placed himself between Tril and his pursuers. Yonny was the first through. Without hesitation, Kitable activated a

spell, trapping Yonny midair. When Kitable gestured sharply, Yonny was pitched backward and crashed into the solid cliff beside the false wall. The moment Yonny hit the stone, the spell dropped, and the diviner who had captured Tril collapsed onto the ledge.

Tril sorted through the visions as fast as he could, searching for the one that would allow him and Kitable to escape, but there was none. The rest of the Watching Circle would not be so rash. They were not going to let them go. In every vision, someone was left behind.

They could not win.

But the way Kitable squared for battle made it clear the wisavi did not know that fact. Kitable never expected to lose.

He was going to fall. Tril could not find a way out.

Finding the tree had been difficult, but Kitable had finally laid eyes on the half-stripped bark of the twisted, scorched oak. A careful search of the area revealed nothing, but with no other leads to follow, he decided to press on. Tohmas wanted the Circle restored. Kitable had to figure out who these new casters were and rescue Tril. That meant going on.

Knowing that whoever had attacked the Circle was also evading Scrys meant his visions could be wrong. There could be more to the tree. He had to check it out.

Appearing in the area, Kitable first examined the tree, which yielded nothing. He was trying to see the top of the cliff face, to determine if he had to go up when the faint feeling of magic made him pause.

The cliff face was the source, as was something behind the cliff. Kitable activated Spell Sight to investigate further, but his enchanted vision revealed nothing, implying the magic he was sensing was concealed. Stepping up to the wall further confirmed it; he could feel the magic from the surface and beyond. There had to be something...

He lost his train of thought entirely with the sound of breaking stone. Spinning, Kitable turned to see a mess of furs rolling through what appeared to be a hole in the cliff. Recognizing the white pelt made him smile, but the sight of the ribbon-robed man leaping after Tril had him immediately activating a force spell. He smashed the spell into the attacker's chest and slammed him against the nearest hard surface.

Tril was rolling to his feet at once.

"More come," Tril warned.

"I noticed," Kitable replied. Spells were appearing above him and from within the hole in the stone. Kitable, with a word, put up a Force Wall to protect Tril just before a fire creation spell struck the defense and was harmlessly deflected.

A woman's voice scoffed, and suddenly Kitable's wall was gone.

When he saw her, Kitable remembered the rest of Kohd's vision. Under a cloudy sky, standing between him and the scorched tree, he saw a blond-streaked woman with Spell Sight over her eyes. Now that she was moving, he could easily see the gems embedded in the corner of her eyes.

As predicted, she was not alone. Another woman floated down the cliff face as Kitable turned, and he got struck simultaneously from the left by a new fire spell. Meanwhile, someone was trying to twist the bindings off his hovering spells.

The woman with the gemmed face was casting, which inspired Kitable to deflect the newest fire spell into her instead of merely dispelling it. She brought up a shield in answer, and the spell exploded without damage.

With the next word, Kitable activated an anchor spell and targeted the person trying to steal the bindings off him. While the attacker was probably hoping to destroy the spells, the person unwittingly connected themselves to Kitable. Kitable was happy to make use of such vulnerability.

He hooked an anchor to the enemy's first shield and activated a dispel, destroying the protection.

The woman coming in from above spoke. It was not a word he understood, and he chose to ignore it instead of searching for a Translation, which he did not have at the ready. The way a Force Bolt was deflected by his defenses made it clear that these were not friends, so her comments seemed irrelevant.

"Stop!" came another voice, this time from the cavern visible beyond the hole that Tril had created. Knowing he had no Translation up, the word must have been spoken in Esparan.

Kitable identified the next shield along his anchor and dispelled it. There was no remaining defense. His anchor locked onto a person.

"Wait, my friend." When Tril spoke, Kitable paused. For a moment, he wondered if a thought domination spell had snuck past him, but no spells were visible to his enchanted vision when he glanced at Tril.

In the ensuing pause, a man about Tohmas' age made his way through the hole by kicking it open into a whole doorway. With his hands out complacently, the man stepped gingerly into the sunlight and repeated, "Stop, please."

Now that there were five recognized casters around him, Kitable thought it prudent to listen to Tril. It was difficult to gauge the skills of his enemies as they did not appear, to his magic sight, to be using hovering spells at all. He had already seen two of them full cast in less time than he had thought possible. His hovering spells would surpass that casting style, but his chances would fall dramatically if they survived until he ran out of hovering spells.

Further confounding the situation was the long drop at their backs that blocked escape. He had a feeling a Seal spell was already up. He could not Relocate with it in place nor rescue Tril.

Narrowing his gaze on the youngest of the gathering, Kitable frowned. "You speak Esparan," Kitable said, "but you are not Esparan. None of you are Esparan."

"I speak Shantanese," the stranger corrected with a half-smile that made his skin wrinkle around another gem, this one at the center of his skull. As the stranger had a completely shaven head, the wrinkles extended over the entire scalp. "Technically, so do you. You call it something else."

"Where are you from?" Kitable asked, willing to carry the conversation while he sorted out a solution. "With that wardrobe and the ability and apparently the desire to fuse crystals to your forehead, you're not from anywhere around here."

The woman above, who seemed to match Elder Ela's age and stature, said something, but again Kitable failed to understand. The younger man sighed and rolled his eyes.

"There is a universal area Translation up," the man said. "If you would just let it—"

"You want me to drop my thought defenses?" Kitable snorted in disbelief. "I would be found kissing Ocea's sandals first! You already kidnapped my friend and tried to kill me several times, not to mention

CHAPTER 9

the other attacks! What makes you think I would *ever* consider making myself that vulnerable?"

The man looked a little offended, but Kitable did not care.

"We wish to speak to you," the man replied, translating another string of words from the woman floating above. "We would plead our case."

Kitable considered the invitation begrudgingly. He was trapped, and he would be dead shortly unless he got off several perfect hits. Having Tril with him might have evened the odds slightly, but the Northlander seemed to be bogged down by visions. If Tril was going to require further defending, the easiest thing would be to get the Northlander somewhere safe.

Kitable worked better alone.

With that in mind, he agreed to hear them out.

Gannon was genuinely surprised when Kitable agreed to listen to what he had to say. Despite being a caster, Kitable knew more about those Tainted powers than most. Gannon hoped he might see the offense the mingling of the two types of magic caused.

When Rean's Binding reached for him, Gannon understood he was to become their spokesperson, as Kitable's defenses continued to keep the Translation at bay. He dutifully repeated the thoughts of the Voice of the Watching Circle but used his own words.

"Your lineage, Kitable, comes from where I come from: the United Provinces of Shantan," Gannon explained. "Your ancestor was Leugan, who came to this world to help drive away the beasts of the Third world. You call them demons."

The little diviner crouched at Kitable's side, interrupted, "Against wishes, against orders, without permission... Derelict Leugan, he is called."

Raising an eyebrow at his companion, Kitable frowned. "Derelict?" he repeated. "How flattering."

For a blink, Gannon saw Rean's thoughts debate trying to force their version of the tale onward, but Gannon argued against it, and as it was his voice being used, he got the final say. Truth, at least in this, was prudent.

"He was not praised for his actions," Gannon admitted. "He is still a shame to his homeland, for he let himself be tainted by this world. Still, he was responsible for bringing our magic to your people."

"Wizards," Kitable said, nodding. "You are telling me all casters in this world descended from this Derelict Leugan. So? What difference does that make?"

Clearing his throat to push away half of the thoughts trying to guide him, Gannon smiled slightly and pressed, "Let me finish, please," to give Rean time to decide. He recognized that she might have been running more than one thought spell, but as Yonny was unconscious, they could not activate the Linking.

"This world has its own magic," Gannon explained. He had to correct the next thought in fear of offending the man. "Tainted," as Rean continued to call it, seemed uncomplimentary. "You know it as untouchable magic," he instead said. "I know you are familiar with it."

Kitable started at the word, but Gannon attributed that to the inherent fear Maybel had said all wizards had of untouchables. The concept made powerful casters cringe, and rightly so.

"Now we come to your Northlander friends," Gannon continued, gesturing to the Northlander trembling at Kitable's side, his eyes blindly tracking visions. "They are a meld of the two powers, Kitable. They are one part untouchable and one part wizard. This makes them unstable and very dangerous."

Knowing that the man understood untouchables and feared them made Gannon hopeful that Kitable would turn from the Northlander now that he knew. But when the wizard glanced at his friend, his expression was not suspicious. Instead, compassion was the only thing Gannon saw cross the wizard's face. They could all see that visions were scrambling the Northlander's mind.

"They are latent casters of both powers," Gannon said, "and their powers are great if uncontrolled. We, the Watching Circle, came from Wanter to see how you were using the magic Leugan brought. You are a pure caster, Kitable, and a good one at that. You are close to Wanter. These half-breeds will only destroy that. We do not want our magic infected."

CHAPTER 9

Kitable considered the argument carefully, staring at Gannon. Was he looking for family resemblance? Gannon wondered. Maybel had said this wizard had no family. Would he want one?

"What we seek to do," Gannon explained, "is understand them but also limit them before they do too much damage. We took this one away from his Circle because the Circle, when complete, amplifies the influence of the tainted powers. We kept him alive to investigate this phenomenon."

They also had kept him alive, Gannon knew, to avoid having the dead man replaced. Thus far, the Northlander Circle had searched for their missing member instead of seeking a replacement. Keeping the man away kept the Circle from being complete.

"You could help us," Fantorn shocked Gannon by saying in Shantanese. "Come with us."

Is she mad or joking? Gannon had to wonder. And when had she learned Shantanese? They only ever spoke Gavorian in the Circle. Where had she learned a language she insisted was beneath her?

Regardless of the source of her knowledge, the Shantanese was clear enough to let both Tainted men understand.

The little Northlander replied first. "Five scores have gone away," he muttered, "but of these, only one will ever return until the day when the one who hears the power crosses the gap and brings love back through." Blinking to clear his eyes, the Northlander looked up to Kitable, who raised a curious eyebrow speechlessly.

"Only one will return from Wanter," the Northlander said, just as he had earlier without context, "and it will not be you, Kitable. If you go, you will die."

Stopping the Northlander before he convinced them they were doomed, as he seemed to be about to, Gannon interrupted, "You must help us keep magic pure, Kitable. This corruption cannot be permitted."

For a long moment, Kitable considered the plea, passing his stare from the fur-clad Northlander at his side to the gathering of strangers around him. When he sighed, Gannon knew he had reached a decision.

Kitable moved to the side in a pensive pace. "Something does not make sense." He pointed at Rean above them, showing he knew of the binding between Gannon and Rean, and accused, "You claim that all casters are from this Leugan, making us all from your world if we can

cast. There have been casters for many generations. By now, most of Espar could be related to your Leugan, however distantly. And if that is true," he threw his hands up, "are they not casters as well? And if they are, but not strong enough to cast, then are they diluted too far? Then they are too much untouchable, making them as mixed as Tril and his Circle! That makes most of the population of Espar guilty in your eyes!

"But even that cannot be true!" he continued with his hands flaring wide and his voice rising. "Because magic is not being diluted! Every caster since the first has been stronger, wiser, and better skilled! We are improving our ways with every generation! How is that possible? Would his bloodlines not be expected to wash into that of the locals?" He gestured at the Northlander by demonstration.

"Or is there another source?" Kitable said, turning to them. "Are you here because others have escaped your world and are sneaking into our population? And if you are, then this is your fault! You have no right to blame the people who are just the product of your mess! It is not," Kitable finished, standing behind his friend and slamming a hand onto the fur shoulder, "his fault!"

Gannon had to blink in the next moment, for he disbelieved his vision. When Kitable's hand touched Tril, the Northlander vanished.

"The Seal!" Fantorn shouted in outrage. "You altered a hole through it!" It had been a given, even without a Linking, that Fantorn would put a Seal over the area to stop their enemies from escaping. Hearing her squeal now made it clear that Kitable had broken through it.

Gannon was tempted to laugh, and Rean saw it clearly despite his attempt to stifle it even mentally. The rant had been a distraction. Kitable had been casting the entire time, and no one had noticed!

"That," Gannon said, modifying Rean's more violent response, "was unwise. You have upset us."

"Upset *you?*" Kitable carried on his tirade. "YOU are the ones who have intruded into our world like some misguided mothers! So your Leugan came here and started a family! How does that give you any right to play with the lives of his descendants? This is our world!"

If he was casting again, the Circle did not want him to succeed, and the Tainted man seemed to recognize it.

He stopped pacing and faced them. "Leave us alone!"

Spells shot out from all side. He had as many defenses as any of the Watching Circle members did, but there were five of them and only one of him. His "hovering" spells, as Maybel had called them, were faster than anything the Circle could conjure, but outside of that, he was weak.

It was useless trying to track the spells. Joining his fellow Circle members, Gannon sought a way through the mental defenses that Kitable had made a special attempt to keep up. In the end, however, Rean got through first. Her wind spell circled him with enough power to keep all remaining spells contained, then took the air from his lungs and kept him from casting. When a final dispel struck him, Kitable fell to the ground, powerless, beside Yonny's unmoving form.

In that moment, Gannon suddenly recognized that, in contrast to the panting Tainted man, Yonny was not breathing.

Despite his profound dislike for the diviner, Gannon grieved for his fallen companion. They were the Watching Circle and, regardless of their feud, they always came to each other's aid. They may not have liked each other, but they had been allies.

Rean must have been able to see his expression in what was now a fading light, as the sun had slipped behind the peaks and was coloring the sky in sunset, for she lowered herself and gripped his arm lightly in comfort.

"We will have vengeance," she told him in Gavorian calmly, "once you have taken all you can from this one."

Memories of his conversations with Maybel sprang to mind, and Gannon smiled weakly. "I know how," he said, and the Voice smiled back as her wind spells wrapped their new prisoner in a sling and dragged him through the broken wall and into the cave, making sure to cut him on every fragment of the wall they could.

"We will send to Wanter for a replacement," she finalized while the rest of the broken Circle followed her in. It would be easy to replace Yonny, for the schools had their best students groomed in case a competition was called. They would find the best diviner in Wanter, and he or she would complete the Circle by morning.

Gannon was the last to follow Rean in, leaving Yonny by the door. By the time he ducked inside, Famni had readied his spell and repaired the hole in Gannon's wake.

Fantorn placed a solid Force Wall over the wall afterward. This time, they all silently agreed, there would be no escape.

Chapter 10

T ohmas was the last to arrive at the long tent, but as that meant everything else was ready by the time he made his entrance, he was pleased. Celebrant Sedgan nodded at the king as he entered, his expression grave. He'd been to trials with Tohmas before. He knew his stance on traitors. But his brow furrowed when he spotted Shimmer Weaver coming in Tohmas' shadow.

Despite his usual approach, Tohmas had listened to Sol and Barnon this time. It was not enough to bring some conspirators to justice for killing the protectors. He wanted them all, every last one. Ordinary lackeys were easy to come by. If more were hiding in his ranks, especially a leader, he wanted them more than any underlings. Only once the entire group was eradicated would he be satisfied.

The Esparan way was better here.

The line of men accused of tampering with the various horns or poisoning protectors knelt in a row before him, hidden in the tent not for their comfort but to keep them from prying eyes. Each twenty-odd man had a surviving protector behind them holding a drawn blade on their shoulder in open threat. Their eyes widened at seeing Shimmer, but none of them moved. Carsh remained outside, Tohmas assumed because he couldn't tolerate the closeness of the magic around the Weaver woman.

"Listen carefully!" Tohmas told the line of kneeling companions, wardens, and occasional tradespeople. "You are each here because you

are suspected of conspiring with Gaidol or Damoria against Galanth. That man in the corner is a Celebrant of Inac, so this is your trial. Those deemed guilty will be executed here and now unless they can name another who played a role in the sabotage and attack. Name someone I determine is innocent, and you will find your death on a starvation post, a far worse fate than a quick knife. Name someone guilty, and you will instead be made a slave to our cause. You'll live, even have a good life, under Galanth slavery laws."

He wished for a moment that Kitable was present. The wisavi could have read the minds of the captives. How many names could he have collected in an instant?

It struck him how casual it had become to rely on the wizard, and he scolded himself. Tamv would not have been pleased with use of mind magic. But for now, using magic would streamline matters. Rydans would have killed first, thinking the fear of retribution would keep the next would-be traitor in line, but he wanted to be feared for more than his temper. He needed them to know he would find them.

"I brought help to make this go quickly. Miss Weaver, you have the floor," he finished.

One by one, their eyes went to Shimmer.

Tohmas was impressed by her gumption as she strode forward. Head held high, she lit a white orb on the palm of her hand. Her voice rang clear and strong through the tent.

"You will always answer me with complete sentences, not just yes or no. You will answer me honestly."

Tohmas smiled broadly behind her, letting them see his bared teeth. "Any liar will be executed on the spot," he said.

He'd not warned her about that, he realized. But beyond the first obvious flinch, she seemed to quickly bury her discomfort and put on an air of indifference he envied.

She was being paid for a service, and she had committed. Turning to the first man in the line, Shimmer placed the light in front of his eyes. "Did you assist Gaidol during the raid?" she demanded.

The man stared at the little white light cross-eyed, his face blanched to match the pale light. When he replied, it was soft. "I did not assist Gaidol during the raid."

The light went blue.

It was nearly imperceptible, but Shimmer flinched at the color change. Tohmas knew the Lie Light spells well enough to recognize the meaning.

"That was a lie," Tohmas said calmly.

Protector Derry, set behind the first man, performed the execution with uncanny efficiency. After expertly cutting the man's throat, Derry lowered the body onto the ground, then dragged it to the side without hesitation. The protector had been a thief once, Tohmas knew. Perhaps he had done more nefarious things than pick pockets. That had been impressive.

The remaining suspected conspirators looked paler, Tohmas thought.

Shimmer swallowed hard but determinedly took the light to the next man in line as the smell of blood filled the tent. "Same statement," she said. "Did you assist Gaidol during the raid?"

"I did not assist Gaidol during the raid," the man said.

The light went blue. Shimmer moved aside quickly.

"Lie," Tohmas said.

The next protector was new to their ranks. Sworn in only the day before, Protector Golnan was a large youth from Lour who had caught the protectors' attention by winning local barehand sparring matches. He had a history of bar fights and betting, but he had impressed Tohmas with his candid personality and had been brought in to bolster the damaged ranks.

Protector Golnan hesitated, and the sword on the traitor's shoulder slipped down. Then the brute of a man cursed, stabbed the blade into the ground, grabbed the conspirator's head, and snapped his neck. The body flopped to the ground.

"Much less messy," the protector said proudly. He lifted the dead body one-handed and dropped it atop the first.

Shimmer moved along the line, but she had only to show the light to the next man.

"I helped Gaidol!" the man squawked. "Stole a horn. I'll show you where I put it! I didn't know it would be that serious, I swear. They said it was just to confuse things! Slow you down! Please!"

The light remained white, and Shimmer let out a small breath. "At least he speaks the truth," she said.

"We are getting somewhere," Tohmas agreed. "Next?"

Of the twenty-six in the room, twenty-two were found guilty by the light. And thirteen named another to take their place. Tohmas assigned a team to fetch those named.

Leaving the damned with their guards, Tohmas stepped outside to escape the smell of blood. Only the first two had been executed. That left many to help flush out more guilty parties. He was satisfied.

Shimmer Weaver joined him in the lamplight, her face drawn.

"I will ask my papa to make you a trinket, King Tohmas," she said. "Or perhaps Kitable can do it for you. I don't think I can do that again."

Tohmas shrugged. "Once word gets around that lies are death, fewer will try. But there are always a few heroics among those thinking themselves in the right." He'd expected it and was surprised she hadn't.

"You could have warned me," she said softly.

"I assumed you were accustomed to death."

He glanced at her. She could hardly speak, her lips pressed between sentences, and her breath tightly controlled.

"I was wrong," he said. "I am sorry."

She did not look up at him but cast her gaze over the tents and bustle of early evening. Fixer City lay not far from their setup although she did not move toward it.

"No, I am sorry," she said. "I can't do this, King Tohmas. I'm not like Kitable. I will not have men die by my actions. A trinket will have to suffice for the next round."

He took her at her word. The trinket, a constant light of white that changed with any lie in the vicinity, arrived at his tent the next day in time to use against the next batch of spies.

The Lie Light found ten of the thirteen guilty. The circle continued until the only names offered were already accused or executed. The only comfort was that none identified spies among the remaining Trullers. But of course, Charger Granton was still missing.

The new slaves were split up and sent to every corner of Espar. Some went back to Trulin to help rebuild damaged cities, including Galvay, which had been conquered and returned to her previous owners. Some were sent to Lour to make safe the collapsed tunnels. Some went to Barlaby to build the cities the new Kingsman Hurtz needed before winter.

The rest were quickly executed. The point of starvation was to make betrayal a public event, but the last thing he wanted was to draw attention to the traitors they had in their midst. He cut them down and buried their bodies without ceremony.

After the trials, Tohmas returned to a vigil on the hill, looking for the scouts he wished would bring him the news of Damoria's withdrawal. It had been nine days since the night raid and his warriors were eager to march. Even though many still recovered in the Healing waggons, the remainder were restless.

He held them back. Walking into the enemy's trap did not bode well, not yet.

As he stood on the ride on the 19th of the 4th cycle, Carsh stiffened, warning of magic, but he did not react as though a spell targeted Tohmas directly. No, Elder Tril made his way to Tohmas' vantage point.

"Elder Tril! You have returned! Wonderful!" Tohmas called. A blink later, Tohmas read the downcast Northlander's face, and he frowned. "Where's Kitable?"

Sure enough, the Northlander grimaced. "We exchanged places four days ago," the diviner admitted with a sad shake of his head. "I have only now managed to be conscious long enough to tell you."

"When I said I wanted you back," Tohmas replied, "I did not mean I wanted Kitable gone. Where is he?"

"Far west mountain range, I believe. Far beyond your reach, King Tohmas," the elder answered.

Tohmas' heart grew heavy. At least the Northlander had not said Kitable was dead, for he had no answer for that. The west mountains were borders to Damoria and Lour. If it was Lour, he could have Kingsman Loritat intervene, but if it was Damoria...

And he had no way to send messages that far. He could send riders, but it would be a quartercycle before they even saw the Dragontail Mountains. Just how long would the enemy wait before slaying the wisavi?

If Tril had been reading Tohmas' thoughts, Tohmas liked to think he would have noticed. Carsh surely would have reacted! Still, when the Northlander spoke, he seemed to know precisely what Tohmas had been thinking.

"He is too far for you, but the Circle of the Raven may be able to send him aid. I learned a great deal while I was their prisoner, and what they inadvertently taught me can be used against them. I came to warn you that Kitable will not join your attack on Gaidol. But you have the Northlanders once more. The DoomDragon is among us again. We are one. The Northlanders will go to war."

"I am glad. And if these casters are not getting involved in this conflict, I see no requirement for Kitable. We can handle Gaidol with Darknim and your people once more. But I want Kitable back."

At this, the wolf-eyed elder smiled weakly. "I see my often-isolated comrade has more friends than he thinks. I want him back as well. We will do all we can."

"I cannot ask for more," Tohmas agreed before turning back to his watching. "Good luck!" Tohmas added in place of the typical blessing he would have offered. Somehow, wishing Inac's blessings on the wizard seemed a bad idea. Kitable hated gods even more than he hated celebrants.

"You too," Tril replied as he shuffled away, passing a rider on his way down. "Oh, and you need to go now, King Tohmas. Your enemy waits beyond the hills, two days ahead of you. Your ploy has worked, but you must hurry."

The scout was grinning as he presented himself to Tohmas. "Yellow and red are breaking camp," the man reported. "By now, they will be on the move."

Tohmas would have waited for more information before committing to the attack, but with Tril confirming the news that Damoria was pulling out, he had sufficient confidence to act immediately.

He sounded the pursuit, ready to press Dorakon before he reached the river. They would never drop the bridge if their prince were on the wrong side.

Kitable woke with bound hands, but he could not see ropes. The uneasy glances of the streak-haired woman let him conclude the powers were force, as she had already identified her preferred element.

CHAPTER 10

There were three men with gems inset in their foreheads watching him. The youngest was the speaker he had dealt with earlier, while the eldest was much more wrinkled and based in fire from what Kitable recalled of the fight. The three stood next to the petite woman Kitable had compared to Elder Ela earlier. Seeing her face, he had to rescind the thought. Although they were of similar stature, the woman dressed in blue-scintillating ribbons was far more crone-like than Ela, and her wrinkles, which Ela wore as laugh lines, were strongest around her prominent frown. There were no gems, but her robe sparkled. A strange symbol pulsed from her chest.

The younger man with the gem in his forehead spoke. "Up," he said, gesturing. "Sit up."

With his back to solid stone and a semi-circle of enemies in front of him, Kitable did not feel ready to argue. He pushed himself into a kneeling position, which seemed to be the only position he could easily hold with his hands tied in his lap by magic.

They had taken all his trinkets and piled them to one side by the fake wall of the cavern, leaving him with nothing. Dressed in only his tunic and trousers, he was without hovering spells. That, more than the loss of his usual objects, made him feel naked.

Despite the relative hopelessness of his position, he kept his back straight and his chin high. But when he opened his mouth to speak, no sound emerged.

"That," the speaker informed him, "would be Rean's doing; she's the woman standing beside Gilan there." He indicated the old woman and her bald fire-based companion. "She remains the best wind caster in Wanter. You have had your voice blocked."

Voxed, Kitable groaned to himself. He knew the spell, and it would not be easy to escape.

"There is a Translation up, and I am speaking Gavorian now, not Shantanese. I will continue to translate for you..." the man continued, *because I do not need you to speak to know what you wish to say.*

The feeling of magic in his mind made Kitable shutter. Thought magic was his least favorite element by far. A Gaes could compel him to obey any order, and if the caster in front of him were talented enough to be finishing his sentences in mind magic, then a Gaes would not be difficult. An unwilling target might be able to resist, but this man

could create the thought required to make Kitable willing. He had no way to stop him.

"You are afraid unnecessarily," the man said. "I will not control you, Kitable, unless you make it necessary to."

Kitable checked himself over and recognized the vague discomfort he felt in his head. His thoughts were being read. Any coherent thought he had would be seen.

But that meant *any* coherent thought would be seen.

He imagined the enemy caster at the center of a crowd of angry, armed Galanth soldiers. He pictured Tohmas' loyal men drawing their swords and slicing the caster into a thousand tiny pieces.

Before the first blade touched down, everything stopped to the waved hand of the stranger.

Kitable mentally cursed. The man was performing thought alteration.

"Do not bore me," the caster said. "I am Gannon, the seat of thought in the Watching Circle. If I do not like your thoughts, I will change them. If I think you are lying, I will dig until I find the truth. I can be very good at that, or I can be sloppy. You have been warned."

Deep thought magic was a category of spells Kitable had never attempted. For each layer infiltrated, the danger of damaging the invaded mind increased. A good caster could avoid doing any harm, but a clumsy one that was powerful enough to perform the spell but not skilled enough to be cautious could turn a normal person into a vegetable.

Determined, Kitable centered his thoughts. If he kept his surface thoughts tidy, it might not be necessary for any deeper thought magic.

"Better," the Wanter caster said. "Now, you have raised several interesting questions and we want answers. You will answer me."

They asked about his heritage, and he mutely laughed at them for that. No, he revealed, his father had not been a wizard, else the man would not have been with Kitable's mother. And no, Kitable's mother had not been a wizard either. Casters did not often have to make their way selling their bodies, not if they were good.

Your theories about Leugan fall short, Kitable told the caster in his mind. I am not from any great lineage.

"It is possible your parents did not know their potential. Explain your training."

Again, Kitable laughed.

Never had any, he thought back.

"Impossible!" Gannon objected, but his rage only made Kitable smile.

I was apprenticed, but the oaf only ever taught me to read. I learned from the books and trial and error. I never had any formal training.

"Schools? Mentors?"

We have no schools. We train by apprenticeships, only mine was to a man who was as daft as he was corrupt.

By way of evidence, Kitable brought to mind memories of the master he had left dead. Kitable had felt no compassion for the thief when he first ran away from the murder, and there was none now.

Seemingly satisfied, the next question was about the Contingency.

Kitable was, for a moment, grateful. The Contingency was a secret he had given up eight years previously, and he felt no need to defend it now.

They followed his memories as he traced how he had come across the idea, then fine-tuned it into a workable form. When Gannon pressed for more information, Kitable revealed all the ways he had applied it initially, to the death of all challengers, then the day he had finally called together all the casters in Espar and told them how it was done. It was found in every magic book in Espar now as the means to change any spell into a hovering spell.

Once he finished, Gannon looked at the woman who had blocked Kitable's voice. "Anything else?"

Apparently, the answer was "yes," for Kitable was next asked for everything he knew about the untouchables and the Northlander Circle.

Kitable willingly handed over plenty of useless hours of conversations and meditations, mostly about Calanor, then tried his utmost to push Loni from his thoughts.

"Who is the woman?" Gannon demanded

You don't want to know about her, Kitable projected his thoughts. She is dangerous... *she is...*

"Another untouchable," the thought caster correctly read. "Tell me about her."

He brought to mind all their interactions. There was nothing valuable in them, but they took up time.

They did not give up, but after extracting every detail they could about Loni, the effort of concentrating took its toll. Kitable's focus slipped.

Ironically, it was to his advantage. Unable to keep his prisoner on a single train of thought, Gannon withdrew.

"I could press you," Gannon said as he pulled some of the magic from Kitable's mind, "but then I might damage you. I will try again later. Fantorn—" The man indicated the streak-haired woman with gems beside her eyes, "wishes you to come to Wanter for her students to examine. So you get to rest."

Since the thought-reading remained, Kitable became aware of something else withdrawing. There had been a spell on him, one he had failed to notice, but it explained why he was so tired. Even without knowing specifics, he would resist magic instinctually as long as he was conscious.

If you go, Kitable heard Tril warn, *you will die.*

He was still bound, even as he collapsed to the ground. Some of their spells during the earlier duels had injured him mildly, and his skin had been scraped until it bled in several places, leaving him sore. But he was not enervated, which was almost embarrassing. He had not even defended himself well enough to become enervated.

"But first," the Wanter caster said, prodding Kitable with a foot and prompting him to open his eyes. "Did you know you killed Yonny? You broke our Circle."

Second time I have broken a Circle. I'm getting good at it, Kitable thought. The last time had been by stealing Tril's wolf skin.

"Rean promised me revenge," Gannon said, ignoring Kitable's vindictive pleasure at hearing of the Circle member's death. "I have chosen to take it on your little red-haired companion."

Kitable brought his thoughts together with effort. *The Weaver girl? Why would you think she means anything?*

"I hear you consider her your 'Heart's Desire.' You took one of ours. Now we take one of yours."

She is meaningless, Kitable objected, finding a last reserve of mental power to concentrate his thoughts. *That spell makes the victim behave*

favorably toward the caster. All it means is that I dislike her slightly less than I dislike everyone else! Considering that I dislike everyone else quite a lot, that is not saying much!

His reply made the man sit back on his heels, but his smile was derisive. "So you will not mind if I kill her?"

I mind, Kitable insisted, knowing a lie would be detected, *but I would mind if you slay anyone simply because they know me!*

"You have precious few friends, Wisavi," Gannon said. "I cannot touch the Circle without better understanding their powers. Tainted powers protect your king. No, I have someone ready to deal the blow I require. Your red-haired beauty makes a good target."

Something in Kitable's mind gave out. The last thought he forced into the fore of his mind was, *If you harm anyone else to get at me, I will make you regret it.*

He vaguely felt a hand on his forehead.

"You cannot have it both ways, Wisavi. Either you come to Wanter and die, or you stay here and never catch me. Either way, I do not fear you."

Kitable was unconscious in the next flicker. He fell asleep with the mocking chuckle of the Wanter man in his ear.

The mountains loomed to the west, snow-topped even in the late summer heat. The run-off from those mountains formed BrokenFall River, one of the largest Tohmas had ever seen. On the march to meet Northlanders last year, they had turned west before this northern border. Seeing the rocky terrain of the foothills, lakesides, and formidable rivers, Tohmas was grateful for that fact. The north part of Espar remained barren and treacherous, making him eager for the rolling, soft hills of the south.

The crossing into Gaidol required they pass over BrokenFall River, and while there were dozens of bridges, the closest and largest was at the covered entrance to the small city of Newar. The city at the mouth of the river was on the lake, backed by mountains.

The rest of the river had tiny footbridges every few leagues, most of which were guarded or blocked by men and gates. Tohmas had heard

from Lance about the style of the smaller bridges, all narrow with high railings, so that horse riders had no choice but to dismount and lead their mounts. Trulin's greatest strength was in its horses; forcing them to walk across the wide water made them easy targets. The only exception was the bridge at Newar. Tohmas had no other way to get his waggons across.

To his disappointment, he failed to catch Dorakon. The Prince of Gaidol left obstacles at every turn, ranging from smaller squads of soldiers to downed trees and broken waggons. Tohmas caught some of the forces with riders, but his soldiers were matched by Dorakon's, and both sides lost equally.

Scouts had been unable to cross the bridge at Newar but surprised Tohmas by continuously reporting the bridge intact. It was a covered bridge divided into three sections to reach across the steep-banked river. At either end, a huge black-metal gate was set, opened only by order of the High Guardsman of Newar. It could have been a rife trade route, with such easy access to the main roads into Trulin and her capital, but instead, it remained perpetually closed and barred, guarded by a hundred men even when there was no war or conquest.

Tohmas had lost all advantage of numbers in the raids, and the space on the bridge was easily defensible; this could become a hard track through. And if Dorakon felt he would lose, then all he needed to do was sabotage the bridge, and Tohmas would be set back by a half-cycle at least.

As the dawn rose on the second day of pursuit, Lance met Tohmas on point and, after giving the overnight reports of harassing the enemy's train, warned, "They'll make the bridge today, and we can't get them in time. Dorakon is heading south fast. He's commanded they bring it down to split your men. No one must cross the bridge."

Tohmas frowned. "He's betting we can't stop him from burning it."

"Not burning," Lance corrected.

Cocking his head, Tohmas reevaluated his guardian. "You know something?"

Lance nodded. "I won't know for sure until we get there, but there is a good chance we will not have issues getting into Gaidol."

Taking his Follower at his word, Tohmas gave the orders to keep all his ranks on the Trulin side of BrokenFall River. He made a point of being at the front of the army when they finally reached the bridge.

Lance and his guardsmen led the way. When they reached the border, Lance called the halt. Already on hand, Tohmas joined the guardian looking down the slope to the bridge, trying for the best vantage point.

It was intact but guarded. Uneasy soldiers on the far side took cover among the houses. Beyond the soldiers, the city appeared deserted and silent, which was unexpected. If they had been planning to ambush his forces once over the bridge, would they have set some semblance of normality to try and fool him? Or was he overthinking it? It looked more like the army had marched straight through. A large dust cloud rose in the distance, likely the passage of a large number of people and animals.

So only a handful of people left behind, Tohmas guessed. Enough to make them fight for the bridge, kill some of his fighters and slow him down at the choke point over the water. And when he got through, they'd take out the bridge from under him. Those on the north bank would have to go around and take another twenty days or more to get through the foothills around the lake. Those in the south bank would die within moments. It would end his conquest.

Tohmas cursed under his breath. He'd worked to avoid this situation, but he'd come too late. Dorakon had the bridge, and he had no choice but to go around to minimize the disaster. Even that delay migh be sufficient to give his enemies time to coordinate.

But as Tohmas examined the area more closely, he noticed a single hunched man with a cane standing on the Trulin side of the bridge facing Tohmas' ranks. The small figure stood with the closed gates at their back.

"You'll be able to cross," Lance reported.

"Someone you know?" Tohmas asked.

Lance's smile broadened. The mustached soldier was on the verge of laughing. "I'll introduce you! Just a moment!"

Kicking his great black stallion on, Lance rode down the slopes unaccosted by arrows from the defenders on the bridge. Once he reached the old man, Lance dismounted. The two men discussed something, the man gesturing more than once at Lance's braced leg. But once

TRAITOR

they had settled the conversation, the two of them slowly approached Tohmas on foot.

His protectors around him, Tohmas dismounted and met Lance. When he saw the man, Tohmas was struck by the family resemblance.

Lance paused in hesitation, as if deciding on the words to use. Then, breaking formality, he said, "Tohmas, this is my father, Hiron Carraway."

Tohmas cracked a smile at the lack of titles. He nodded his head respectfully. "It's an honor to meet the man who raised one of my best guardians," he said. "Am I to assume you are responsible for the lack of resistance from Prince Dorakon that I am currently enjoying?"

The older man had two scars over his face, evidence of battles long since ended, but he spoke with a voice of a born leader. Although he did not smile, his eyes brightened. "My sons hold the bridge behind me. They will open it to whichever side I tell them to. I have come to take your measure."

Tohmas raised his chin. "How do I fare thus far?"

"One of my sons, albeit one of the younger, foolish ones, fights at your side. That elevates you. How is it you earned his loyalty?"

He had to think back to find the answer. Their paths had crossed in Gaidol during Tohmas' march north, but the later battles against the Northlanders had forged the relationship. There had not been a moment that had made him accept Lance as a friend, rather a million flickers.

"Your son's honesty shocked me," Tohmas replied. "There are few who will speak the truth others do not wish to hear, nor do it with such eloquence. But he did, and so I returned the favor." Letting drop the formal words of princes and politics, Tohmas finished, "He's been following me around since. As he is my Follower, and I am his Leader, I will provide for him anything he desires that is within my power to give." He glared at Lance. "He doesn't tell me what he wants very often."

"Don't need anything," Lance said softly.

"Need and want are two different things," Tohmas said. He turned his attention to Hiron once more. "In short, I treated him like a friend. For some reason, that surprised him."

Lance's father nodded sagely, his eyes narrowed in thought. Something more than his words was being assessed, Tohmas was certain, but he knew he had no control over that. He was what he was. This man would accept or refuse it.

"Did he tell you about us, his family?" Hiron asked.

"No," Tohmas answered. "I understand he had a big family but not who or where they were."

Hiron critically examined Lance this time. "Well, Lance?"

"It's the right thing," Lance immediately replied. "Dorakon remains a threat. If… when you leave us, father, those who defend you will turn a blind eye, and he will hunt us down. I am here, on this side, to save us."

Hiron nodded then cracked a very broken smile. "Well, I figured one of you boys would do it. I assumed it would be Brandin, to be honest." He sighed and turned back toward the bridge. "Come on then. The bridge is yours." He glanced over his shoulder after one tottering step. "I want your word, Prince of Galanth and would-be king, that you will spare Gaidol as much as you can and give her back to us when you move through."

Tohmas nodded. "As I did in Trulin. I want a Gaidolon ruling Gaidol."

"But one answering to you," Hiron challenged.

Tohmas shrugged. "I was not hiding it. Yes, answering to me. Because I am the only person both willing and able to bear that responsibility."

Hiron eased his unsteady feet down the road, his cane lightly touching the stones. "Able? We'll see."

Lance waved forward a far crier, but he waited for Tohmas to give the final word.

"You ever going to tell me what the hell just happened?" Tohmas asked first.

Lance laughed. "If you want, sure. But it's complicated. Suffice to say, I have a lot of brothers."

Tohmas sighed. "Lead on, Guardian Carraway. I trust you. The path is open. Sound the march."

The next stop was the capital.

Chapter II

To Prince Dorakon's surprise, the gates of his capital did not immediately close behind him once his army was within. Tohmas was not far behind him and was gaining. They did not have time to wait!

He was equally shocked when his order to see the doors shut and readied was followed by, "Shall we close the other gates too, my prince?"

Tohmas and his forces had not been delayed at Newar, nor had they been broken by the sabotage on the bridge. He did not know how or why, but the enemy was on his tail closely. Since the departure of Damoria from his ranks, Dorakon had been in a steady retreat that bordered on flight. He kept control, knowing it was a close thing. But all the fighters wanted the safety of the city. They fled as one coordinated mass. They had expected the city to be ready to repel a siege.

Instead, the conqueror of Espar was less than a candle behind him, and SwordWood still had the gates open! What had High Guardsman Bosul been thinking?

After he ordered all the gates shut and readied against the siege, he sought the high guardsman and immediately understood. His messages warning of the failure in Newar had never reached Bosul. Instead, Bosul had been told Gaidol was victorious and to expect a celebration.

They performed admirably considering the sudden disadvantage. The gates were sealed by the time the green tabards appeared on the road to the capital. The relaxing guardsmen were pulled from revelry and put on duty manning the walls and preparing the defense of SwordWood.

Dorakon rushed up the northwest tower, nicknamed Eagle's Nest, the embarrassed high guardsman in tow.

Up until the false message had gotten through, High Guardsman Bosul had been readying the city for war. The machines installed along the wall were primed to attack the invading army as it advanced.

But Tohmas did not follow the road down to the west gate, instead trampling a path through farmland, aiming for the smaller, less defended south gate.

Had he noticed, when he had entered by that door last year, that the gate was less defensible? Had he compared it to the west gate he had departed by? Or had High Guardsman Carraway told the invader to use the south gate? But Lance had not been in Gaidol since the improvements. He could not have known they had not finished the south approach.

It did not worry Dorakon. The south gate did not require as many defenders because it was smaller and so limited the number who could move against it. The doors were more robust, being stocky, and the entrance was narrow. Enemies could not invade in great numbers, and Dorakon would be dropping arrows or stones on them the entire time.

"We can fire the catapult by the west gate," High Guardsman Bosul offered. "I know its range. It is one of Prince Neillen's finest. It will strike them even at this distance."

"Do it," Dorakon commanded, and runners carried down the order.

A few moments later, a stone was loaded and launched over the west wall.

The moment the arm of the machine was vertical, the wood groaned and, with a shocking "crack," snapped. Despite the machine's death, the stone hurtled toward Tohmas' forces with perfect accuracy.

The army scattered, but the stone still rolled many down. Dorakon would have expected them to hesitate now, as they had no way of knowing the machine had broken under the strain of the first stone, but they marched on, undeterred. With no more boulders crashing down, their courage was rewarded.

At first, Dorakon blamed shoddy construction, but a breathless runner arrived with a surprising report. "The lever arm had been sawed," the young man announced. "Cut almost through under the lashings to hide it."

Two possibilities jumped to mind; either a spy had gotten into Gaidol and weakened the machine, or Neillen had been so cowed that he had sabotaged his machine before selling it to Dorakon. But the timing didn't work for the latter. He had a spy in his city already?

"To the hells with the machines. Move the archers from the east to the south wall and shoot them down. Get the portable machines assembled in the streets. My guardsmen can dictate where. At least those will work."

The Galanth forces halted on the edge of arrow range, but Dorakon ordered volleys high to force them behind their shields.

Meanwhile, the newly returned army assembled the war machines. It was surprisingly tricky. The people were panicking, a runner reported. Galanth had been spotted within the city already.

"Get me a witness!" he insisted.

A shaking woman in an apron came before him, her hair frizzed around her head. Her voice squeaked as she told him she'd heard of Galanth soldiers between the south and west gates. But when pressed, she had not seen them herself, only heard others make the claim. In the end, no soldier had engaged anyone in the area either. More misinformation?

Dorakon selected a high guardsman to investigate. If their enemy had already breached the city, had it been by magic or deception?

A horn sounded among the enemy's ranks outside the wall, and Dorakon saw the red light of the invader's sword go up. At the head of the charge, Tohmas rode with his enchanted blade high.

In a random street somewhere between the south and west gates, Valia paused. She'd deliberately lost her guardsmen as soon as the alarms had sounded, which had recently become an easy, well-practiced trick. She had seen the immense stone that Neillen's machine had thrown. The fact that only one stone was fired made her smile. Her efforts with the saw had been effective.

As she had suggested to him, Lance was heading for the south gate, which put the attention in the city's center.

Having worn her plainest clothing, she felt she fit in nicely with the city people. Messing her hair slightly and hiding her jewelry completed her deception, and she was ready.

There was an art, she thought, between being incoherent enough to make her fear seem real and being coherent enough to make her words heard.

She chose a starting place by locating a quiet, empty street, where she started to run. At a sprint, she turned the corner into the busier, populated area and started screaming.

"Galanth! They are here! West gate! HELP! Galanth is invading!"

The people paused, and more than one tried to calm her, but she maintained her hysteria. Panting, shaking, shouting, and checking over her shoulder frantically, she continued screaming and running until she finally got to another empty area.

Behind her, she could hear the shouting people as they gathered their friends and family and rapidly retreated toward the town center. More than one person started running, and soon she had a crowd on their way south.

She swept herself out of the crowd, then made her way to the manor, replacing her jewelry and fixing her hair as she walked. She ran the last distance, however, to make herself breathless.

Sure enough, she found High Guardsman Bosul on a mission from Dorakon, and she fell into his arms in mock exhaustion.

"The east," she panted. "They say Galanth is already in the east side of the city, near the temples!"

She then fainted dramatically.

She overheard the orders for men to move into the city seeking these invaders and others for messages to be sent to Dorakon in Eagle's Nest farther south, but further eavesdropping was thwarted when she was carried to her room. She rose and went to the window as soon as the door was shut.

If all went well, the crowd from the west would pull Dorakon's attention in one direction while Bosul would be looking to the east.

Meanwhile, Lance and Tohmas would have their enemy divided and could put their forces against the south. If she were lucky, the Gaidolon forces would be pushed back to the manor by nightfall. Surrender would be inevitable. The city would be Tohmas'.

As much as some part of her mind tried to convince her that her behavior was abhorrent, her heart overruled everything it said. It did not matter to her if a strange Galanth conquered her city so long as Lance was not kept away. Dorakon could die for all she cared. He had done enough to deserve it.

She smiled as the first Gaidolon soldiers moved into the city's quiet, peaceful west side. Last night was the last time she would ever suffer a high guardsman in her bed. From this night onward, she would allow only her guardian to touch her.

Lance's heart panged to see the capital of Gaidol once more, standing impenetrable and strong among the fields of wheat and barley. It had been his home since birth, and he still knew every one of her streets well enough to walk them blind. Even from where he stood, he could hear the calls of the merchants and see the great temples lit against the evening sky. He vividly remembered the parade grounds where he had once been trained as a defender. The manor equally stirred memories of old duties and friends and with those memories came Valia.

She was in there, safe, he prayed. If she were wise, she would be hiding in the manor by now and leaving the fighting to others. She had done enough already.

None but Lance knew the extent to which she had helped Tohmas and his forces, first by identifying the new horn commands to Lance, then by giving reports on all the preparations taking place in SwordWood. Recently, if the final note could be believed, she had done her best to sabotage the defenses. The single shot from the catapult testified to her likely involvement. Despite his wishes, she was probably not far and still doing what she could to help Tohmas.

Not Tohmas, Lance corrected. She was not betraying her father and her people for the king's sake. Although her letters had been only ever factual and frank and certainly never said anything about his promise or the desires they knew the other shared, he knew she was doing it for him. She wanted him back.

But it was not quite that simple. They might take SwordWood, even capture or kill Dorakon, but that did not mean Lance was any freer to

fulfill his promise than he had been the day he had left. Could he walk in and claim her the way a Rydan would? Would she even want him? He was crippled, despite how much he tried to hide the brace and use the leg. Bolt helped conceal it, but even the great Trulin warhorse could not make it untrue. Lance could not walk unaided. What woman would want someone like that?

He had to laugh and shake his head once he realized how far ahead of things he had gotten. They were still outside the city, and the gates were barred.

The lines upon lines of archers along the walls did not support Lance's suggestion to attack the south gate primarily, but Tohmas did not seem concerned as he drew SoulBurner and charged.

"I hate when he does that!" one protector objected when Schlavarai dashed forward with Bashuran in her wake, and Lance sympathized. While the rest of the forces had been given a hold command, the protectors were required to follow. The red light would keep Tohmas and those nearest him safe, but many more would be exposed.

Thankfully, the arrows focused on the king, and the fiery aura immolated the majority. Cleverly, the protectors made a spear-shaped formation in the king's shadow. The light protected them partially as they ran.

The rest of the army began their slow, calculated march forward at a horn call. The Northlanders accounted for half their ranks.

The king reached the small gate, a large single door, and set SoulBurner against it. Before the archers could adjust back to let other defenders deal with the charge, the king turned away from the gate at a gallop.

When the horn sounded the charge, Lance did not hesitate. Like his men, Lance moved Bolt up and started the run at the sealed gate.

Bolt had taken only three strides before Lance understood. Having cut through the hinges and the bar, the king had hooked a rope into the door and pulled the gate off. He and his protectors held their place, letting the army charge into the gap.

It was going to get ugly now as war tended to. Lance prayed again Valia was clear by now.

Without another thought, Lance forced his way into the city at the head of the army, leading Arrow's fyrd.

As Tohmas entered, the city of SwordWood was a mess. The entire city was ready for them, from east to west and north to south, but the people confused the matter by alternating between running and cheering. It helped further that the forces of Gaidol had divided themselves for an unknown reason. While Tohmas pushed back the south-facing men headed by Dorakon's standard, the rest of the Gaidolon forces seemed to be running around aimlessly. It was odd but very obliging of them.

Tohmas' men adapted quickly to moving from street to street. Horn calls kept each party aware of the others and had his fyrds marching in perfect cohesion through the foreign city. When they met pockets of immovable enemies, Tohmas answered the call. But when he saw how the people reacted to Lance, he changed his strategy and brought the ex-high guardsman with him everywhere.

Lance was a source of changeable reactions. Half of the people who recognized him immediately hailed him as a hero while the other half doubled their efforts to kill him. The Gaidolon's various ex-guardsmen (now wardens of the fyrd of Arrow) helped by calling to everyone they knew. Even Tohmas did not know who was an ally by the end. Large sections of Dorakon's defenders were changing sides at an alarming rate.

By nightfall, the various pockets were being killed or routed, and the only major obstruction was the manor itself.

Dorakon had not been caught; however, Tohmas heard reports of at least five high guardsmen killed and a sixth who saw Lance and promptly pledged to follow the renegade high guardsman. Tohmas let Lance decide whether the oath given so quickly was valid. Galanth gained over three hundred men within a single afternoon thanks to similar defections.

The manor's gates were initially a barrier, but they opened as Tohmas' forces prepared their assault. Lance met another apparently familiar face, a broad older man with a bristled blond beard.

Lance laughed aloud. "Tyron, you old goat, what the hells are you doing out here?" He jumped off Bolt and clasped arms with the man, his smile mirrored on the man's face.

"Giving you a hand, of course. Seems like you got in over your head again."

Lance's brow dropped, his amusement gone. "But how did you know?"

The man laughed and wagged a finger at Lance. "I figured out who was prettier than my Kaylie when your sweetheart sent me a note. She'd got a good head on her shoulders. A keeper." Using their clasped arms, Tyron pulled Lance forward. "Come on. I brought the team from WaterBranch."

Lance's eyes went wide, and he checked over his shoulder on Tohmas. "All of them?"

"Just my closest relatives," Tyron said with a wink. "Let's go, High Guardsman. Seems the greatest threat today is our own prince. We're overdue a rebellion, don't you think?"

Tohmas chuckled and followed Lance in, pleased to let someone else lead for the moment.

The rest of the manor went relatively quickly.

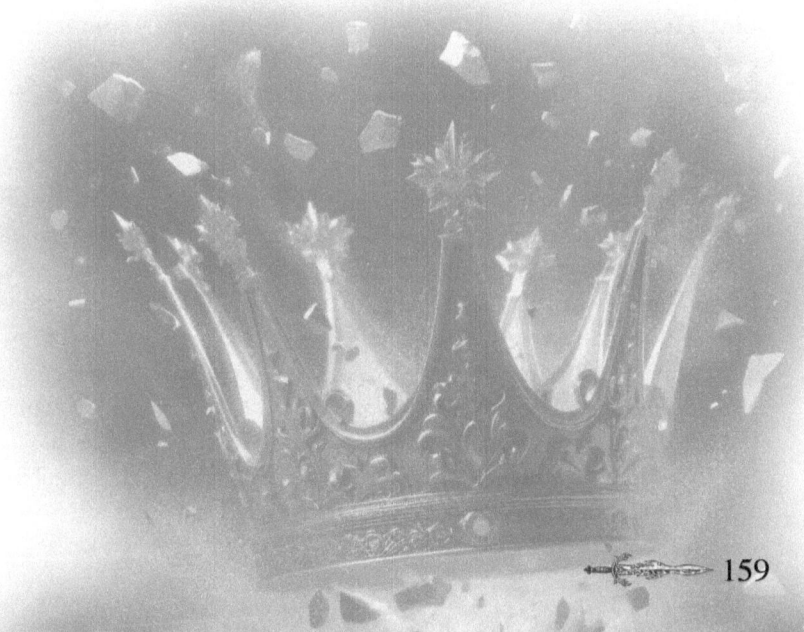

Chapter 12

T hey had defended Gaidol as well as they could, but in the end, Dorakon watched his city fall. High Guardsman Bosul was missing, presumed dead, and his assortment guardsmen were spread too thin to defend the manor properly. Still, he had expected the walls to slow them.

Until a small group of guardsmen and visitors intervened, chasing his loyal men off the defenses and opening the doors to the invader. His people rapidly surrendered.

In fear for his life, Dorakon did not venture out. There was no point. He'd seen his own blue and white fighting against him in the city, brought to the enemy's side by the traitorous scourge of a Vont son. Those within the manor would be the same ilk. *Should have wiped them out years ago,* he mused as he pulled two small scrolls from the writing desk. He swiftly crossed the manor's grounds, sending his guardsmen to cover his back. He pushed the noises out of his mind. At least there was *some* fighting. Someone was still loyal to their true prince.

Lance had been a high guardsman as his eldest brother had been. Others of the Vont line had been guardsmen too. Dorakon had been responsible for their training and giving them purpose, yet now they and all their affiliates turned against him. Perhaps it had been a ruse all along, designed to get close to him. *But I didn't fall for it,* he thought. He'd kept Lance at a distance, never trusting him fully. He'd even corrected that mishap that had put Lance in charge of Valia's defense. No son of Minette Vont could be trusted. This proved the point!

In the barn, not far from the dovecote, he located the pigeons' enclosure. Selecting the three he needed, he loaded the notes and loosed the birds. It was not a job for a Prince of Espar, but he trusted no other to do it, not after what he'd seen today.

He had plans to aim for an escape tunnel, but the fighting crossed the courtyard while he was in the barn, and Dorakon instead had to retreat into his wife's garden cottage on the grounds behind the manor.

A group of Galanth soldiers found him. With too few defenders remaining, Dorakon did not fight. Instead, he greeted the Galanth with a smile and offered his sword.

"I surrender. I am willing to become a kingsman."

It took the prime warden by surprise. Wisely, the blue and silver-roped man sent a runner for Tohmas in answer.

Dorakon found a chair by the fireplace, where rows of herbs hung low over swept stones. A brew of roses stood on the mantle, perfuming the room. He waited.

He waited more. To his irritation, Dorakon remained in the Galanth soldiers' company for far too long. Eventually, the Galanth ushered in High Guardsman Bosul, turning the quaint cottage into a respectable cell.

"He's the last one alive," the Galanth prime warden acting a gaoler reported with a grim smile. He'd wrapped his knuckles and flexed his fists as he spoke as if looking for an excuse to hit something. Dorakon gave no reply, feeling the man did not deserve one.

Dorakon scowled at Calus as he took a seat on a bench. He'd been disarmed but was unwounded, which spoke ill of his devotion as far as Dorakon was concerned.

Calus waited until the Galanth had returned to their post at the door and outside before leaning forward and confiding, "Dansin's alive. But he's with Lance now."

Dorakon fumed to hear the news. Had High Guardsman Dansin Gandal been responsible for the sabotage of the machine? It seemed unlikely: the man had been with Dorakon in the field. But someone had been sending false messages during the attack on the city. Where had the misdirection come from?

While they waited, Valia was escorted in with Lady Melodi, Dorakon's third wife. Melodi took a seat in a corner, looking scandalized,

but Valia refused to settle, pacing the cottage as if admiring the drying herbs. She'd been spending time down here the last few quartercycles, Dorakon knew. Melodi had claimed she wanted to learn about the gardens.

They waited longer, passing a hungry, hopeless night in the cottage. A spattering of uncooked vegetables became their dinner as their guards refused to allow them to light a fire.

Tohmas Galanth finally entered the cottage with the dawn. Dorakon recognized many of the faces he brought with him; they had once been princes. Except for Lance, who shadowed the would-be king, those present were Tohmas' kingsmen.

Finally, Dorakon rose from the seat he had slept in. The younger man stood across the table from him, echoing their first meeting over breakfast in the dawn a year before. Dorakon's stomach grumbled at the thought.

With care, Tohmas laid a sheet of vellum on the table.

"It took us all night to decide if we would let you join," the king said with his hand still on the page. "Most want to gut you, Dorakon, especially because of your very successful raid, but I promised to try and keep the current leaders in their places, so I will offer you this. You will sign, then tomorrow you will swear the oath, and the gods will keep you honest. If you can pass that, I will take you as kingsman."

It must have been taking a great deal of effort, Dorakon guessed, for Lance to stand there, saying nothing. He was not even looking at Dorakon.

"Read it, carefully," Tohmas prompted. "I do not want your signature if you do not mean it."

Dorakon ran his eyes over the dreaded agreement in the dawn's light. He knew it already, and his stomach churned over the promises, but he could not refuse it now.

While he pretended to read, Dorakon felt High Guardsman Bosul move away. Valia had spent the night curled up on the floor, but she was now standing by the fireplace. Calus headed to her, bringing himself between her and the invaders and putting a hand on her wrist.

Of course, Lance would not meet Dorakon's eyes: he was watching Valia! With longing, he stared at Dorakon's little girl. *Damn him!* Minette Vont's line should never have been allowed to persist. Dorakon

cursed Hiron Carraway for having talked him into letting the daughter of his rival live and cursed him again for marrying the sprite of a woman. More conspiracies, perhaps. Had Hiron planned for his wife's return to power all along? He'd taken a long time to reach that goal, but here it was, at long last, the final victory of the Vont family over that of Lodaton.

There was desperation in Lance's stare as he stood beside the King of Espar. But what could the disabled man do? Walking in here had revealed a prominent limp, and closer investigation now showed that Lance used a cane and a leg brace. He was no longer a fighter.

Finishing, Dorakon replaced the vellum on the workbench. "I agree."

He had the impression he had disappointed the kingsmen with his declaration. Someone, he felt, had just lost a bet.

He was reaching for the quill beside the treaty when Tohmas placed a hand over the vellum and leaned in.

"One final requirement," he amended.

Dorakon frowned. "All sign the same treaty! You said so yourself."

"I also said those who opposed me would die, Dorakon," Tohmas replied. "Would you like me to hold to that as well?"

The threat closed Dorakon's mouth instantly.

"You fought us," the king further justified, "and I want to ensure future generations do not do that. I want your daughter."

By the many confused expressions, Dorakon could tell the king had not discussed this caveat with anyone, not even Lance. For once, the ex-high guardsman looked like he might harm his new patron.

"Gods, man!" Dorakon snapped before he had time to consider the proximity of the many hostile weapons. "You are already married!"

At this, Tohmas chuckled. "Not for me. I want your daughter to marry Lance Carraway."

Had it not been for Lance's reaction, Dorakon would have believed Galanth's newest guardian had set the arrangement up mooncycles prior, but the crippled ex-high guardsman was as speechless as the rest of the kingsmen.

But Dorakon was a prince, and he was not easily silenced. "At least let her decide for herself," he said. "I heard it said you let your own wife decide. Is it not—"

"She will marry him," Tohmas interrupted. "I cannot ask her to decide between you and me. She has to live with you. I could kill her. Hardly fair."

As the only thing that would take the hand off of the treaty he had to sign to save his life was agreement, Dorakon forced himself to nod. Tohmas released the vellum and invited, with a gesture, for him to resume making his surrender complete.

Valia's face was impassive when Dorakon turned around. The high guardsman with her had clenched his teeth against rebuts. There was nothing to say anyway.

Business concluded, Tohmas collected his treaty.

"We will return you to your quarters," Tohmas told him with a half-smile. "Come tomorrow—"

At last, Dorakon heard the voice of the man who had betrayed him. "My king," Lance said, "I heard there were plans made for a wedding between High Guardsman Bosul and Lady Valia. It was to be soon."

Undeterred, the king smiled wider. "Then they can push up the arrangements and have you married tomorrow. Dorakon will say his oath after the wedding. So long as he does not falter, we will be riding for Polthian by the end of the quartercycle. Objections?" Lance shook his head, and the king clapped him on the shoulder. "Good!"

He was gone back out the way he had come without another look around. The kingsmen filed out, including the burly Northlander leader. Lance was the last to follow, and Dorakon was left with the man who had destroyed his princedom.

But no one had given him back his sword, and there was nothing he could do directly to repay the insult he had been dealt.

"Calus," Dorakon ordered his loyal high guardsman, dropping the title as it seemed invalid now, "take Valia to her room. She must be exhausted and has a big day ahead of her tomorrow."

With a nod, the high guardsman directed Valia out the door by her forearm. A gathering of Garanth soldiers followed them out.

Gaidol had won the first battle, Dorakon thought, but lost the second. The third would be trickier, but Dorakon was still confident. His messages were already on their way to Polthian and Damoria. He did not have to defeat Tohmas' army here to still be instrumental in their demise.

"You think you win?" Dorakon said with a snarl. "You know nothing."

To his amazement, Guardian Carraway laughed. "I *know* we win, Dorakon," Lance said. "We always knew we would win."

"I will be a kingsman," Dorakon warned. His rank would still give him authority over Gaidol. Lance would still be his subordinate.

Lance shook his head. "I do not care. Either you obey Tohmas and do what is right for the first time in your life, or you disobey him and die. I have just been made the happiest man in the world!"

But Dorakon would get the final laugh. He knew what Calus, outraged at having his bride stolen from him, was planning. Lance would not like what he found. Tomorrow would be too late.

As if reading his mind, Lance raised an eyebrow. "I am not nearly as crippled as you think. And I'm faster than Calus."

Without a glance over his shoulder, Lance walked out smoothly.

Dorakon sat back down, taking the treaty in hand. If he made an error in the recitation, they would have their excuse to cut him down. Gods be damned; he could recite anything if it meant keeping his head. Retaliation would come later.

Lance left the room briskly, his cane and brace stabilizing him in a long stride. He stumbled into Darknim and the other kingsmen who were lingering outside.

"I need to...."

"I'm with you," Darknim interrupted. "Can't have you gallivanting off alone. Lead the way. The rest of these have work to do." He eyed the other kingsmen meaningfully, and Lance wondered what they had been discussing, but he did not take time to think about it.

He cut through the yard, catching the high guardsman and Valia on a path before the manor's gate.

Valia's call made the high guardsman stop. "Lance!" Her voice held more surprise than plea.

Lance did not know what to say. He had never told anyone about his longing for Valia, not by name, and he did not see how the king had figured it out. He'd only told Tohmas that he had a woman waiting for him in Gaidol.

TRAITOR

As she had not been asked, Lance feared Valia did not want him.

In the next moment, Valia twisted her arm out of the high guardsman's hold, ran the distance between them, and jumped into Lance's arms, clarifying the matter.

Lance was grateful for Darknim's support, as he did not think his brace could have balanced him against the onslaught. With the Northlander's grip on the back of his tunic, Lance caught Valia's flying leap and easily held her off the ground.

Before he could speak, she pressed her lips against his, kissing him passionately. For that moment, nothing else mattered.

When she finally came up for air, he was breathless. The first words out of his mouth were, "Valia, will you marry me?"

She wiggled down to stand in front of him, still with her arms around his neck. "Yes, yes, yes!" she insisted, kissing his mouth with each word, bouncing off the river stone path. "Of course! I don't know how you convinced Prince Tohmas! I swear, I will pay you back whatever you paid him!"

Lance shook his head. "No need. I am his Follower, meaning he will spend his life trying to figure out what I want so he can give it to me. I did not ask. He just gave."

"Then I owe him a kiss too!" Valia giggled into another kiss. With his feet under him and her weight now on her own legs, Darknim gently released the extra support.

There was a loud throat clearing from down the path, and Lance found High Guardsman Bosul glaring at them.

"Hardly appropriate behavior, fair lady," the high guardsman scolded.

Her arm dropped to loop around Lance's waist as she faced the high guardsman with a scowl. "You are a fine one to talk!" she snapped in a voice he had never heard her use. "He," she went on, tugging his embrace hard, "is now engaged to me. He gets to do whatever he wants with me!"

Lance tensed as, like the firedrake he wore, Darknim growled. What did she mean by that? High guardsman Bosul had been engaged to Valia.

"Hardly," the high guardsman said. "Crippled through the hip, I heard. I wonder if everything works. The man cannot even stand on his own two feet!"

"The man who stands with the help of others," Darknim interrupted, "stands with more strength than any who stands alone. Watch yourself, high guardsman. Lance is not just one man."

It was an echo of words Lance had once heard Prince Dorakon say, but this time they sounded like a compliment.

Puffing himself up, Calus dismissed the warning and said, "Come along, Valia." The high guardsman indicated the path between the poplars. "You need to get some rest."

She hugged Lance tighter. "No," she said simply and without concern. "I am not going with you."

Lance gripped the handle of his sword in readiness. The high guardsman's face was flushing red.

"Your father..."

"My father handed me over to be raped, and tonight, I imagine, possibly murdered. So no, I am not going to do what my father says. I am not going with you."

The words "raped" and "murdered" stopped Lance's heart. His grip on the sword tightened. It took effort not to attack the high guardsman outright, but he knew his ire should be directed at Prince Dorakon.

Calus stepped forward. "I said—"

"Leave her," Lance replied. "She will not be going with you tonight."

"Says the cripple!" Calus mocked. He seemed to reach for a weapon but had none on hand.

Letting his hand fall from Valia's waist, Lance drew his sword out of the sheath hooked into the brace. The sword's removal initiated Kitable's enchantment, and his leg was immediately dropped into a bent, fully supported position.

"How does it feel to know your firstborn might be mine?" Calus taunted.

Before Lance could react, Valia dropped her hand from Lance and stomped over to the high guardsman boldly. Lance missed catching her arm to hold her back. Did she not recognize the threat? Or had her fury overruled her senses entirely? The man was disarmed, but that did not mean he was not dangerous.

Darknim, standing by, watched on with amusement, an axe in hand.

"What sort of infant do you take me for?" Valia snapped. "This," she informed Calus at a half shout as she thrust a leafed plant she had

retrieved from a pouch under his nose, "is what I had been taking every three days since you first came to my room. You thought I was just a sensitive virgin! I was purging myself!"

Before he could recover from the assault, she threw her plant at his feet and pulled another like a dagger.

"And *this*," she cried, "this is what I have been sneaking into every drink I have ever brought you! Every cup of tea, every mug of ale, every sip of water, Calus, I have laced with gensom's seed." She slapped the plant into his available hand. "You dared to try and steal my joy, so now I take yours. I will never bear a child of yours, High Guardsman. *You* will never sire *any* child!"

Lance was just as speechless as the assaulted high guardsman. He was impressed yet knew her admission should have scandalized him.

Valia spun on her heels and marched back to Lance's side, the river stone path crunching under her slippers. She picked up Lance's hand, put it on her waist, and leaned against him.

Belatedly, Calus seemed to regain his senses, and he made as if to follow.

There was no doubt that Darknim's new powers had given him speed, for even Lance had not seen the Northlander move. Darknim was suddenly behind Calus, catching the man by his belt and pulling him back.

"We should give the newly engaged couple a moment alone," he said amicably. Without effort, he dragged Calus from the trail back the way they had come.

Once the pair were gone, Lance let out his breath and replaced his sword. Doing so deactivated Kitable's spell on the brace.

"I will take you to Lady Arnika," Lance told his love. Now relying on the springs and hinges of the brace, he led her out of the manor's grounds. "She will be able to find you a place to stay tonight that is far from them."

Her eyes were clear when she looked up at him, but tears ran down her cheeks. She tucked her head against him and did not let go until they were among the Galanth forces outside the city.

As soon as the manor was declared safe, Arnika demanded she attend to her husband. Tohmas, his usual complacent self, invited her to sit with the kingsmen as they debated their choices for Dorakon, and she was there when they finally accepted that so long as he could speak the oath, he could join them. It was, interestingly, Tohmas who pushed the most for acceptance, relying on the oath to prove loyalty. Sol and Barnon warned against trusting Dorakon ever, but they caved to Tohmas' confidence in the gods' supervision.

They could have remained in the manor, but practicality won out, and they returned to the camp's command tent and usual residence.

Tohmas was the first back from the encounter with Dorakon.

"He says he'll sign," he told her as he arrived. He grimaced. "And I made him agree to give his daughter up for marriage."

Arnika bristled. "Doesn't sound kind to her."

His smile was mischievous. "I think it is."

Pulled away by messages, they did not get to the topic again until Lance Carraway arrived, Lady Valia Lodaton on his arm.

The moment Tohmas saw the guardian, he broke into a grin. "Was I right?"

Arnika frowned, trying to read Prince Dorakon's daughter's expression. The woman was Arnika's age, if a little older, and matched Arnika in height. Unlike Arnika's brown, embroidered dress, the woman wore a wrinkled blue and white dress with pearls and jewelry to match. Long blond-gold hair flowed well past the girl's shoulders, making Arnika envy her. Her eyes were wide as she surveyed the camp, but she didn't sense fear in her. She certainly did not seem upset. And neither did Lance.

Guardian Carraway rolled his eyes and nodded.

Lady Valia's jaw dropped. "I know you said you didn't ask for the favor," she said to her beau, "but don't tell me this marriage was *a guess*!"

The king bowed his head, still smiling. "I had a pretty good idea, but he never specifically named you, fair lady."

"Just as you never named your lady," Lance pointed out, making the king lower his head in concession.

"So we are both stubborn fools," the king agreed. "I'm still glad I was right."

"So am I," Lance replied. He faced Arnika and gave her a respectful bow of his head. "My Lady, we seem to have everything arranged for a

wedding tomorrow, but Valia has expressed concern over her dress as it appears the previously made one is not to her liking. Could you recommend a seamstress who could prepare something for tomorrow?"

Feeling herself blush slightly in recognition, Arnika forced herself to smile at the new bride-to-be. "I fear I do not know the women who made my dress, but if we seek my Lady Mother, I am certain they can be found."

She extended her arm to Lady Valia in welcome, and the Gaidolon hesitantly let go of her fiancé's arm. She checked with Lance, but the guardian was already turning to Tohmas, more than happy that Arnika's assistance would be sincere.

Of all the men Tohmas had at his side, Lance seemed to be the only one who never doubted Arnika. It seemed fitting as he was as much an odd ally as she was, but she was still grateful.

"I would also ask that she stay with your Lady Mother tonight, Tohmas," Lance said. "Gaidol is not safe for her these days."

The king and his wife both lifted their eyebrows in surprise.

"I have been receiving letters from her since Trulin," Lance confessed with a laugh at their bemused expressions. "She told me the new horn commands, without which I would have been as blind as any of you. She also stirred up a fair bit of upset during the attack, apparently."

"I sabotaged the siege machines, too," Valia added. When she got a smile from the king, she justified, "Am I not to be proud of myself? I think I did very well, thank you!"

"Indeed you did," Tohmas agreed. "We are grateful."

"Gaidol," Lance added, "is not as grateful."

"That, and I just finished poisoning the man who took from me the right to wear white at my wedding," Lady Valia added, puffing herself up like a proud hen.

Lance flushed. Under the querying stares of the rest of the gathering, he admitted, "That has got to be one of the most attractive things I have ever heard a woman say." His grin grew. "I love this woman!"

Apparently unable to resist, Lance pulled Valia against him and kissed her. The way the woman sank into the embrace made Arnika take her turn flushing. Tohmas had not been guessing, she decided. He had seen the way the two people looked at each other. It was just that obvious.

Eventually, Lance let his bride go, and Arnika extended her arm again.

"Shall we seek my mother-in-law? She will make you feel at home, have no doubt. She once told me she wore blue to her wedding."

The king's mother had already proven her skills at wedding organizing. They would have everything arranged by morning.

It was not until they arrived at Lady Fayela's waggon that Arnika realized just how momentous the day had become. Her Lady Mother met her with tears in her eyes.

As Arnika explained what they needed, the Lady Mother smiled.

"I should have a portrait done," she said, wiping away the wetness of her eyes. "I may never believe it happened otherwise!"

"What happened?" Arnika inquired.

Fayela's smile warmed. "A daughter of Gaidol has just walked to me, arm in arm with a daughter of Trulin! Look at you two! Your families have been fighting since before you were born, and here you are, together! The women of Espar will heal that which this war injures."

Valia found her voice. "I, for one, have had enough of fighting. As far as I am concerned, there should always be peace between Trulin and Gaidol."

Stepping between them and looping her arms around each of their shoulders, Arnika's mother-in-law nodded. "Here," she said, "let us find you a place to stay. Then we can see about that wedding!"

Chapter 13

While tradespeople sought to replenish supplies and make sales in the conquered SwordWood, Shimmer was content to open Match and Mixer and deal with the curious people who eventually left their city to investigate the encamped army. There were the typical disagreements between local and Fixer City merchants hawking the same goods, but there were still enough customers to go around. The majority of the people accepted Tohmas' dominion without interest. As long as the king did not try to change too much too fast, Shimmer assumed he would be tolerated. Few cared who ruled day to day.

The dancing show at Match and Mixer was well-attended, and Maybel did exceptionally well. They were closing for the night when Maybel came to assist. Shimmer was taken aback as she had already paid Maybel her share of the profit from the dancing.

"No partner tonight, Maybel?" Shimmer asked, trying to keep her voice light.

"You do not have to approve," Maybel candidly informed her, which made Shimmer laugh. She had told plenty of people the same over the years.

"I was just trying to make small talk, oh overly-sensitive one," Shimmer said. "I am not disapproving. You just have never helped with closing before. I thought I would be friendly."

Maybel pressed her lips and went on with closing the wooden window covers of the waggon. Dust stuck his head out to confirm that everything was locked and enchanted, then disappeared inside.

Shimmer tightened the last latch. She could not offer Maybel a place to sleep—the waggon was too small—but if she wanted to come in for a cup of tea...

Power rolled over her. Shimmer spun in search of the caster, activating her hovering Spell Sight in the next instant. To her surprise, her spells vanished as if an Eight-Layer Dispel had cut through her defenses. Even her Spell Sight did no more than flash across her eyes before falling away.

She'd heard no activation word, yet these were potent spells. Her heart jumped into her throat.

There was no one around her. The clearing they had used for dancing was empty. Not even the fire pit remained.

Maybel had been there, and Shimmer did not believe the woman had moved off so quickly or silently. This wasn't right. She was not even sure she was still standing next to Match and Mixer. Everything, from the tilt of the torchlight to the feel of the earth under her feet, felt wrong.

She opened her mouth to call for her father, but something pierced between her shoulder blades as she drew breath.

Her muscles collapsed as the pain shot through her. Her chest spasmed, and the words on her tongue were lost as breath left her. Consciousness lingered. She was aware enough to know that she was bleeding as she lay on the ground. Lying mute, she spotted feet and recognized Maybel's charm anklet.

Magic echoed off everything, churning in her mind and scattering her thoughts. Enchantments, she was confident, but then no, the pain was real. When had Maybel learned an Eight-Layer Dispel, and how had she readied it without Shimmer noticing?

The satisfied snort she heard made her believe the woman was smiling as she turned away.

Without a voice, for it was all she could do to breathe shallowly against the pain in her back, Shimmer could not cast or call for help. Without help, she'd bleed out.

The magic left like the retreat of a wave over a beach. The world came back into clarity, down to the trampled grasses under her nose as she lay on her side, gasping. The fire pit smoke drifted low around her.

One hand would not move when she tried, but her left hand was responsive; she reached into her bag. Pulling out things randomly, she found herbs and powders primarily, but one snap-bang found its way into her hand.

They were used in her father's show to distract and entertain but needed to be hit against something hard to explode the grey powder inside. They were dangerous close-up, but with her arm losing strength, she could not throw it.

With all her energy, Shimmer turned the snap-bang against a nearby stone. The movement shifted something behind her, and pain exploded. She blacked out.

The wedding was far from perfect as the many superfluous things Valia had arranged to delay her marriage to Calus took time and attention. However, the essential parts remained: a Celebrant of Ocea to marry them and the man she loved to marry. They chopped the guest list quickly to allow for Galanth kingsmen to attend.

King Tohmas arranged to have High Guardsman Bosul surrounded by kingsmen during the ceremony, and despite his glares, the man never so much as blinked out of place. While weddings had traditionally forbidden weapons, Valia had heard about Arnika's marriage and, as such, was not surprised when every kingsman carried his sword in, and the protectors took strategic posts around the temple's aisles. SoulBurner, Arnika had told her, never left Tohmas' side except when on the altar during prayers. It was a comfort to have that protection at the ready when the king stood beside Lance.

However, they needed none of the weapons as the wedding progressed, and Celebrant Corolys confirmed them as husband and wife. They retreated to the side, giving Tohmas the floor, his four celebrants at his back in observance.

The attention turned to Prince Dorakon, who stepped up and then knelt as was proper of a man taking a new patron. The first part of

the oath, recited by every soldier from protector to companion, went smoothly. Dorakon then paused before beginning the second part, specific to the title of kingsman. He glanced around as if expecting something.

Her father went back to the oath, but the words seemed unsure. Only two sentences in, Dorakon paused again and looked around in irritation. He seemed to search for something but found nothing with each investigation.

As he tried to resume the oath, the murmurs began among the Galanth kingsmen. No doubt they knew the kingsman oath well. Dorakon had made a mistake.

King Tohmas' expression fell.

Dorakon seemed to realize his error, and he came to his feet. "Distractions are hardly fair!" he objected. "Who keeps whispering?"

Valia had heard nothing, and she and Lance were still a bear stride from her father. Everyone had been listening to Dorakon.

In the pause, the red-robed celebrant with the fire scars of Inac on his chest stepped forward, and his compatriots followed. They formed a semicircle that included the king as they confronted Dorakon.

"Celebrant Calanor tells us the voice you hear, Dorakon Lodaton, is that of the Wind God Totho," the fire celebrant declared with a gesture to the white-robed, feather-decorated wind celebrant of the group. "If the god has something to say, you can be forgiven for mistaking the oath, I am sure. Tell us, Dorakon Lodaton, what did the whispers say?"

With his face covered by a scarf, only Celebrant Calanor's ashen eyes were visible, and the stern stare directed on Dorakon made Valia shiver. Lance drew her against him. She believed they were doing the will of their gods, but the consequence of his mistake was slowly dawning on her. If he could not make reparations, his oath would be rejected and his life was forfeit.

Her father paused, clearly unwilling to repeat what the whispers had said.

Banked by celebrants, the king drew his sword and rested the tip on the ground. The red light of fire surrounded them.

Dorakon flinched but held his ground.

"Try again then," Tohmas invited. "In the presence of the holy light of Inac, if you believe the words you say, speak the oath."

The four celebrants nodded concession and allowed Dorakon to kneel. He examined them each for some sign, but when his eyes hit the holy light in front of him, he launched back as if he had been struck.

"That was the warning of the Wind, Dorakon Lodaton," the Celebrant of Ocea said, her alto voice firm instead of sweet as it had been during the marriage. "If you will not repeat the whisper, I shall. Totho has declared that your lies will not be accepted."

The word "lies" made the entire crowd stir, a wave of muttering rising until it was an ocean's worth. What had been speculation was now confirmed.

A voice echoed between the temple's pillars, a voice that belonged perfectly to her father, yet his mouth was closed.

"I'll say what has to be said and wait for them to stop paying attention. Arrogant brute, Tohmas will believe anything."

Dorakon blanched, his eyes wide.

"Your oath," the Celebrant of Pari added as he stepped up to reform the broken semicircle his companions had made, "is false, and under the eyes of the gods, it is rejected."

When Valia had been a child, Dorakon had been infallible and wise, and she had to, for a moment, wonder when that had changed. He had two possible reactions to give, and he chose the one least likely to see people support him. It was not the decision of a rational, wise man. It was a fury born of desperation. He had been trapped by his lies and presumptions.

"Damned demon-kissing fools!" he snapped at the celebrants. "How could you know? What voice have you—"

The Celebrant of Totho was the only one to move, but the moment the arm gestured, Dorakon's tirade ended, and he fell onto his knees.

The voice of the Lord of Secrets will not be slighted, Valia heard with her mind, not her ears. *Your thoughts betrayed you. Now live with the consequences.*

Although she did not see Celebrant Calanor's mouth move, she knew the words were his and that everyone at the assembly had heard them.

Tohmas lifted SoulBurner and put away the holy light. Answering his wave, the protectors took Dorakon away.

Lance turned his head to Valia as if to ask a question, but she shook her head pre-emptively.

"I have nothing to say to him," she said. "He lied under oath. So be it."

Her new husband—how she loved that idea!—had not even turned his head from her when King Tohmas' voice rose over the assembly.

"Lance," the king shouted, "I need a Kingsman of Gaidol. You feel up for giving an oath today?"

It was Lance's turn to be unsteady, but Valia was there for him, and his mild shake was only visible to her. He took only a blink to consider it, probably going over the oath in his mind, before nodding.

Valia escorted him but left him when he took his weight entirely on the brace. He could not properly kneel with the injured leg, but no one seemed to mind when he bent his right leg low and let the left hover off the ground behind him in half-kneel.

He recited the oath without fault. When it ended, a cheer went up as his guardsmen, who had followed him into Tohmas' service and were now wardens and companions within the Galanth forces, let loose their joy.

Tohmas helped Lance rise, then turned his attention to the assembled crowd and declared her husband the Kingsman of Gaidol.

The cheer doubled in volume. Tohmas passed Lance the coveted black braid and helped him tie it in place.

The only unhappy face in all the gathered people was High Guardsman Bosul.

The first time Kitable woke, he endured another list of questions about the untouchable and the Northlander Circle. He got to meet the newest member of the Watching Circle, a little woman by the name of Minet, who was apparently Kitable's age and appeared to be half that. She was a new graduate this year and the current expert in Divination.

Kitable figured she would be no match for Tril, and he wondered if she knew that.

He did not let them drive him to complete exhaustion during the following inquisitions and instead took his mind away from his body. In thought, he sought the black space of the mind, where he could

watch the spiraling magic across the great, impossible gap. The first several times he performed the feat, he was allowed to sit and watch the blackness in rest but after what he had to guess was a few days, Gannon followed.

It wasn't easy to recognize Gannon. In the black place, in place of his gem, Gannon wore a prominent black mark at the center of his forehead. His robes had been replaced with the simplest shift, but tendrils extended from the third eye down Gannon's skin in a writhing, shifting pattern that made Kitable's skin crawl. The darkness seemed to grab at the Wanter caster and the world around as one.

As there was never any sound in the space between, he did not notice the Vox spell's continual presence as more than a tickle in his throat.

I had her stabbed, in case you were wondering, Gannon told him. The thought wizard seemed to appreciate the chance to speak away from the other Circle members, especially the little Minet. With Gannon the closest to her age, she had been paying particular attention to the thought master, and Kitable had already gotten the impression Gannon resented it.

Gannon shared a vision of Maybel stabbing a knife into Shimmer's back. Shimmer collapsed, but the vision faded before Kitable could confirm the blade had struck anything vital.

Gloating, are you now, Gannon? What are you looking for? I told you she meant nothing to me, Kitable replied in mind.

Nevertheless, Gannon pressed, *you would seek her attacker if given a chance.*

I resent Maybel's presence on principle. I promised that if our paths crossed again, I would kill her. I keep my promises. Kitable analyzed Gannon and added, *Please remember that.*

In mind, Gannon had grown in height and muscle, but Kitable knew that to be an illusion, not fact. A projected ego could not change the man's skills.

Well, you can be certain Maybel means nothing to me, Kitable, Gannon boasted. *But I doubt you will have the chance to exact your revenge on her. Fantorn will take you to Wanter tomorrow, where you will be left while we resume our destruction of the Northlander Circle.*

Your attempted destruction, you mean, Kitable goaded. *Two of them handed four of you your asses if I remember correctly.* He deliberately

remembered the stories in detail, imagining some of Darknim and Ela's accounts vividly to make the point. He focused on Ela because he could already tell how much that failure had vexed the thought wizard.

But we are a complete Circle again, Gannon replied.

So are they! Thanks to me! Kitable snapped.

Unable to let Kitable have the last word, Gannon ended with a final, *But not for long,* before fading out of Kitable's mind. He had been generous in offering rest when Kitable needed it, although Kitable assumed it was because they did not want him dying prematurely.

That could have been what Tril had meant, but Kitable was uncertain.

He had gotten out of being without hovering spells before but not while Voxed. The only Vox he had ever had locked onto him had been worse; Master Terant had put a Black Agony on him as well. Kitable would have traded the Vox for the Black Agony. He could cast through the intense pain of the Black Agony, but he could not cast through a Vox.

He had escaped that too, but that had required aid, and he was too far from help here. Who would show up soaking wet to cast their first Eight-Layered Dispel and save him?

The memory made him smile.

Kitable had deliberately kept his thoughts in sentences for Gannon, but once the presence was gone and he was free to think, Kitable reviewed the conversation in detail. Shimmer Weaver was not dead. Firstly, Gannon had said Shimmer had been "stabbed," not "killed." Further, he had told Kitable he would want to go after her "attacker," not necessarily her "killer" or "murderer." Had it been a ploy to keep him hopeful, or had Gannon feared Kitable would catch him in a lie? He'd not shown Kitable her body either. Was that because Shimmer had found help?

Shimmer was resourceful, and Maybel was incompetent. It seemed unlikely the Weaver would die. That made Kitable feel slightly less guilty over her inadvertent involvement. It was her fault. She was the one who kept drawing attention to herself!

His thoughts were still on Shimmer when he spotted movement in the dark space between minds.

Out of the gloom of the shadowless light, Tril walked with his white wolf at his side.

Words were not possible, Kitable was frustrated to remember. What would they discuss anyway? There was nothing Tril could do for Kitable from where he was. Hells, the Northlander could not even target Kitable this way. Northlanders were not good at targeting!

To his surprise, Tril gestured for him to follow and started back the way he had come.

With no landmarks, it was hard to say how long they walked in the blackness. They had left the great gap behind, and the spiral had seemingly shrunk by the time Kitable sensed a thinning of the black around him and suddenly found himself in a room of golden light.

Having adjusted to the dark, the glittering, shimmering surroundings blinded him, and he covered his eyes against them. Before he could blink the spots out of his vision, he heard the Northlander speak.

"How are you getting on?"

Kitable rubbed his eyes and eventually made out the elder in front of him. Like Gannon in the mental world, Tril had changed forms and now wore his wolf Aspect heavily. Visibly half man and half wolf, it was only the voice of the elder that let Kitable identify the man through the long-snouted, furred beast in front of him.

"Where are we?"

The wolf face smiled to reveal a complete set of teeth. "You have just left the magic place behind, my friend. For the first time in twenty years, you are dreaming."

"Then you are not here," Kitable said with a sigh.

The wolf-man laughed. "I am here, my friend. I am dreaming too."

The explanation fell remarkably short. "We are dreaming the same dream? And we are not creative enough to come up with anything more than an expanse of golden light? I am decidedly disappointed."

"This," Tril said, gesturing to the vastness around them, "is where everyone dreams, Kitable. We are between dreams."

Kitable's head started hurting. "Tril," he said, "I am less than a day from being taken to their world. They have stripped my mind of everything they remotely consider valuable, and I am powerless to stop them. If I am going to die shortly, I want a better dream!"

"But you are not going to die shortly." Tril smiled again with plenty of teeth. "I have just given you a way out."

Kitable eyed the wolf-man skeptically. "If you say something about wishing or dreaming a solution, I will leave."

Tril would not be dissuaded. "This world," he pressed, "is the untouchable world, Kitable. You draw your powers from the spiral in the dark, and the untouchables draw from this golden world. This is why wizards occasionally wake dispelled: they have been dreaming! This is why you cannot always target a sleeping person: they are here! You are close to the wizard's side of things, but you still hold the potential for Dreamer magic."

Kitable looked at the golden expanse but slowly shook his head. He felt naked and vulnerable, not empowered. He was, as Tril said, close to the wizard's side. He did not belong in the golden light.

"I am not able to use untouchable powers, Tril," he refused. "It is too different."

A furry hand shoved him playfully. "I am not suggesting you suddenly master another art of magic, my friend. All I am saying is that you have been touched by untouchable magic, the power of emotion and hope. That is all I can offer you. You are dispelled."

With a golden twinkle in his beast eyes, the elder added, "Of course, that means all of you is dispelled."

Kitable straightened in understanding. The tickle in his throat was gone.

Tril turned toward the light and roamed away. "We will be waiting for you when you return, do not fear."

Left alone, Kitable retraced his steps and found the black world. From there, he made his way back to his body.

Gannon arrived breathless, skipping through a portal to heed Rean's recall. He was met by the Watching Circle's scowls. They had been waiting for him, Kitable standing ready with his hands bound by Fantorn's force magic.

"Where have you been?" Rean demanded, her voice low so the younger member would not hear her disapproval. Appearances mattered.

"Dealing with contingency plans," he replied honestly, not knowing how much she already knew. Although Kitable was their prisoner, losing

the Northlander elder had given him a new job: breaking the Circle of the Raven again. Knowing direct conflict had not gone well, he had started alternative plans. He'd intended to discuss them with her once they bore fruit, not on the fly between things.

Rean narrowed her eyes on him, her squinting orbs of white reduced to slits that vanished among her wrinkles. She pursed her lips as if wanting to chastise him but lacking a specific topic to attack. Instead, with a sneer, she said, "Make the portal. Kitable goes to Wanter now."

"Of course," Gannon replied. All of them knew the portal spell well, although it was one kept from the annexes for students. But any Watching Circle member working off world had to be able to get home. It was a simple thing, so often had it been practiced.

Vindictively, Gannon made the portal to Wanter a step high in the wizarding world, and he watched the Wisavi of Galanth be pushed forward. There was no point in reading any more thoughts. They had learned all they could. It was time to see how others fared with the specimen.

Fantorn stepped up to the portal awaiting her prey while Gilan and Rean passed along the belongings they had taken from Kitable. They had been tempted to dress him once more to show Wanter what the strange Tainted wore, but the danger of his items kept him minimally attired and his hands bound. His trinkets lay atop his robe. It would not do well to have the man activating them.

Kitable was calm as he approached the portal, but Gannon knew without looking into the mind that it was a facade. Not knowing what he was about to face, but with the prophecy from the Northlander in his mind, Kitable was scared. Some people, Gannon thought, became agitated when frightened. Some fled, some wept, but this man stepped back from his emotions and marched on. Although his movement insisted he was present consciously, Gannon would not have been surprised to find some part of Kitable's mind still walking around in the black space between their worlds.

There was nothing he could do about it. Gannon would return to the Esparan camp in a short while and finish what he had started. He had new tools to use in this battle with the Northlander Circle.

When Kitable broke from his detached march to his doom, everyone jumped. Several facts struck Gannon at once, not the least

of which was that Kitable's hands were inexplicably free from the force shackles. The subsequent realization was that they had never bothered to decipher Kitable's items. When Kitable lunged at Gilan and pulled a crystal pendant from his belongings, they did not know what to expect.

Thankfully, it was not a great blast of magic or a dispel. Instead, Kitable was suddenly gone.

He had waited with his hands in front of him as if still bound, knowing the Seal had to come down to permit the portal. The item activated a Relocation spell instantly, and although more than one of them tried, none of them could cast fast enough to stop him.

Gannon was quietly impressed. He must have planned it in the farthest reaches of his mind or only just decided to attempt flight, for even Gannon, who had been sharing the man's thoughts for days, had not seen the escape. How had he broken Fantorn's spell?

Fantorn was not one to be denied a prize. With curses worthy of Shantanese sailors, she sought his anchor and put together a Relocation spell. Namni and Tranvin were not far behind with Gilan and Rean rapidly following.

The little Gavorian brat Minet turned her pretty head his way. "Where have they gone? We must follow!"

Gannon shook his head as he considered the events he had just seen unfold. "They have just walked into a trap," he told her. "Follow if you want. I'm staying here."

She went pinker still and stomped her foot like a spoiled child. "You are the Watching Circle! You must act together! Help them! You must deal with Kitable, or he will end our world!"

Gannon paused, eyeing the little divination caster closely. Casters drawn to circle positions were often attuned to their elements or domains well beyond the normal residents of Wanter. He expected Minet to be good at divination, but he was suddenly unsure if her final sentence was a casual prophecy. Had she accidentally come across something?

Still, Gannon shook his head. "Do a Scry," he invited, "and I bet you will see their imminent demise. I cannot change that future. I could get myself killed, or I could sit here and wait for those who are going to escape to escape. It is too late, and I do not need divination to tell me that!"

She debated the choice for far too long—had she been able to make a difference, it would be too late now—and eventually decided not to bother even trying. When she finally did a Scry and divination on the matter, she found he had been right.

The Watching Circle had walked right into the Northlander Circle.

Rean made it back, but Gilan was gone. Fantorn returned as well, sparing the entire female side of the Circle, with Tranvin slinking back with most of an arm missing but no sign of Namni. Their accounts matched Gannon's fears: the beasts and the Northlanders had been waiting, ready, for them. Their divination master had foreseen the Watching Circle's actions. It should have been impossible through the shields they kept, but it had been done. Gilan and Namni had paid for it.

Fantorn had taken a blow to her leg from a horse, she claimed, breaking the limb. Rean continued to stagger until Gannon finally sat her down and worked his way through the thought magic that had scrambled her mind. Eventually, she could focus on him without becoming dizzy, but it took until the powers of the portal had dropped before she could walk.

Without a complete Circle, for they had been broken two-fold this night, they could not cast a Linking, but the consensus was still clear: they would move and wait for new members and plan. The northern Tainted were coming into their strengths too fast. They would have to catch the Northlanders apart and take them down one at a time if they wanted to succeed.

And they would do their best to kill the treacherous Kitable if they had a chance. He could not be allowed to assist the Northlander Circle any longer.

Gannon set up his own Scry, focused on Kitable. Once he was not protected by the others, Gannon would be ready.

Chapter 14

It was a shock to Relocate to his anchor in King Tohmas' command tent and be surrounded by Northlander Elders. They encircled the cleared area where a table had once stood, each facing in as Kitable appeared. Their Aspects, glittering in golden light from the Dreamworld, were already manifested in readiness.

"Move aside, Kitable," Tril called and, still disoriented and dispelled, Kitable obliged.

As the Wanter Circle pursued him, they met the readied Northlanders.

Kitable contributed very little to the conflict, his assistance unnecessary. Tril had prepared all of the Northlander Circle members. With their animals projected, there was a veritable army awaiting the attackers. One by one, the Wanter casters were run off, their magic falling away under the powers of the Circle of the Raven. Darknim was among them as well, his axe driving the enemies out when the powers themselves failed. Two of the Wanter Circle members were dead by the time the last of the intruders withdrew.

Kitable watched them drag away the bodies, finally feeling it was safe enough to pick the crystal shards from the palm of his hand. He would have to find another medium for the Relocation spell. Not only was the trinket now revealed, but each prick of lead crystal in his skin threatened him with poisoning. He'd never expected to use it so much.

Outside, the Northlanders dropped the bodies into two holes Tril had suggested be dug before the battle started.

He could not admit it aloud, but the accuracy of Tril's predictions unsettled Kitable. He could only be grateful Tril had decided to support Galanth.

Tril came up beside him, a thundercloud of magic invisibly around him. Kitable's arm hairs stood on end as he approached, the strength of the magic palpable to him. The wolf eyes were clouding, and Kitable wondered if that was age or visions. The way Tril looked around him now implied he saw visions layered upon visions, and the thought worried Kitable. How far could Tril push it?

But Tril's words were kind. "Go see to her," he said. "You have unfinished business there."

Her. So Shimmer Weaver had indeed lived. And Tril was right; he needed to see it himself.

Kitable took one step, then paused. "How long has it been?" he asked. "I remember only a few, maybe four, days, but that bastard was playing in my head."

Tril's eyes did not focus as he replied, "Twenty-one days since they took you, three since she was sent to a Healing waggon."

"Twenty-one?" Kitable exclaimed. "That son of a—"

"Go see to her, Kitable," Tril interrupted. "You have unfinished business there." The voice was the same as before, each word spoken with the exact emphasis as before. Did he even remember having said these words already?

Kitable opened his mouth to argue but recognized before he said a word that there was no point. Nothing would reach Tril now, not when the elder was so lost in visions.

And he knew Tril was right.

Still without robes or trinkets, Kitable sought the Healing waggon nearest the Match and Mixer shop, casting as he walked.

Dust was with Shimmer as she lay on a mat against the far wall, her bright red hair forming a soft pillow. Despite what he had told Gannon, seeing her prone and injured made Kitable's heart ache. Knowing she had been attacked to get at him rapidly changed that sadness to anger.

Healing was the realm of the celebrants. He could only deal in vengeance.

CHAPTER 14

He cast a Scry and searched out the blond woman he knew was responsible for Shimmer's state. Removing any supporters of the Watching Circle would be prudent anyway. And he had a promise to keep.

Finding Maybel hastily walking a road not far away, Kitable locked an anchor ahead of her. He added Spell Sight, but Dust Weaver stepped up to address him before he could cast his Relocation.

"See to your daughter," Kitable told the apothecary. "She will need you."

"Not me she's needing," Dust replied, "and I want Maybel dead as much as you do."

Kitable sensed the man's determination, but he had to try. "I have killed plenty of casters. You do not need to taint—" He paused because of the irony of the word, but the apothecary seized the opportunity to interrupt.

"Stop fussing about my innocence, Kitable. I am no more pure than you are. You can either take me with you or accept that I will show up shortly."

With one part of his vision still on the distant road, Kitable glanced at the angry father.

He was taken aback by the sternness of the man's stare. As much as he wanted to argue, he could see it would be useless. Someone had hurt Dust's daughter. Nothing in the world would stop the father from getting revenge.

Giving in, Kitable nodded and extended his hand. "I found her, and I happened to have gotten very good at two-person Relocations recently. However, I have a price."

"Rather appropriate," the Weaver said vengefully. "Name it."

"Keep Shimmer away from me. It was because of my affiliations that your daughter was targeted. I want you to make sure it does not happen again."

Kitable felt the terms were very reasonable, but the father sank back and chewed his lip for a long moment before answering.

"What she does is her choice," Dust insisted. "Being a caster is dangerous, and she knows that. Let her run her own life."

"Try," Kitable insisted. "I want nothing to do with her. Convince her of that."

"I will try," Dust agreed. He extended his hand.

In taking Dust's wrist, Kitable felt the Weaver drop some of his defenses to let the Relocation take effect. With a few dozen words, they were standing beside a road farther south.

Maybel froze on the road, her eyes going wide as coins.

"Please," she said, her hands out. "Let me—"

Kitable struck her with an Eight-Layered Dispel. His next spell Voxed her. Dust's spells wrapped her feet in magic, so she fell when she turned from them.

In the pause, Dust wondered, "Vox?"

"I do not like listening to them," Kitable admitted as they walked to where she was flailing like a fish on the bank. If the Dust thought him cruel, he did not care.

Dust cast a force spell across the girl and pinned her down. Her mouth continued to try to make a sound, but Kitable's spell kept her silent. He had time to consider his options for a quick execution.

Magic flared to his right, an unexpected burst potent enough to make Kitable spin and fire another Eight-layered Dispel in reflex.

His stomach dropped as he recognized Gannon with his focus gem glowing blood red. He'd assumed the Northlander Circle had done enough damage to keep the Wanter casters busy tending their wounds. Seeing him interfering to help Maybel was doubly unexpected as Kitable had believed Gannon's assertion that he had no interest in the woman.

But as Kitable's Eight-layered Dispel took out a shield, Kitable realized that Gannon's appearance had nothing to do with Maybel. In leaving the Northlanders, Kitable had made himself vulnerable. Why had Tril not mentioned it?

His spells were fewer than usual. If he ran out of hovering spells, Gannon would easily defeat him. *At least I have Dust.* Even just having two targets for the Wanter caster would help.

Dust made the point by spinning on his heels and shooting six balls of light at the intruder. Kitable's Spell Sight showed them all to be illusions, but the Wanter caster either did not have Spell Sight up or did not have time to think about the attacking balls of light. He dropped low to dodge them.

Kitable activated a Force Wall behind Gannon and reflected the illusions. A dispel destroyed the spell, but in his hurry to defend himself

from the illusions, Gannon failed to notice the Force Wall was an open spell. Kitable pivoted the wall to push the man into the ground.

When they matched their strengths, they were even. With Gannon pushing up against the wall and Kitable's force pushing down, nothing moved. Dust had time to do something, but he was nowhere to be seen for a moment.

As he pushed, Gannon cast. His spell shattered the Force Wall. Kitable turned his attention to defenses next, for Gannon took that instant to fire a thought alteration at him. The last thing Kitable wanted was the thought master of Wanter in his head again. He activated a hovering spell to defend himself, but it marked the last thought spell he had pre-casted. He had to take a moment to put another one up.

Dust proved he had not been entirely idle by rushing at Gannon, waving a branch as a weapon. Gannon's attack on Kitable, which could easily have destroyed the defense he was putting up, had to be turned against Dust. Thought magic reached out, and Dust stopped in his tracks. The branch lowered as the apothecary's expression became confused.

Kitable had no idea what spell that had been or how to counter it.

With his defense up, Kitable fired off a five-way dispel that was deflected, then dispelled, by Gannon's defenses. With only a few words from the enemy caster, Kitable's new thought shield was also gone. He was again vulnerable.

It took Kitable over forty words to put up a defense, but it took the Wanter Caster only ten to pull it down. In this exchange, Kitable was going to lose.

He fired a Drill spell and cut a hole through Gannon's remaining shields, but the thought wizard merely stepped to his left to avoid the damaging part of the spell that would have drilled into the caster. Kitable sent a Dart into the hole as his last action before a layered spell destroyed his shield and let a new thought spell stab into his mind.

"Dust!" Kitable shouted as the thought alteration spell clamped down his muscles, starting at his feet and working its way up. "This is the man who sent Maybel against Shimmer!"

Kitable turned his focus inward, trying to force the mind magic out of his skull. His mind made more thoughts with every moment, and even Gannon could only alter or destroy so many. Kitable was

not helpless this time, not bound as he had been. But organizing his thoughts became a struggle.

"You were not ready for a duel, were you, Kitable?" Gannon gloated, taking advantage of the lull. Dust stood frozen to his right while Kitable could not move from in front of him. "You thought you were my match."

Kitable laughed, the amusement rising too quickly to be stopped by the spell. *Gloating takes time. Time makes your attacks weaker and lets us adjust,* he thought, certain the Wanter man would see it.

Seeing what Kitable did, Gannon jumped forward to dodge the stick Dust swung, but Dust was an illusionist. Kitable's Spell Sight saw both the force line that made the branch stronger and the illusion that made it appear shorter than it was.

The reinforced wood cracked into Gannon's ribs. The Wanter caster collapsed.

The spell connecting Kitable's mind to Gannon's lingered long enough to let Kitable scoff. Gannon was not just offended; he was surprised by the concept of pain. He could not fathom it.

Tainted casters, Kitable made a point of thinking, *know spells are pain. I dare say we handle it better.*

Dust reared back for a second swing as the mind spell dropped from Kitable. With a word, Kitable threw another Dart into Gannon's shoulder, passing through the defenses against magic.

Dust's swing crashed into the prone man vindictively, hard enough to break ribs. By Gannon's cry, he probably did.

Instantly, Gannon disappeared. Without a Tracker at the ready, Kitable could not follow. Dust pounded the place where he had vanished, but when his swings struck only stone and dirt, they both knew Gannon had escaped.

Kitable put up a handful of thought magic defenses before going to see Maybel. She was already dead. A minor earth destruction spell had pierced her skull.

Dust came up beside Kitable and shrugged. "I didn't want her getting away," he said. "Not nice to leave her trapped either."

Kitable shrugged back. Leaving the body to thieves and beggars, if any traveled this road, he walked away.

"Our agreement stands, Weaver," Kitable said as he located his waggon's anchor and bound himself to it. He extended his hand to take the man home.

"I will do all I can to keep her away from you," the father agreed. "It's for her own good anyway."

Kitable had hold of the man's wrist and Relocated them back to the camp by the time the man decided to add, "The hard part will be convincing her of that."

The quiet of the waggon was a welcome relief after too many days in a cave robbed of his magic. It took Kitable the rest of the day to see to his injuries, change his clothes, and get cleaned. As the sun set, it felt as if nothing had changed. The Northlander Circle was again complete. He was home and surrounded by his magic. Tohmas was still on his march to glory and conquest.

Days passed without evidence of the Wanter Circle. Tril promised he had a final plan for them and that, as a unit, they were finished. This gave Kitable time to look into a promise he had given Fayela.

As the army marched southwest for the next few days, Kitable used his magic to unravel the past around the man he had sworn to follow in Habal's place. What he saw did not surprise him, although it contradicted much of what Tohmas had told him. He was left with the impossible question of whether to tell Fayela the truth. Would she hold it secret? Would the kingsmen follow if they knew?

Through his Reflections, Kitable heard the lies Chief Tamv told Tohmas about his bloodline. Tohmas Galanth had died fifteen years prior and was buried under a swamp tree in the Black Marsh. The man who carried his name had been groomed to take up the position so thoroughly, Kitable wasn't sure if Tohmas knew the truth or not.

As he reviewed the Reflections from the safety of his vardo, Kitable had to wonder, did it matter?

He'd already decided Tohmas' role in his father's death did not change his opinion of Tohmas, not after what they had accomplished in unifying Espar. Tril seemed to think the cause worthwhile enough to guide his people to it. Whatever the reasoning behind it, the goal of bringing order to Espar was noble.

And he thought he knew Tohmas well enough now.

Finally putting away his candles, Kitable made a cup of tea and decided to keep this secret. The support of the Esparans would likely break if the truth were known; Sol and Barnon would surely break off if they discovered Tohmas was not their nephew and had played a role in the death of their brother.

But Kitable believed in Tohmas' good intentions. He would see this conquest through.

Once Dust returned to the Healing waggon, Shimmer was conscious enough to ask where he had gone. He told her the truth and repeated the wisavi's insistence that she stay clear of Kitable and end any contact for her protection.

It made her smile.

"He worries about me?"

"Promise to stay away for a bit, Shim. He's busy right now, found himself some new enemies. Give him at least that. He did avenge you, after all. Next time we reach a good city, we will stay there. I haven't been to Wayburn for a while. Be nice to catch up with the locals." He paused, checking her expression. "Promise me, Shim. We need to back off from this."

With her eyes closed and her focus on her breathing, she nodded. Not wanting to press her, Dust sat back and tried to be satisfied.

It was not the first time he had been forced to defend his little girl, but it had been a while since the last. He did not consider himself a vengeful person. Still, he had taken Shimmer from her mother by force and was willing to demonstrate that same determination to keep her safe from any other threat. No one would take his daughter from him even if that meant he had to keep a host of more aggressive spells at the ready. He would do whatever was required. That had always been true.

He felt no compassion for the woman he had killed with a spear of destructive earth magic. Maybel had used their hospitality and Shimmer's generosity to stab her in the back, literally. The cutters had seen to her right away, and the news had been tepid: had Dust not heard the snap-bang and gotten to her when he had, she would undoubtedly be dead. The healers still had to empty her chest of the blood pooling

in it day by day. They confessed that there was nothing they could do to stop the bleeding, but at least they could prevent the blood from suffocating her.

She was weak but woke every evening when he brought food, which was a good sign. Her smile tonight was the greatest sign of life he had seen in three days. She was still there, if feeble, and that was good enough for him.

They drained her chest one more time, but there was less blood. She would take days to recover from the blood loss, but they prayed she would regain her strength over time.

He was not one for gods and prayers, but Dust laid tribute to Pari in thanks for her recovery. He said the prayers to Inac, wishing to see passion return to his beautiful girl. Then he lingered in the waggon of Ocea. He left the largest tribute there, praying her heart would find its way out from the love ensnaring it.

High Guardsman Ranth Prem, commander of the armies of Polthian, was unmarried. He had already had two wives, both dead to childbirth, and his two children were both grown enough to no longer require his attention. He still found time to visit his newly wedded and now-pregnant daughter Mari, and only Mari dared ask him about his work. When she asked about the concerns about their southern border, where a new Rydan village had formed last year, he was only able to say that Prince Polthian had been keeping the Rydans at bay for more years than either of them had seen and probably would continue to do so for many more. But when she asked about the invaders from the north, he admitted Prince Tohmas, the conqueror of Espar, had left Gaidol, easily crossed Nothor, and was now in the Princedom of Polthian.

With Prince Dorakon usurped and the princedom-turned-province controlled by those loyal to Tohmas, Ranth had expected Prince Neillan of Nothor to oppose the army's advancement through his land. But amidst rumors of religious fervor, instead Neillan had personally met King Tohmas on the border and helped him steal the border town of Caritan from Polthian. Reports confirmed Neillan had given the oath flawlessly that afternoon.

Now Polthian and Damoria stood alone.

"Why did we not fight?" Mari asked over dinner, her husband on duty on the walls.

Ranth could understand her worry. Mari herself had been born during one of Ranth's early years as a high guardsman, when the Second Clan Rydans had been invading before Ranth had finally managed to convince them trade worked better than raiding. Ranth had missed Mari's birth because of that war and so missed the death of his wife, and he remembered having the same worries when he held his daughter for the first time. What kind of place was this for a child?

But Mari had survived, as Mari's child would. Times could be challenging, but the Esparans would survive. That was, and always had been, the way of things. Tohmas may have been wearing a different set of skins than the Rydans, but it was the same thing.

He did not have the heart to tell her they had not opposed Tohmas because, officially, they still claimed neutrality. The concept sat poorly with him for two reasons; for one, he didn't think they *should* be trying for neutrality. And for two, it was a lie. Prince Polthian was quietly opposing Tohmas, supporting Damoria as her forces passed through their lands to join Gaidol in attacking the self-declared "king." But so long as their involvement remained secret, Prince Polthian continued claiming they had not taken a side. The loss of the border town made Ranth doubt the ruse was even working, but Prince Polthian was the politician, not Ranth. He controlled the soldiers.

At least in principle he did. Prince Polthian, increasingly jittery, had been steadily taking control away from him.

"Raiders come and go," Ranth told his daughter as they finished their dinner visit. "It has always been that way. He will move on."

Ranth did not believe it, but neither did he think Tohmas could take the capital CloudWater. It had been attacked hundreds of times over the years, and none had breached the towering walls. A siege against CloudWater would take years, time Tohmas did not have. If he lost his momentum, Damoria would move in, and despite the many names on his treaty, Tohmas' forces were increasingly spread thin. He could not match Damoria.

Prince Polthian was satisfied to delay the man with useless communications for now. A delay was in their favor, so he did not plot

grand counterattacks. Instead, Ranth went home, satisfied with the set defenses of his city.

With his family fledged and his wives gone, Ranth lived alone in the Manor of CloudWater. As most of his guardsmen did not even know where his room was in the maze of corridors, it was always surprising to have a visitor. However, having a visitor waiting for him in his room was unprecedented, as was the intruder's identity.

The Rydan did not attempt to hide his knives or bracelets, flaunting his heritage. In the moonlight, for the man had lit no candles, Ranth did not know him at first. But when Carsh chuckled and leaned into the lamplight Ranth carried in, he was easily recognizable.

They had been enemies since Prince Tohmas had made his treaty announcement in Narsol, whether the king had realized it or not. Before that, they had met during the Galanth's march north, and that meeting had been enlightening. They were now enemies, but Ranth respected Carsh and his skills no less.

He had always had a healthy respect for Rydans. While most people dismissed them as uncivilized and crude, Ranth considered them proud survivors of a harsh climate. His dealings with them had been courteous, and he had been well received over the many years. Thanks to his efforts, Prince Polthian traded with the Second Clan often. At Ranth's recommendation, they had sent a messenger into the Outlands to ask for aid from the Second Clan, knowing Tohmas and his Rydan allies were First Clan. They had not heard back yet.

He wondered for a moment if the Rydan knew Prince Polthian's lies. Carsh's loyalty to Tohmas was unmistakable, yet Ranth found his enthusiasm for life inspiring. Most impressively, Carsh had a careless, playful charisma that initially took Ranth off guard but later endeared him to the man. He liked the energy and sincerity of the Rydan. It was refreshing after Esparan politics and dealing with Prince Polthian.

As odd as it was seeing the Rydan in his room after dark, Ranth did not feel threatened. He knew the Rydan's reputation. If the Prime Protector of Galanth wanted to kill him, the younger, lither, faster Rydan would have already done so.

Instead of launching a fated-to-fail assault or calling in the guardsmen outside his room, Ranth laughed and closed the door behind him. "How, by the hells, did you get in here?"

"I climb," Carsh informed him with a gesture to the window, a mere slit in the wall. "I be va goh climbin'."

"Demon shit," Ranth replied. "You are not that skinny," he pointed out, pulling off his coat and putting aside his knife. He had visited his daughter without any weapons on him but knew precisely where his two swords were mounted on the wall. Unfortunately, the prime protector was between him and the weapons. "No one is that skinny," he added. "Drink?"

There was a pitcher of wine beside the bed with several cups. He only ever used one at a time, but having multiple cups meant he always had one without mold to drink from.

The Rydan slung a wineskin off his shoulder and tossed it to Ranth in answer. He knew the contents and chuckled again. He could *still* taste the burn of wildwater from the first time he had tried it, but he did not want to squelch the offer. He found the cups and poured them both a drink. While he sat, not surprisingly, the Rydan remained standing.

"So," Ranth tried pressing the taciturn man, "is this how Tohmas has been pulling this stunt off? Sending you in and taking out the positions of power before the army even shows up? Clever, I admit, but I should have heard someone saying something about assassinations. Dorakon, I heard, was executed, although very few people claim to have seen it. That because it did not happen or because Tohmas wanted to keep it quiet?"

The Rydan tossed one of his knives in the air and simultaneously put away the other. Having only one knife out was another form of compliment, Ranth knew.

"I am not going to kill you," the Rydan said in perfect Esparan. "Dorakon messed up his oath and was executed. Everyone else has been killed in battle or is still alive."

Ranth could hardly believe his ears. "Since when do you speak Esparan, you sly dog! You have had me asking for you to repeat yourself four times in a row when I couldn't make sense of your rambling!"

The Rydan stretched slightly, then sat in the chair opposite Ranth. In a blink, Carsh had both feet on the table and the chair balancing onto two legs.

CHAPTER 14

"I know Esparan as well as Tohmas does," he said. "I don't like using it. But you need to understand, so I will speak properly to you in your language."

There were multiple parts of that statement that Ranth wanted elaborated, but he had to choose the most relevant one. "You want me to turn against Polthian, I take it." He shook his head. "Not going to happen, Prime Protector. I am loyal to the princedom."

The Rydan merely leaned into the shadows and tossed back his cup of wildwater.

"Do you think Prince Polthian is a wise man?" the Rydan asked.

"He's one of the greatest scholars in Espar, so yes. He is very intelligent."

"But do you think him wise? The Rydans to your south readily made themselves known to you, Tohmas declared his intentions in writing, and every ally he has earned has been public. Polthian *knew* you were surrounded and outnumbered, yet he moves against us. Do you think that wise?"

So he knows, Ranth thought. Polthian's ruse could end now. That was a relief. At least everyone knew where they stood.

"My prince has made his decision and follows it through," he said obliquely.

"And now that Gaidol has fallen, Nothor is an ally to us, and Damoria has retreated to their territory, do you think Polthian will surrender?" the Rydan asked with a lop-sided, goading grin.

"No," Ranth replied immediately.

Dropping his feet from the table and leaning forward, Carsh let the moonlight silhouette him. "Do you think he should?"

That was the crux of the matter. Polthian, the man and the princedom, were going to fight Tohmas, to their demise. There was still hope. Was it worth laying down one's life over?

As Ranth hesitated, the Rydan grinned further. "Would you surrender CloudWater?"

Hearing the challenge bluntly brought Ranth's loyalty to the forefront once more. "Would you surrender, Prime Protector?" he answered. "If you were surrounded and outnumbered, would you give in?"

Having the question turned on him made Carsh sit straighter. He considered his reply, giving Ranth hope that the response would be honest. "My home is my clan. I do not surrender my clan."

"Of course not!" Ranth answered. "And Polthian, by my oath, is my clan. You would not betray your father," he pressed, remembering the social importance of the family in Rydan society, "and I will not betray my prince."

Perhaps Carsh was finally finding the strange language a little much; he took longer. Ranth held hope that they might reach an understanding. He could not begin to guess what that would mean in the fighting to come.

At length, the Rydan said, "I would not betray my father or my clan, but if my chief were a fool, I would seek to replace him."

That was how the Outlands worked. The chief held power so long as he was the strongest. If his influence waned, another took his place.

It had not been, Ranth saw, the idea of loyalty that Carsh had taken time to understand, but the process of applying his values to an Esparan.

Proving he had come to understand Esparans, Carsh added, "You gave your word to Prince Polthian, but that was when war was not at hand. Your prince is not fit to run a war. He is a foolish man if he thinks he can stop us. He is not leading well."

"Not leading well" was an insult. A man who could not be a decent leader would never have his name glorified. Power, to them, was about earning Followers and working a network. Alone, no Rydan lasted long, fortifying their notions of family and clan.

And it's true, Ranth finally admitted to himself. Prince Polthian had become obsessed with the war against Tohmas since Ranth had passed him the treaty from Narsol. Most of the talk revolved around attacking Tohmas, not necessarily the army.

But Ranth's oath was still there, nagging him, and he knew he could not take the action the Rydan expected.

"We still have hope," Ranth said.

"I had forgotten. Yes, you sent me a message. I also came to respond to that."

Ranth's heart dropped. There had been a message, but not to Carsh. He'd sent it to Second Clan, the traditional enemy of the First Clan that was allied to Tohmas.

"We sent you no message," Ranth corrected.

Carsh, still unconcerned, stood as if to stretch stiff muscles. Ranth had to wonder how often the man sat down for any length of time. Was he sore already?

"You sent a message south," Carsh said. "You asked for Rydan aid against Tohmas."

"That was not sent to—"

"I am the second son of the chief of the Outlands. All dealings, or 'foreign affairs' as you call them, are my responsibility. So, I am here."

"We sent a call to the Second Clan. That you intercepted the messenger is—"

"Second Clan," Carsh candidly explained, "was slaughtered several years ago by the first son of the chief of the Outlands, whose duty it is to defend and extend the power and land of the chief. There is no Second Clan for you to call upon, nor any Third Clan either. Only the First remains."

Unable to find his voice, Ranth sat dumbfounded.

"In other words," Carsh finished eloquently, "I fear I must decline your request. None in the Outlands will aid you."

The moon chose that moment to move behind the clouds, and the room darkened. Ranth felt the effect on his heart more than his sight. When he jumped, he jostled the lamp and it went out.

"I will still not turn on him, Prime Protector," Ranth forced himself to say as he fumbled for the light, trying to remember where he had put the flint and wishing he had thought to light the fireplace. "If you want to kill me for it, then so be it. I will—"

"I am not going to kill you," Carsh said from a place by the gloomy window, "for you are the only person in CloudWater we can count on to do the right thing. Your chief is weak and must be replaced before he makes your land weak as well. Only you can do this."

By the time the light of the moon returned, the Rydan had gone and left Ranth with a room full of thoughts. He shakily relit the lamp, then the fire.

He chased away every thought that wondered if the Rydan was right and replaced them with the words of the oath he had made over three decades prior. It had been a different world, he had to admit, but that did not invalidate his words. He had to believe it.

Despite the attempts to convince himself, he hardly slept. What snippets he managed to grab were filled with visions of the future he was making for his daughter's unborn child. With Prince Polthian leading them, the only future he saw was sword and fire.

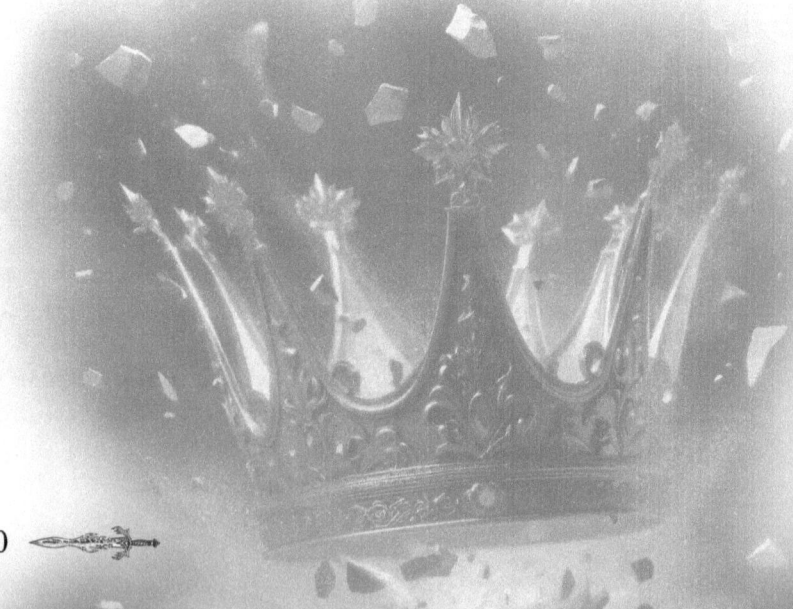

Chapter 15

The camp settled outside CloudWater, the conversation strained. Carsh returned, giving cautious reports that they had a likely ally within. Sure enough, their forces met little resistance, and one supporter on the wall helped leave an open gate. But once they reached the streets, it became apparent why: the city had already been emptied. They located High Guardsman Prem in a cell within the manor.

Polthian had known of the imminent insurrection. He'd marched his forces and war machines out, avoiding a panic by claiming it was to defend them against the invaders. Instead, the army's trail led west sharply.

"Polthian's forces are heading to join Damoria," Sol declared as they took their place around the table. He'd stepped in to ask the high guardsman for more information, now able to relay the findings. Rumors were already circulating. Their unopposed arrival caused a panic almost as effective as a formalized defense as people clumsily attacked or fled when they saw the invaders, causing chaos.

Barnon had been left in CloudWater to sort it out with Lance and Talbit. "The city is split for loyalties," he reported. "They will not be easy to organize. It's safe enough; there aren't any trouble we can't handle, but they don't even have a local militia left or peacekeeper. We're dealing with more thieves and thugs than soldiers. I prefer soldiers."

Tohmas digested the information. "Even if we get Ranth Prem in place, he doesn't have the support of the population. And he doesn't have the forces to keep them cowed."

Ironic that a surrendered city could be more of a strain to his forces than a contended one, Tohmas mused. He hated how much he had to devote to settling the city and the province now that it was without its prince.

Feeling he had no choice, he assigned Lour's fyrd to CloudWater. It left nearly twelve hundred soldiers behind as the rest headed into what Tohmas expected to be the final battle to claim Espar: Damoria on the border of Galanth. But if Polthian's army joined with Damoria now, he would sorely miss those twelve-hundred soldiers.

He still had the Rydans to assist, those helping the Galanth hold Damoria at bay. His soldiers were matched, if not outnumbered. Although he had faith in their skills, he needed to improve his odds.

"We will commandeer soldiers from Forsinth as he pass through," Tohmas decided. "That will make up the difference."

Kingsman Talbit shifted noisily in his seat, drawing the eyes of the table onto him. He pushed his glasses up and seemed to check that no one else would speak before caving and saying, "We must be careful. The season grows late. The men will be needed for harvest. We cannot have our people starving over winter."

It was an annoyingly true statement. Tohmas' campaign had been delayed time and time again. With summer ending, it was still warm, but the crops needed harvesting soon, and winter was not far. Rydans had a history of fighting whenever they needed, but the Esparans would want to move indoors when the cold came. There were also many more of them; they needed to be home for the harvest, or winter would see them starve.

Before Tohmas could address the issue, Protector Golnan loudly cleared his throat from the entrance. Tohmas made a note to have Carsh remind the new protector about protocols to help avoid him running afoul of the kingsmen.

Showing no remorse, Golnan flatly said, "Some big Rydan wants to talk to you. Might get messy if we say no. Want me to toss him out?" His Lourite accent was particularly thick this evening.

CHAPTER 15

"As entertaining as that might be to see you try," Tohmas replied, "no. Please let him in."

Expecting to see Burlotak representing the Rydans with Tohmas' forces, Tohmas was shocked to see Chief Tamv, the head of all the Outlands, stride in.

Tohmas shot to his feet. "Out," Tohmas commanded. "All of you, out. Protectors too." When had Tamv arrived?

Most of the kingsmen calmly gathered their things and filed out, but Sol hesitated. "You all right?" he asked.

There was no denying the chief was an imposing sight. Just as SoulBurner was always within Tohmas' reach, the chief had his two *hooknyes* on hand. He was not a knife dancer like his youngest son, but Tohmas knew where Carsh's aptitude with the blades had originated. The red-stained grass bracelets around Tamv's wrists were mostly bones, as the chief had more Followers than any other in all the Outlands. Additional knucklebones hung from both his *hooknyes* and a series of necklaces that lay over the intricate tattoo of a small dragon clinging to his chest.

From an Esparan point of view, Tamv looked the part of a legendary monster.

"Fine, Sol," Tohmas said, his words loosening the knot in his throat. "I just know he will not want people listening in."

Nodding, the Kingsman of Solta followed the others out. Only Carsh remained, his constant companion. But with a gesture of his head, the chief sent Carsh out. There was no hesitation; once Carsh recognized the order, he left at a brisk walk without looking back. He would not go far, Tohmas knew. They always eavesdropped on any meeting between the chief and the other and had since they were children. What one son of Tamv knew, the other knew.

Rather abruptly, Tohmas wondered if Tamv was aware of that minor disobedience.

Once alone, Tohmas came out from the table and dropped into a ready position, kneeling with one leg bent and the other knee not quite touching the ground, not unlike Lance at his oath-giving. As he took the position of obedience and willingness to act, his fist went to his shoulder to identify Tamv's title.

That's something else the chief doesn't know, Tohmas considered. The Pack Runner had marked another as the Shoulder, which traditionally superseded the previous one. Only Carsh, Sabian, and Tohmas had seen it happen, and as far as Tohmas knew, Sabian still did not understand the meaning of the scar on his shoulder, which was for the best. In the eyes of the Pack Runner, however, Tohmas' salute was no longer valid. The Shoulder had been replaced.

After a long enough pause, Chief Tamv strode past Tohmas.

"Relax," he said in Rydan, making a dismissive wave toward Tohmas but giving him leave to stand.

Tohmas quickly pulled a seat away from the table to best mimic the *traon*—the throne seat—the chief would typically sit on. Tamv took the seat imperiously, sitting straight and resting his hands on his knees. Although sitting across from his father was tempting, Tohmas lowered himself into a crouch on the ground instead of taking another chair. Tamv's seat was not elevated, and sitting at the chief's level would imply equality that would be both offensive and wrong.

"You are doing well," the chief said as Tohmas took his place at his father's feet. "I am pleased."

Compliments from the chief were unexpected. Tohmas' ego soared. He brought his fist to his shoulder again in gratitude.

"Where do we stand?"

They had discussed plans for Espar last winter. He'd not expected the chief to need more information, but he did not hesitate to recite, "Gaidol, Nothor, and Trulin are ours, controlled by kingsmen loyal to me. Polthian is ours, but the prince emptied it and joined our enemies. Our path is to Damoria."

Faint optimism snuck into Tohmas. The chief thought the situation on the border to Damoria secure enough to travel away from the frontlines. That boded well.

"We can take Damoria at any time," Tamv said, making Tohmas' hope swell. "Prince Wevan is within our reach."

"Then we will have it all by the end of the mooncycle," Tohmas answered. He had many questions but knew better than to voice them. It would be obvious in time, he was sure. And how it was done mattered little. The important thing was that it was happening. He could

take Damoria despite his weakened army. All of Espar would be his to give to Tamv.

But if Damoria were as ripe as Polthian, he would have it all before autumn. That resolved the issue about harvest for the Esparans.

"What has become of the Pack Runner, Tohmas?" Tamv interrupted Tohmas' thoughts to ask. "He has not been seen lately."

"He was wounded outside of LandWater," Tohmas replied. "Laorn says he lives but has been nursing his wounds." It had been seven quartercycles since the Pack Runner had returned grievously wounded and missing two hounds. They still occasionally heard of kills made in the area, but no one had seen either the Pack Runner or his mate since Tohmas had accepted Laorn's child from her.

"And what became of their newest child?"

Tamv still had an interest in Laorn as leverage over a minor rival, Tohmas assumed. He could think of no other reason the chief cared what became of her.

"She carried it to term" was all Tohmas said initially. More was needed, but he had to decide which lie to use. Part of him was shocked he was considering lying to his father, but he knew the truth would not suffice.

"Boy or girl?"

He could say the child had died and leave it at that, but it was possible the chief already knew Laorn had come to him. She would have no reason to report her child's death. But she would have brought him the child if it had been a girl.

"Girl," Tohmas lied. "I gave it to one of my Followers to raise." Despite Laorn's current life with the Pack Runner, she was of a good family, and the offspring of the Pack Runner were highly regarded. It made sense for Tohmas to have offered the girl child to someone he trusted.

"Who?"

Tohmas was surprised by the question, especially as he had said the child was a girl, but he had no problem providing the answer. Thankfully, baby Degan, the true boy-child of the Pack Runner, had a sister identical in age.

"Darknim DoomDragon."

The double name made Tamv raise a half-shorn eyebrow. "An Esparan."

"A Northlander," Tohmas corrected. "Leader of the Northlanders, Elder of the Circle of the Raven, and Kingsman of Meloch in the north. A good, strong man. He had a son around the same time and has many wet mothers for the children. Layla has grown well. I am certain you could see her whenever you wished."

Would Laorn have told Tamv otherwise?

The chief seemed pensive for a moment—the way his eyes narrowed betrayed it—then pressed on.

"You have many Esparan Followers now. You think highly of them."

"I think highly of *some* of them," Tohmas confessed and corrected in one. He did not hear disapproval in his father's voice, which was another relief. Thus far, his Esparan Followers had done well in the eyes of the Rydans. The chief would know as much by now from Burlotak.

"You even took one as a wife," the chief finished. This time, disapproval was evident.

Unable to deny the fact, Tohmas lowered his head and did not move, not even when the chief stood and struck the back of his head.

"You did not tell me! You did not ask! An Esparan woman! I am insulted."

Knowing defending himself now would only infuriate his father further, Tohmas moved into an obedient waiting position and held it in silence until he was asked directly, "Who is she to be worthy of my family?"

"She is Arnika," Tohmas answered, avoiding her last name to make her sound a little less Esparan. "She was daughter to the greatest of the Esparan leaders and sister to their greatest warrior, whose head my Followers presented to me in honor. Both men of her family are dead by my hand."

Taking Trulin, when told in that manner, sounded Rydan. Although the chief circled him once more, he then retook his seat. To Tohmas, that meant endorsement. He slowly released a nervous sigh and added, "She is a strong woman."

The chief snorted. "You, like your brother, have always liked the spirited ones."

Arnika was nothing like Darcina, but Tohmas still nodded.

"They say she is small," the chief pressed. Tohmas nodded again. "Then it will not last. When she bears you a child, she will die with it."

Tohmas' stomach tightened. The chief would try to make his prediction come true; Tohmas had seen that strategy before. But Tohmas could not allow anyone to harm his wife.

"I will test her," the chief decided with a firm nod. "If she is as spirited as you think, she will survive and be free to return to you. As I doubt she will live through birthing, that will suffice."

Tohmas' breath stuck in his throat like sap, his heart frozen within his chest.

"You would test her?" he stammered with more hesitation than he ever wanted to show to the Chief of the Outlands. "She is Esparan!"

Would she survive an encounter with Tamv? Physically, perhaps, but her spirit would not. That was what Tamv expected of a wife, but it was not what Tohmas wanted. He loved the shy, occasionally assertive woman he had married. If she was going to change, he wanted her to become stronger, not meeker. A night with Tamv would break her heart.

"You said she was worthy of notice. I thought ill of Darcina before, and she tested true. She pleases Carsh. I think ill of your choice, Tohmas. I will test her, and we will see."

Tohmas' heart restarted at a steadily increasing rate but without panic. He had known little fear in his adult life—Rydans had no patience for it—but he had not forgotten the feeling. He felt as if he stood, the Second Clan at his heels and the Third Clan camped before him, staring down at the battlefield of dead, knowing he had to go forward to free the capital from the Third Clan killers. A great battle awaited him, an unavoidable battle he was not confident he could win.

But as he considered the chief's words, the fear changed. Arnika was in no danger. Tohmas would not let Tamv take her. That certainty shook Tohmas to his core.

His heart was Rydan, but even that Rydan heart had fallen for the little woman who had accepted his offer of marriage to save her homeland. A Rydan who betrayed his father could never be expected to be loyal to anything. If Tohmas disobeyed Tamv...

When a horn sounded over the camp, Tohmas jumped up. It was an alarm call, not a military one. There was a fire. If someone was sounding the horn, it had to be significant.

"Fire," Tohmas translated for the chief. The voices of his protectors reached his ears.

A green-roped man appeared through his door in the next blink. "Fire in the corrals," the protector reported. "People are saying sabotage."

"I must call Schlavarai," Tohmas said. As the protector was already gone, Tohmas saluted the Shoulder formally.

He knew Tamv's dismissive gesture was a bad sign, but he did not care. Freed from the decision he did not dare make, he left searching for his horse and a saboteur among his forces.

Carsh was not waiting outside as he left.

Gannon was the first to wake, meaning no other Circle members heard his shriek as he sat bolt upright. The morning light seeped through the opened ceiling, casting grey shadows over their dim carven hall, a new abode that hid them from the Tainted. It was cold in the room despite the enchanted ground. He touched the stone below him, finding all the heating spells had left them.

One by one, the other Circle members woke, each startling awake. Fantorn and Minet both screamed. Tranvin rolled right out of his bed. His bandaged arm crashed into the stone, and he cried out as the pain hit.

Like their first cavern, the new hiding place had been massively enchanted to protect the occupants from divination, including Scrys. To Gannon's disappointment, the defenses had failed. They had been attacked while they slept.

Visions, terrible visions, had assaulted them. Gannon was conscious enough to begin casting to track the assailants, but he paused mid-spell in confusion. His spells were missing. It would have obviously been necessary to bypass his thought magic defenses to force the visions into his mind as he slept, but he was surprised to find every single protection, regardless of element or domain, gone.

The others also struggled, stumbling as they tried to use spells or enchantments that no longer existed around them.

Proving him right, Minet voiced it: "I am dispelled!"

The others had not wasted their time with dismay but cast defenses immediately as Gannon did. But as time passed and no further attacks

manifested, they each confirmed their lack of bound spells. Once they had placed enough spells to secure the area and themselves, the Circle slowly came to their feet, one by one.

Gannon's searching revealed nothing. There was no hint of mind magic left in his or any of the Circle members' minds. The attacker had left no trace.

He turned to Minet. "I can find no sign of thought magic. What does your divination show?"

She was flustered, and it frustrated him to see it. *Was I ever so slow?* he wondered. To be fair to Minet, Gannon's arrival to the Watching Circle had been at a time of nothing but watching. Now was a time of action, and she could not keep up.

Obediently, she searched, but her divinations failed.

Nothing to find or is she being blocked? There was no doubt in Gannon's mind that the Northlander diviner was better than Minet. He could have intercepted her.

Gannon went to join Fantorn in resetting more defenses, but memories started creeping in as he moved. He'd not just seen things; he'd felt something too. He drew back his sleeves to search for the talon marks of the hawk that had attacked him. He had seen Fantorn's eyes pecked out by a crow in his vision, but seeing her now made it clear her sight was fine.

But he could still feel where the hawk had struck vividly, and the way Fantorn put her hand to her face made him wonder if she had seen the same as he had. Were these shared visions? That was complicated, even for their mind elder and her owl Aspect. But if mind magic had been involved, why could he find no trace of it?

However, they all knew one thing with certainty: they did not want to go back to sleep.

The replacements were coming, but adding so many young members would weaken the Watching Circle. Gannon was not keen to set the new members against the Northlander Circle, expecting them to die as their predecessors had. Although he had been considered the adolescent of the Circle recently, Gannon had suddenly become one of its veterans and so was included when Rean called aside Tranvin and Fantorn with him to discuss the situation.

"We need to track them down!" Fantorn insisted. She winced and touched her forehead, her gem-stoned knuckles glittering with the movement. They were tinged in gold.

"If we don't know where all of them are, we can't be sure the one we find is truly alone!" Tranvin replied. He was jumpy, checking over his shoulder repeatedly and adjusting the tussled ribbons on his robe like a new graduate. He'd helped Yonny capture Tril initially, but since Yonny's death, he seemed to think the Northlander divination seat was right behind him at every turn. It made some sense; despite all their efforts, they had failed to locate Tril in any Scry. Occasionally, they found the others, particularly the imposing DoomDragon. They located Kitable, hoping to see the Northlander visit, but all they saw was a series of rude gestures from Kitable, who seemed to know they were watching.

"We just need one," Fantorn reminded them.

"Yet the more we watch, the less likely it becomes that we will get that one," Gannon pointed out. The owl and firedrake had proven themselves strong enough to defend themselves, the horse had kicked hard enough to make Fantorn reluctant to go after her, the walrus had matched Gilan's fire to Gilan's demise, the fox kept sneaking in and out of their sights, and the crow was too fast to follow, let alone catch. The weakest member still seemed to be the wolf, but they could never find him. Minet's best divinations were still revealing gibberish. "We need to use others from this world. We cannot confront them directly and hope to overpower them, but this world is already divided. If we aid their enemies..."

Rean sat back and shook her head. "We dare not spend another night here. We return to Wanter."

"We are giving up?" Gannon heard himself question. "But they are still—"

Rean frowned, deepening the many wrinkles over her eyes. "Their leader will die soon. They have someone to lead in her place but no one to complete the Circle. We will wait until that time. We are no match for them right now."

Looking relieved, the Watching Circle took their turns walking through the portal.

Gannon crossed his arms and stood by. "I will not let them get away with what they have done." Nodding to add certainty to his decision,

he said, "I think I have a way to disrupt them without coming into direct contact."

Rean shrugged and followed the others through the portal. There was nothing she could have said to convince him otherwise, and she must have known it.

He was going to have his revenge on Kitable. He would succeed where the others had failed.

Tril sat back from the Circle, glad for the wall behind him. The rest of the Circle elders smiled, but Ela rose swiftly to assist Tril as he flopped backward. He was only half awake when she reached his side, but he knew she was there and tried to grin at her. It had worked. He had protected the Circle. The *visaln* showed him the results of their efforts; the Watching Circle was leaving.

In the haze of visions, he saw their eventual return and the hatred they carried with them when they did. There was only one pleasant thought among those visions, where Kitable knocked the thought master Gannon off his feet with a punch.

Knowing he was tumbling into visions despite his wolf's efforts, Tril rattled off the words to the spell to block the images. It was time for a rest. He could not take any more visions now.

To his terror, the shield failed.

It had been too much. In his plotting to save Kitable and drive the Wanter Circle from his world, Tril had neglected himself. With every snippet of mental power he possessed, he had been driving his *visaln* to plan the attack. He had taught the Circle how to enter the golden untouchable world through their Aspects and shown them how to manipulate the enemy's dreams. Nightmares of every description had been their weapons, a vicious strike for a race unaccustomed to dreams.

Coordinating the efforts and passing on his powers to the others to guide them had finally sapped Tril of his last energy. Now that the danger passed and would not return in his lifetime, he was spent.

Ela knew. While the others celebrated the victory, she knelt beside him and placed a concerned hand on his brow. He shivered and could not stop.

He knew she would die within the year and never be replaced. This act, his *visaln* told him, had been the last the Northlander Circle would ever accomplish. Their legacy was over. It broke his heart.

The visions came in torrents now, and he slipped along the black of the empty place, drawn toward the spiral of light. The gap was waiting for him, but the wolf would not let him fall. Together, they retreated to the golden world where the visions could not follow.

The threat of visions waiting to jump him should he set foot outside the golden world lingered no matter where he went. There was, to Tril, a dragon on the doorstep, and he could not get past it. He was dreaming and could not wake.

Chapter 16

The fires burned out overnight, leaving little damage but plenty of confusion. The only clue they found was a report of a Rydan being seen in the area before the arson. As Burolotak's fighters tended to steer clear of Esparan camp and had no interest in the Esparan horses, it was suspicious.

Tohmas left the investigation to others, swiftly heading back to his tent and summoning Kitable. Unsurprisingly, Arnika met him, eager to hear news of Polthian's withdrawal and the plans for the ongoing march.

Tohmas waded in and started collecting her belongings. As soon as Kitable appeared, Tohmas said, "I need you to take her to Wayburn and keep her there."

"But I am to travel with you!" Arnika protested before Kitable could reply.

"It is not safe where we are going," he replied as firmly as he could to her hurt expression.

Hands on her hips, she answered, "I know Gaidol got close, Tohmas, but we survived that, and you know the protectors have doubled their watches. No one will get so close again!"

"I know," he conceded, "but there is still danger." Despite Kitable watching with mouth agape, Tohmas admitted, "I could not stand to lose you."

"You are afraid," she stated with a pout, seeing through his haste. "You have ridden full speed into the middle of a thousand enemies

without hesitation, and now, when the danger is almost past, you fear? Why?"

His heart ached to see her anger, but he could not tell her. "There are things—"

She tossed her hands in the air and turned from him. "After all your nonsense about getting your kingsmen to trust me, now I find it is *you* who does not trust me!"

He caught her in his arms and pulled her against him with unsteady hands. Sniffling, she buried her face against his chest and whispered, "You said I would go with you." Her eyes brimmed with tears.

Her heart beating against his chest, his mouth went dry. That she wanted to come with him made him elated, but the thought of seeing her taken by the red-grassed hands took the breath from his lungs. Could he refuse his father and chief?

He did not have the answer. Avoiding the question was his best hope.

"There are things even I cannot defend you from, my love. I beg you, go with Kitable."

She pulled away from him gently with her tears still falling, but she pressed her lips together and looked over at their audience, Kitable still silently watching. There was a chill to her voice when she curtsied, bowed her head, and said, "As you command, my king."

It broke his heart further. Words left him. She couldn't know why he did this, and neither could Kitable.

Kitable cleared his throat and, bowing politely, ushered her out. The wizard's brow furrowed low.

"Please stay with her and protect her," Tohmas said.

Kitable nodded stiffly, looking awkward at what he had witnessed. "The affairs of magic appear to have ended in this conflict," he said formally. "The Northlander elders have chased off our enemy wizard. But if you need me, call for me, my king. I will be listening from Wayburn." He pivoted, leaving the tent briskly to chase the young woman who had stormed out. He'd already been about to head for Wayburn to take Elder Tril to healers there; this would be no change to his plans. It seemed Wayburn was to be a sanctuary for them both.

The march through Forsinth was lonely. With Lour's forces left to stabilize the newest province, the forces grew thinner than Tohmas liked. But Kingsman Deiton surprised Tohmas by becoming a gracious

host. Despite Deiton's uncertain relationship with the sons of Zayban, Deiton hosted all the kingsmen with a smile, and they moved on without mentioning Deiton's courtship of Arnika before her marriage to Tohmas. Not having Arnika present was for the best, Tohmas tried to convince himself. There appeared to be no hard feelings; Deiton did not hesitate to pledge soldiers and then offered to come himself into battle against Damoria as a final sign of his support.

Their march to Galanth was filled with excitement from border to border. As much as he was tempted to visit the capital and his wife, who was now setting up home in the manor, Tohmas led the forces around Wayburn. The chief still traveled with Burotak's Rydans.

Tohmas caught news of the Weavers breaking off from the forces and heading to Wayburn, and he could not blame them. Now on home ground, Fixer City was thinning rapidly. It was clear that, whatever the outcome, the war for Espar would end on the border to Damoria. Tohmas sent the rest of Arnika's ladies along with them to keep his wife company.

If the chief's promise were fulfilled, Damoria would fall. But if he took Damoria, he no longer had any excuse to keep Arnika hidden.

Gannon stood, visible yet unnoticed, in the corridor of the Manor of SwordWood outside a dungeon door. He kept an aura of insignificance around himself, not concerned if people saw him so long as they didn't care about his presence. It was more effective than trying to manipulate light and hide himself directly and far easier for a thought master.

He was aware of the armies marching around the world but had moved his attention to this cell, this place. With no experience with battles on a large scale, Gannon needed someone more knowledgeable in the mundane and barbaric. Nowhere on Wanter utilized combat anymore. He couldn't remember ever seeing a sword except in history books. What was the point of a weapon when a word could end any battle?

The guards in the corridor had changed over twice since he had been standing there, too irrelevant to be questioned. When a servant appeared down the hall bearing food, Gannon moved into the man's shadow. Manipulating the servant's thoughts was simple enough. The

servant handed him the food and walked back the way he had come without a word. Adjusting the guard's thoughts, Gannon made himself look like the servant. The guard opened the door for the food.

Once the gap was wide enough for him, Gannon applied a Loop spell to the guard, wrapping the man's thoughts into the same pattern. The stiff-backed guard froze, trapped at the moment when he held the door for the food plate to be placed within.

Gannon passed into the cell this time. Once in the shadows of the dimly lit room, he dropped the Indifference Shield.

The man in the corner jumped up as a cantrip had gone off under him. Eyes wide over his overgrown beard and mustache, he spat, "Where did you come from?"

Conveniently, the language was Shantanese, and Gannon did not need to waste any energy translating. He also did not require spells to make the man do what he wanted; their goals matched.

"You would not believe me if I told you," Gannon replied. He watched the prisoner's eyes narrow as the man tried to place the accent. It was strange, but he had discovered this world consistently judged accents. In Wanter, languages differentiated the peoples, not mild differences in inflections or word choices. Here, some claimed they could narrow down a person's upbringing to a hamlet by their speech. Of course, with his Shantanese accent, he baffled those people.

"Well, then what do you want?" the man demanded. His once-fine clothes had not changed in the dozens of days since he had stood before a crowd and fumbled his words, earning himself a death sentence. He reeked of sweat and dirt, reduced to sitting on the floor in the small cell. On the poor rations, his strength was failing; Dorakon Lodaton was not as impressive as he had once been, but Gannon thought he looked pretty good for a dead man.

"We have a common enemy," Gannon said. "You sent an animal to the south with a message, rallying others against Tohmas Galanth."

"An... an animal?" Dorakon said softly, his face screwed up with confusion.

"A flying one," Gannon confirmed matter of fact. "I could recite the message you put on the creature's leg, but you know what it said. You will be pleased to know that the recipient of the message immediately allied with Damoria, and that Forsinth will wait for an opportunity to

join. They are all three now setting up to fight, but Forsinth, that man called Deiton, has not declared himself yet Tohmas' enemy. In fact, it seems King Tohmas considers Deiton family still." As a show of good faith, he handed the ex-prince the food tray. It was some kind of gruel that smelled like swamp water to Gannon. Dorakon took it without looking down. He stared at Gannon expectantly.

"Divided, you cannot oppose Tohmas. With me uniting, you can."

"Why?" The word was accusatory.

"Because I need the Northalnder Circle gone," Gannon admitted readily. There was a certain degree of freedom in knowing he could remove any given thought from someone if he happened to say something he didn't want them to remember. He could repeat the conversation if he had to later, if it didn't go the way he wanted. But there was no reason to hide his motives; they complemented those of this coalition. "It's simple," Gannon continued. "Tohmas Galanth is allied with Northlanders and the Circle of the Raven. I want that Circle broken. The best way for me to do that is to have you kill them all. To do that, you have to win against Tohmas. All the better if this alliance falls apart along the way. You want to reclaim your lands, maybe expand them. And you want your daughter back. I will assist you to achieve your goals if you aid me in mine."

Finally, Dorakon's stare released to look Gannon over from head to toe. Gannon figured he did not look too out of place in the basic garb of a Tainted man. He was not wearing his focus gem and while he blended in better, it had the disadvantage of making him look less impressive.

"And what do you bring to this alliance?" Dorakon asked in a croaking voice.

Gannon smirked. "I've already convinced the entire city that you are dead, Prince Dorakon of Gaidol. Most of them believe they saw your execution, in fact. I am standing here, in a cell, unopposed. Think of everything else I can do."

Dorakon raised a bushy eyebrow. "Wizard?"

"The best," Gannon confirmed.

"Better than Kitable?"

Gannon's smile grew. "I intend to prove that. For now, my priority is getting a sizeable force opposing the Northlanders. You did well, but none of the Circle elders died in your attack. My discussions with the

others will go better if you can introduce me, Prince Dorakon." He hoped it sounded adequately subservient. He wasn't used to telling anyone he wanted their assistance.

But Dorakon seemed appeased. He nodded, his head bobbing like a market toy. "Is there better food where we are going?" he asked.

"Even if there wasn't, I can make gruel taste like a four-course meal," Gannon said. He swept his arm behind him. "Shall we?"

Dorakon eyed the guard, who still stood mid-motion, hand on the door in readiness to close it.

"He won't move until I release him," Gannon explained.

Tossing the tray over his shoulder, Dorakon marched out passed the guard boldly. Once he and Gannon were at the far end of the corridor, Gannon released the Loop spell, and the man calmly closed the door and locked it, then retook his post.

Gannon felt Dorakon's eyes on him as they left the corridor, suspicion filling his stare. Opening a portal before the man probably did nothing to assuage his concerns.

"This leads to Wayburn. We have business there."

"Tohmas' capital?" Dorakon asked, aghast. "Just like that, you're halfway across the world?"

Gannon shrugged. "No, just like that, we are many strides away, but not across the world. You idiots have no idea how big your world is. Now, come on. The longer I hold it, the harder it is to keep Kitable from noticing!"

They stepped through.

When he emerged from his tent, Sabian felt as though the entire weight of the rising sun sat on his head. Memories of the night were blurred; the only thing he was sure of was that he had enjoyed it. The Rydans had worked their way across Damoria and joined the border defenses with Chief Tamv's main forces, spurring a grand celebration of victory. Reintegration had led to a few altercations, especially as the returning raiding Rydans ran into the Esparan forces working on this side of the Black Marsh. Sabian prided himself on keeping the peace between the

two sides. His association with Carsh helped; the Followers of Tamv's second son came running if anyone threatened Sabian.

But if there was a way to drink that much wildwater and not get profoundly hungover, Sabian did not know it.

A Rydan woman met him at his fire, offering a cup of something steaming.

He refused it, and she lowered it into her lap.

"You are slower when you are hungover," she said with a shrug. "Do not think the others cannot tell."

Sabian did not know her name or whose wife she was, but she seemed to be bold for any rank. His hackles rose.

"Do not—"

"That was an observation," she interrupted, her smile easy and unconcerned, "not a threat or insult. And you are far too sensitive, but I suppose, being Esparan among Rydans, you have to be." She extended the cup again. "I am not poisoning you. Had I wanted to harm you, you would be dead, or do you not remember last night?"

Flashes of the night before passed through his mind. He could not help but smile. For one so small, she was surprisingly creative. He warmed.

Seeing she was still offering the drink, he accepted it and sat down.

"I am Sori," she introduced.

"Sabian," he answered. The mug, filled to the brim, smelled sweet, but it burned the entire length of his throat as he swallowed it.

Knowingly, Sori handed him a wineskin of water.

He assumed he had not erred in taking her, but he did not know who Sori was within the ranks of the First Clan. If he had offended someone, he needed to know.

"Whose wife are you?"

She laughed like a songbird's call for a mate. "Not a wife," she answered when she saw he did not understand her mirth.

"Then how are you ... here?" Rydan women did not leave the Outlands unless in the company of their husbands on a campaign. Only wives were found in the camps.

"I have nowhere else to be. Forgive me; I thought you knew. I am Second Clan." She had retrieved a purse from her bag and took to sewing up a tear as she answered.

"Second Clan is dead."

"I am not dead." She said it simply as if it was the most obvious thing in the world, and he was a child asking silly questions. Her expression was one of amusement when she looked at him.

He could not find a reply. The Second Clan had died after attacking the First Clan, but Sori did not seem to be a threat. He could not decide if he had a responsibility to First Clan to kill her. He did not want to.

The water and the drink seemed to clear his head, and he finally remembered her.

"I recognize you. You were with Lance."

Sori looked up from her stitching and smiled again. "He never wanted me, treated me like a daughter." She shrugged, but her smile did not fade. "I am alone now, like you."

"Me?" Sabian replied. "I am a Follower of Carsh. I am never alone."

Her hands paused, and her expression fell slightly. "A Follower?" she echoed. "You? An Esparan?"

"You did not know?"

She shook her head, dropped her stitching into her sac, then stood and threw the bag over her shoulder in a single action.

"You don't live with the First Clan," he realized, standing to match her. "You didn't even know—"

"I should go."

"What did you expect of me if you didn't know my rank?" he demanded, catching her arm as she stepped away. For the first time—a testament to how hungover he was—he noticed that she carried three blades openly instead of a woman's single *shanye*. Her clothes were also beaded differently. He was ashamed he had not recognized her as not being First Clan.

"What did you expect of *me*?" she replied. "You did not know my rank either, did you?"

He dropped his hand, letting her leave, but she went only two steps before pausing.

"Two parts hellweed and one part miracle flower," she said over her shoulder. "Boil it until it lightens. Clears the mind and encourages you to drink the water that will cure your hangover."

Before he could find words, she vanished among the other tents. Not surprisingly, she headed away from the Rydan camp.

He sat back down on the stone and finished the drink. He then finished most of the water.

It didn't make sense. Sori had expected to gain nothing from her association with him. She had not known his rank and assumed he held none.

I have to find out what she wanted from me!

The golden light his prison, Tril was trapped. Exploring lead him into the dreams of others, but leaving the Dreamworld brought on a torrent of visions. He heard the echoes of the elders' concerns through his half-consciousness. He was barely able to swallow water without choking. He could not focus long enough to eat. His body weakened.

Dreams moved at a pace all their own, and Tril had candles upon candles of time to spend in the golden light in his half-wolf form, a white wolf at his heel for company. As he wandered the gold, searching for another way out, he discovered he was not alone.

He had already met many of the dreamers, although he doubted any of them would remember him after they woke, but seeing a person stand in the golden light itself without a dream around them ... was different. The woman was slight, as short as Tril's son, but had an air of non-Esparan about her. Unlike the darkest shade of blond Tril had ever seen, the stranger's long hair was the color of fir bark. She wore a tunic of white that reached her ankles, tied at the waist with a cloth belt.

Like the Wanter Circle he had so recently repelled, the woman had a mark at the center of her forehead, but the symbol was a circle with four spokes, not a gem.

Tril immediately missed his visions. He had not seen this stranger in any prophecies. He did not even know if the woman was a friend or foe. As much as the visions had overwhelmed him, they still had allowed him to understand the world better than most. Tril felt blind.

"Wandering one," the woman said in a language Tril did not know, yet understood, "what are you seeking?"

This was not a dreamer. Like him, the stranger was a visitor to the Dreamworld.

"I seek a way to control my visions," he answered in Northlander, feeling confident that the stranger would understand him.

"You are living in darkness, torn between the blackness you can see and the gold that protects you. Too much time has been spent looking forward with too little of your attention on the present. You are unbalanced."

The words, Tril felt strongly, were divinations. He could not deny any of her statements.

Around him, like a dream forming, the gold shimmered. The light dimmed to lamp light, and the clouds of golden light took on substance. He saw himself lying in a room where the Northlander Circle tried to sustain him until his mind settled. The wolf, walking at his side in these dreams, whined in frustration at being kept from her family and pack.

Like every man, woman, and child of this world, Tril could freely tap into the dreaming place. But, like wizards, he also had an attachment to the blackness and the spiral of power beyond. That connection had become stronger with the use of his *Visaln*. Where once he had kept the powers of the spiral and those of the Aspect wolf even, the spiral now dominated.

Tril looked up at the dream of Ela, his heart heavy. He knew he would never see her again with his own eyes. His mind was too broken by magic to recover before her heart gave out. Feeling he had lost his mother, grief swelled.

"I stand too close to the darkness," Tril admitted. "The spiral promises to take me away, so I hide." He suspected the stranger already knew all this, perhaps better than Tril.

The stranger walked among the Northlander Circle in the vision, examining each with child-like curiosity. "We can show you how to strengthen your attachment to the Dreamworld. We can help you."

Tril and the wolf both started to attention. "At what cost?" he asked.

The woman tossed her head with a sigh. Her attention was now on Ela, frozen by Tril's side in the vision. "We cannot help you where you are. You must come with us."

He had been, Tril reflected, around Esparans too much of late; he had expected a cost in coins or services. Northlanders would expect nothing from another; all Northlanders were family.

But the woman was not Northlander, and as far as he could tell, she was neither Esparan nor Rydan. Why would she assist without wanting something? He did not even know her name.

"I am called Pitiscil," she told him.

"You can see my thoughts," Tril realized. "I do not even speak, and you know—"

Her smile broadened. The golden light of the Dreamworld reflected over her skin, making the symbol on her forehead glow. "I am the messenger of the One God of the Nurmi. Like you, I am a prophet, and yes, I can see the thoughts of a mind in the Dreamworld. You need me, Tril of the Northlands, and I need you. My people will soon face a great tragedy. We cannot prevent it, but if we are to recover from it, I need your assistance. You can reach a place I cannot. I can keep it from overwhelming you. Together, we can keep my people from being lost."

He could not help but feel flattered, yet sadness threatened to overwhelm him. Tril looked through the frozen room. What of Ela? What of the Circle? His wife, his child? Leaving meant abandoning them all.

Seeing his hesitation, Pitiscil placed a hand on his furred arm. "You can visit them whenever you wish through their dreams, but to teach you the secrets of the Dreamworld, you must come to our groves."

When he still did not agree, she let her hand fall.

"Consider it, Tril. I will return when you have made a decision."

The dream of the Circle faded from sight, replaced by the golden light. The woman walked into the distance, eventually being encompassed by gold and disappear.

Somewhere farther afield, he heard a lone wolf howl.

Arnika tried to turn the Manor of Wayburn into an adventure, exploring the corridors and rooms until she knew them by heart. She was baffled by the basement; her home in Cainton had been on stone as most of Trulin was. Here, where the ground was soft, cellars were apparently reasonably common. What shocked her was that there was an entire complex under the manor, much of which had been created by Kitable. His room was in the maze, but she'd yet to find it.

With few duties, Arnika tried to find a place somewhere in the daily activities without causing disruption. She started missing Tohmas within a few days. It was strange since she had spent most of her time wishing to see less of the man, but now that he was not sleeping beside her, her bed felt empty. It did not help that she was now living in a foreign, empty manor in a princedom she had never so much as visited, waited on by people she did not know. She was thus elated when Altana and Valia turned up with Lady Fayela. As much as Arnika respected and liked her mother-in-law, Lady Fayela was rapidly whisked into lunches, teas, and meetings with old friends, and Arnika was left behind as the manor quickly reverted to Lady Fayela as the mistress of the household. Arnika found speaking to Lance's wife challenging due to her brusque manner, but Altana was a steadfast listening ear. When Arnika found a neglected herb garden within the manor's walls, she took it upon herself to see it restored with Valia and Altana's help. It was the wrong time of year to be planting, but she bought some winter vegetable seeds, which the gardener said had a decent chance of growing this time of year. Galanth was more southern than her homeland; it was still mild although the autumn was coming.

After four days of working on the garden, Arnika felt ill. At first, she attributed it to her nerves, but when she was overtly sick at breakfast, Lady Fayela smiled comfortingly and suggested she speak to a midwife.

Arnika locked herself in her room immediately.

She had to know. One way or another, she had to find out if she was pregnant.

But who could she talk to? Altana often referred to her marriage as "forced" and would not be a sympathetic ear. Lady Fayela had been hustled off right after breakfast. She went to her garden mindlessly, filling her day with tasks, but she could not think.

Arnika waited for Altana to head out for the afternoon, claiming her back was sore from weeding but likely boring of the dirty work, before telling Valia her fears.

Valia squealed, clapping her hands like a child at play. "Wonderful! This is great news!"

"Only if it is true," Arnika cautioned, a knot forming in her stomach. She wasn't sure if she was hoping it was or wasn't.

"Well, then we'll ask Shimmer," Valia suggested.

Although she initially opened her mouth to refuse, Arnika reconsidered before she could utter a word. Shimmer Weaver was in the city, performing with her father's show. She was a caster. She could find out.

Calling out the protectors Tohmas had assigned her, Arnika declared that she wanted to visit Wayburn and seek out a show called Match and Mixer, Valia at her side. Not surprisingly, many protectors knew the show. Before the sun had entirely set, she stood among a crowd watching the end of a juggling act.

Their presence raised plenty of eyebrows, but the show did not pause for it, and soon Arnika was watching the woman who saved Master Kitable dance. They had last met at Arnika's wedding, and she had found Shimmer charming and well-spoken then. Now, she had to reconsider.

Her dancing was suggestive and crude but elegant and graceful in one. The crowd of men cheered her on with coins and promises as she moved across the cleared area with attention Arnika envied. Valia even made Arnika nervously laugh when she leaned over and suggested, "Wonder if she could teach me that one! I bet Lance would love it!"

Arnika could not respond through her blushing, but she was grateful Altana was not present. As the night went on—the dancing continued in firelight and under lit stars—doubt seeped deeper into Arnika. She was the wife to the king. She could not be seen with a dancer like Shimmer Weaver, not when she now understood the type of performances Shimmer did!

Despite Valia's encouragement, Arnika turned away from the show. "We'll do this properly," she decided.

She assigned a protector to deliver a message, then headed for bed, knowing she would not sleep.

Chapter 17

It took Sabian all day, but he found Sori working in the Esparan camp. This time he was sober and fully able to analyze every word she said. He still found no purpose. He asked her a dozen questions, demanding to know her reasons for lying with him, and she evaded or insulted him until he ran out of inquiry.

She was nothing like the other women he had taken to bed among the Rydans. Rydan women were fierce and assertive, but their every action had layers. Every gesture had meaning; every word had two. Although he felt he was improving at interpreting the many subtleties, he found it exhausting.

When his words ran out, desire replaced them.

Sori smirked at his advances, but she spent the night again. Come morning, she cooked breakfast like a wife and then set to fixing a tunic she had been hired to repair.

That was her survival; sewing, cooking, cleaning, and anything else the Esparans needed and didn't want to go into Fixer City for. With Wayburn behind them and the army on its home ground, there was little demand for Fixer City, and the gathering was dwindling. Even Match and Mixer stayed in Wayburn, which meant no more red-haired beauty to annoy him, and Sabian's tingling hand was grateful for that fact. Word came that Tohmas' forces had finished arriving and another celebration was due in the evening among the Rydans as the chief was now back with his people.

CHAPTER 17

"You do not wonder what the others will think?" Sori asked, her voice light by the evening fire. "I am not First Clan, and now you have favored me two times."

"I can do what I want," Sabian replied, throwing stones into the fire.

"So what *do* you want?" she asked. "I cannot see what you are looking for, Sabian. You sought me. Do I remind you of someone? Did I please you?"

"You want a compliment?" Sabian replied, sitting straight. "Is that it? Recognition?"

She shook her head as she laughed, making her long hair tangle in the wind. "I seek to understand you," she said, "and now you seek to understand me."

She leaned forward over the fire, her eyes intense. He could not doubt her sincerity.

"I want nothing from you, Sabian," she said. "I want to enjoy my life. You are fun. I do not want to be a wife, and I have no interest in being accepted by First Clan. I don't care what they think, and I don't want them trying to run my life. Does that help?"

It did. A weight, one he now recognized as suspicion, lifted. There was no need to watch his belongings or his back. All the pressure vanished. He even believed her.

"So what do *you* want?" she asked, leaning back and returning to her sewing.

Having no reply, he shrugged and said, "Right now, I want to repeat last night. I'll decide about later later. I..." He glanced toward the main Esparan camp. "...I think I owe Lance a drink."

She stuffed the tunic back into her bag and rose. Sabian liked the look in her eyes.

Without another word, she pulled him back into the tent.

Carsh knew why Tohmas sent Arnika off, but it was hard to tell if Tamv did. It might not even occur to the chief that Tohmas would keep his wife from him; there was no reason for Tohmas to do so in the chief's eyes. But Carsh knew his brother had succumbed to *faluv* and was vulnerable. If the Rydans found out, he would become a joke among them.

No man let a woman control his life, not if he was strong. Tohmas was not as strong as he had once been.

After another quarter cycle of marching, bypassing the capital, the remaining army joined the defenses on the border of Damoria. Damoria warriors had chased the Rydan raiders back and set up camp on the west side of the Black Marsh while Galanth forces kept the border on the east side of the damp dark of the marsh. Tohmas' scout confirmed Polthian's army encamped with Damoria's, doubling their numbers.

The remnants of Tohmas' forces joined those on the marsh's border, including the Rydans. If it had not been for Tamv's assurances earlier, Carsh would have been less optimistic about their odds, especially with Polthian strengthening Damoria's position.

The army set their camp, ready to push the Damorians back to their capital and take the final princedom. Then, from the DragonTail Mountains to the Ice Ocean, Espar would be Tohmas,' and Tohmas' duty as the first son would be done.

He would give it to Tamv, the greatest expansion of Rydan territory in history. Carsh was proud to have been a part of it.

There would be a grand celebration this night as battle loomed and the two halves of the First Clan reunited, their chief now in attendance to assure victory. It was time to celebrate their imminent success, and it was a party Carsh did not plan to miss.

Tohmas left the kingsmen to their preparations and sent the protectors away, despite their many objections. Carsh was grateful the chief had not been present to see the hesitation. Men should obey without questioning his Rydan heart told him. Esparans were foolish that way.

Tohmas and Carsh made their way alone to the camp beside the Black Marsh. Despite it being midday as they arrived, the bonfires blazed in expectation, the smoke filling the region as the still air failed to clear it. The sky above was a granite grey, the sun invisible behind high clouds, making it feel like autumn although the season had not changed in earnest yet.

Their Followers met them—just as new to the camp by the marsh as Carsh and Tohmas—but they fit in more than Tohmas did in his green tabard and thick leather armor. It was familiar and light-hearted as they joined the throngs of Rydans in seeking the bonfires and, most importantly, the chief *shella*.

The chief stood in glory on the threshold of the small building, his bare chest displaying his tattoo of the dragon in black ink. The step at the doorway amplified his already-respectable height. It looked as though he had re-stained his grass bracelets, for they were a brighter fiery red interspersed by the many knucklebones of his dead Followers.

This time, there was no challenger. No one dared oppose Tohmas or Carsh as they approached and knelt in a ready position in the dirt before Chief Tamv.

"Come, my sons," Tamv called grandly, then turned and stepped into the *shella*. Tohmas followed first as the eldest, and Carsh came second. Their Followers remained outside although the bustle rose as they dispersed to visit with others.

As Carsh stepped into the *shella,* something seemed amiss at once. There was magic in the air.

"Leave your sword, Tohmas," the chief called. Carsh was aware his brother obeyed and laid SoulBurner by the entrance, but his attention was at once on the occupants of the *shella*, not Tohmas.

Two unknown Rydans stood next to the chief's *traon* as the chief took his seat on the raised chair. Both of the older Rydans, dressed in hide clothes and wearing sparse grass bracelets, carried only a woman's simple *shanye* each. It did not escape Carsh's notice that they were relatively unmarked by weapon wounds. Rydans alive today had survived the annihilation of the Second and Third Clans, and every man able had seen countless battles.

These two had not. At a glance, their lack of weapons and their slight build made them seem weak, but the creeping feel of magic assaulting Carsh's senses made it clear where their strength stemmed from.

Carsh pulled a second blade and dropped into a fighting stance, but Tohmas calmly knelt into a waiting position with both knees down before the chief and addressed the strangers mildly:

"Wisavi Gagn, Wisavi Bast, it has been a long time."

The first to incline his head was Gagn, the younger of the two wisavis. His head and face were covered with small scars as if he had fallen among thorns at a young age, but his exposed arms and hands were clean. The scars extended over his scalp, which he kept trimmed short, and over one eye, giving him a permanent squint and scowl.

The second man, Bast, was older than Tamv and shared the chief's white hair although Bast wore his long. His eyes had started to cloud. Carsh had the feeling it did not interfere with his vision at all by the way the Rydan examined the room.

Since they had met at the age of eight, Carsh and Tohmas had been separated only a handful of times, yet Tohmas knew these two, and Carsh did not. It had to be from when Tohmas had initially gone to Galanth to become their prince. Bragn, Carsh's original brother, had been cared for by two wisavi just as Tohmas had first come to the Outlands with two protectors. They would have been there when Tohmas had first gone to Espar.

Yet even that surprised Carsh. Had the wisavi who had escorted, educated, and defended Bragn been casters? None in the Outlands would have put trust in a magic user. Until Carsh had met Kitable, he'd believed all casters were evil flyers aiming to destroy the Outlands and all its inhabitants. Tamv would never deal with flyers. So were these wizards like Kitable? It was not a distinction he had ever had to make in the Outlands but one he had started to grasp in Espar. Flyers could do anything they wanted. Wizards only did what was right.

Carsh fidgeted with his second knife, unsure if he needed it.

"Carsh!" Tamv snapped, and Carsh, despite his knife dancer training pleading he not lower his defenses among unknown casters, immediately dropped into the waiting position. His knife went away, and he saluted the chief, trying to make amends for his lapse.

"Relax, my sons," the chief said graciously, allowing both to rise now that Carsh was behaving appropriately. Carsh came slowly to his feet, wishing he could draw another blade without offending his father. He felt under threat. Even Tohmas stood at attention with tension in his stance, but Carsh thought it more likely he was wondering if the topic of his wife would come up.

"My forces are ready," Tohmas said stiffly, his eyes on the chief alone. "We await your command."

Tamv's smile was a long, drawn-out grin that seeped across his face like mud from the marsh. "I have a better way."

He signaled Bast, and the older Rydan gestured sharply. The magic flare made Carsh flinch forward, his palm itching for his knife.

A new person appeared beside the wisavi. He wore fine Esparan clothing in elegant yellow and red, golden trinkets decorating him. He had two prominent golden bands over his right arm. Although he had never seen the man before, Carsh had learned all the ranks and colors of the princedoms of Espar when Tamv prepared them. This was a Damorian, and by the two golden bands, this was their prince, Wevan Damoria.

At first, all they could do was stare.

Tamv had claimed Damoria was within their grasp when Carsh had been eavesdropping on his conference with Tohmas in Polthian. He had never imagined they had captured the prince already.

Tohmas seemed just as confused, his eyes narrowed in a familiar, pensive manner.

Prince Wevan stood immobile where he had appeared, staring vacantly forward. His sword hung on his belt, but the prince held his arms at his side as if frozen. Carsh wondered for a moment what was happening in the man's mind.

The longer the pause, the more irritated the chief appeared to become. Did he expect them to congratulate him? Be impressed?

At length, Tohmas said, "Prince Wevan of Damoria. This is what you meant when you said he was within your reach. But killing the prince will not end this. His son will inherit."

Tamv sneered, tossing his hand dismissively. The knucklebones rattled like rain pelting on a mud field. "I do not intend to kill him, not yet at least."

Again, Tohmas hesitated, making Carsh's stomach flutter. Magic? He didn't understand how Tamv could tolerate these two and how he had hidden them for so long. Rydans did not use magic!

A year before, Carsh would never have dared doubted Tamv, but doubt now crept in. Still, Carsh could not find the words to voice his confusion. He would not show weakness.

Tohmas spoke while Carsh stood on in silence.

"If we win this war by trickery, we lose the Esparans. They will not follow me. We must be victorious in Damoria by the sword."

The silence that fell came down like a boulder. But although he could not have failed to notice the chief's disapproval, Tohmas did

not drop into a submissive position. He made his point by remaining standing, his head above the chief's seated position on the *traon*.

Tamv rose on the platform, standing in front of the *traon* to tower over Tohmas. "This war must be won, whatever the cost."

Tohmas should have lowered himself, but he stood firm. "Victory at all costs," he conceded, "but if we take this by magic, there will be no unified Espar. They will fracture, and we will have to take them each in turn again."

It was cold logic but clearly unwanted. The wisavis shifted in place as if expecting more, magic drifting between them and the prisoner like a sinister fog. It made his skin crawl, but Carsh did not dare move. If Tohmas did not defer to the chief, would this come to blows? Carsh had been on the receiving end of Tamv's rage in the past and had plenty of scars to show for it. And the chief's word was still law; opposing Tamv set the entire First Clan against Tohmas. Surely Tohmas never planned to take things that far! And with two casters working with the chief, what hope did Tohmas have? It was mad that he considered such events even possible.

Carsh suddenly didn't know who he would fight for. His chest panged.

"We will control him," the chief said, his hand openly on his *hooknye*, "His words will be our words on the battlefield. Then his forces will perish, and Espar will be mine. Damoria and Polthian work against you; your position is one of disadvantage. You cannot win without this."

Tohmas eyes flashed between the wisavis and then to the prisoner and his blank expression. By casting asperities on Tohmas' skills and hope for victory, the chief had brought their disagreement to a head. Saying Tohmas needed the very subterfuge he objected to if he was to complete the task set for him was profoundly insulting.

Tohmas' calculating stare returned for a blink. Carsh had no doubt a dozen options were turning in his mind. But then, with great care, Tohmas bowed his head. He lowered himself into a waiting stance, capitulating with a gesture. "This is wise," he said. "I obey."

Yet Carsh did not entirely trust his brother's tone. Feeling forgotten, Carsh remained standing at the side, for a rare moment in a position of rank above his brother.

Tamv nodded, drawing his hand away from his weapon, and the tension, palpable in the changing magic around the wisavis, released slightly.

"May I bring in my wisavi?" Tohmas requested lightly, his eyes down and his head bowed still. "His wisdom can aid us."

Tamv's eyes narrowed, his sneer returning. "Yes, let us see what this *Esparan* can offer if you have such confidence in him."

A test, Carsh interpreted. If Kitable could not contribute to their efforts, he would be deemed unworthy of the rank of wisavi.

Swallowing hard, Tohmas said clearly, "Kitable, I need your assistance."

It took only a flicker. With a burst of powers, Kitable appeared behind Tohmas, garbed in his green and silver robes. He had not bothered to don boots and was barefoot.

His grey eyes swept through the room, taking in the scene slowly. Recognizing the chief, Kitable, with hesitation, placed a fist to his left shoulder and half bowed his head, but he was stepping away as he saluted.

"My king?" he asked in Esparan, talking to Tohmas' back.

Having not been permitted to rise, Tohmas turned his head but did not stand. "We have magic at play. I want your council."

Kitable searched the room again, his eyes flickering through colors, boldly showing his Spell Sight to the Rydans before him. He seemed confused, focusing the most on the two wisavis, then on the prisoner. "Casters among the Rydans?" he finally stammered.

Tamv had taught Tohmas and Carsh Esparan and would know every word, but the two other wisavis were unlikely to understand the language.

"These are the chief's wisavis," Tohmas said to introduce them.

Kitable's voice darkened. "When I asked you if a wisavi was allowed to use magic, you said 'no more than any other Rydan,' Tohmas. What are these, then?"

"Your wisavi asks too many questions," the chief said in Rydan. He turned his sour expression to Kitable and said in Esparan, "They are our way into Damoria. They are my Followers and will not be judged by you, Esparan. Mind your place."

"Kit, down," Tohmas warned, but Kitable shook his head and stepped away, proving the chief was right; the Esparan would be no help.

"What do you mean they are your way into Damoria?"

Carsh suddenly understood. The magic he saw in use was making Kitable uncomfortable. Carsh felt renewed anger at the wisavis, but confusion held him back.

The chief seethed at the disobedience.

"I'm seeing domination auras, Tohmas," Kitable objected. "Multiple threads, combined with destruction. With these elements, they control this man." Kitable squared himself proudly, staring down the chief. "They are using the exact spells I told you I will not associate myself with. No, this is foul magic."

At Kitable's challenge, Gagn held out his hand. The palm proved to be as scratched as his head. "We hold the mind of your enemy," he said in halting Esparan. "We offer you the chance to defeat Prince Wevan."

Kitable took a final step back. "I told you," Kitable said to Tohmas, shaking his head, "that I would never deal in dominations! This is torture! Worse! You have locked this man into a corner of his mind and are controlling his body without even giving him a chance to scream in frustration. I will not condone this!"

"We are not asking for your permission," the chief informed the wisavi, and Carsh felt the *hooknyes* would soon be out.

Surprisingly bold, Kitable stood his ground. Carsh already knew that any knife from the chief would be deflected, but he did not know what the wisavis would do in answer. He did not know these wisavis, but they were his father's Followers. Kitable was already in the wrong; he had refused to lower himself to the chief.

"This magic," Kitable said with complete finality, "is cruel and unnecessary. I will have no part of it."

"Kitable!" Tohmas called, still from his knelt position.

Kitable walked out. Tamv must have known that his attacks would be futile, for the chief did not send his *hooknyes* at the wizard as Kitable left without permission and without paying proper tribute.

The other wisavis looked to the chief for a sign, but the chief looked at Tohmas.

He'd failed this test, yet Carsh didn't think Tohmas was surprised by any of it. Carsh did not see what calling Kitable in had accomplished.

"Let me speak to him, Chief," Tohmas requested, his words soft. "I am certain we can come to an understanding."

The chief considered the request through a long pause. If Kitable would act against them, then he had to be dealt with soon. As he was Esparan, Tamv would have no qualms about having him slain.

The idea got muddled when Carsh remembered that Kitable was Tohmas' Follower. Tohmas was responsible for the man and his actions.

"Go, enjoy the celebration, my sons," the chief said. "Deal with it, Tohmas. We finish this in the new day."

Carsh's chest tightened again, and a shot of pain flashed down his arm, making him take a short breath. He hoped no one noticed. *Finish?* But to be finished meant giving up everything. Tamv was their chief. Tohmas' victories were Tamv's victories. He should have been excited, yet Carsh was now uncertain.

Tohmas saluted, rose, and left swiftly, pulling his sword up from the ground as he passed out into the party beyond. They had always known it would come. If they won, Tamv won. Their every action had been at his command. There would be a King of Espar, but it would not be Tohmas.

Heeding the dismissal, Carsh saluted and left the *shella* quickly, desperate to be away from the magic lest he succumb to his instinct to attack it. But he glanced back despite himself. Prince Wevan still stood by the *traon,* immobile. This felt, in his heart, wrong.

It was easy to get caught up in the celebration outside the *shella.* Carsh's Followers were keen to mingle with those who had remained in the south: warriors on defense and unmarried women. Now, even the lowest ranks could find partners and friends.

Carsh sought Sabian, only to be told his Esparan Follower had been bedding a woman and left early. He deliberately lost track of Tohmas in the bustle, knowing his brother would be dealing with Kitable and wanting to distance himself from that. Tohmas excelled at plotting, but Carsh preferred his conflicts simple: kill or be killed. Until this night, he had never doubted the authority of his chief or the way of the Rydans. Even if it took an entire wineskin of wildwater, he would not drown out his uncertainty.

Kitable sat at his campfire, drying his feet out by the fire before putting on the boots he had retrieved. His vardo had stayed with the army and was in easy proximity when he decided to stay in the camp instead of heading to Wayburn. Colt had chosen a place uphill from the marsh to set the vardo, giving him a view of the bonfires below and the marsh beyond. With only a smattering of Fixer City left, he could not hide his waggon but relied on the defenses woven into it to keep him safe as he pondered his next move.

The same conclusions repeated in his jumbled mind again and again, not stopping until the king, wearing his green and silver, walked up to his fire.

It was odd to see the man without protectors. Most notably, Carsh was absent, but that did not change Kitable's reaction. Kitable stood to leave for his waggon. "Not up for discussion," he informed Tohmas. "Domination magic is not uncommon because it is tricky; it is vile! The worst kind of torture! I would rather have a dozen Black Agonies on me than the most basic domination! It is wrong! I will not have—"

"I agree, Kit," Tohmas calmly said, taking a seat by the fire as if joining Kitable, although Kitable was no longer there. "How can we stop them?"

Kitable stood at the top of the stairs to his waggon with the door open. Had he done a thousand divinations, he doubted he ever would have predicted that response. The way the king had behaved in front of the chief had convinced him that action against Chief Tamv would be impossible.

Tohmas slowly looked up at Kitable, his expression downtrodden. "I do not know much about magic," he confessed. "What can they do to Prince Wevan? Can you block them?"

Hesitantly, Kitable walked back to the fire and sat on the stone he had vacated. His throat was dry, but he forced the words out.

"With two of them holding the enchantments, it would be practically impossible to block. The spells I saw were woven together. I don't know how they did it, but I suspect they cast by instinct like a Northlander. The problem is, my casting is layered. One element will hit first. But if any part of their spell is disrupted, the destruction is released. It would kill Prince Wevan. And if they suspect something is amiss, they could kill him with a thought. I'm surprised they haven't already."

Tohmas swallowed hard, but his words still sounded choked. "Tamv may have accepted using casters, but most Rydans have not. He plans to have Wevan under his control during a battle and use him to destroy Damoria and Polthian's alliance. He underestimates what will happen when news spreads. He thinks he can kill all witnesses." Tohmas lifted his eyes, his jaw tense as he added, "You and I know that will be impossible. I called you into the *shella* so you would see the powers they were using, Kitable. I need your council. If you cannot block them, what can you do?"

"Without wanting to sound overly suspicious, my king," Kitable said cautiously, "why would you move against Tamv?" He met the king's stare, confident in his defenses but not knowing what to expect. He had sworn his life to Habal Galanth and transferred that pledge to Tohmas, Habal's son. But all that was a lie. Kitable knew Tohmas was no son of Habal. Kitable's oath was invalid.

If he disobeyed Tohmas, their relationship was over. It was a price Kitable was willing to pay, but one he hoped would not be necessary.

Tohmas said nothing, holding Kitable's stare as he considered the reply.

"I have been doing a great many Reflections recently at your mother's request," Kitable confessed. "I saw your life among the Outlands. I saw you grow up Rydan and heard you call Tamv 'father.' I know you are loyal to him above any other, Tohmas, and you have been since childhood. You fear and honor him; you are Rydan more than Esparan at heart. Rydans will never betray their chief. To help Prince Wevan, you must disobey Tamv. Why would you commit this great crime?"

Tohmas dropped his gaze to his clenched hands on his lap and did not reply for a long moment. When he finally spoke, it was softer than any speech Kitable had ever heard from the imposing man. "If I do this his way," Tohmas said, "the war ends, and Espar is his. I will have done my duty as the chief's first son and expanded my father's land. I will be a hero among the Rydans. I will have done everything I set out to do."

He paused as if that was all he had to say.

"Therein lies the problem," Kitable pointed out.

Tohmas nodded and drew in a long breath as if the words that followed needed additional pressure to be forced from him. "Inac charged me to bring peace to Espar. I cannot believe she wanted it won through

treachery like this. She has been silent recently, and I fear that is because I have fallen from her grace. When I married..."

This time, Kitable let the silence linger, knowing more would follow.

"As my chief," Tohmas said, "Tamv claims all I have earned. That means Espar will be his." He finally lifted his head, his sharp eyes flickering the reflections of the fire as he stared into it. "I once said I was the only one who could lead this conquest because the Rydans would never obey an Esparan. Now I find the same is true of the Esparans! They will not allow Tamv to take control of Espar without a fight." Tohmas' smile was bitter. "I have taught them to think for themselves in battle as Rydans do, only I did it without the Rydan sense of clan and rank to control it. Now, they will look at Tamv and decide he is unworthy. We will not have the peace Inac tasked me to achieve."

It made sense, Kitable had to admit. The kingsmen had learned to work together, sometimes to Tohmas' disadvantage. They knew they were stronger now, and their confidence was showing. Where the chief refused to allow any subordination, Tohmas' men often questioned the king. None of the twelve kingsmen would survive under Tamv as a king.

"So you will not surrender Espar?" Kitable clarified.

"If I try, it falls apart. You said I was Rydan, Kitable, but that is not true, not anymore. He may not know it, but I have already betrayed Tamv twice to save the people I care about. Rydans do not do that, especially not for an Esparan." Tohmas shook his head. "I am already damned for it!"

"Twice?" Kitable pressed.

"I am complicit in ending the tradition of the Pack Runner; I lied about Crawthran's son to save the child. And I sent Arnika away to keep her from him, Kitable. The danger I warned Arnika against, it was him. Once this ends, how can I protect her?"

As much as he had expected to doubt, Kitable believed the king's sincerity.

Tohmas leaned back and released his sword from his belt. He held the scabbard between his hands, the red and gold glistening in the firelight. "Somewhere along the lines, I picked up an Esparan heart. Now my chief asks me to choose between the woman I love and his way of life. He has just lost."

Kitable unclenched his fists, trying to be confident SoulBurner wasn't coming into play. He believed Tohmas. The alliance, and all the work put into securing it, was doomed. If Tohmas sought to save Wevan, the Rydans turned against him, and any hope they had of adding Damoria or Polthian vanished. But if Tohmas handed Espar over to Tamv, he lost the kingsmen just as surely.

"Well," Kitable said, slapping his knees and smiling, "if we're to be damned, at least we can be damned while doing the right thing." He looked around. "Where's Carsh?"

The Rydan might be hiding out of sight, waiting for the conversation's outcome to attack. Although Kitable thought he and Carsh had come to an understanding over the years, he did not doubt Carsh's hatred for wizards could be reactivated easily if his chief had commanded Kitable's execution.

Tohmas shook his head dejectedly. "Celebrating below," he admitted. "I do not think we can count on him in this."

The decision to stand against Tamv had clearly been hard on Tohmas, but the realization that he would do so without his closest ally seemed to have broken the king. Carsh, unlike Tohmas, was Rydan through and through. Having seen the history of the friends, Kitable understood that Tohmas was acting alone for the first time in almost two decades. Even speaking the admission aloud made Tohmas slouch.

Kitable's eyes went to the sword still in Tohmas' hand, wondering if it was an adequate replacement for Tohmas. He had claimed faith in Inac, but the loss of Carsh...

Tohmas seemed to follow his gaze and asked, "Would SoulBurner undo the magic in the right order?"

Kitable nodded thoughtfully. "Likely. Untouchable powers are exactly what I was thinking."

Tohmas grew pensive as if envisioning the camp by the marsh's edge, full of Rydans. "If I draw this, it is a challenge to the chief. Then the entire clan comes down on me."

Kitable felt his eyes widen. "All of them?"

"Most of them," Tohmas corrected. "I might hold some Followers." He let out a long sigh. "I don't know if I can get close enough with it. Tamv has been very careful to keep it out of play. I..." Tohmas' words trailed off as a woman in a red and gold dress stepped into the firelight.

Tohmas shot straight onto his feet. Loni was scantily clad as ever, with breasts that threatened to break free of their corset at any moment, but Kitable was glad to see her for once.

"Champion," the celebrant cooed, kneeling at the unexpected presence of the king, "I am honored, as always."

Confused, Tohmas looked at Kitable, who kept his seat with great determination. As much as the presence of the untouchable made him nervous, he was not going to start the night by running from her. After all, he had asked her to come.

"You asked me," Kitable explained, "what I was going to do to help Prince Wevan. I don't have SoulBurner, so I thought I would ask for divine assistance."

"The Lady of Fire awaits your wishes, Champion," the woman with the bees-nest hair said.

Kitable finally saw the king smile in relief. Yes, Loni could get close enough when SoulBurner couldn't. They would have to move quickly once it was done, but it was possible.

"He will not keep Wevan there long," Tohmas said quickly. "This happens now."

Kitable joined him, keeping a safe distance from Loni, wondering what they should tell the woman. He was certain Tohmas could come up with something that would suit her, and sure enough, Tohmas quickly told the celebrant that a man loyal to Inac was being held against his will. A kiss would no doubt free him although they had to navigate through Rydans first. She happily followed as they left the campfire, ranting passionately against the foul heretics who dared oppose the goddess' will. Leaving her to her tirade, Tohmas briefly conferred with Kitable, confirming that Tohmas would go in with Loni while Kitable waited outside to avoid causing upset. Once Wevan was freed, Kitable would protect him from further attacks. No bloodshed was required. They would have to retreat to Esparan ranks quickly though.

As the Rydan celebration reached his ears, Kitable paused. "You ready for the consequence of this?"

"Doesn't matter if I am," Tohmas replied without breaking stride. "There is no choice."

Chapter 18

I t was the strangest walk of his life. Although Tohmas kept his head held high, trying to give no sign of hesitation or weakness as they headed into Rydan camp, he felt as if his insides had turned to mud. The most familiar sights now felt wrong. Rydan drum beats filled his ears, chaotic and irritating. Food was being circulated, an evening feast to prepare them for the morning's battle. The wildwater flowed freely, fresh batches of wineskins hanging from wooden frames beside the fires for anyone to take. The sun had touched the tops of the trees, making the shadows long and light, no longer deep and dark. Smoke hung low, not adding mystery but providing cover. Whenever a Follower noticed him, Tohmas sent them away. With Kitable and Loni in his shadow, Tohmas made his cautious way into the camp, dreading every step.

To Tohmas' surprise, he spotted Carsh not far from the *shella*. He'd apparently taken the time to get as drunk as possible, something Tohmas had not seen in many years. For a man who practiced killing, being out of control and emotional was dangerous for everyone. Sure enough, his Followers had moved in, shielding him from interacting with others. Further, Darcina seemed to be trying to coax him into a tent, likely to remove him from the party. But he was obstinate and resisting until he saw Tohmas. He broke from Darcina and rushed over.

Darcina met Tohmas' eye behind her husband's back, and for the first time, Tohmas saw her clearly. He'd never paid her much attention. She was pretty enough but tall and muscled in a proudly Rydan fashion,

unlike Arnika. Carsh had laid claim to her the moment they had met, leaving Tohmas no need to get to know her. But as he saw her efforts to protect Carsh from his stupidity, she had an intelligent, calculating look in her pale eyes.

He'd assumed she sought only to maintain her rank and position through her ongoing relationship with Carsh. Breaking from him would see her killed, as she would be a Second Clan survivor without a husband to make her First Clan. But as Tohmas saw the concern flash through her eyes, he suddenly realized there was more to it.

Carsh denied it, but Tohmas knew his brother loved Darcina. Was the reverse true?

With a lift of her chin, she passed Carsh to him, trusting him to protect him as she had been doing.

Tohmas' stomach dropped as he recognized he was about to betray that very trust. And if he took Carsh down with him, he damned her too.

"On our way to see Chief Tamv," Tohmas said in Esparan, wanting Kitable to hear it and hoping most nearby Rydans would ignore a conversation in the foreign language, even if they knew Esparan. Carsh smiled lopsidedly at the celebrant and did a sort of bow that ended off-center. Tohmas caught his arm to steady him.

"I come then," Carsh declared. He tried to turn quickly toward the *shella* and stumbled, but Tohmas' hand on his arm kept him from falling.

He'd never lied to Carsh before. What one knew, the other knew, that had always been their pact. But, as he had told Kitable, Tohmas did not think he could count on Carsh in this.

At least he was sufficiently drunk not to suspect what was going on. That thought sat sourly in his stomach.

"Stay here, play and dance and sing, brother," Tohmas said. "This, I can do alone."

Some sense reached out from the glazed, stupefied eyes. Was that suspicion? Perhaps not speaking Rydan among the crowd had been a mistake, or maybe it had been the overt use of "brother" when an Esparan was present. He might have no idea what Tohmas was hiding, but he seemed to know he was hiding something. They knew each other too well.

"I will come with you," Carsh said in perfect, unaccented Esparan. Beside him, Tohmas saw Kitable raise an eyebrow. Since they had met

two years prior, Carsh had spoken in an accented, slurred bastardization of Esparan and Rydan to annoy the Esparans. But he knew Esparan as well as Tohmas did, and now he showed it to make his point.

"As you like," Tohmas conceded. Trying to keep Carsh out would raise alarms. Where one went, the other followed. It had been that way for years before plans for Espar had been in place. The last thing Tohmas wanted now was undue attention.

As he put an arm around Carsh and brought him along, Tohmas met Darcina's gaze over Carsh's shoulder and wished he could tell her something was amiss. She was bound to Carsh's fate too. But she turned away, content and unaware.

Leaving the drumming and dancing, Carsh and Tohmas headed for the chief's *shella*. Kitable waited, staying outside as Loni hooked Tohmas' arm from the other side to accompany them.

"Might as well see yourself," Tohmas said defeatedly as he led Carsh into the *shella*.

The *shella* was hot in the evening, making Tohmas sweat swiftly after entering and envying the Rydan's more sparse attire.

The wisavis knelt behind the *traon*, their backs visible as they crouched around something at the back of the tent. Drawing his attention before he could find Prince Wevan, Tamv rose from the *traon*, his scowl deep. "No blade, Tohmas," he warned. The command was sharp, almost as though the chief feared something from leaving Tohmas armed. Furthering the thought, Tamv did not command Carsh to remove his weapons.

It seemed obvious now; the chief doubted Tohmas. Perhaps he always had, knowing Tohmas was Esparan blood regardless of his upbringing. He'd spent his life trying to please the chief and prove his worth, and now, after fifteen years, Tohmas was about to show Chief Tamv he had been right all along: Esparans were weak.

Tohmas paused at the entrance and removed SoulBurner obediently as Celebrant Loni advanced into the chief's *shella* as if she was visiting an old friend. Tamv opened his mouth to speak again but paused with mouth agape, his thought unfinished. She was not necessarily beautiful, but Loni was distinctive in any company with her bright red lips and golden makeup.

"Celebrant," Carsh helpfully told Tamv as Tohmas was busy placing his sword by the door, standing the sheath up against the inside of the frame. "Celebrant to Inac." Carsh smiled widely, keen for all that Loni represented. Tohmas knew his brother had spent his share of nights with Loni when Darcina had been in the Outlands and enjoyed himself on every visit. Although they both knew they had to watch her temper, which could rise and fall unpredictably, she tended to be enthusiastic and as fiery as her goddess.

Loni bowed in Esparan fashion, and the chief stepped down from his *traon*, acknowledging the celebrant. From behind the *traon*, the wisavis rose and approached. Tohmas' heart skipped when he caught sight of Prince Wevan, who had been crouched between the two casters. He had his hands over his head as if sheltering from a blow and did not rise as they moved away, but he was still present in the *shella*. That was a piece of luck. He didn't look physically injured. Had they been casting? Laying down magic for the next day? Tohmas didn't know what the wisavis had to do to take control of a man. Kitable would know, but it was too late to ask him.

Loni's words were sultry. "A blessing for the day ahead," she offered. Somehow, whenever she met a man's eye, she made her smile seem like it was exclusively for them. Celebrants were uncommon travelers in the Outlands, but they were always respected and heeded; even the wisavis deferentially nodded their heads. If the will of the Goddess of Fire was being spoken, they had to listen.

She drifted in like smoke off a fire, swirling between the wisavis. They exchanged worried glances over her head. Kitable had said before he could feel the shake of magic when an Untouchable was around. Were these two able to tell what she was?

Fear, real and ugly, climbed through Tohmas. This defiance could cost him his life in a blink. Bringing Carsh had been a bad idea. If Carsh stood with Tamv, Tohmas would be dead the moment his disobedience came to light.

"And this? Is this a sacrifice for Inac?" Loni cooed, moving past the wisavis and approaching Wevan.

Tohmas advanced as well, needing to be within reach. Even if they did not know what Loni was, they would recognize the dispel of their magic when she touched Wevan. There would be little time.

CHAPTER 18

"He is a prisoner here, celebrant," Tohmas said carefully, hoping she would connect their earlier conversation to the words he chose. He felt the narrowed gaze of the chief on him but ignored it. "He is bound to these."

The older wisavi started as if realizing something, and Tohmas took a chance; he stepped between the man and Loni. "Is that not right, wisavi?" Tohmas asked innocently, using his bulk to hide what Loni was doing.

"My chief..." the wisavi began, his voice high in alarm.

"Tohmas!" Tamv snapped instantly, already on edge and eager to correct him.

Chastised, Tohmas dropped low, but instead of going down into a waiting stance, he fell into a ready position, muscles poised. He spotted Carsh's confused frown as he made what looked to be a mistake. But the next moment, it became apparent why he had not let both knees touch the ground.

Celebrant Loni placed a kiss on the prisoner's cheek.

Both wisavis squawked in alarm, their magic gone in a flicker. Prince Wevan crumbled like a tossed rag.

Tohmas launched himself, slashing at one wisavi as Loni, shrieking about the offense to Inac, lunged at the other. The attack was fated to fail, as these were well-protected flyers, but Tohmas and Carsh had fought wizards several times now, and Tohmas did not let the failure of his first swing stop him from making another. Although invisible shields deflected his dagger, the force knocked the man off his feet. Tohmas immediately grabbed the fallen's man ankle and stabbed the wisavi's sole.

The wounded man screeched like a rabbit snared by a hawk. Loni put her knife into the other wisavi's neck, making the other man scream although that cry seemed to be petering out quickly.

Tohmas spun to face Carsh, expecting him. Without SoulBurner, he was at a disadvantage, yet he stood firm, ready to face his brother in a final deadly spar.

But Carsh was not acting, seeming frozen by indecision for the moment. Then, with a snarl, he joyfully drew a second blade and launched himself not at Tohmas but at the wisavi trying to cast through his cut throat. His knife took the wisavi through the back, between the ribs, and into the heart. Without shields to defend him, for the celebrant had connected during her attacks, he died instantly.

"Carsh!" Tamv snapped, his weapons drawn and a grimace making his sharpened canines visible. To his dismay, scolded, Carsh went down into a waiting position, looking surprised.

"Tohmas!" was the next shout.

Tohmas snatched up Wevan and threw him over a shoulder as Loni devotedly kicked the wisavi Tohmas had wounded, undoing his spells and preventing immediate retaliation.

But they could cast again in time. He needed to get to Kitable and get protections in place.

Tamv stepped up, making Tohmas acutely aware of the *hooknyes* in his chief's hands.

"Not like this, chief," Tohmas said as he adjusted the weight of the man on his shoulder and planned a path to the exit. "This is not war. This is treachery."

"Traitor," Tamv scoffed. "You would betray me, your father, your chief, for an *Esparan*?"

"Assassinating him would not be victory," Tohmas declared, and Loni, representing the Goddess of Justice, Victory, and War, stepped up to his side to confirm it. She had retrieved her knife from the dead wisavi's neck and held the blood-stained blade at the ready. The second wisavi, in testimony to his cowardice, did not rise from where Loni had kicked him but instead held his injured foot and whimpered.

Tamv stood firm in their path.

Into the shocked stillness, Tohmas threw his blade at Tamv directly, aiming for the heart. Lacking Carsh's skill, the attack was easy to deflect. But it gave him time to bolt. Loni slashed at the Rydan as Tohmas passed, but both attacks managed only to block and delay, not draw blood. He remembered to snatch up SoulBurner as he passed through the door.

The chief's words at his back sent a chill through Tohmas.

"Geddit, Carsh."

Tohmas put on a burst of speed, knowing his destination and counting on the crowd to slow Carsh. Kitable quickly fell into stride behind him, muttering spells. Although he could not sense magic as Carsh did, Tohmas assumed he was doing as they had planned, defending Wevan immediately from additional attacks. He lost track

of Loni but was unsurprised by that. She was a survivor. Hiding now would be the best chance.

He couldn't hide.

Kitable at his side, Tohmas made it through the camp without a *hooknye* carving out his kidney. But as they reached the quiet edges of the Esparan forces, Tohmas heard Carsh calling after him. He pushed on, climbing the steep slope up to the Esparan defenses and leaving the Rydan camp at his back.

Running with a full-grown man on his shoulder took its toll; Tohmas halted and laid Wevan down on a patch of dry grasses between primary defenses. His head was still spinning. He'd tried to kill Tamv. He had wanted no bloodshed, but he'd thrown his knife to kill. There was no going back from this.

"How did it go?" Kitable asked, finally able to check on Wevan, who was breathing steadily with his eyes shut, looking asleep.

"Killed one, hurt the other," Tohmas said.

"I've got him defended best I can," Kitable commented. "Should I be rallying the troops?"

Tohmas looked back the way they had come. While there was undeniably a separation of Rydan from Esparan, the slope was no battlefield. Tents and fires littered behind him, with Rydans, Northlanders, and Esparans milling around in trade and conversation. But a long rumble approached from the marsh's edge, a rallying call that people would soon recognize. And having the king standing among them with his most powerful wizard and a seemingly dead body was attracting attention.

"Where's the nearest Far Crier?" Tohmas shouted, and a tiny bald man with a long thin braid bravely scrambled out of a tent carrying an ox horn. "Call my protectors," Tohmas told him. "And sound the all up and ready for the rest."

A scramble followed as the forces in all corners of the camp responded to a possible threat. Protectors appeared from all directions, directed, Tohmas eventually recognized, by Kitable's light above them. As they arrived, Tohmas sent some off as messengers to the kingsmen. "Tell them I've just deeply offended the most powerful man in the Outlands. They must be wary of a Rydan attack."

Each of the protectors took a blink to blanch. One swore. They all rushed off at a sprint.

Once done, Tohmas optimistically whistled for Schlavarai, but it was Carsh who first crested the top of the hill. Farther behind him, visible down a slope toward the marsh, a crowd of Rydans were advancing.

"Tohmas?" Carsh called.

Kitable spun as if he had been kicked and shot a spell. Tohmas started, reaching out to stop the wizard but knowing it was already too late. Carsh dodged sloppily, but the flashing ball of light tracked him and crashed into his chest. Tohmas' heart stopped entirely, the air frozen in his lungs. *Not Carsh...*

But Carsh only blinked as the magic light faded. His glassy eyes were bright, the confusion gone from his face.

"It's the best I can do," Kitable said, standing tall facing the Rydan. "You're stone-cold sober, Carsh. Now you decide."

They stared at each other for a long moment as the people around continued their controlled chaos. Then, allowing Tohmas to let out his breath, Carsh broke the glare with Kitable and addressed Tohmas in Rydan.

"*Wadhap? Wevan be Esparan. Wad ya be doin'?*"

Tohmas had to tear the words out of his mouth one by one, knowing with each that he was breaking away from everything he had known. His life had been in the Outlands. His family had been Carsh and Tamv. He'd never been without his brother.

"I cannot do it. I cannot turn things over to Tamv. I will not give him Espar," he confessed.

"*D'aems,*" the Rydan muttered, his expression a scowl and his words swapping from Rydan to Esparan and back. "Arnika. *Foluv! Ya phaecok!*"

Tohmas could not explain. There were not enough words in either Esparan or Rydan to make Carsh understand.

When even the insults did not get a reaction, Carsh pushed forward two more steps. Below, a mass of Rydans had come into view through the smoke. Tohmas was still unsure if they were spectators or a war party, but there were a lot of them. Behind Tohmas, the protectors had assembled, and more soldiers made their ranks in haste.

Carsh had both blades in hand still, Tohmas noticed, hinting that although Carsh used his words, he felt threatened.

"*Fa 'er, ya daern ta chief? Ta fahta?*"

For her, he would betray the chief and his father?

"*Ya,*" Tohmas replied, feeling his heart pang. "*Fa 'er, fa Espar.*"

It took Carsh a dozen heartbeats to sort out what to do next, and by the time he had, Schlavarai had joined Tohmas. Below, the Rydans stared up, curiously wary as ever. Behind him, the forces of Espar quieted, ready.

"I guess we see now, Kit," Tohmas said, "if it's the whole clan."

"*Followa' ta me!*" Tohmas called. He could not let himself be responsible for avoidable deaths. They could leave his service if they knew, and the chief could forgive them. He was not the man they had sworn to follow; too much had changed.

The Followers answered, coming to the front of the Rydan crowd, but just as they stepped away from the Rydan camp, the chief's voice boomed out.

"*Sta!*"

Everything stopped. Even the soldiers behind Tohmas in the Esparan ranks paused in surprise. The Followers froze in their tracks, heads pivoting from Tohmas to Tamv, confused.

Tamv had stepped up onto an outcropping and stood above the crowd, his arm raised high to show off the red bracelet. "Carsh!" he shouted, summoning his son. The chief had his surviving wisavi with him at the base of the rocky section. The wisavi held Darcina close to him, his hand suspiciously at her back.

Carsh turned as if by instinct and took a step but then paused, as if unsure who had called him. His eyes fell onto Darcina openly, and he flushed. For the moment, she stood unharmed among them, but the proximity of the weapons made it clear they could turn the threat into action if they had to. Darcina, like all Carsh had, belonged to Tamv.

Carsh took one more step toward his father but stopped again when he seemed to suddenly realize Tohmas had not also been called and would not be called. He looked back over his shoulder, pleading, "*Arnika be Esparan. Wevan be Esparan. Dey just Esparan!*"

As much as it tore his heart to say it, Tohmas had to respond, "I am Esparan."

Carsh snorted in disbelief. "*Ya be Ryda!*" he declared for all to hear.

The booming voice of the chief interrupted, "*Ee be Esparan!*"

That was it; the last of his hold in the Outlands was gone. No Follower would obey an Esparan Leader. The chief could not have an Esparan son. Tohmas had been disowned.

Carsh, crestfallen, faced the Rydans to answer his father's call. Gone was the eager, quick response the chief required. His hesitation spoke more words than all the Rydan language.

After three steps, Carsh stopped, his eyes on the chief and the wounded wisavi beside him. At the distance, Carsh should have been able to feel the magic of the flyer below. Was that the pause? Or was it for Darcina, who was defiantly baring her teeth?

Tohmas saw Carsh's grip on his knives tighten, the muscles twitching in readiness.

Straightening, Carsh raised his knives above his head and declared, "*Ee be Ryda!*"

With a quick pivot, the prime protector marched back to his brother's side.

Darcina moved, her short knife taking the wisavi in the face, or at least knocking the blow against his new defenses. Her kick knocked the next Rydan who tried to grab her off his feet. Someone threw a knife, but she dodged low and pounced, racing to the Esparan side. One last blade caught her arm, but she clutched at the wound and kept running. As she reached the top of the rise, Carsh extended his hand, caught hers, and wheeled her behind him defensively.

Carsh had permitted her to carry that knife, Tohmas realized with a smile. Hells, Carsh had probably helped her become such a surprisingly good fighter.

The tightness in Tohmas' heart was instantly gone. Carsh was with him. As impossible as it was to believe, his brother was at his side.

But Carsh was not finished. Seeing his wife free and the flyer still alive, he surprised Tohmas by grabbing Tohmas' wrist and lifting his scarred hand high. His Rydan was sharp.

"*Da 'And be 'ere,*" he declared. "*Da Arm be here!*" he added, lifting his own scarred forearm. "*Da chief be wid Flya!*"

Cries went up from the Rydans, Carsh not the only one who considered a flyer unacceptable company. But instead of a Follower making the first movement to join, the Pack Runner stepped out from the Rydans, his pack of black hounds at his heel and Laorn behind him.

Tohmas' stomach tossed. He had not even known Crawthran was around. But seeing the feral man gave Tohmas an idea.

"Sabian!" he called to the crowd of Esparans, whose rough formations were progressively breaking down as people fought for the best viewpoint now that there was no direct battle. "Sabian, come forward!"

Where precisely the Vait boy had been standing, Tohmas never knew, but when the crowd of protectors parted, the boy and his baldrics of knives stepped out. With a steady step, a sure sign he had gained confidence with Rydans, he came to stand at Carsh's side.

Without needing to be told, the boy removed his baldrics and tunic. The scar he had received from the Pack Runner was almost a year old, but it was still pink and obvious against the tanned skin. He had fought the knife dancer and impressed him enough to be marked. He had usurped Tamv's position as the Shoulder although the chief had never known as much.

But the Pack Runner remembered. Following strength was the only thing Crawthran knew.

Carsh grabbed the boy's shoulder and declared for all to hear, "*Da Shoulda be 'ere!*"

The only other knife dancer in the Outlands, followed by his pack of hounds, crossed to the Esparan side and settled into a space the nearest Esparans retreated to provide for him. He did not acknowledge the chief, paying all his attention to the three marked men atop the rise.

From within the crowd, a shout of agreement began, the Followers all promising to support each other. Both Carsh and Tohmas' Followers made to leave the Rydan mob. When other Rydans tried to stop the movement, the group came together and created a path to their Leaders' sides.

Tamv commanded they leave in the wake of the disobedience. Any who dissented now would be labeled *dearn'd,* traitors.

Several hundred *dearn'd* men, women, and horses were waiting for Tohmas by the time the Rydans camp was gone into the marsh.

The next morning, Shimmer sent word she was coming to visit. At Arnika's insistence, the protectors left Valia, Altana, and Arnika alone

with Shimmer in the opulent chambers. Arnika found a seat on a stool, a position that had become familiar and comfortable after being on the road with Tohmas. It made her feel in control, poised, and active in the conversation.

Altana and Valia found lower seats. While Valia sat up, paying attention and ignoring the book she had been reading, Altana worked to untangle thread for a dress she was making. The dress reminded Arnika of what her mother would wear: a deep shade of oak brown with fresh lace on the collar and cuffs. Arnika had already teased her that it must be to impress a protector although she got a scathing look at that suggestion. The silver thread for the embroidery had turned into a large, uncooperative knot, delaying the finishing touches on the dress.

"Oh, they are going to complain about this one," the dancer laughed as the protectors closed the door with great frowns. She tossed her head as she turned, the bangles in her hair clattering and shining. "Probably are on their way to Kitable right now. Too bad he left yesterday evening. I wonder if they know."

"Kitable left?" Arnika choked out.

Shimmer shrugged, her bag sliding off her bare shoulder and onto the floor smoothly. She had worn a thick cloak to cover her scandalous attire but now let the cloak hang open and revealed her beaded vest, short blouse, and layered skirts. "Tohmas called him, I think. Had some magic dealings by the Black Marsh. As far as I can tell, no one's injured, but I don't understand exactly what happened. Saw some magical Rydans, which I still haven't got my head around." Shimmer glanced at the door. "They'll be back soon. You have something you wanted to ask me?"

The words burst from Arnika: "Am I pregnant, Shimmer?"

Altana's face went ashen, although she did not look up from the tangle. On Arnika's other side, Valia sat up eagerly, her face alight.

Shimmer, without missing a flicker, replied, "You don't look pregnant."

"Can you tell, with magic or something? I cannot be sure... I just... I need to know, Shimmer! Please!"

"I assume you don't want the old-fashioned response, do you?" Shimmer coyly replied.

Arnika released her hands from their tight grip on her lap, desperate to leave the stool but knowing it would give away her anxiety. "What's that?" she asked.

"Wait a few cycles!" Shimmer said. But she hooked her foot on her bag, pulled it up as she spoke, and rifled through it. She first pulled out a deck of cards, then met Arnika's eyes. Seeing her expression, the dancer laughed. "Well, if you start getting a big belly, it'll be obvious, won't it!" She handed the card to Arnika. Altana brought her gaze up from the tangle, starting at the cards as if they might bite Arnika.

"Shuffle them, please," Shimmer said as she pressed on through her sack. Eventually, she had a small orb in hand. Arnika offered back the deck of cards, but Shimmer instead said, "Cut them and show me the card. Just my curiosity."

Arnika cut the cards and showed the dancer.

"Moon card: that's Ocea's card. The cards think you are indeed pregnant! How about magic? Lady Altana, could you hold this, please?" Shimmer extended the black orb to Altana.

Altana stared up from her work, glowering. "Why?"

"It's a comparison check. Needs a baseline," Shimmer explained, rushed.

"No, thanks," Altana said.

With no hesitation, Valia extended her hand, bouncing in her seat like an audience member at the nightly performances. "I'll do it!"

But Shimmer pursed her lips. "Doesn't work right if you are pregnant too. Any chance of that?"

Rather than shy away, Valia shrugged. "Lance doesn't exactly spend our time in bed simply *looking* at me, ladies. So, sure, possible."

Shimmer cracked a smile. "I'm no good as a baseline; I'm shielded."

Arnika turned to her cousin. "Please, Tana."

Altana pressed her lips, clearly debating with herself. Altana had always loved attending shows in Trulin, Arnika thought. She didn't think Kitable had ever been mean to her; though, he had once snubbed her advances. Surely that wouldn't mean she feared magic all of a sudden? Perhaps it was dealing with Shimmer that made her uncomfortable. Altana was accustomed to manor halls and formal affairs. Shimmer's beaded hair and layered, mix-matched attire might offend Altana's sensibilities.

But after meeting Arnika's wide, pleading stare, Altana caved and extended her hand. She doggedly avoided Shimmer's eyes.

"Perfect, hold this."

Altana kept the black orb at full arm's length as it slowly shifted to red. Once it had swapped into a deep crimson, Shimmer gently removed it from Altana's grip and, reaching tentatively toward Arnika as if expecting protectors to tackle her at any moment, touched it to Arnika's forehead.

Arnika felt no different, but Shimmer stepped back, blinking rapidly, and started assessing something only she could see, the orb again black in her fist. Arnika's hands had tied themselves into her dress as they wrung in apprehension. She had promised Tohmas, but now that it was a possibility, she did not know if she wanted it to be true or not. A baby? *His* baby?

Shimmer's green eyes narrowed on her, Arnika waited. Shimmer checked her top to bottom more than once before finally letting out a breath and saying, "I think you are pregnant. There are a few things in your blood that are not in Lady Altana's, and more importantly, I would think, I can see a concentration of something in your womb." The topic seemed to unsettle Shimmer, and she quickly retrieved her bag. It was as if the dancer expected Arnika to become cross or violent, but Arnika herself did not know how she felt besides suddenly very nervous. Her hand went to her navel in horror and excitement. "I—" was as far as she got in her response.

Shimmer spun to the door, dropping into a half-crouch instantly. But rather than protectors storming in, something went over her head and crashed into the window behind them all, breaking the stone frame and tossing it into the courtyard below.

Three men blocked the entrance now.

Arnika recognized two of them but didn't believe her eyes. Prince Dorakon of Gaidol, who had trimmed his beard short and wore a servant's attire, stood on the left. On the right was Charger Granton, the man who had disrupted her wedding and then disappeared after the Gaidolon raids. He had not changed his appearance except to forgo the brown and silver he had once worn with immense pride.

Neither made sense. Dorakon had been executed after failing to make the oath—the story of it had been all over SwordWood. And

Granton had been missing since the Gaidolon raid, lost into the mountains in the south of Trulin. How could either of them be here, now?

Shimmer answered with magic, throwing a bright green orb. It occurred to Arnika that she didn't know what had broken the window. A spell? Was that why Shimmer was casting? And where were the protectors?

Beside her, Valia shouted and took a defensive place between the attackers and Arnika, although the action seemed foolish and futile in one. What did she plan to do against three? At least Shimmer had a chance with her magic.

But Shimmer's spell flashed out of sight before striking its target. Shimmer's attention shifted instantly to the smallest of the men, whose only action had been to tilt his head. It was clear he was a caster; Arnika was shocked she hadn't noticed it before. His head was shaven, and there was a gem implanted, somewhat implausibly, in the man's forehead.

Two spells followed from Shimmer although neither seemed to do anything. The stranger retaliated with one clear spell. Shimmer collapsed. Arnika's heart sank with her, her voice caught in the constriction of her throat. She leaped from the stool and checked on Shimmer while Valia moved up, continuing to shield her.

"She is not dead," the man with the gem said, his voice accented in a manner Arnika had never heard before. "I need her for information and as bait."

Valia squared herself against the stranger, challenging him with the edge of her stare more than physically. "There are a hundred protectors in this manor. All of them will come for your head if you dare—"

The caster waved his hand, and Valia's voice left her. She placed a hand on her neck in surprise.

"Quiet, little bird," the stranger said. "That's enough."

The next movement was Charger Granton, who stepped forward. Arnika pulled away, gathering Valia up, although she found it hard to pull the woman back.

"Come, my lady," he said firmly. "Willingly or unwillingly, you will come with us." He reached out to take her arm

"Be gone!" Arnika snapped, yanking her arm away.

"Unwillingly then," he said simply.

"Traitor!" Arnika declared, backing away. But she could not pull Valia with her this time. She'd locked eyes with the stranger with the gem and did not respond to Arnika's pulls. She looked for help; Altana had stood but was otherwise not moving. Arnika expected her to be screaming or fleeing, yet her cousin was still timidly waiting by the stool, her unfinished brown and silver dress in hand.

Brown and silver, Arnika recognized. Precisely the sort of thing her mother would have worn because it was the typical attire of a Lady of Trulin. Altana was unafraid. Was she affected by magic, or was she familiar with these three?

Valia was frozen, Shimmer collapsed, and Arnika had a terrible feeling Altana was working with these three and would be no help. Seeing no choice, Arnika ran, screaming all the while for the protectors she prayed would burst through the door and come to her rescue. But there was no way out passed the people. Once they had trapped her against the corner, Charger Granton placed one calloused hand over her mouth while another worked to put a hood over her head.

She bit the hand in spite, but they did not let her go. She was carried screaming and struggling from her room.

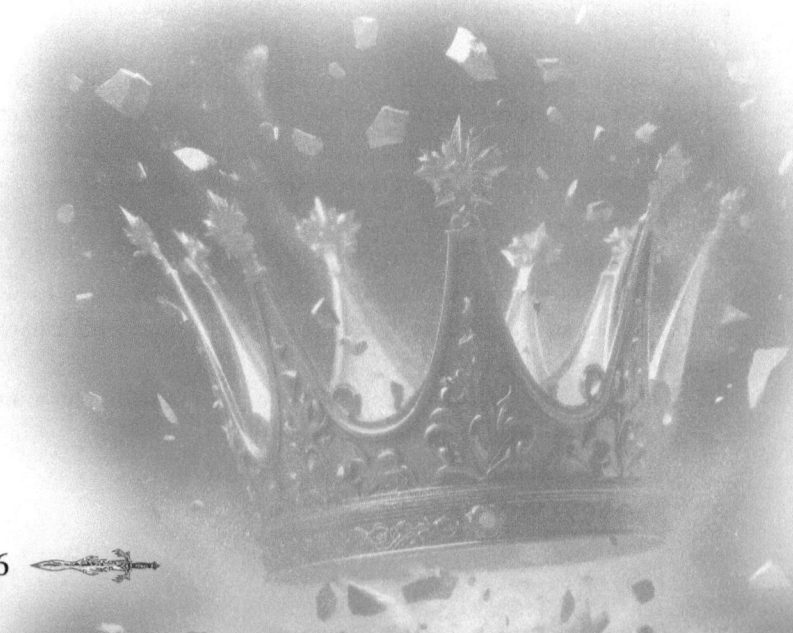

Chapter 19

Sedgan debated his visit to the king for most of the day, but as the day drew to a close and the darkness reminded him that Loni was most active in the night, he finally gave in. The protectors, he sighed, were probably getting nervous by now anyway. He had been pacing outside the king's tent since noon.

The protectors never stopped the Celebrants of Galanth, knowing their purposes with the king at any time took priority. As expected, they gave Sedgan leave to enter immediately. The king and his kingsmen were redistributing the forces using tokens on the table now that the Rydans had withdrawn.

King Tohmas immediately straightened to see Sedgan. The kingsmen did not need to be told: they quietly filed out and left Carsh as the only witness. Sedgan was grateful.

"I would ask you to sit," the king offered before picking up a cup of wine and extending it to Sedgan, "but I do not think you will. The protectors said you have been out there all day."

Sedgan put the cup right onto the table and made his point.

"I do not know what you did in the Black Marsh, Tohmas," he said, "but you have managed to inspire Loni fiercely. She is..."

It was almost too much for him. Inac was his life, and he had seen enough of Loni to know she was blessed in the Goddess' eyes, but things were slipping out of his grasp. The last time Loni had taken her inspiration to action, three Temple waggons had burned, and two celebrants

and nearly fifty acolytes had died. It had taken them mooncycles to undo the damage, and as much as he had benefited from the fires, he did not want the event repeated.

"She is preaching another purge," Sedgan said, words spilling from him, "and I cannot talk her out of it! She is not listening!"

It was the closest Sedgan had ever come to fully admitting his involvement with the earlier fires, but Sedgan had always assumed Tohmas had known. At the time, they had needed the Fire waggon to be free from blame, or else all divine support would flee the army. The evidence had been there. Tohmas had deliberately ignored it.

"If she's left to her own devices, she'll burn Ocea, Totho, and Pari again, my king."

"You are certain?" Tohmas' voice was barely louder than a whisper.

"I have tried everything! She is bound and determined that Inac is losing interest in the forces of Galanth, and she claims the Rydans saw it first, which is why they left. She believes only fire can bring the goddess' attention to us, and she means to take out the other Temple waggons. She wants Inac as the only god, Tohmas. No balance, no equality! I have kept her from acting for mooncycles, but now she will not be called down. You are the only—"

"Runnah!" Tohmas bellowed, and a protector immediately stuck his head into the tent. "Get me Celebrant Loni."

As the protector ran to obey, Sedgan finally sat down. "It's not the first time she has spoken about it," Sedgan said. "I have always succeeded in distracting her before. She thinks I am still under her control, you see. Still drugs my wine most nights, but it keeps her happy, so what do I care?"

He realized too late that he had confessed too much, but when he looked up, neither the prime protector nor the king looked surprised by the admission. He picked up the cup of wine and eyed it. He had given up wine after he had found out Loni had been poisoning him daily to confuse him and make him easier to handle, and the sight of it now reminded him again of that time and that headache. But he'd been both sober and free of drugs for mooncycles now.

"I have sent her on pointless missions, pretended to have visions, flattered her ... all to keep her quiet and content. She inspires people," he repeated the king's words from years ago to him, "I know, but she is

mad and getting worse. She has more fits, almost one daily. Sometimes she does not remember who she is. Right now, she is talking about Barga again! Barga has been dead for a year!" He dropped his head into his hand, wishing the memories would not surface with the name of the celebrant of Pari he had helped kill.

Tohmas cleared his throat softly. "I will admit, Celebrant Sedgan, that I do not feel Inac as close as I once did. Perhaps Loni is correct. I think Inac dislikes my marriage to Arnika. I've not seen the goddess since the marriage."

He should have been shocked to hear that Tohmas had seen the Goddess of Fire at all, yet it failed to reach him through the wall of defeat closing in. "No one gave you permission to fall in love with your wife. That was what Loni said on your wedding day. She believes that your attention to Arnika has weakened Inac's hold."

King Tohmas nodded in admitted culpability. "It has. I now have Ocea's hold on my heart as well. I still honor my Goddess above others, but..."

The appearance of the woman in red and gold stopped the conversation. Sedgan jumped to his feet guiltily as Loni sauntered into the tent as if marching in a funeral parade, then knelt before Tohmas and refused to rise until Tohmas bid her to.

"I have seen little of Inac these days, Celebrant," the king said soberly.

"Her sights are on you, Champion," Loni declared, her voice full of enthusiasm, "but her voice competes with others. You must make your camp clean and devout!"

"I saw a time when your four-cornered table was incomplete," Tohmas insisted, "and I did not like it. I want balance, not domination. I need all four gods, Loni."

Her head came up. It seemed her green eyes darkened. Even Carsh moved up behind Tohmas cautiously as if expecting an outburst. Tohmas gestured to call off the Rydan protector, willing to confront Loni without lethal force, for now.

"You require only Inac!" she snapped.

While many cowered before Loni during her rage, Tohmas stood unflinchingly before her. "Life does not come into being with only one element. Even I, Inac's Champion, know that. We need a balanced four."

When she stepped forward, Sedgan wondered if she had lost her sanity enough to strike the king. That, he knew, would not end well.

"The light is dimming! You saw the deception of the wizards! Your favor wanes! The Rydans have deserted! You cannot see! You fool!"

"I see enough to know we cannot be divided when—"

She swung at him, her shining silver blade bared. Carsh did not bother reacting; Tohmas caught her hand easily. He twisted his grip and broke her hold on the knife, deftly pulling it from her hand, his eyes on hers with renewed determination as if seeing her for the first time.

He kept the knife but let her hand go, stepping back. The king's voice tightened. "You are right," he said. "So be it."

"Fire burns true! There will be flames tonight!" she declared fanatically. Sedgan's heart went cold, as if a blast of the north's frigid wind had swept down his throat. Surely King Tohmas would not *allow* this? Sedgan had come pleading for action, yet now Tohmas seemed willing to release her to her purpose. Not only were the other Temple waggons at risk, but also if Loni ever learned Sedgan had spoken against her, his life would be forfeit.

She tossed her head as she turned, her sparkling jewelry casting specks of light over the canvas around them. Sedgan met her stare, and the chill in his chest took over his entire body. He saw pure, complete sanity in her eyes for a moment, and he was certain that she knew he had derided her. She also knew, with that look, all the lies he had told to appease and control her. He was now a known hindrance to her and would no doubt face the same fires she plotted for the other Temple waggons. None but her gathering would survive.

But, in a blink, the glare was gone, and Loni winked at him suggestively. He felt sick at the thought of laying a hand on her.

"Anything in service to the Fire," she cooed in a low, calm voice completely at odds with her earlier fury and passion. She strolled out with her hips swaying enticingly.

"'So be it?'" Sedgan asked as he faced Tohmas. "Will you condone this?" Sedgan's faith in Inac had been shaken before, but this time it felt as if it had been utterly collapsed. If the goddess was manifest in Loni, Sedgan was damned, for he could not believe the correct course. That meant he did not believe in Inac. He was left feeling empty.

But as he saw Tohmas' face, he let his accusation fall off. The king's expression had become stone. In a choked whisper, Tohmas said solemnly, "Carsh, *geddit*."

Carsh seemed to understand yet left slowly, like a boy being called in after a day at play. He checked back at the door, staring at Tohmas to confirm something. Tohmas' nod sent Carsh on his way.

Once Carsh had vanished into the dusk, the king sat back down as if he had gained weight since those final words, sinking deep into the chair. "Carsh will take care of it," he said softly. "She will be dead by midnight." King Tohmas returned to his tokens as if his admission was no more notable than a comment on the weather.

"Dead?" Sedgan snapped, unable to stop himself. "You cannot find a way to reason or..."

He had never seen the king look as tired as he did when he looked up from his tokens. His weight was heavily forward over the table like something was physically pressing on his shoulders, crushing him. There seemed to be more lines around his eyes already.

"I just gave up my clan to preserve Espar as I have created it," the king said, his voice rough, as if overused recently. "If she stands in my way, I will move her. Nothing else is sufficient. Ready yourself for the backlash. We are not ruled by Inac now; we are ruled by the four."

A frown pulled on Sedgan's mouth, confusion reactivating his brain slowly. This was Inac's will, he hoped. But if they were wrong...

Sedgan closed his mouth. He was not entirely certain if he surrendered because he agreed with the king or because he could not find a way to argue.

Satisfied but miserable, Sedgan rose to leave, feeling his conscious nagging as if prepping for the later onslaught. He was tempted to seek a jug of wine to calm that nausea, but the thought of drinking left a dry taste in his mouth. No, he sighed, he would just have to deal with knowing she would die tonight. There would be work to do come morning, and he had to be ready.

Just as Sedgan reached the entrance, he heard the king add, in a more familiar sincere voice, "I am sorry."

"Me too," Sedgan replied as he headed into the night.

"You demon!" Sori shouted at Sabian when he finally found her. She had been sitting by someone else's fire cooking within the Esparan camp uphill from the deserted Black Marsh. He kept his distance; she was shaking a ladle at him, wielding it like a club. "You didn't tell me what that scar meant!"

He stared blankly for a long moment, trying to see why she was so angry, but the answer was slow in coming. Finally, he remembered she was not First Clan, and she did not recognize the Hand, Arm, or Shoulder in the same manner. She knew the Pack Runner—everyone feared him—but she was unaware of the honor bestowed on Sabian through the scar on his shoulder.

He didn't want to fight. Not caring whose campfire he was intruding upon, Sabian collapsed onto a log by the fire opposite her.

Sori lowered the ladle slowly as if expecting him to jump at her at any moment. When her glare garnered no response, she went back to the large pot of soup hung over the coals.

He sat in silence for a long time. The smell of rabbit and wild spinach reached his nostrils, flavored with something spicy.

"What do you want?" Sori asked into the silence.

Finding he still had no reply, Sabian settled for the two words that had been haunting him since the night before. "I'm Esparan."

"I noticed," Sori replied flatly.

"So is Tohmas now," Sabian pressed, trying to find a way to explain why that admission left him so hollow. "And so are Lance and Kitable. There are lots of strong Esparans."

"You want permission to be Esparan?" Sori asked, one eyebrow raised as she stirred. "Why? You have always been Esparan. Now you will have to be a Leader too. So?"

"I don't know how to be a Leader," Sabian confessed, the words rushing out before he had time to rein them in. "I don't even know why I want to tell you that. I don't know why it matters! You can't help. No one can."

With a glance at the tent beside her, Sori sighed and pulled the pot off the fire. She left the cooking on the ground as she found a seat beside Sabian.

"Let me try to help," she said with a light smile, her ire gone as she slid into fluent Rydan. "You came here because I am like you, an outsider. We fit but don't. I am of the wrong clan. You are of the wrong blood."

She waited, but Sabian had nothing to add. It was the truth.

She placed a kind hand on his knee as she continued, "You have lost yourself. You were Rydan at heart, following another Rydan, but now the clarity of rank and position is gone. You do not know your place." She paused, tilting into his line of sight despite how he kept his head bowed. "Where would you like your place to be?"

Tohmas' separation from the main body of Rydans had left Sabian adrift. If he wanted to be Rydan, would he follow Chief Tamv like a proper Rydan or stay with the *dearn'd* Rydans who stuck with Tohmas and Carsh? He'd already seen the Followers changing. Many left Tohmas' following, unable to accept being a Follower to an admitted Esparan. Carsh's Followers were unwavering, claiming he would be their chief although Carsh himself deferred to Tohmas still and refused to don the red bracelets of chiefdom. Sabian wondered if the prime protector still hoped for reconciliation with Tamv, knowing that daring to call himself chief would immediately make that an impossibility.

Sabian could go to the Esparan side, follow Tohmas' example, and try to be satisfied as an Esparan. Or he could continue to follow Carsh, making a name for himself as a Rydan with the wrong blood as Tohmas had done for years. Lastly, he could try to make himself a Leader, but that seemed the most terrifying of all. How would they follow him if he was Esparan?

"I don't know," he admitted. That was the crux of the matter. He didn't belong in any position.

"Then you need to seek guidance," Sori informed him. Her bright blue eyes narrowed as she considered the options. "Esparans do not have knucklebone bracelets to speak to their supporters. What do you use?"

"We don't have—" Before he could finish the sentence, Sabian remembered his brother Ciene's candle. He still carried it around, tucked into one of the holsters of his baldric, even though he had never used it. There had not been much time to think about Ciene or his hometown of Vait in a long time.

He retrieved the red candle and presented it to Sori. She accepted it with reverence, turning it over gently in her callused hands.

"It belonged to my brother," Sabian explained. "He taught me to throw knives for playing at the pub. He died a long time ago." It had not been that long, he realized. Ciene had died during the Northlander War only two years ago, part of the early casualties as they faced DoomDragon.

"It has not been lit," Sori pointed out. "What is the point of having a candle if you do not light it?"

"It's a candle for the Gathering of Inac," Sabian explained. "Lighting it is meant to bring Inac's attention to you."

"But you did not want Inac's attention?" Sori asked, cocking her head at him.

The thought made Sabian pause. There had been plenty of times when the favor of the Goddess would have helped him. Why had he never tried? In fact, it now seemed odd that Ciene had never lit it either. He'd raised Sabian after their parents had died. There had been plenty of times for prayers and desperate measures. Yet he'd always left things to fall as they would. He'd stood on his own two feet.

Sabian could still remember the expression on his older brother's face when Sabian had beat Ciene for the first time at the target in the pub. He had not competed after that day, always passing the challenges to his younger brother. He had been proud of Sabian's skill then.

Would he be proud now?

There was quite a difference between a betting game in the corner of a tavern and the kind of knife-throwing he did now. He had gone from gambler to assassin to wizard slayer, and he had not even noticed.

"I didn't want my brother paying attention," Sabian admitted. Thinking about what Sori had said about finding guidance, he leaned forward and touched the wick to the coals. A small flame sprang to life, biting into the wax as Sabian stuck the candle into the dirt by the fire to stand on its own. This was no time-keeping candle. This would burn swiftly, as brief as Inac's favor.

Seeing the flame flicker in the wind, Sabian pressed his lips, his mind turning over. The words fell from him. "I think he would be ashamed of me."

"You?" Sori answered. "Ashamed of the Esparan who walks with Rydans?"

"He'd be proud, Sabian," another voice interrupted, startling Sabian to his feet and bringing a knife to his hand. The candle flickered again, but did not go out despite the kick of dirt nearby.

Lance stood by the tent, just outside of Sabian's peripheral vision. The kingsman had traveled with Rydans long before they had joined the army, and Sabian knew his Rydan was good enough to have understood the entire conversation.

Smiling at Sabian's shock, Sori rose and went to the pot. She pulled a wooden bowl from a stack, dipped her ladle into the stew, and rationed out the meal. She offered the first bowl to Kingsman Lance, who took it with a grateful nod.

"Sabian," he said, "your skill ended a war; you brought Darknim to where we could meet him. You're a peacekeeper between the Outlands and Espar, at least you were until Tohmas messed it up. Don't be hard on yourself. Your brother would be bursting with pride to know the Shoulder of the Outlands."

Lance sat next to Sabian on the damp log, his stew held low in his lap. "Are you ready to admit defeat yet, or do you want to ask Sori why she sat with you?"

Three mooncycles ago, Sabian had challenged Lance to prove his theory that the world still contained genuine generosity, something Sabian had lost faith in when dealing with Rydans. Yet here he was being proven wrong, by a Rydan no less.

To Sabian's surprise, Sori made a face at Lance. Lance shot the Rydan woman a glare, but it was playful. He caught the small spoon when she threw it at him.

"I did it," Sori replied tersely in Esparan, "because I wanted to. He is a good man, Lance. Do not be mean to him!"

Lance held his hands up in surrender, then, once he was certain Sori had gone back to doling out the soup for the other Gaidolons who were congregating from between the tents, he turned back to Sabian.

"You might not want my advice, Sabe, but here it is anyway. As the Shoulder, you need to become a Leader. You need to start giving to your Followers."

As Carsh's Follower, Sabian had been given anything he wanted by his Leader. Now, with the rank of Shoulder, it fell to Sabian to become

TRAITOR

a Leader. Sabian had to give his Followers what they wanted. That was the trade they agreed upon.

Lance had been right. Giving was at the very core of the Rydan hierarchy.

"Demons," Sabian grumbled in defeat. "You were right. But I'm Esparan."

Lance shrugged. "Then prove to them that there are strong Esparans," he replied, cracking another smile. He gestured at the pot. "Want to stay for dinner? Sori's cooking is particularly good now that we're closer to the Outlands. I think she knows these plants better for the seasoning or maybe—"

The ladle smacked Lance's arm.

"Not that it wasn't good before!" Lance corrected.

"I would be glad to stay," Sabian interrupted before the feud got out of hand. He carefully retrieved the candle by his feet and, with a pinch, extinguished it. He'd received the help he required.

"I know you would," Lance replied, glancing between Sabian and Sori. "But if you hurt her, I'll break your legs."

"Another adopted daughter?" Sabian asked, trying not to think about why Lance assumed that Sabian would be taking on Sori.

"A friend," Lance answered. "Now sit down and eat."

Loni woke in an empty place. A red light, like firelight without a source, shone all around her, but she saw no walls, no trees, and no earth. Beneath her feet, a metal surface reflected the light. Her eyes hurt from the glare.

Her eyes were not the only thing hurting. Her head ached, but she knew immediately that it had been hurting for a long time. She had never noticed it before, but the pain had been there for years.

The back of her hand ached too, the pain tracing familiar lines. But when she looked, the scar on the back of her hand was gone. For the first time in her living memory, the skin of both her hands was smooth and unmarked. Her right hand felt like it burned, still stuck in the fire, the flames burning in two waves along her skin, but there was no sign of damage. Rubbing it did not help.

Nothing made sense. She knew she had been by her campfire only moments before but now could not even tell if she was indoors or outside. Listening, she detected voices in the distance, but she could not hear what they were saying.

Slowly, more memories came through. Just moments ago, she had entertained the prime protector for the first time in mooncycles. She smiled; he was such an enthusiastic lover! Carsh had always been one of her favorites.

But how had she gone from there to here? And where was here? She had to assume it was magic of some kind, this place of emptiness and red light. She had never sensed magic on her before, but...

In a flash of recollections, she saw how her touch had dispelled Master Clarin on the hill when the Northlanders had attacked. She saw Kitable skitter away from her, suspiciously keeping his distance from her during every interaction. She had destroyed Kitable's spells when she had attacked him to get revenge for his assault on one of her girls; her knife could never have cut through his defenses without it. Every time magic touched her, the magic vanished.

I have never felt magic before, Loni suddenly realized, *because I am immune to all magic.*

The cascade continued. In her newfound clarity, Loni recognized all the lies. Kitable never even went near her girls; it seemed unlikely he had harmed one of them as Melody had claimed. And the castings she had heard and seen from the hole during their confrontation proved someone had used her presence to nearly kill Kitable. She had been used to distract and dispel him.

Her life had been filled with lies, Loni abruptly knew. Everything seemed clearer in the red light she did not understand. She remembered her every fit of fury and heard the nonsense she seemed to sputter perpetually. She saw the wonder of the girls she had inspired but, at the same moment, knew their envy to be unfounded. She played a hundred men once more in her mind and took their money for herself, not for her Goddess.

Deceptions followed. She drugged a cutter into betraying his temple, stealing his secrets to blackmail others. She dressed a poor man in fine clothes to fool a Celebrant of Pari. She had one of her girls seduce the Celebrant of Ocea. She told a pimp he would go far and convinced

hundreds that they were worth so much more. She, without remorse, slew those who offended her. She sabotaged a waggon and stepped into a fire to bring a message to a prince's wife.

Her mouth dropped open, her heart now pounding up her throat.

She had impersonated the Goddess Inac! In front of Nothor's envoys, she had dressed in fine clothes and made her hair lie flat and spoken as if she was the Goddess herself! She had even used the fire tricks she had learned in Pariway to add weight to the "vision."

She brought her hand to her mouth as more memories flooded in. She had done it before! She'd been in King Tohmas' tent—and his bed—in the same guise. In front of the entire army, she had meticulously rigged a waggon to explode, protected herself with blankets and ment, then presented a sword to Prince Tohmas dressed as Inac.

Perhaps it had been Inac all along, she tried to convince herself. She had been acting out Inac's will, surely. SoulBurner had needed to be in Tohmas' hand. The Goddess had given her the blade, then manipulated her mind and...

No, the memories interrupted. Loni herself had gone to StonePeak and sought out the best weaponsmith in the princedom. At first, she had paid him with rubies and golden wheel coins she had earned with her whoring, preaching, and dancing, but then she had paid him with her body. She was an experienced Lady of Lust. He had appreciated it.

Then she had killed him for it.

Feeling nauseous, she went down onto her knees, full-body tremors shaking her.

SoulBurner was no goddess-given blade. It had been fashioned in StonePeak, as real as any sword.

She had taken SoulBurner—she could remember every step of the journey back to the north—and presented it to Tohmas herself, pretending to be the Goddess. She had then retraced her steps and lain in the freezing water until she had been found and brought back to the army, supposedly having been found near death.

"Why?!" The word burst from her, taking a part of her heart with it. Nothing made sense anymore.

She could see *how* she had done all of it, from the night she had locked the celebrants in their waggons and set them alight to the

evening she had drugged Sedgan and burned the symbol of Inac onto his chest. But she did not understand why!

She tried to center herself, her heart pounding like runaway horses and her body shivering. The answer was there: Inac. She had been doing Inac's will. It *had* to be that, she repeated.

That was no Goddess, her panicked heart answered. Loni *was* the Goddess. When Tohmas saw his patron goddess, it was Loni dressed in fine clothes and new makeup. Those had been *her* words! Nowhere in any of the now-too-real memories could Loni see or hear Inac's influence. All attempts to find Inac's wishes had Loni listening to herself, her crazed, deranged voice!

The ground was cold to her touch when she collapsed to cry.

She finally understood where she was.

During her time in Lour, she had given her deepest attention to the blade she had commissioned. It had taken up her power, stolen some of whatever it was that made her immune to magic. Like Calanor's ability to project his wind, she had the ability to bring out firelight and gifted it to the sword. In the process, however, she had transferred some part of herself into the blade. She felt as though she had locked only the sane part of her mind away, happy to revel in the madness that remained in life. She had been mad; she saw quite clearly. In fact, just this evening, she had campaigned for murdering the other Temple waggons once more, even going as far as to strike King Tohmas with a blade. She'd seen his reaction yet dismissed it, confident she had convinced him of Inac's will. Yet now, she recognized the hard stare as something else.

He'd sent Carsh after her. She had been mad, and Carsh had killed her for it.

Now, lacking a tie to life, the soul in SoulBurner had awakened. This was all that was left of her; a piece of a soul within the sword.

Why? Why kill her? Why had they not tried to explain to her!? Why just slay her? After all she had done to bring Tohmas' to glory, how could he discard her like that?!

Furious, she launched to her feet. She would find a way out, she decided. She would find a way back. So long as her soul remained, she had a chance.

TRAITOR

She struck out through the red-lit place, long strides over the smooth silver surface covering a great distance quickly. Over the horizon, she discovered she was not completely alone after all.

Tohmas, dressed in green and silver and wearing a silver rope over one shoulder, stood in the red light. He was smaller than usual and almost appeared transparent, but he was undoubtedly present, staring blankly ahead. Even when she stood in front of him, he did not move even to blink.

She pressed her hand against him and felt resistance but not substance. The sound of voices became clearer. They were discussing tactics. This instant, out in the real world, Tohmas and his kingsmen planned attacking Damoria's entrenched forces.

Projecting firelight and being immune to magic was something, Loni considered, but maybe it was not the limit of her powers. She had given magic to a sword unknowingly. Could she not project further, as Calanor did? Tohmas was here, trapped in the blade as she was, or at least part of him was, unaware of her. He was still connected to the sword.

Loni reached out, finding a tether that led from Tohmas up and out of the red-lit place. Seizing it, she pulled herself up. Hand over hand, she left behind the red light and entered a strange new space, a darkness so deep it seemed to eat any of the glimpses of light that appeared. Voices rang around her, bouncing off invisible walls and losing all meaning in echoes. She focused on one, and it seemed to slow in answer, pausing as if at her command.

She heard Tohmas' voice now; thoughts passed through before her, each curated to find the correct words to say. He dismissed much of what he thought, knowing the kingsmen would disapprove, desperate to hold onto what power remained.

Loni dismissed the current conversation as irrelevant. She was in Tohmas' mind now. On a whim, she wondered what else she could find. Leaving the thread that burned red-gold in the darkness attaching him to SoulBurner, she traveled away from his voice.

New voices and memories rose; focusing on them clarified them one by one. One jumped out when she recognized it.

Disguised as Inac, Loni held SoulBurner before Tohmas in the command tent. She had commanded him to take Espar and then sire

an heir. But there was more in the memory. Now, Loni could see the tether that bound Tohmas to SoulBurner as she held it, its power over him persistent. The red tether pulsed as Loni spoke and made the command bind him as tightly as SoulBurner did. He was compelled to obey, controlled by the sword.

The realization seemed to summon another of Tohmas' memories. Loni was not the only one to hold SoulBurner—hold Tohmas' soul—and control him, albeit unwittingly. Fayela Galanth had SoulBurner in her admiring grip as she mused about love and marriage. Within Tohmas' mind, the red light flashed up the tether. He was tied to her will.

Who gave him permission to fall in love? Loni had once asked. Now, she saw she had asked the wrong question. Who had *made* him fall in love? According to Fayela, and thus Tohmas because of SoulBurner, he could only marry if he loved his wife. As soon as he decided to marry, he fell in love.

I had the power in front of me all along, Loni thought. She only needed to hold SoulBurner, and she could have given him any command. She could have controlled it all, if only she'd been wise enough to see it!

Frustrated, she stormed away from the memories of SoulBurner, seeking something useful. She could not take up SoulBurner now, not dead. But there had to be something within Tohmas' bound and broken mind that would serve her better in her vengeance against the man who had slain her.

Chapter 20

"Warrah is a brat!" Sol exclaimed, slamming his fist onto the table. His older brother had been prone to the same outburst, Tohmas thought. Once Sol inherited the position as eldest Galanth brother, Tohmas had noticed him doing the same.

"It's not Warrah we need to deal with," Tohmas pointed out.

"Prince Wevan is, somewhat understandably, not keen to get involved directly. He claims there is magic afoot still and wants Kitable sent away. So he leaves it all to his son, meaning Warrah *is* the person to deal with. And he wants exemptions, which none of us are keen to give out. He demands to speak to you only."

"Then I will have to speak to him," Tohmas answered calmly. Fighting with Damoria while the Rydan hovered just over the border was a dangerous prospect. For once, Tohmas was hoping to avoid battle and find common ground with peace talks. It seemed a faint hope considering the animosity historically along their border.

"Will that even work?" Kingsman Deiton, a scholarly man with glasses and a permanent tremble in his hands when in Tohmas' presence, squeaked his question. Next to the immense frames of Sol and even Barnon, Deiton looked mousey and weak, but he had brought soldiers. He had a place at their table for now.

"It is worth a try," Tohmas said complacently. "Time and place?" he asked Barnon and Sol.

Disgruntled, Barnon snorted. "He will not deal with any sons of Zayban, Tohmas. He claims he will leave the moment any of our colors appear."

"So I will have to be careful who I take with me, is that right?" Tohmas interpreted.

Barnon rolled his eyes. "He claims the sight of green and silver make him nervous, so that means no protectors either!"

"The more rules he puts up, the less I like it," Lance added from the seat across from Tohmas.

"Have we arranged the meeting?" Tohmas asked, remaining unconcerned. There was still merit here; he could make them see reason. He'd saved Prince Wevan. He just had to explain that fully, he was certain.

Lance miserably nodded and slid a parchment across the table to Tohmas. "Wants to meet for one last chance at making the treaty work. Just you, no other kingsmen, no wizard, and no Rydans. Sounds traplike. Very annoying."

Tohmas chuckled with a shrug. "I can take Gaidolons and Trullers with me," he said. "Or the men from Forsinth even," he added to Deiton. The man jumped at the name of his province but nodded like a puppet. "Lance," Tohmas continued, "I will need some—"

"I'll get a couple of squads to you," the Gaidolon Kingsman agreed at once. He let out a long sign. "I wish you luck, Tohmas. You'll need a miracle to convince either Wevan or his son you were not involved in the prince's domination."

"I'll pray for a miracle then," Tohmas replied. The words stuck in his throat slightly. With Celebrant Loni's recent execution, he had less confidence than ever that the Goddess Inac would be answering any of his prayers. But a feat of arms would be hard-pressed to cross the Black Marsh and push out Damoria's forces. Words were better here than swords. He just had to believe it.

Loni watched through Tohmas' eyes when it suited her. She explored in the moments between, following his memories back, watching his life in reverse, not caring how long it took. She found snippets from

him casting aside Chief Tamv's influence recently, then wandered back through the conquest of Espar from his perspective.

Reveling in battle, she brought up the Northlander War memories. Curious, she went farther back still, bearing witness to his arrival in Wayburn on a flea-covered horse from the Outlands. Farther back still was a war Espar had not known about—a battle between clans that brought down two of the three clans of the Outlands in the end. Tohmas fought countless battles, Carsh at his side, and Loni finally fully appreciated the extent of their bond. She followed their interactions back again, all the way to their first meeting outside a leaning wooden house, throwing stones at birds.

And there, it stopped abruptly. Beyond that memory, there was nothing but a white fog in Tohmas' mind, no matter how much Loni sought them. She had to conclude he had no memories of the days before meeting Carsh in the Outlands. No memories of Galanth, his family, growing up in a manor with a prince for a father ... nothing at all. A lost childhood.

She returned to the mind, listening to him plan a conversation with Prince Wevan's son, a final bid for victory when a strength of arms would be too close a thing.

I won't be alone for long, Loni decided. With her help, SoulBurner would overcome him and, in the end, claim every shred of his mind. It was just a matter of time.

In the back of Tohmas' mind, Loni laughed.

Loni curated his thoughts from that moment on, pushing aside the ones that did not suit her purpose. *Forget the Outlands,* she insisted. *Ignore them. Ignore all the thoughts that warn Chief Tamv would never walk away from a challenge. You're safe, of course you are. No, there's nothing spurious about Prince Deiton's odd behavior. You are invincible....*

She was looking forward to seeing Tohmas' surprise when the people nearest him betrayed him.

"What do you want?"

The question spun like a tethered raven in the depth of Shimmer's mind. At the end of its leash, the bird fluttered in frustration, but it

was kept distant by the rope that bound it. She had just awoken from her involuntary slumber when, with a victorious squawk, it broke free.

The voice sounded in her ear as she got to her feet in a vast space of perfect white. "What do you want?" it asked.

The answer was simple.

Shimmer felt a presence behind her, followed by hands on her hips. When next she heard a voice, it was Kitable's soft tone, although it was strange to hear him speak without irritation or disapproval in his voice.

"You amaze me, Miss Weaver."

"Shimmer," she corrected as the hands slowly started to make their way over her waist and up her sides. Every muscle he touched tightened under his fingers, and her stomach knotted. She felt her body flush from belly to cheeks. Her heart was pounding.

His touch was soft, entreating.

"Shimmer then," he agreed, and she trembled to hear him speak her name. "You amaze me, Shimmer," he repeated in her ear, his mouth close enough for her to feel his warm breath. "You are such a magnificent woman: strong, intelligent, beautiful..."

His hands walked up her ribs, and as he finished, he brushed the hair from the back of her neck, which sent a shiver straight down her spine. She swooned under the pressure, her stomach fluttering as if filled with drugged butterflies. She wanted to face him but feared disrupting this perfect moment.

"And a talented wizard as well," he added. A light kiss was placed on her neck, a warm caress she savored. She forced herself to breathe, trying to control her shaking ecstasy. "Here you were, all this time, and I nearly missed you."

One hand stayed cupping the side of her neck while the other wrapped around her waist, turning her to face him.

Everything about Kitable was glorious. Strong grey eyes that she had only ever seen pensive in her presence were filled with longing. For the first time in her memory, he was even smiling as he leaned toward her for a kiss.

The sensible part of her mind interrupted. As much as it hurt to say it, she could not deny the truth.

"This is not real," she whispered, pulling back from his embrace and wishing that speaking the words quietly would make them weak enough

to be untrue. But no matter how soft they were, they were more real than anything else in this blinding space of white. "As much as I want it to be true, this is not real!" she said, raising her voice.

But Kitable did not change. The feeling of hands on her hips remained.

"I can make it real," he said, but this time, his voice was not quite right. It was familiar, but it was not Kitable's.

She covered her eyes, trying to hide what she was rejecting. With tears creeping in, she pulled herself from Kitable's grasp and put her back to him. Her side went cold as his touch fell from her skin.

"No," she said softly. "No amount of magic can create love. You are not him. This is not real. I deny you."

When next the man spoke, the voice was entirely different. Although she did not turn, she knew Kitable, the man she loved, was gone.

"It has been done," the stranger told her. "He has done it."

"Impossible," she refused, wishing she could doubt that statement.

"But he accomplishes the impossible on an almost-daily basis, Shimmer. If any can do it, it would be he."

She could believe that easily.

"How would he do it?" the strange voice asked.

Her head was beginning to hurt, a familiar pain she could not place. Gradually, she realized she did not know where she was or how she got here. The more she considered it, the less confident she was that she was anywhere at all.

But the throb of her head stopped her from following the realization through, and despite the distant ache of her skull, she found the reply to the question she felt she had to answer.

"There was a theory," she said, remembering the books as if they were before her. She'd read hundreds of tomes written by wizards, memorizing many. "If a wizard could alter the thoughts to change the definition of love in a mind to fit their thoughts of someone they did not love, they would believe they were in love."

"So it could be done," the strange voice said from over her shoulder.

Shimmer shook her head once more. "It is too complicated."

"But he is Kitable. He could do it, and if he could do it, so could you. I will help you."

"Even if I could get past his defenses—" she objected.

"His defenses are nothing to me," the voice declared boldly.

"It does not matter!" Her voice rose to a shout, and Shimmer threw her hands down to her side, catching them in the folds of her skirts. "It would not be love! He would just believe his disapproval of me was called 'love.' That is not the same thing!"

"But it would suffice. At least it does for King Tohmas."

The implications of those words were deep enough to convince Shimmer to turn. She feared seeing Kitable standing behind her once more, for she doubted she would be able to refuse him a second time, but when she spun to face the strange voice, she found no one.

"This isn't real!" she realized again with even more force. "None of this is real!" she screamed, her voice cracking. There was no echo in this place, her scream disappearing as if muted by thick blankets.

Her next thought was again the pain in her head, but to her relief, it came with a sudden flood of sensations. She was lying, she realized a moment later, on a stone floor with her back pressed against a wall and her hands bound.

The empty white space vanished, replaced by the regular blackness of her closed eyes. She could hear and feel. It all came back to her. She remembered coming to see the king's wife. She remembered seeing the magic around the unborn child, and, in a moment of clarity, she remembered the intrusion of three men, one of whom had cast spells at her. She had been knocked out by thought magic, she recognized now. The dream she had experienced must have been a spell. The headache was even familiar: the night before the raid on the Gaidolon border. No wonder she'd known the voice.

She had just taken stock of her position when she heard the voice once more.

"It can be done," the voice that had interrogated her stated. His footsteps withdrew from her. "By magic, he can confuse her thoughts until she believes she is in love."

"I knew it! So you can do it, Master Gannon?" another voice exclaimed. A host of other agreeing voices brought Shimmer's count of men to five.

"It means it is possible to permanently enchant a Tainted," the stranger from her dream—the master wizard—said. "That means I can fulfill Prince Deiton's wish. So his armies are ours without a doubt."

Shimmer was confused; Prince Deiton hadn't been brought into the conquest. He was family to the sons of Zayban by an old marriage although widowed now. What did *he* have to do with anything?

New footsteps approached, hard boots clattering on the stone floors. A hand smelling of sword oil touched her face. "So what do we do with this one?" a brisk voice said.

The hand ran down her cheek with a sigh, and Shimmer's stomach twisted. *Not helpless,* she silently asserted. *Never helpless, never again.*

"She's a pretty one," the man above her said, and she kept her grimace from surfacing. Men wanted participation: sleep was a sanctuary. She had to exploit her supposed slumber for as long as she could. If it was long enough, she could ready a spell. If she was lucky, and they did not heed the caster's warning, she may even be able to get a hovering defense up too.

"Pity she's a viper," Master Gannon's voice said. "If she speaks, assume she is casting."

The hand pulled from her cheek as the viper searched her memory for spells she could cast with her hands bound.

Arnika did not see where they took her, but she never stopped screaming for assistance. Why the protectors did not hear her, or why the magic-user among the kidnappers did not silence her as he had Valia, she did not know. No aid had appeared by the time they pulled the hood off her head. As she had not yet fully investigated the manor, she did not recognize where she was in the grand building.

The room where they finally released her was windowless, lit by lanterns, and seemed to be a prison of some kind. One part of the room had been sectioned off by bars to form a cage, and it was here they placed Shimmer's unconscious body, with the strange man in robes ducking in after her to cast more spells. Other people milled in this room and the one that opened on it. Although they did not wear their colors, she recognized some from Trulin. The others seemed to flock to Prince Dorakon as he chained Valia to the wall beside the cage and made a show of ignoring her venom-filled stare. The spell on Valia's throat had worn off or been dropped, for she muttered curses softly. Her fury at

her father seemed to choke her voice, but that was probably for the best. Arnika feared if Valia said too much, the caster would replace the spell, perhaps making it permanent, if such a thing was possible.

Once he was done, Dorakon headed through an archway into another room, his Gaidolons going with him.

As Arnika was placed on a hard stool facing the cage, the stone at her back, she realized Altana was still with her and free to move about. She decided upon a place beside Charger Granton as he sat at a small table nearest the door, and much of her cousin's behavior made sudden sense. Altana leaned affectionately against Denvan Granton's knee, but his hand on her shoulder seemed more possessive than loving to Arnika.

The thought of the two of them made Arnika's stomach twist uncomfortably. Clearly, Tohmas' convincing had failed to change Charger Granton's opinion. And Altana... how long had she known about this plan? How long had she been loyal to the Truller charger?

"Traitors," Arnika whispered.

Altana's head shot up, her pale face flushing in the lamplight. The hand on her shoulder visibly tightened, keeping her in her place at his hip.

"She is helping you, my Lady," the charger told Arnika, his voice short and factual.

Rage lifted Arnika to her feet, but the other Trullers forced her back to her seat against the wall. They were not rough, but neither were they willing to be gentle enough to let her confront Charger Granton properly.

"You have kidnapped me!" Arnika accused. "How is that helping? You are betraying your king!"

"You are sick," Altana objected meekly. "He has bewitched—"

Arnika slammed her fist into the wall behind her in frustration, and the gesture interrupted her younger cousin's half-formed insistence.

"I am not sick!" Arnika objected as the Trullers, remaining within easy reach of her, withdrew their hands now that she was not actively fighting them. She used her voice instead. "I am not bewitched! You are putting all of our lives in danger! How dare you!"

Her shouts made Altana shrink back, and Arnika felt vindicated.

Bristling, the charger stared across at Arnika. "Do you love him?" he inquired, and that, more than his tone or the proximity of the strangers, made Arnika's tirade stop.

Do I?

When she had married Tohmas, the answer had been a simple "no." But after almost a mooncycle as his wife, she did not know the answer anymore. She knew he loved her—she had seen that every day by the look in his eyes—but did she return the affection?

She thought of the nights with him. She thought of the child she carried and how excited it made her knowing she was to bear his heir. Was it just her pride at being able to fulfill the oath she had made to keep him loyal to her? Or was it that she wanted a child? She was the right age. All the rest of her family was gone. Was she longing for company and a new family, or did she want *him* and *his* child?

The last time they had spoken, he had told her to stay in Wayburn. While she had been furious at him for not trusting her to be with him, she understood now: he had done it to protect her. He was afraid, and rightly so. He was facing Damoria and Polthian on the border now, yet this room contained Trullers and Gaidolons. He had made more enemies than he even knew.

And that worried her, worried her all the way to her toes. She feared for him. She did not want a world without him in it, without his sneaky smile and calming presence. She closed her eyes, envisioning him at her side, his hands brushing her skin. A desire rose so powerfully through her that her breath caught.

"Yes," Arnika said in soft disbelief. "Yes, I love him."

Charger Granton snorted. "That's your evidence right there. Her mind has been altered. She is under a spell." But his voice was flat, not victorious. Arnika was unconvinced he believed his words, and by the way the other Trullers smirked and looked away, she was not the only one. It was a ruse, she knew. He was saying it for Altana.

The wizard leaning over Shimmer chose that moment to step away and leave the cell.

"It can be done," he confirmed with a tired sigh. The gem on his forehead, which had once been red, was now a gentle blue. "By magic, he can confuse her thoughts until she believes she is in love."

"I knew it!" Charger Granton exclaimed, with echoed agreement and excitement from the others in the room. "So you can do it?"

"It means it is possible to enchant a Tainted permanently. That means this I can fulfill Prince Deiton's wish. So his armies are ours without a doubt," Gannon, the stranger with the gem in his forehead, said.

The caster went to the table, took the empty seat opposite Granton, leaned against the wall, and closed his eyes partially. Arnika wished she was a caster, if only to be able to tell what he was doing. He seemed to be facing *her*, but she didn't know why. There was no spell on her, she was sure of it. Why would they want anyone to be enchanted to fall in love?

One of the two men around Arnika left to check the cell, bent over Shimmer's still-sleeping form, and laid one hand on her head as if to check for fever.

"So what do we do with this one? She's a pretty one."

"Pity she's a viper," came the immediate reply from the caster. He did not move, not even to open his eyes. "If she speaks, assume she is casting."

The Truller ran his fingers down Shimmer's cheek with a sigh as Arnika struggled to remember his name. Bansin, she suspected.

The Truller rose, closed the cell door behind him, and locked it with a key that he tossed to the table, well out of reach of any of the women except Altana. He returned to his post next to Arnika.

Prince Dorakon returned from the side room, now armed obviously and carrying a sack. The Gaidolons followed behind him. He scowled when he saw the wizard sitting back.

"We need you disrupting their alliance, Gannon," he said grumpily. "You have better things to be doing than playing with emotions."

Gannon laughed, a sharp, high laugh that cut through the room and made Arnika jump. "King Tohmas has done my job for me, you will be pleased to know, Prince Dorakon. He has alienated himself thoroughly from the Rydans, so he faces your friend Prince Polthian and the forces of Damoria with limited support. It gets better every day; Damoria readies a trap for him, one he appears ready to walk into. We will see more of his support failing shortly. Prince Deiton has his forces supposedly allied with him and will be in a position to change the flow of power in a moment. I will confirm I can provide his payment; this Tainted woman will love him. We also have Rydans assisting us now, and the chief has shared some wonderful secrets I will disseminate." The man

laughed again. "The alliance is dead, Prince Dorakon. Your princedom is free. I will deal with Kitable, and my part will be done. As for yours..."

"I guess I have a job to do," Prince Dorakon said. His voice grated like riverbed stones. "You sure you're right about the location?" he asked the wizard.

"I would not send you after the Circle of the Raven, my dear Dorakon, unless I was confident. The unconscious one is in the city in the healing temple. Kill him swiftly. I will manage the distant affairs, assuming King Tohmas does not end himself for us. That is seeming increasingly likely as this day goes on!"

"Very well," Dorakon said. He nodded to the door, and the majority of the men, armed as he was, left swiftly. Two guards remained with Arnika, with the caster seated at the table, his hand lying flat against the rough surface and Charger Granton in his seat across from him.

Dorakon glanced over his shoulder as he reached the doorway, his stare finding his daughter. He frowned deeply, then called, "Calus, she's yours."

He walked out without looking back.

Arnika saw Valia's expression change from silent determination to solid stone when High Guardsman Calus Bosul entered the room through the side door. His grin became feral, his eyes fixed upon her like a stalking wild cat. Frozen as she was, Valia did not protest when he pushed her against the wall roughly.

"Leave her!" Arnika shouted, knowing well no one would obey her.

But when Arnika had expected fear, Valia's stone expression contained only hatred.

Valia's fist went up, but the high guardsman caught her wrist and slowly forced her hand down. Arnika thought Valia was losing until she realized the Gaidolon woman had just been waiting for the man's full attention to be on her fists to keep him from expecting her kick.

Her knee snapped up, caught him in the crotch, and knocked him, staggering, back.

"Does that actually still hurt?" She sneered brutally from the limit of her chain. "I didn't think you had enough left to feel it anymore!" She had to stretch to get her next kick, aimed at his head, to connect. It did not have much force, but it pushed him back a step.

Arnika couldn't help herself; she cheered.

CHAPTER 20

Altana paled and recoiled against the wall, looking miserable, and Arnika was not the only one to see it. No doubt the charger knew his support from Arnika's cousin—his way into the ruling family of Trulin—would wane if Valia were harmed unnecessarily. As Valia was adamant that no man would lay a hand on her without being castrated, the charger interrupted as High Guardsman Bosul made as if to approach again.

"Give her time to cool off," he suggested to Bosul. "Once Lady Trulin is back to normal, we can leave, and you can have the men assist."

The way Arnika's guards sidled away from Valia made her think they were not keen to go anywhere near her. They had called Shimmer a viper, but it was rapidly becoming evident that there was more than one snake in the room today.

Arnika didn't know how, but she wanted to make the count rise to three.

"There, I've got it," the wizard's voice said conversationally. His piercing eyes, which now matched the color of the shimmering green stone fixed to his forehead, landed on Arnika. His words chilled her through.

"Your turn."

Chapter 21

Something felt wrong as Tohmas traveled. More than once, he stopped to check his surroundings. By the third time, the guardian with him asked if everything was alright. The man was from Forsinth, with a long mustache that was drooping lower the longer they rode uncomfortably through the Black Marsh to the meeting place.

"Just a headache," Tohmas finally admitted. He felt as if his head was spinning. As much as he knew he should be watching his surroundings, he could not decide why and so kept dismissing the nagging suspicion that lingered. As a result, an ache had started at the front of his head and was getting worse.

"Shall we postpone?" the guardian—Tohmas could not even remember his name—inquired.

"The sooner this is settled, the better," he said, the thought becoming words almost instantly. He guided Schlavarai onward. He was not going far, and he had his men with him. Schlavarai was on hand, SoulBurner on his hip, and it was midday. He had done far stupider things! So why did this seem so off?

They found Warrah, Prince Wevan's son sitting on his horse beside the lone willow tree beyond the marsh, just as they had agreed. Again, Tohmas' mind wandered: the willow hung low behind Warrah, obscuring the distance. That seemed important but also irrelevant. His head throbbed again, trying to reconcile conflicting ideas. Why did everything seem strange today?

CHAPTER 21

"About time," Warrah said, and Tohmas pushed his headache aside to focus. They were similar, he and Warrah. Both raised to be strong fighters and carrying their bulk in their wide shoulders; both tall enough to mount a horse without stirrups, both with short cropped hair to keep it out of the way. They could have been mistaken for brothers under different circumstances.

"How is your father?" Tohmas replied. He had been hoping to talk to Prince Wevan after what had happened. He and Warrah had apparently fought since childhood although Tohmas could not remember any of those meetings. But the protectors had always believed Damoria and Galanth could never be allies; they had a long history of blood. His only hope was the older generation, the calmer one than Warrah and his hot-headed approach.

It took Warrah's glance to show Tohmas that Prince Wevan was present. In his yellow and red, the prince sat on a black horse dwarfed by Schlavarai's bulk, looking on from beside the willow's trunk. Tohmas had failed to notice him.

Although Tohmas and Warrah were similar, Wevan looked nothing like Tohmas' father Habal. He was squat and wide, with a thick belly that pushed against his yellow and red tunic. He wore no sword, looking more the part of disgruntled cook than a prince. But then, Tohmas realized, he had not fought in person for some time. With his son to carry the sword, he no longer needed to do battle.

That was good. Tohmas didn't want to fight either. But the sour frown on the prince's face worried Tohmas that he was in for a different fight.

"Well enough now, no thanks to you," the prince replied.

"I had nothing to do with your enchantment," Tohmas said patiently. "I broke it."

"A good story," Warrah interrupted, bristling like a porcupine, "but not the only one we have been hearing."

"Story?" Tohmas pressed, his head throbbing hard enough to blur his vision. He brought a hand up involuntarily before forcing it down in Rydan denial of pain or weakness. "You were there, Prince Wevan."

"It was the perfect setup," Warrah interrupted, keeping his father from answering. "Made you into a hero."

Damn. Warrah's already leading....

Despite the ache in his head, Tohmas understood. "Do you honestly think I arranged it? Why would you...?"

He stopped at the sound of a horn. Without turning his gaze from the two men in front of him, he heard and felt the movement of his allies. The nearby Forsinth soldiers were lowering their spears, but not at the enemy, at Schlavarai.

"I can hardly believe that worked," Warrah said with a laugh. "Off your horse. Hand over the sword." There should have been an "or else" to that command, but the rest of the statement was so obvious it did not need to be spoken.

Surrender and die, or die now... a voice said clearly in his head.

Tohmas' headache instantly cleared. Memories cascaded in, including the warnings he had overlooked, from Kingsman Deiton's sudden military support to Tamv's uncharacteristic lack of immediate retaliation. In his memory, he could even see the unease of the men who had come with him. They had known, from the beginning, that they were not there to defend but to take him down. He'd seen it.

Celebrant Loni's strike returned to his memory, and he understood. He had offended Inac. He had killed her celebrant. He would die for the insult.

Oddly, he felt he deserved it for a moment. The feeling passed in a blink as if it did not belong to him at all.

He heard a woman laugh.

Now, you understand, her voice said. *Now, I will watch you die.*

"How?" Tohmas stuttered.

The word was not directed at Warrah, but the prince's son grinned and answered, "People lie, Tohmas. People lie even under oath, like Prince Deiton. Get off your horse, and we will let her live."

Not that the horse would have returned the favor, Tohmas realized. Schlavarai was well aware that something was wrong and might have even been able to tell they were discussing her, for she tossed her head with a stomp of her foot to tell them what she thought of the idea.

For a moment, Tohmas envied the horse. To her, every fight meant victory. She did not believe there could be any alternative conclusion to a battle. There had never been before.

Consciously, he chose to follow her example.

You'll die, the woman's voice said in his ear, and he finally recognized it: Celebrant Loni. So this was her revenge, a ghost haunting him. *This is hopeless,* she continued. *You're a dead man, even if you deny—*

With a steadying breath, Tohmas pushed out her voice and the headache coming with it. There was blessed silence so long as he focused, and he would use that. He had enemies to kill. With the three ranks behind him training their spears, his best chance was forward.

He spared a moment to meet Prince Wevan's stare. "I broke my alliance with the Rydans because of what they were doing. If I am to bring Espar together, it must be done right. I hope you see that." He slowly unclenched his fists, readying to fight. He met Warrah's eyes next. "I will not be cut down like an animal. If I die, I die fighting."

Schlavarai lurched forward. With a shout from Warrah, arrows shot out from behind the veil of the willow. Tohmas blocked with his left arm—always faster than his right—and did not regret it even when the arrow sank into his forearm to the bone, knowing that the arrow had been about to take him through the throat. For now, he could ignore that pain with his life on the line.

His right hand found a side grip on SoulBurner, which was awkward and did not let him draw the blade but was enough to get the sword to glow for him. The next set of arrows was burned up, sparing him entirely, as he burst through the willow's hanging branches.

Ranks upon ranks of Damorians greeted him.

Maybe Inac is not so forgiving, he thought.

Schlavarai aimed and charged as Tohmas finally drew his sword fully, ready to die.

It took Gannon much longer than he liked to find the solution to the problem of permanently enchanting a Tainted, knowing their strange practice of sleeping overnight seemed to dispel them. The spell would have to pulse, the goal to have it return to the person after a dispel. He had learned the Renewing spell at school, but it had been some time since he had used it.

"You finished?" Denvan interrupted for the second time. Thankfully, he had, but Gannon still felt the need to roll his eyes at the man.

"If you people were normal," he pointed out, "this would be child's play. As it stands, it's tricky. You should be grateful I am as good as I am. I doubt any caster on your world could pull this off."

Angry at being chastised, the man replied, "Kitable has," by way of argument. "Supposedly," he added, glancing at the young woman at his side. The blond-haired girl was heavy-lidded by now; Gannon did not think she heard him, too close to falling asleep on her partner's lap.

"If he is doing it," Gannon corrected, "he is refreshing it daily. I will be putting up a spell that will renew itself."

To annoy them, he went back to reviewing his code. He was confident it was perfect, but he did not mind making them wait a little longer.

"Gannon," one of the other men interrupted, "your viper is awake."

Sure enough, although she had not tried to cast anything, Shimmer Weaver had risen to stand at the edge of her cage and was watching him from behind the bars.

He understood what Kitable saw in her. Fiery to a fault, intelligent and capable, Shimmer Weaver was a treasure. He wondered if Fantorn would like to take the girl to Wanter. Shimmer was not as powerful as Kitable, but she would be entertaining, and Gannon's vengeance would be enhanced by condemning the object of Kitable's affection to that fate.

It was too bad he intended to kill Kitable. Fantorn would have to be satisfied with the female counterpart.

"Well then, it is fortunate I have finished composing my spell," he replied, standing and moving to where it would be easiest to focus on the woman he had to define. The king's wife was, unlike the distinctive Weaver, plain. But she was unlikely to use an illusion at any level, making it easy.

The moment he knelt in front of Arnika, the redhead in the cage spoke.

"It will not work."

"Sit down and shut up, girl," he replied, "or I will put a Mute on you."

She raised one sarcastic eyebrow at him, a smile pulling at the corner of her mouth. "We call it a Vox."

The name surprised him. Wanter had replaced the term "Vox" during the Standardization Phase several hundred years ago. Here, the archaic word had survived, yet he knew the Tainted casters changed the spells they had inherited from Leugan extensively. He wondered briefly

which bits were preserved in their original form and which had been perverted beyond recognition.

He would not have time to investigate that, he admitted. Wanter would be happy with his work once the Northlander Circle was finished. And after that, any effort to return to the World of the Tainted would be scrutinized.

"Just get on with it," Denvan interrupted. "Tohmas ought to be dead shortly, which means Kitable will know something is up. I want to be out of here before he gets involved."

"Kitable won't do anything until I want him to. I've redirected his monitoring spell from Tohmas. Even if the king draws his sword or is attacked, Kitable won't know," Gannon corrected, his attention still on the Tainted women.

Gannon re-evaluated Shimmer as he spoke, trying to decide what to do with her. His wind spells were not bad, but it was not his strongest element, so silencing her would be annoying. He did not want to waste his time or energy managing her.

She helped him by tossing her hands slightly and turning away from them. "Fine, go ahead," she grumbled. "What do I care? She is just a spoiled noble brat."

She sat down with her back to the room, her eyes on the stones of the wall. As she made no further movement or sound, Gannon was satisfied. He kept an ear out for her casting but focused on his target.

The little Tainted woman, very much like Minet, squirmed when he went to touch her. With a wall at her back, she could not get far enough away to stop him from diving his magic into her mind.

There was nothing wrong with Arnika Galanth's mind. He knew perfectly well no magic manipulated her thoughts, at least not yet, but that didn't matter. They needed her to be receptive to Prince Deiton to be certain of his cooperation. It had long since occurred to Gannon that Prince Dorakon appeared to be doing what King Tohmas had attempted to do: bring together several princedoms under his control. The others knew it as well, he was sure, but so long as they got to continue to rule or, in the case of Charger Granton, started to rule, they did not care.

"Please don't," the young woman whispered.

Gannon ignored her.

As a result of being in her mind, Gannon was stuck seeing her thoughts as they came to her. More than anything, Arnika felt frustrated. The men who had brought her here had not had trouble catching then carrying her. Her attempts at helping her friends had fallen short. Shimmer had abandoned her. Altana had betrayed her. Only Valia had stood up for herself, a feat Arnika could not duplicate.

As Gannon sought the part of her mind that defined the word "love," he saw her frustration change to envy for Valia. Valia had fought. She alone had been strong.

"No!" Arnika snapped. For an inexplicable moment, he saw the flash of a braid of hair in a fire in Arnika's memory.

Gannon was ejected from her mind. It was so swift, it took him a moment to get his bearings.

"How do you people *do* that?" he exclaimed, replacing his hands on her head and pinning her against the wall. "A memory, one simple memory, and suddenly you manifest Tainted powers. Stop it! Hold still and be quiet."

He tried again, and she failed to replicate the expulsion although he saw her try. He weeded through her fleeting thoughts until he found the foundations of her mind, where she held her beliefs, ethics, views of self, and definitions. Sorting through them, he sought "love."

She shifted under his touch, he thought to adjust her position against the stone. Instead, she lunged and bit him. The need to withdraw his hand stopped his spell. He was ejected again.

He was bleeding when he checked his hand. One of her guards stepped up and struck her for the insult; it had not occurred to Gannon to hit her back. He had to admit that it seemed to be the practical thing to do, but people did not go around biting and hitting things in Wanter. They had far better ways of making their point.

Well, I don't need to touch her, he decided. It would take longer to channel it across the space between them, but it could still be done. He had to keep his distance.

He cast the spell for a third time and had just started to get tangled in her definitions of love (there were *how* many?) when a flare of magic appeared behind him, the guards were slammed back under a force spell. There was no time to think about the thought spell he was dropping for

the third time. The door they had so carefully locked and warded flew wide and admitted Kitable.

He is early, Gannon thought. He'd have to kill Kitable now and enchant Arnika later.

Kitable paused in surprise as he entered, his stare landing on Gannon. Gannon still benefited from the shielding the Watching Circle had established. If he had investigated the room before entering, Kitable had not seen Gannon.

Gannon read the wizard's defenses and cast swiftly. To his delight, his spell sliced through Kitable's meager thought shields and buried itself right into his mind. Gannon sent a potent destruction spell up next. It would only destroy Kitable's mind, leaving his body intact, but what good was a wizard without his brain?

He was eager to return to Wanter now. Wait until they hear how he single-handedly killed the Northlander Circle and the legendary Kitable! He would be leading the Watching Circle by spring.

As Schlavarai shoved her way through the Damorians, Tohmas snapped the shaft off the arrow, leaving the head in his forearm. In that flicker of hope for escape, he had a moment of doubt. Why would they have made it that easy?

Turning along the slant of the slight rise, having managed to get through the first column of Damorians, Tohmas found himself facing Rydans in a long line.

So this is where the "story" of Wevan's enchantment had come from, Tohmas realized. No wonder Tamv had not been active; he'd been working to ally himself with other Esparans. Did he hold the same hope that he could control them adequately and still take Espar? Or was this now just vengeance, a chance to kill Tohmas for his disobedience? Tohmas spotted the chief among the mounted Rydans who were ready to intercept him, the chief's glower firmly set on Tohmas, here to witness revenge.

Schlavarai could have defeated any Damorian steed, but setting her against Rydan horses was a different matter. Even she could not outrun them all.

Despite knowing their chances of escape had gone from unlikely to nearly impossible, Schlavarai held her charge. They could not go backward. It seemed fitting that he would die among the Rydans; they had put the sword into his hand as a child and taught him to fight. They could be the ones to take it from him when he fell.

Some threw their spears as he approached, but SoulBurner's aura burned up the shafts, and none hit their mark. Once he was among the Rydans, their weapons reached for him. Knowing the charge had been lost, he dropped from Schlavarai's back, his chances best on the ground with her at his back fighting in the crowded chaos, using their great numbers against them. She would stay with him.

Tohmas lashed out, unseated a nearby rider, and slew him, then moved with the enemy's horse as it tried to get at him. SoulBurner fended off the incoming Rydans on his left while his knife guarded his right, his wounded arm working well enough through the dull pain. Despite clearing some space, Schlavarai became separated from him, but he could see her fighting for a way back to his side. He wished for a moment that he had a way to order her to leave, but no such command existed. She probably would not have heeded it.

Schlavarai gave an infuriated scream and went down. Desperate, Tohmas fought to reach her, but the enemies closed in around him, keeping him back. They were pulling away though, creating a circle to cage him among the bodies he left. The battle calmed. Only one or two attackers would challenge him at a time now, wearing him down. He was flattered by their compliment to his skills, although he feared it would not take as long as he would have liked to tire him out. He was still bleeding from where the arrowhead was trapped by his bone. A tingle had started in his arm, hinting that its strength was fading.

To his satisfaction, the first attacker underestimated SoulBurner's impossibly keen edge and died when he tried to block instead of dodge. At least, Tohmas felt he could cost them a good number of weapons and, hopefully, warriors before they brought him down.

But that was what would happen, he knew, as the second challenger slunk forward, dodged, and made Tohmas defend himself before sneaking out and letting another follow in. Tohmas might slay some of them, but he could not go forever. Carsh was too far away to answer

his call. Kitable should have come when SoulBurner was drawn, yet he was nowhere to be seen.

Tohmas was truly alone.

Run!

The word struck like a push from behind, not an audible shout but an idea striking him like a sling stone. Kitable was only vaguely aware of the blackness around him, of the darkness near the spiral, his mind clearly in retreat from the thought magic assaulting it. Before he could get his bearings, something nipped at Kitable's heels.

He broke into a run, fleeing from the attack. Tril was at his side within a stride, belying his age by sprinting faster than Kitable could follow through the darkness. The wolf was on his heel—he glimpsed her white fur when he glanced back.

But coming up from behind her was a tremendous gusting spell of orange thought magic. The sight of it shot fear through Kitable. As the wolf snapped at it, trying to fend it off, Kitable fled, feeling it gaining like the pursuit of a wildcat.

Then, just as the magic created pressure between his shoulder blades, Kitable stumbled out of the darkness and into the golden light. He careened into Tril, who had stopped within the golden Dreamworld. Kitable crashed, tripping and falling through the golden mist into a grove of trees.

Lying on his back in a puddle of rainwater and staring up at a canopy of ancient trees, Kitable let out a long breath. He should have been winded, but it seems the panic and flight of his mind had nothing to do with his physical form. He was tired but physically fine as he pushed himself up. His robes stuck to him in the cool air.

Tril walked out between the trees, grinning from ear to ear, his wolf at his side.

"I didn't see him," Kitable confessed, events catching up with him. "Shimmer warned me that Arnika was in trouble. I checked the room, Tril, and I didn't see the caster! Gannon was right there! He knew I was coming!"

"Yes," Tril said, "the Watching Circle has ways of hiding."

"So..." Kitable pivoted, searching the grove he stood within. The trees were odd here; these were not species he was familiar with. Even the smell of them was different, colder. "A dream? Am I hiding in a dream? He's going to kill me if I linger. I am dispelled!"

Tril shrugged. "Time doesn't move the same in dreams, Kitable."

"Fair... but now what?"

A shape appeared behind Tril, trailing golden light as it stepped into the grove. The form became a short woman dressed in a white shift, a golden mark on her forehead shining in the late sunlight of the forest. Her steps moved without the barest trace of sound as she stepped up behind the Northlander. Without turning, Tril seemed to know she was there, and he gave a sigh that dropped his shoulders. His smile was instantly gone.

"Time to go, Tril," the woman said in a deep alto. "If you wait any longer..."

"There is never enough time," Tril said. "I am sorry, Kitable. There was no other way, my friend. This is all I can do."

The complete lack of joviality in the Northlander stopped Kitable cold.

"I must go," Tril continued. "Visions have pushed me to my limit. I might have found a way out, but I must leave to use it. The Circle of the Raven will be divided. We are broken once more."

It was not the first time there had been a gap in the Circle, and it did not worry Kitable as much as the elder seemed to think it should. "Another can—"

The Northlander shook his head. "There will be no replacements this time. By the time another takes my place, Ela will die. Perhaps another thousand years will pass before any Circle can be completed in our world."

"Divinations are not certain, Tril, especially not so far in the future," Kitable objected.

"This one is," Tril said sadly.

"And the Watching Circle from Wanter?" Kitable pressed. The idea of losing their only defense against the strangers from the magical world sat poorly with him. Alone, he could not defend his world from Wanter. He was not sure how to defeat even one of their members.

"With the Circle gone, they have no interest in our world. One day," the Northlander confided, "they will come again, and you will get your revenge. Worlds will be different then. Times will be different. You will be different."

Sensing the beginnings of rambling, Kitable interrupted, "And what about now?" His gaze searched the trees, the soft northern light that sent long, cool shadows between the trunks with the bark that hung off them in strips. "How do I stop Gannon?"

"Tril, they are approaching your body," the woman warned.

Tril nodded. "Enemies approach, Kitable. Just remember: you are not alone."

Tril turned to follow the woman, who hooked her arm through his and led him away. "I am sorry to leave you, my friend," Tril called over his shoulder. "I wish I could be present to see your great adventures."

"I do not want adventures!" Kitable called back as a break in the woods surrounding them turned golden. The pair walked out into the gold light of the Dreamworld.

Not alone, Kitable reminded himself as the grove faded. He was entirely dispelled, and an enemy wizard was right in front of him, one spell away from killing him. He could not retreat into the Dreamworld if the wizard tried to kill his body instead of his mind. He would have only a moment to act.

The basement cell came into view.

Chapter 22

Feeling Tohmas would want to speak to the kingsmen once he returned, they had not dispersed after the king sought Warrah and his father. Instead, Sol invited all the kingsmen to stay for drinks. With Carsh joining them, they sat around the table talking about the war and what they planned to do when it ended.

They were all family men, Sol discovered. Lance was the newest to be married, and even he was keen to have children. They were all surprised when Carsh admitted he would have his family soon enough too. They asked him about the woman who had struggled against the chief's men and been wounded, but he told them that nothing would slow Darcina down. She would be healthy shortly, and then they would have their family.

The mood continued to be light until Carsh's single knife became two, and he sat up sharply. They all knew that meant a caster or other threat was nearby, but nothing happened for a long moment. Carsh's eyes seemed to track something above, which then slowly lowered onto the table.

Words appeared, burned by magic into the wood.

Tohmas is in danger.

Silence fell over them.

"Now?" someone asked, but Carsh was already heading for the exit, and Sol scrambled to follow.

The Rydan whistled, and his magnificent black horse rushed over, the protectors not far behind. Before he could mount, however, a horn sounded.

"Divide," Sol interpreted absently, trying to think what the signal meant under the circumstances. It had no identifying caller.

There was movement among the ranks, then a horn of alarm. It took Sol another flicker to sort out what he was seeing.

The men Tohmas had collected at Forsinth were moving to join what he now saw were Damorian red and yellow forces on the marsh's edge. And they were not alone. A spattering of others had set themselves on the edges of the army and were now turning their attention toward their fellows. A large retinue of Polthian's blue and red soldiers was visible on the east flank.

"Trap," Sol grumbled. "Demon piss."

"Gentlemen," a meek voice cut in behind Sol, "we need to talk."

Sol turned slowly, confused to find the speaker was Kingsman Deiton. He'd hardly recognized the man's voice. Short of his oath, Sol wasn't sure he'd heard the Kingsman of Polthian speak this loudly.

"Not now," Lance interrupted on Sol's left. He spun to Carsh, who looked like he feared they would ask him to take command. "Take the protectors and get Tohmas. We will handle this." Leaving them to do what Tohmas had trained them to do, Carsh kicked Bashuran into a run, the protectors in his wake.

Sol spoke next. "Lance, your men take center; they're best against those horsemen."

"Then you take my riders to the west. It's flat enough for a charge," Lance countered.

"I'll take archers to the east hills," Barnon added as the next horn sounded.

"We'll set up reserves," Darknim added.

"Gentlemen," Kingman Deiton said firmly, "they won't attack until I send the signalor if I am cut down."

As one, the other kingsmen turned to stare at the timid man who had joined them late in the conquest. Sol stood unbelieving. He'd known Deiton since he'd been a quiet but successful merchant in the territories around his father, Zayban. He'd never understood what his sister saw in the man but had supported him because Zayban had

requested it. They had taken land for him. They had supported his claim to the central princedom, a pivotal piece of land that controlled trade on all sides. He'd been their brother by marriage.

But the man looking back at him was not the same one Sol had seen marry his sister Elinea. That man had been excited to join the family of Galanth. Now, the man looking at him scowled with disgust.

"How could you swear an oath and break it, you demon!" Sol snapped, blood rushing to his cheeks. He knew battle and commanding, but he had tried to leave his anger in his youth. Now, it all cascaded upon him. Furious, the only thing keeping him from strangling Deiton was the worry that the armies would attack if he did. They needed time to sort their defenses.

Deiton sneered. "None of us made an oath to 'King Tohmas Galanth,' Sol. You can't. There is no 'King Tohmas.' Habal's son died years ago. You swore an oath to an imposter."

Curses for Deiton died on Sol's lips. Beside him, Barnon was similarly afflicted, his mouth hanging open.

"Liar," Barnon choked out, but it lacked confidence.

"The fact that you have not replied," Deiton said, his stare on Sol, "tells me you doubt Tohmas' bloodline, Sol."

And despite himself, Sol knew the man was right. He did doubt. He saw so little of Habal in Tohmas. Tohmas, who struggled with Esparan, who seemed so much more at ease among Rydans, who never called him "uncle..."

"Tohmas Galanth was replaced," Deiton said. "The chief of the Outlands confirmed it himself. It was a lie from the beginning. Your nephew died. Chief Tamv replaced him with a slave so he could keep control. Through him, he planned to take all of Espar."

"*Dearn'd* man, we cannot trust a word you say," Lance cut in.

"Agreed," Darknim grumbled. "I do not have the patience for this."

But Deiton's eyes were on Sol and Barnon as if his words were exclusively for them. "He killed the other princes, Sol. He killed Kelland, Rairn, Dragal and even Habal."

The dismissal, readied on Sol's lips, paused when he heard his brothers' names. Even Lance and Darknim started back as if a blow had been directed at them. A chill ran through Sol, his anger extinguished by grief.

"I will swear it to the Flame, or to the Gust, or any other holy oath you want," Deiton went on. "It is the truth, Sol. Tohmas killed Rairn by poison. And he was standing beside Dragal when the arrow struck him, only no one saw the archer. What archer takes only one shot in those circumstances?"

"It was a Tanbie arrow—" Barnon tried to argue.

"Ask any protector," Deiton corrected. "Carsh had one stuck in his splint, then it was gone. And what of Habal? He died as if bleeding out, but the cutters could not find the source. The Rydan wisavi were in the room. They hid the wound Tohmas inflicted."

"Sol, Barnon," Lance said softly from outside Sol's line of sight, "remember who you are talking to! Deiton has just betrayed us!"

Before Sol could reply, images flooded over him. He felt the others nearby and inexplicably knew he was to share this experience with them.

Magic of some kind washing over him, Sol witnessed each murder, one after another, through Tohmas' eyes and mind, seeing everything he saw and feeling everything he felt.

He stood at the doorway to a Temple waggon. Prince Rairn lay within, shaking in fever and delirium as Tohmas, without guilt, replaced the poisonous tarol root in his pocket for later use. He felt no remorse for poisoning the prince; the man had betrayed him.

Next, Sol heard the news of Prince Kelland's death. The prince's death during the battle for LandWater had been an accident, one that grieved Tohmas. Had the prince lived, Tohmas had wanted to try again to convince him to join and avoid further bloodshed. He had admired Kelland, even if he had not agreed with him. Tohmas' hope for peace turned to the man's daughter.

Sol now stood in the shadows of a tent's awnings, overhearing Dragal's request that his brothers help him die in the upcoming battles. Sol and Barnon refused, but Tohmas' thoughts proved the younger prince willing. Not only could he honor the dying man's request, Tohmas wanted Dragal's illness out of his camp. He was determined to fulfill the dying man's request.

The scene shifted, the opportunity on hand. He and Dragal stood isolated behind a wall of protectors, their backs to a window. Knowing the murder would never be seen in the light he wanted, Tohmas used an enemy's arrow to deal the deadly blow into Dragal's back. With his

loyal Rydan prime protector, he created a ruse to fool the protectors into believing the shot had passed through the window.

Lastly, Tohmas sat with his father, Prince Habal of Galanth, in a small room, conversing with three Rydans. Tohmas' thoughts identified Bragn, the youngest Rydan, as the chief's son and so a form of brother. When Bragn suddenly drew a blade and stabbed the then-Prince of Galanth, Tohmas hesitated. His loyalty to the Outlands was plain in his mind, but his heart was torn to see his supposed-father slain. Tohmas' hesitation was seen as disloyalty, and Bragn turned the blade on Tohmas. Tohmas answered the only way he knew how; Bragn lay dead in a moment.

Flustered wisavis took Bragn away and disguised Prince Habal's fatal wound. Prompted by the wisavi, Tohmas watched in muted horror as the cutters tried to heal the injury they could not see.

Although Tohmas had been told Habal was his father, he did not know the man. Part of the memory wanted to feel something at the stranger's passing, but the more practical Rydan thoughts dismissed the death as inconsequential. There had been enough other deaths to make the current one irrelevant.

It took a long moment for Sol to get his vision back. By the uniform bewilderment among the kingsmen, it seemed likely the others had seen the same memories.

Truth, but lies as well. Now you know.

Hearing the voice of the Celebrant of Totho, Sol spun to find the four celebrants standing together beside the kingsmen, each frowning. When they had arrived, he did not know, but he was confident Celebrant Calanor had been responsible for the memories.

Deiton was pale as ash, clearly exposed to the same magic. In a faint voice, he said, "He is a murderer many times over. What makes you think he will spare any of you? There are no blood ties to protect any of us!"

A cold wind swept around them in the silence. Sol hesitated. The Damorian and Polthian forces, bolstered by Forsinth, would be a formidable foe. It still seemed possible that the combined efforts of the kingsmen would push back the attackers, but to what end? If Tohmas was already dead, the campaign was...

DoomDragon growled. "Prince Rairn could not be trusted. He fought for himself and no other. I never put faith in him, even when he claimed to be my ally. It does not surprise me that Tohmas felt the same. The man was a traitor more than once. If Tohmas had not done it, I would have."

"Prince Kelland's death was a mistake," Lance added. "Had he properly identified himself, no one would have harmed him."

"Dragal," Barnon surprised all the kingsmen by adding, "came north seeking death. He asked us for it, but we refused. Tohmas did not."

Silence fell as Sol turned the arguments and the visions over in his mind, lingering the most on the night Habal had died. He felt Tohmas' conflicting emotions, saw his confusion, and then shared his grief. Even if it had been a lie, Tohmas had believed Habal was his father. He had regretted the event.

The silence lingered. Sol realized the others were waiting on him, he cleared his throat and said, "It was not Tohmas' hand that stabbed my brother; it was a Rydan's, and that Rydan is dead by Tohmas' blade."

Deiton looked as if Sol had suggested the horses were not expected to walk. "He stood by and let his father be murdered!" the Forsinth man snapped with surprising authority.

Sol had never seen the man this livid. But then, Deiton had gambled against them, trusting that the truth of Tohmas' past would break the union. If he had guessed wrong, he stood to lose everything.

Sol's voice gathered confidence as he continued. "By your own admission, he is not my brother's son. All he did was watch helplessly as a stranger died. He was used by the Chief of the Outlands. It took him this long to stand against it. It is a miracle he succeeded even then!"

"But—"

Feeling the part of a kingsman once more, Sol drew his sword. "Nephew or not, Tohmas has pulled me out of more than one scrap. I'll ask him about it when I see him next." He glared at Deiton. "I intend to see him again shortly. Call off your forces, Deiton, or we will ensure none are standing by nightfall."

The remaining kingsmen drew their swords in solidarity.

"We swore an oath to a king," Darknim finalized. "I will not squelch on it."

"Neither will I," Lance and Barnon echoed.

With a teeth-baring grin, Barnon added, "Start running, Deiton. Because if we have enough time to ready our soldiers, you will die with the rest of your traitorous slugs."

Deiton hesitated only a moment more. Faced by the resolute kingsmen, he fled.

They let him reach the edge of the camp before dispersing to their ranks, from where they would control the defense of the camp.

The horns sounding an attack cut through the still air. The enemy moved in.

Arnika was too pleased with the success of ejecting the wizard from her mind to be worried about being slapped. She liked to think the changing colors of the man's gem was his frustration. If she could do it once, she told herself, she could do it again. The taste of blood in her mouth—she had bitten her tongue—was almost sweet.

The third time magic entered her mind, she tried to reactivate the force that had pushed him out but found it difficult to think about anything for more than a moment. One thought suggested he was blocking her, but even that idea did not last long. She could no longer remember what had worked to resist the magic, nor remember why she would want to.

But then the magic in her mind was suddenly withdrawn. The attacking wizard, Gannon, spun to face the door. More magic swept the men off their feet and into the stone walls, but it did not hit the caster. Gannon was standing at the center of the room when the door flew wide.

Armed men would shake their weapons at the enemy or flex their muscles, but Kitable had only to step forward to menace his opponents. Even when faced with the strange man with the gem on his forehead, his calm confidence did not waver. Magic exploded between them.

Arnika was instantly on her feet; she had had enough sitting around. Like an arrow, she shot across the room and snatched up the key to Shimmer's cage. A glance showed the dancer was at the lock already, but Arnika saved her a spell by tossing her the key as Denvan stirred by the bars. Arnika was at Valia's chains next, where she was stopped by High Guardsman Bosul, who had scrambled back to his feet.

When he grabbed her, Arnika dug her nails into his arm as hard as she could and drew blood. He did not seem willing to release her and was in the process of dragging her into a place as a human shield when Valia swung her chains like a flail into the man's head. When he released, Arnika pivoted, kneed him hard, then snapped her kick into his forehead as he bent forward. He flew back and struck his head against the wall beside Valia. She vindictively slammed her foot onto his chest, and he stayed down after that.

They had the chains off Valia shortly. Arnika grabbed the knife from Calus Bosul's belt.

"When will you learn to wear more thought defenses!?" Gannon's voice cut through Arnika's concentration, and her gut wrenched as she reassessed the conflict between the wizards. She had assumed Kitable would be victorious. Defeat for him had seemed impossible. Yet, to Arnika's disbelief, Kitable stood unmoving at the end of Gannon's pointed finger, his stare vacant.

Panic seized Arnika, her grip tight on the blade.

Something in the air snapped. Gannon stepped back sharply, allowing Kitable to fall onto his knees. The wisavi looked exhausted as he lifted his stare, first finding Gannon before him. The enemy wizard's face had twisted into a sickly snarl although his mouth was open as if the word "how" had become stuck.

Kitable softly said something as he broke the stare with Gannon and glanced around the room. It sounded a bit like "not alone," but it was too soft for Arnika to be sure.

He spotted her, his eyes dropped to the knife in her hand, and he nodded all in the time of a blink.

"Strike!" he called, lurching to his feet at Gannon. It seemed to take the wizard by surprise, and he stumbled back, into Arnika's reach.

She had not had many lessons yet with the blade, but she remembered enough to adjust her grip to be strong, brace her body and arm, and stab with conviction as the protectors had instructed her.

The dagger's point cut through the man's simple shirt and then through the flesh of his back. By some miracle, she missed his ribs, finding the soft spot between them and plunging the silver blade deep. He pitched away from her, a trail of blood following him down. Kitable was casting—Arnika heard his words—but before he could finish, the

enemy wizard collapsed onto the stone. The moment he touched the ground, he vanished.

"Contingency on unconsciousness!" Kitable snapped, the words making little sense to Arnika. "That's my spell, you bastard!"

Her heart pounding in her ears, Arnika spun in place. Valia kept vigil over Bosul, looking as though she might carve out his heart if he dared move. Belatedly, Arnika remembered her cousin had been in the room with Denvan. She found Altana under the table by the door, cowering and unlikely to emerge. Denvan lay writhing on the floor, Shimmer watching him placidly from the opened jail cell door.

Gingerly advancing to look down at the charger, Kitable cast quickly. His eyes changed, now draped in shifting colors. He assessed the downed man, who was starting to squeal and clutched at his groin in panic.

"A five-way alteration?" Kitable inquired. "Looks like a modified Reduction."

"It's area targeted," Shimmer said proudly, stepping out to stand over Denvan as well, "but only about so big." She made a circle about the size of an apple with her hands. "Works against men when I aim it well."

With sudden realization, Kitable winced. "Remind me never to piss you off! Impressive! But for his sake..." Kitable rattled off a series of incomprehensible words, and Charger Denvan went still. He was breathing but otherwise not moving.

"Kitable!" Arnika interrupted, pushing her way between Shimmer and Kitable, "they are attacking Tohmas! They said he should be dead by now!"

The wisavi's face went dark. He cast another spell quickly, and a light burst out, then vanished out the door and down the corridor. A red thread trailed behind it.

"This will lead the protectors to you all. I need to..."

"I warned the king," Shimmer interrupted.

"When?" Arnika demanded. Gannon had been watching her since she became conscious, and no one had heard her cast anything.

"When the oaf with the forehead jewelry was playing in your head," Shimmer replied. "What did you think I was doing? Admiring the masonry?"

Relief flooded in, and Arnika felt as though she could finally breathe after panting for the last while. Her heart still had to slow down; it pounded hard enough to make her body shake. She began to notice the blood all over her hand was drying, making her skin prickle. The smell was getting to her; nausea was rising.

Oblivious to her increasing discomfort, Kitable eyed Shimmer. "King Tohmas cannot be targeted so long as he carries SoulBurner. How did you get a message to him?"

Looking embarrassed, the dancer's hands played with the bottom of her blouse as she replied, "I targeted Carsh. Defined him by his bracelets, his knives, and the black root poison in his heart." Shimmer shyly glanced up to check for Kitable's reaction.

He stared at her as if she had just spoken Rydan. His jaw was half open for the brief moment it took him to shake his head in astonishment. "Have you ever considered making a proper study of magic, Miss Weaver?"

Shimmer's eyes went wide, and her jaw dropped. "Like an apprenticeship? Wha—"

Kitable waved her sentence aside, "Once I have dealt with Tohmas' apparent danger, talk to me about it. If you are inventing spells and casting under the eyes of a Wanter caster without his knowing, we should talk."

Turning to Arnika and leaving Shimmer in stunned silence, he continued, "I will anchor to the camp and seek Tohmas out, my lady."

"Take me with you," she demanded, grabbing his arm in determination.

He seemed to want to form an argument, but if Tohmas was meant to be dead, they could already be too late.

"Very well." He glanced through the room, taking in the unconscious high guardsman under Valia's heel and the charger lying at Shimmer's feet. As he did, a pair of protectors rushed in, stumbling into what must have been a bizarre sight.

"Protectors," Kitable said, "Lady Valia and Shimmer Weaver here have things in hand. Follow their directions in cleaning this mess up. I have no doubt there are others. Miss Weaver, feel free to use that Reduction spell if they don't listen." Shimmer blushed fiercely. "I am

TRAITOR

taking Lady Arnika to her husband." He placed his hand atop hers, still clutching his arm.

The last thing Arnika saw before the magic whisked her away was the protectors bowing their heads to Valia and Shimmer respectfully.

Her next sight was a camp in full activity.

From the place pinned in the Rydan circle, Tohmas slew enough warriors to lose track by the time fatigue seeped in. The Rydans let their tactic lapse, attacking him with an increasing number of opponents simultaneously. They did not dig deep but cut to bleed out his fortitude. His aching left arm had all but failed him now. In the end, a slash ripped across his shoulders, and he fell to his knees.

He could not rise.

"Back!" a familiar voice shouted from behind him. The Rydans obeyed, leaving Tohmas kneeling in the trampled grasses. He was in the shade of the willow tree, the light sliced into speckles by its multitude of tiny leaves. The breeze cut cold across his aching skin, the sweat catching it and turning it to near-ice. He lacked the energy even to shiver.

A fresh, deep pain burst through his shoulder, and the chief's *hooknye* appeared above his collar bone on his left, cutting through the arrow scar from Gaidol a year ago. Tohmas' grip on SoulBurner broke. The red aura vanished as he let fall the sword. Someone snatched it up, and someone else took the knife from his right hand. He could not stop them, his mind too shaken by pain and his body broken by blood loss to even recognize the Rydans.

Another slash cut across his back, angled shallowly. *Not aiming to kill, not yet*, Tohmas thought. He did not cry out, but the pain of the strike knocked him forward onto his hands. His left arm crumpled under him, but his right held him on his hand and knees. The pain intensified, building to an impossible strength until his mind seemed to let go of it entirely.

But where he expected to pass out, instead, his mind cleared. *Ironic*, he thought. The headache was gone. He was perfectly aware of the mistakes he had made to lead him into the trap. He had seen deception

CHAPTER 22

in the guardian's eyes. He had known the circumstances sounded con-trived. It had been obvious, and he had ignored it.

You will watch. You will suffer.

"I am chief." To Tamv's voice, Tohmas looked up. The chief stood before him, his garb of traditional Rydan hide left wide to show his tattoo. It seemed the red of his bracelets was uncommonly bright. Any more blood in them, Tohmas thought, and they would be dripping.

The chief sneered down at Tohmas. "I always win."

Tohmas shook his head despite how much it hurt to pull the mus-cles against the *hooknye* still in his shoulder. He saw it all now.

"You lose," Tohmas answered in a soft voice he had meant to make firm. "You cannot take them now. The Esparans are united."

He wanted to make the words convincing, but the ache of breathing broke his sentence into fragments. But he spoke the truth.

With his head lowered, Tohmas' eyes went to his damaged left arm. His hand had been scarred many years ago, but now the arrow cut his forearm, and, thanks to the *hooknye* in his shoulder, he had a mark there too. He had become Shoulder, Arm, and Hand in one. *More ironies.*

Feeling numb from fingertips to blistered feet, Tohmas dropped onto his right elbow. Out of sight under his hunched body, he grit his teeth, swallowed any cry of pain, and pulled loose the half of an arrow embedded in his arm. It brought the arrow tip with it.

He dragged his eyes up. Tamv was talking, his words meaningless and dismissed, until Tamv crouched in front of Tohmas, his eyes wild and his teeth bared like a mad dog. "I will take them. If I must, I will kill the Esparans, every last one. Think I can't use the flyers again? Your Esparans are pathetic. We can warp their minds as we did before. I will conquer them, and your name will be erased from all memory. Never my son. Never my clan. *Daern'd* man, you will be forgotten."

It was meant to be a threat but lost its potency in its falseness. Espar would remember him. He had made his legacy. The Rydan tradition of keeping the names of the damned from the gods did not hold in the north. In Espar, he was eternal.

"You..." Tohmas said, his voice coming in a whisper, "...you forgot."

For within three strides of Tamv was Prince Wevan, still sitting on his horse in the shade of the willow, his jaw clenched hard enough to

crack rocks. There was no doubt by the hatred in his eyes that he had heard Tamv's casual admission.

Tamv turned to follow Tohmas' stare, and into that lapse, Tohmas lurched up. The arrowhead in his bloodied hand dug deep into the gut of the immortal chief of the Outlands just under his dragon tattoo as he turned toward Tohmas. Opening his hand, Tohmas left the tip there as he collapsed.

Everything fell apart in his mind. Blood from his back, shoulder, and arm covered him in burning heat against his prickling skin. The cool breeze seemed to go through him and linger in his core like an icicle.

His vision blanked even as he fell. He heard horns; an Espar call to pull out, but all he could think of was how tired he was now.

The protectors had never ridden as fast. For the first time, every one of the horses matched Bashuran's speed. It was never going to be fast enough.

Carsh and the protectors found the Rydans standing beside a copse of trees in silence, a tall willow at the center of their circle. The protectors fell into an offensive formation, but it seemed unnecessary; no one appeared ready to fight. For a long moment, there was no movement. Eventually, Burlotak and his horse stepped out to meet Carsh. There was no Prince Wevan or Damorian forces to be seen.

Carsh checked the crowd, looking for his father, but saw only grim faces. Tamv should have been the one to confront him. And where was Tohmas?

"Bones," Burlotak said simply.

Carsh's heart shook until his chest ached. The Rydans moved aside, creating a corridor. The message was clear: Tohmas was dead. In honor of the dead man who had accomplished so much, Carsh was being granted the chance to attach himself to the spirit by collecting his brother's knucklebone.

In dismounting, Carsh's presence pushed the on-looking Rydans back several steps. He walked the corridor with Bashuran at his side and protectors in his wake, each still armed and ready for conflict. And there, under the falling leaves of the willow, Carsh found Tohmas in a pond of

blood. Schlavarai stood over Tohmas, her head lowered. Sliced muscles bled and stained her coat to match Bashuran's black, but she remained by Tohmas' side, her nose at his shoulder, as if grieving. With her master dead, none of the Rydans seemed to have any need to finish her off.

As Carsh approached, Tamv came into view, lying on his back away from Tohmas with his hands gripping a still-bleeding gut wound. No one moved to help him, and Carsh did not either. The injury would kill and explained at once why Burlotak had come forward. Burlotak would wait until Tamv breathed his last, then claim the red bracelets of the chief. There was no wisavi to be seen.

Schlavarai let Carsh approach and did not stir as Carsh pulled his knife to extract a knucklebone. His brother's wounds were extensive: a *hooknye* still embedded in his shoulder, a deep puncture in his forearm, and his skin nearly flayed with the cuts from a long fight.

Carsh's heart tensed again in his chest. For a moment, he felt unable to breathe.

Tohmas' spirit would be a good guide, he told himself.

But the muscles twitched under his touch when Carsh lifted his brother's hand. The weakened man drew breath.

Answering Carsh's shout, the protectors assembled, several dropping from their horses and pulling their supplies from various pouches. Before they could reach Tohmas, the Rydans closed in, Burlotak standing over Carsh.

"Bones," he insisted.

With Tamv dying, Burlotak's command was his alone, not the chief's will. If Carsh took the knucklebone and left, he would be accepting Burlotak as his superior.

Never.

One-on-one, Carsh thought himself the better fighter, but Burlotak was a strong Leader, and Carsh did not have his Followers.

He thought his odds poor until the protectors moved. As one, they spread out, clearing back the Rydans with a powerful shield push. One shouted, "We stand with you, prime protector."

They were the best of the Esparans, and Carsh knew they were a match for Tamv's Rydans. He would never tell them that, but it had become truth somewhere during the war.

Carsh refused to break the stare he held with Burlotak, making the challenge. Burlotak lunged, drawing his blades.

Carsh knocked aside the attack, thinking it almost clumsy. Burlotak was counting on his allies to press in, but the protectors had shields of solid wood and banding, holding the Rydans back. In a blink, Schlavarai pivoted sharply and drove both hindfeet into the would-be-chief of the Outlands from the side. He hit the ground and rolled but was unstable in rising.

Fearing nothing from Schlavarai, Carsh followed Burlotak down. While the protectors defended Carsh's claim, Carsh pounced on Burlotak, leading the attack with both knives. One was knocked aside, but the other hit the chest. It cracked into a rib.

Flung back by Burlotak's kick, Carsh had to adjust his grip on his knife as he was tossed through the air. He threw his blade as soon as he landed, immediately replacing it with one from his baldric. The knife hit below the ribcage, giving Burlotak a wound to match that of his dying chief.

When Burlotak fell, however, Schlavarai was on hand to shorten his suffering. She knocked him prone with a snap of one foreleg, then stomped both onto his chest.

Leaving the warhorse to trample the enemy, Carsh spun around to face the Rydans. The protectors had formed a defensive circle, but the Rydans disengaged instead of pressing them. It was clear Burlotak was not going to lead.

When no other stepped up to challenge him, Carsh had the protectors fetch their horses. Together, they rolled Tohmas onto Schlavarai and began the journey back to camp. No Rydan touched their blades as they departed. No one was brave enough to.

The body hardly breathed, and Carsh felt his chest tighten again. *Not dead, not yet*, he told himself. He hurried along as quickly as he dared, fearing every breath would be the last and ignoring how much his shoulder and arm hurt.

Kitable appeared in the bustling army with Lady Arnika at his side, picking a location back from the front lines but in a position to see the

many ranks engaged below. They appeared among the reserve, now consisting of soldiers with minor wounds that would not stop them from fighting but required some tending to start. In assessing the battlefield, it occurred to Kitable that there were more enemies than he had expected. Still, his first duty was to Tohmas. Inspired by Shimmer's idea, Kitable targeted Carsh with a Scry, not Tohmas, and quickly had an aerial view of a solemn march of protectors, Carsh leading with Schlavarai. Tohmas lay limp across his horse's back. The procession was already reaching the edge of the army, heading home. Whatever had happened was over.

As a protector held SoulBurner in the Scry, Kitable targeted Tohmas and Carsh and Relocated both of them to the nearest Healing waggon. He was content when, once Carsh got his wits about him, he dragged a group of cutters over to tend Tohmas. The healers rushed Tohmas within the waggon.

Kitable dropped the Scry, letting out a sigh. There was nothing for him to do now for Tohmas. Reading Arnika's anxious stare, he said, "I found him. Carsh is with him. I... I brought them to the Healing waggon."

Her face blanched, and he knew she had heard the words he had not spoken.

"I'm sorry," Kitable said.

She bit her lips, holding back tears, but nodded. "Finish this, wisavi," she answered, gesturing to the enemy army. "I will see to my husband." With an escort of wounded soldiers determined to defend her, she marched off.

"You heard her," said a disgruntled voice. Kingsman Sol had found Kitable and was now to his right. He gave the wizard a wide berth as if expecting him to flail his arms again. Mud clung to Sol's left leg below the hip as if he had fallen hard on his shield, and his face was spattered with blood. His mouth set in a grim line, his brow was deeply creased with worry and concentration. "We're losing ground fast on the east. Polthian's set polearms. And Forsinth split us down the middle."

"Wasn't Deiton on our side?" Kitable asked, trying to see what Sol explained in the banners and colors below. But in the thick of things, there were no clear ranks and divisions. It was now a mass of brown leather armor and sparkles of silver weapons.

"Was. Isn't now."

From what Kitable could see, the battle wasn't going in their favor. Vastly outnumbered now and divided by the Forsinth's forces, the kingsmen struggled to hold control on all sides.

"Right," Kitable said.

Casting quickly, he made a dragon burst into view behind the Polthian forces. Next, Kitable added the illusion of more Galanth fighters among the masses, setting his fake green-clad soldiers in the spaces. Allies would not bother with them, but the enemy would struggle to tell the real from the fake, distracting them. He hoped it would be effective. The veterans would recognize the ploy; he'd used it in campaigns with Habal.

Kitable was contemplating what new addition he could make when new horns blasted over the region. The effect trickled through the forces like a river suddenly pooling back off a boulder. The red and yellow of Damoria halted advances. A banner rode in from the back, the horns blasting ahead of it. As Kitable watched, Damoria heeded the commands and pulled back.

"Damoria's retreating," he said.

"Miracle?" Sol said bitterly.

"I doubt gods had anything to do with it," Kitable answered.

Through his tense glare, Sol briefly laughed. "You don't think he talked his way out of it, do you?" he said. "Did Tohmas convince Wevan?"

"Maybe," Kitable replied. He searched the masses, trying to understand what he was seeing. "If Damoria pulls out..."

"Then I'll trust him," Sol said. "Far crier! I've got new commands for you!"

Waiting drove Arnika to madness. By Kitable's tight words, she knew Tohmas was in trouble. But when she went to his side, she found the region around him too crowded. A lump in her throat threatening to choke her, she had to watch from a distance. There was blood everywhere, far more than she had ever seen before. A host of cutters, the Celebrant of Pari among them, tended to him.

At first, she was determined to watch, but as the blood continued to flow and the number of stitches they placed stopped being counted,

she shook too much to remain standing. With the protectors now in her shadow once more, she found her way into daylight, away from the metallic smell.

She stepped into twilight, the entire day gone. Most hard days, she considered in the softness of the sunset, were extended. When she had to do chores or make unwanted decisions, moments passed like candles, and the day seemed never to end, but this day of hardship had been short. Had it not been only moments ago that she had been in Wayburn, fussing over whether she carried a child? She felt as if the sun should be rising, not setting.

The battle had ended. The protectors who had entered the fray carried the news that the Prince of Damoria had withdrawn and, shortly after, offered the signed treaty. The provinces had to unite against their common enemy: the Outlands. But the Rydans had set camp apart from the others and were left in limbo until Carsh went to them. Arnika noted he returned bearing red bracelets but was quickly ushered into a tent by his wife, Darcina. While the men joked about all the rewards he would be receiving, something sat uncomfortably in Arnika's stomach. There was something about how quietly Carsh had gone into Darcina's arms and she into his that felt wrong.

Arnika contemplated seeking out the celebrants, but she could not bring herself to step into any of the Temple waggons. Every one of the four gods felt too distant to help her. It all came crashing down upon her in the silence of the early night. Even the protectors could not defend her from her sorrow.

With the evening air filling her lungs, her tears, held at bay for so long, fell. It felt as if every tear she had denied since her father's death was suddenly loose. Fear for her life, for the life of her husband, and fear for her child all swelled, filling her until there was no room for anything else. She collapsed to her knees above the battlefield, surrounded on all sides by defenders but entirely alone within.

At length, the tears ran out, and her fear with them. She'd never wanted this, any of it, but this was her world now. And as much as she hated the people who had kidnapped her and attacked her husband, she had to admit they had accomplished one good thing; they had shown her how much she loved Tohmas.

And so, after the newly lit stars peeked their way through the first brushes of darkness, Arnika stood back up, pushed her hair lightly out of her eyes, and took a long, shuddering sigh. She had to go back to him. With the battle finished, that was where she was needed.

As she approached the Healing waggon, she caught sight of Shimmer standing at the corner by the lit entrance. With a nod, the caster handed something to someone around the unlit corner. Whoever it was quickly retreated into the darkness.

Shimmer smiled when she saw Arnika. While the smile looked genuine, Arnika knew it had to be false.

"Just got in," Shimmer said. "Cast my first Relocation!"

"And what are you stowing in your bag right now?" Arnika asked. Shimmer had been slipping her hand back under the flap of her sack to replace whatever had remained after her shadowy transaction.

Shimmer pressed her lips in thought, then gave a slight shrug. She leaned in close to Arnika, and her voice dropped so low even the attending protectors would not hear her. "Darcina took some herbs for Carsh. His heart is struggling. She's got him resting. We'll—"

Shimmer's words cut off as the kingsmen left the Healing waggon in a pensive silence. "Later, my lady," Shimmer finished swiftly. She retreated down the dark alley Darcina had used, her cloak melding into the night.

The four men paused outside the Healing waggon, noticing her but seeming to struggle with how to respond to her presence. Lance came forward first, taking her hand gently in his. She hadn't realized how cold her skin was until his warm touch enclosed her icy fingers. "I have seen him take wounds as severe as this, if fewer in number. He never stayed down."

"But he did not even complain this time," Sol grumbled behind Lance. "Not a word! No telling Darak off for wasting his time or passing off the pills—"

"You are worrying his young wife," Darknim interrupted in his rumbling voice. Fixing his lizard stare on her in the gloom, he added, "Go see him, my lady. Perhaps you will enliven him."

Some part of her did not want to step foot in the waggon, for she feared the sight of him would bring more tears. Still, she knew she

would never forgive herself for abandoning him after fighting to come back to him.

Her head held high, she passed the kingsmen and entered the dimly lit waggon.

They had cleaned around him, and the blankets hid all his wounds except the stain of blood in the linens holding the great hole in his left shoulder. In the dim light of the lamp the healers were using to watch him, he looked like a ghost. His eyes sunken and his skin clammy white, she feared he lay dead before her.

But when she whimpered, he opened one eye and groaned. His hand lifted ever so slightly, and Arnika immediately reached for it. He was colder than her.

"I will ensure you are taken care of," he said. For the effort it seemed to take, it should have been a great shout, but the words were so soft she could barely hear them.

The promise only made her eyes fill with tears once more. "Don't you dare! I will not be left behind like this, Tohmas. I need you! I promised..."

"Forget your promise, my love." He closed his eyes as he spoke, lacking the energy to keep them open. "I will not hold you to it."

Stricken, she tightened her grip on his hand as she felt him distancing from her.

"You release me now," she objected with another tear. "You are too late, damn you," but even her curse lacked force.

With his eyes falling shut, she tugged on his hand and said, "How am I going to raise your son without you, Tohmas?"

Celebrant Darak arrived beside her, checking Tohmas' opposite wrist before she could find anything further to say. With a sad smile, he shrugged.

"He is sleeping. It has been a long day. He needs the rest."

Without letting go of his hand, Arnika pushed aside her most recent tears and asked, "Can I stay?"

"I will have a bed made at once."

She fell asleep holding his hand.

In the earliest part of the morning, Arnika woke groggily, wrapped in blankets with a hard pillow under her head. The bed in the Manor of Wayburn had never become familiar enough to feel like home, so

TRAITOR

her mind brought her back to Trulin instead, and she, for a moment, thought she was in her room, in her bed, alone.

Shuffling feet nearby made her sleepy mind wonder about the cats that used to chase the mice out of her room until someone whispered, "I have enough holes in me already. I do not need more."

The chuckle she heard was from Celebrant Darak, and she remembered at once the entire ordeal of the day before. Her hand was empty. She pushed herself up.

Tohmas lay in the grey light of the early morning, looking at her. "Demons," he groaned as he turned his head back and waved Darak off. "I told you not to wake her." Glaring at the celebrant as he started fussing with a new tool, the king grumbled, "Put that away, would you? I am not in the mood."

"But," the celebrant said as he carried on re-stitching a wound despite the king's disagreement, "you cannot do anything about it. Stop whining."

Wincing at the celebrant's ministrations, Tohmas gritted his teeth but then smiled. "Just wait until I can," he threatened.

"I will be elated when you can clap me upside my head, my king."

Tohmas laughed, then winced and stopped, breathless. Turning to her once more, he extended the hand she had dropped.

Taking his hand, Arnika held it to her chest.

"Arnika," Tohmas said, his whisper sounding stronger, "I heard you say something last night that made me very happy, but I cannot remember what it was."

She placed his hand onto her navel, lacking the words to explain. He squinted in the low light, his brow knit low. Seeing he did not understand, she stuttered, "I would have said anything to keep you, Tohmas. But this, this is the truth. Shimmer checked. I am pregnant."

Had he been strong, she knew he would have swept her up and kissed her, but from his place on the mat of the Healing waggon, he could do no more than tighten his hold on her hand and lay his head back with a smile.

"I hope she is as beautiful as you." He sighed as his eyes shut, and sleep seemed to retake him.

"I hope he is as steadfast as you," she countered, but he was already sleeping.

In the days that followed the battle on Damoria's border, there was no more fighting. Prince Deiton surrendered and was stripped of his rank and influence, while Prince Polthian was found dead in the dawn. Kitable could have tried to find out if the man had deliberately fallen on his sword as the surviving officers insisted, but it didn't matter enough to put effort into. With High Guardsman Prem the highest-ranked Polthian officer, the forces were dismissed to return home. Indeed, many had been unaware of the reasoning behind their march and battle and seemed relieved there would be no further war.

The Rydans crossed through the Black Marsh to the south and seemed to set up a new village, as they often did when moving about. Carsh emerged from his Esparan tent to resume his duties as Tohmas' prime protector, assigning Sabian to be his voice among the Rydans. Kitable didn't know what to think about the young woman Sabian called to join him, but she seemed confident in walking at his side as they plunged into the Black Marsh.

And that appeared to be the end. With all of Espar in his patron's hands, Kitable alternated between looking for the Wanter caster who had escaped and defending Tohmas. The armies, however, were released to travel home. Espar was united.

Tohmas began to recover, and he insisted he preferred the fresh air over the Healing waggon's stagnation. Kitable took the opportunity to enjoy the late summer sun, sitting on a barrel of water and leaning against the Healing waggon to keep an eye on his patron. He was reconsidering how to best contact Tril. He'd heard nothing of the Northlander except that the assassins sent to kill him had failed because no one could find him. As Kitable pondered how to find someone he could not see with magic, the protectors started moving aside. Since that meant either a guardian or a kingsman, Kitable sat up to watch.

What he saw, however, was not what he had anticipated. He knew Arnika had already recounted the tale of her abduction and subsequent rescue, in which Shimmer Weaver had played a central role. Still, seeing the overly defensive protectors usher the Weaver forward welcomingly was a surprise.

Tohmas either did not notice or did not bother to turn, the latter being more likely, but the woman's eyes were for Kitable only.

She stood before him in her colorful skirts and beaded headband, her wrists covered with golden bangles, looking the perfect part of a traveling showman. But her stare was stern when she demanded, "Were you serious?"

"Silly question," the reclined king said, but since the man still did not pivot in his seat, Kitable could not see the smirk he heard in Tohmas' voice. "Kitable is always serious." King Tohmas tilted his head toward the apothecary's daughter. "Any chance I get to know what he was serious about?"

Her stare was still on Kitable intently, leaving Kitable to answer for them both.

"Nothing you need to concern yourself over."

Tohmas settled back into his padded bed. "Then I suggest you go discuss nothing in the command tent. At least then you will not be intruded upon, and you can offer her something to drink."

It took him a moment to decide if he wanted to take the king up on the offer, but Kitable concluded that he would appreciate the privacy. Nodding, content that the defenses already around the king would keep even the Watching Circle at bay long enough for him to return if needed, Kitable led the way to the command tent nearby.

He could feel her glare as he walked away, but at least the creeping feeling of being watched confirmed that she was following him as he ducked between the two protectors and into the tent.

The enormous table was there, stained, dented, and burned. Kitable selected the two nearest chairs by turning them to face each other. He gestured for her to sit, which she did gingerly.

She did not speak but watched him with wide eyes.

Feeling awkward, he tried a light topic of conversation as he searched for wine among the king's chests. "Where did you learn magic?" he asked.

"My father," she replied.

"Demon shit," Kitable said. He found a wineskin, pulled the stopper, and confirmed the contents with a grimace before replacing the it. Wildwater was not appropriate. "You are three times the caster he is." He pulled a second skin and was pleased to hear it slosh instead of ooze.

"Once I showed an interest in it, my father made a point of acquiring any book he could on magic."

He did not have to look far for cups; they were next to the wineskin. "So both book-taught and apprenticed to your father," Kitable clarified, and Shimmer nodded stiffly while he put the cups on the table.

I'm making her nervous, he realized, but he did not know what to do about it. They had moved beyond that awkwardness at some point, but he did not know how. Having her fawn over him made him uncomfortable. How had they gotten to wit and warmth, and how could he repeat that effect?

"What about your mother?" he asked as he filled the cups.

He got a slight chuckle that was as tense as her clenched jaw.

"My mother would rather forget that I exist."

There was a story there, he was certain, but he did not think she wanted to discuss it, and he did not feel the need to press her.

"Any other casters teach you?" he asked instead.

Her head dropped with a small sigh, and although she smiled slightly, it seemed sad.

"That explains it," she said. "You want to know if there are other wizards out there. That is why you asked me."

He sat back abruptly, surprised by the conclusion that could not have been more wrong. "I asked you to talk to me because I thought you a talented caster with the potential to be an amazing wizard given some guidance," he corrected.

His reply, given matter-of-fact, made her start out of her slouched posture. Her mouth hung half open when her face paled. She was so seldom seen without a sparkle in her eye and a smile on her face, the absence seemed like a void.

"I have enough enemies already," he added before pushing one cup toward her and picking up the other. "I do not need to go looking for more."

"But... you..." She was not usually incomprehensible, so he decided to wait for her to finish the sentence. After a few more stutters, her shoulders slumped, and she shook her head. "It does not matter," she said. "No way I can afford an apprenticeship, no matter how..."

"The king provides everything I could ever need," Kitable interrupted. "Why would I charge you anything?" Her eyes went wide again.

"By the same logic," he continued, "I cannot reasonably pay for your room or board, so you will have to provide your own accommodations."

He had come close to making the offer before, but he had always talked himself out of it. Now, he could no longer find the words to argue it was a bad idea. Affiliation with him was dangerous, but she knew that. Further, she had survived every trial to date. She had helped him more than once and, through it all, remained the only caster in the world over that he actually trusted, even if just a little. And she had proven herself to be creative.

He wanted to give her the chance to do more.

Since her slack jaw seemed to preclude any further comment, he took a deep breath, made up his mind one last time, and formally said, "What I am suggesting is an exchange of services. I would expect you to assist in my work daily: coding spells, transcriptions, cleaning, investigations, defensive casting, and the like. In exchange, I will teach you until you run out of things to learn, or I run out of things to teach, whichever comes first. You must come to Wayburn, follow wherever I travel, do what I say, and..."

Her gaping jaw was beginning to grin, and finally, her smile surfaced. "You are serious!" she chirped, and he shrugged.

"Despite what the king says, I am not always serious. I am, however, most certainly serious in this." It took another deep breath and a sip of wine to settle his nerves sufficiently to allow him to continue, "This is not an offer I make lightly, Miss Weaver—"

"Shimmer," she corrected.

He paused. He could not have her correcting him every time he addressed her if they were to be working together.

"Shimmer, then."

His concession gave her courage, for she finally took the wine, and the sparkle in her eyes returned. His words came easier as she relaxed.

"I have never had an apprentice before," he said, "but your potential has intrigued me. You have a good mind for magic."

She beamed under the praise, but then her expression grew apologetic. "I am going to destroy your reputation."

"I do not see how. You have already proven that you are competent and highly intelligent and—"

"Not in skill," she corrected gently. "Wisavi Kitable, I am a dancer from Fixer City. Do you not wonder what people will think of you for taking me on? Your reputation—"

"I have never in my life worried about what people think of me." When he had been young, he had been too isolated to have anyone's opinion matter, and by the time he had been around others more often, it had been too late to train himself to care what people thought. He only worried about people's opinions when they might be trying to kill him.

This time, she laughed with a toss of her crimson hair. "As rare of a talent that may be," she said, "I believe you."

"So, are we in agreement?"

She took a moment longer, and Kitable's nerves tensed once more. He was unusually worried that she might refuse. He didn't need her around. He'd never *needed* an apprentice. But he wanted her to join him.

Finishing her wine, she stood and extended her fist.

"I will work for you as your apprentice," she agreed.

He stood to match her. "And I will teach you as much as I can in return. We start," he finalized, "upon our return to Wayburn, to give you time to get your affairs in order."

"Deal," she confirmed, and the knock of his fist against hers finalized it. With the greatest smile he had ever seen on her face, Shimmer skipped back several steps in half dance and laughed lightly. "You will not be disappointed. And do not worry that you have not had an apprentice before. Treat me as your master treated you, and we will be fine."

He chuckled and swallowed the last mouthful of wine. "Shimmer, I assure you that is the last thing you want."

Curiosity made her tilt her head, but he was unwilling to discuss it further. His wave sent her on her way. Soon, he was free to sit back in the chair and wonder if he had lost his sanity or found it.

THE END.

Sneak Peek of
A Tale of Espar
His Last Name

Chapter 1

L ying on her back in a pile of scattered pillows, most of which had slipped out from under her, Shimmer woke to the sight of a distinctive ceiling. The smooth, white wizard-stone of the new Manor of Trulinar above her was already marred by various stains, splatters, and two curious green lines she had never quite gotten around to identifying. There was nothing like it anywhere in the world.

If she had passed out on Master Kitable's floor, her master would be annoyed. Needing an excuse, Shimmer reviewed her memory of the most recent study session.

They had cast a Scry, the tricky art of moving one's consciousness and limited senses independently of the body. She remembered being extra careful because a kingsman's son had weaseled his way into accompanying them. They had come across wards, defenses left by a long-since dead wizard. Leading them, Shimmer had disarmed two Distraction Wards and one Memory ward, then approached a seemingly simple Dispel Ward. Then...

Her Dampening Shield pulsed nearby, and she remembered further.

Shimmer had accidentally set off a Fear Ward. Her Dampening Shield had taken half of it outright, but she had been subjected to the other half. It had knocked her out.

"Feeling better?"

She flinched upon hearing his voice but had been expecting it. The odds of Master Kitable being knocked out by any spell were slim. A measly Fear Ward had probably not even made him blink.

Sitting up, Shimmer found her master perched on a chair at the table nearby, teacup in hand. For a master wizard, he was young. Only fourteen years her senior, his beard showed little signs of the silver of age in the short blond trim. On most days, she enjoyed being the target of his grey stare, but today, his expression was a scowl, and she felt worse still.

Straightening her blouse as she rose, Shimmer replied, "I felt better when I was unconscious."

As a training wizard, Shimmer usually slept without dreams. The black of unconsciousness was refreshing.

Gaten Galanth lay in a slump in the pile of pillows, his contorted expression showing how much he did not share her opinion. Unlike her, Gaten had barely been brushed past magic thus far. He would be capable of dreaming, and with a Fear Ward in his recent memory, the dreams would be unpleasant. Rare people had died because of their imagined terror, especially if the spell had augmented any portion of the ward.

The boy was always scowling anyway. The grimace he wore in his unconsciousness was no different.

"Is he...?"

The stormy eyes of her master glared at her from over the teacup's brim. "You honestly believe I would let a kingsman's son walk around with us in a Scry without defending him?"

Taking to fixing her long auburn hair, Shimmer pointed out, "I did not expect you to let him tag along at all. And who knows? You can have bad days."

Glancing at where the boy still lay sprawled on the cushions, the wizard shrugged. "The king can be very convincing when he wants to be," he said, sounding bitter.

"But what my Dampening Shield let through was nasty enough. He didn't have a Dampening Shield. If the thought spell wasn't blunted..." Shimmer trailed off.

"I had a Full Deflection on him. Did you not check before we left?" Kitable's eyes narrowed. "Careless, Miss Weaver. Were you not aware that I am prone to having bad days?"

CHAPTER 1

"Full Deflections are dangerous!" she snapped, fear for him making her jump. "What if I had triggered a Death Ward?"

Slamming his cup onto the table, he came to his feet. "I would never have allowed you to walk into a Death Ward, Weaver!"

"So you let me walk into the Fear Ward?" she retorted. "How could you—?"

"You should—"

The groan from the floor stopped them both. Gaten rolled over, disoriented.

The boy would have no actual damage. With the Deflector up, all the magic aimed at their tagalong had been redirected at Master Kitable instead, then absorbed by his other spells. Gaten had been knocked out by his fear, but it had not been magically enhanced or even directly targeted in his mind. It was nothing like that which Shimmer had endured.

She would have helped him to his feet but knew the spoiled brat would resent her offer. It had taken Kitable's assertions to convince Gaten that Shimmer was indeed the wizard's apprentice, and it would take the same amount of influence to ever persuade him she was not the whore he imagined. He was one of the few who had connected Shimmer to her past. As such, she was a dancer to him, not to be trusted.

She suspected allowing Gaten into the session had been Kitable's way of trying to appease the boy and keep the secret. Shimmer did not need more of the nobility of Espar noticing her double life.

"Stay seated," Master Kitable told the boy when he tried to get up. "Take a moment to settle."

Rather than assisting, Kitable went back to his tea. Shimmer began rearranging the pillow around the circle they had been using. She knew the pattern; they had plenty of practice with falling over when performing a Scry. The position of each pillow was strategic.

"You know better than to use a Full Deflection," she grumbled at him as she turned away.

"You should know better than to walk into Fear Wards," Kitable retorted, both speaking too softly to be heard by their visitor.

At least Gaten got his desired taste of magic, Shimmer thought. Hopefully, he had found it sour and would leave it. Shimmer suspected that was what the master wizard had intended.

Kitable needed no other apprentice. He had never wanted one anyway.

Glossary

Barlaby: Far north princedom of Espar. Overrun by Northlander
    CURRENT PRINCE: Prince Lorian Rairn.
    COLORS: White and White.
    CREST: None

Calendar: Universal calendar pre-dates the Demon Wars. Roughly
  based on the moon's phases:
    YEAR: Eight mooncycles of forty days, and one mooncycle (the
      ninth) of a variable length, thirty-five or thirty-six days.
    MOONCYCLE: forty days.
    HALFCYCLE: twenty days.
    QUARTERCYCLE: ten days.

Celebrant: Esparan priest, traditionally assigned to a single deity of the
  four. Overseeing a group of Acolytes.

Clandac: Central Esparan princedom.
    CURRENT PRINCE: Prince Dragal Galanth. Eldest son of Zayban.
    COLORS: Blue with Gold.
    CREST: Scythe

Companion (Black rank rope): Esparan Companions are not soldiers
  by profession. They become soldiers when they are required, but
  have other occupations.

Currency (Esparan)

> LEG: Wedge-shaped copper coin with a hole in it for threading on a string.
>
> TABLE: Eight legs strung together.
>
> SLIVER: Wedge-shaped silver coin with a hole in it for threading on a string.
>
> SLICE: Eight slivers strung together.
>
> SPOKE: Wedge-shaped gold coin with a hole in it for threading on a string.
>
> WHEEL: Eight spokes strung together.

Damoria: South west princedom of Espar, corner of DragonTail mountains and Outlands. Enemy of Galanth.

> CURRENT PRINCE: Prince Wevan Damoria.
>
> COLORS: Red with Yellow.
>
> CREST: Dragon

Espar: The overall region north of DragonTail mountains.

Esparan (race): People of Espar. Pale skinned and featured peoples. Religion of four elemental gods.

Forsinth: Princedom of Espar, known for pottery and claywork. Close ally to sons of Zayban

> CURRENT PRINCE: Prince Deiton Darvin-Galanth. (Widower of Elinea Galanth)
>
> COLORS: Brown with Silver.
>
> CREST: wine pitcher

Galanth: Southern Esparan princedom on borders with Outlands.

> CURRENT PRINCE: Prince Tohmas Galanth. (Son to Habal Galanth)
>
> COLORS: Green with Silver.
>
> CREST: Tree

Gaidol: Princedom of Espar with prolific trading routes. Borders contentiously with Trulin. Close ally to Nothor.
 CURRENT PRINCE: Prince Dorakon Lodaton
 COLORS: White with blue.
 CREST: Shark

Guardians (Red rank rope): Each Esparan city had a single Guardian named by the Prince. A Guardian may or may not have a Prime status, depending on the size of the city.

Inac: Esparan fire god. Female. Also known as the Bitch Goddess, Dame Justice, Lady of Lust, Warrior Queen.

Knock: An Esparan gesture of agreement. Originally from a time of blood-bonds, where the two people would press their fists together and cut across the two hands to bind their words and spirits. More recently, no cut is used, just the knock of fists.

Lour: Western princedom of Espar along the Crescent and DragonTail mountains. Deep iron mines. Finest metalsmiths in Espar
 CURRENT PRINCE: Prince Loritat Naygan.
 COLORS: Gold with Grey.
 CREST: Anvil

Meloch: Far north princedom of Espar, currently overrun by Northlanders
 CURRENT PRINCE: Prince Garit Carnilan. Deceased.
 COLORS: Black with Red.
 CREST: Raven

Northlander (race): Race of the far north; a hardy people organized into clans but united by a Circle of the Raven, which comprises of magic-users. When the circle is complete (7 members), they name a DoomDragon (all clan leader).

Nothor: Eastern coastal Esparan Princedom. Known for shipping and mechanical innovation. Close ally to Gaidol.
> CURRENT PRINCE: Prince Neillen Lodaton.
> COLORS: Green with Gold
> CREST: Ship

Ocea: Esparan water god. Female. Also known as the Maiden, The Benevolent Mother, the Weeping Goddess.

Polthian: Esparan Princedom on southern border, close to Outlands.
> CURRENT PRINCE: Prince Emacen Polthian.
> COLORS: Blue with red.
> CREST: Eagle

Pari: Esparan earth god. Male. Also known as the Mountain King, The Beast Lord, The Traveler, Healing Presence.

Prime (single strand of silver in a rank rope): A distinguishing rank above the main associated one in Esparan ranking. For example, a Prime Protector would be one step above a protector and command them.

Protectors (Green rank rope): Bodyguards of a Prince of Espar. Commanded by a prime protector.

Rabarch: Esparan Princedom.
> CURRENT PRINCE: Prince Barnon Galanth (youngest son of Zayban Galanth)
> COLORS: white with red
> CREST: Dragon head

Rydan (race): Tribal people of the south Outlands, consisting of three clans (First, Second, Third), each ruled by a Chief. Primarily raiders and nomads, with a strong emphasis on horsemanship. Rydan horses are powerful warhorses, bound to a given master for life.

Solta: Central princedom of Espar, currently under siege by Northlanders.
    CURRENT PRINCE: Prince Sol Galanth (Second youngest son of Zayban)
    COLORS: Red with back
    CREST: Shield

Tanble: Northern Princedom of Espar, currently overrun by Northlanders.
    CURRENT PRINCE: Prince Vornan Marfaie (believed deceased)
    COLORS: Black with grey.
    CREST: Sword

Totho: Esparan wind god. Male. Also known as the Tempest, The Gust, North Star.

Trulin: North East Espar Princedom. Breeders of powerful warhorses.
    CURRENT PRINCE: Prince Kelland Trulin.
    COLORS: White and Brown.
    CREST: Horse

Wardens (Blue rank rope): Under the Guardians, these are permanent Esparan soldiers who guard the city and maintain the peace. The number of Wardens answering to a Guardian depends on the size of the city. If a call comes from the Prince, the Wardens become responsible for a company of ~20 companions.

Wisavi: A wise-man and advisor to a Rydan Chief.

Author Bio

At a young age, Deborah's rampant imagination kept her up, lending great detail to all the terrible things lurking in the night. In desperation, her mother suggested she invent her own stories to distract her brain. She has been doing that since, channeling her ideas into sword and sorcery-style fantasy novels and shorts.

In her other life, Deborah is a veterinarian. She lives in Sooke, BC, Canada with her husband of 13+ years, their two sons, and three demanding felines.

WWW.DLAMBERTAUTHOR.COM

INSTAGRAM: @dlambertauthor
TWITTER/X: @dlambertauthor
FACEBOOK.COM/DLAMBERT42

Book Club Questions

1. What options did Arnika have that didn't include marriage? How does this make her a strong/weak character?

2. Discuss Loni's character arc. Do you feel she was right? How do you feel about where she ended up?

3. Do deeds matter more than blood? Give examples of how that played out in *Traitor*.

4. Wanter casters do not dream. What impact might never dreaming/imagining have on a society?

5. Darcina and Carsh's relationship differs sharply from Tohmas and Arnika's. Contrast them. Are they both true love? Why or why not?

6. Who demonstrates the greatest loyalty to Tohmas in the series? Why did you make that decision?

7. How broken is Tohmas' mind? Is he fit to lead? Who do you think should be in charge of Espar going forward?

8. Which scene has stuck with you the most? Why?

9. What do you consider the biggest theme in this book? What scenes or characters best demonstrated that theme?

10. Would you read another book by this author? Why or why not?

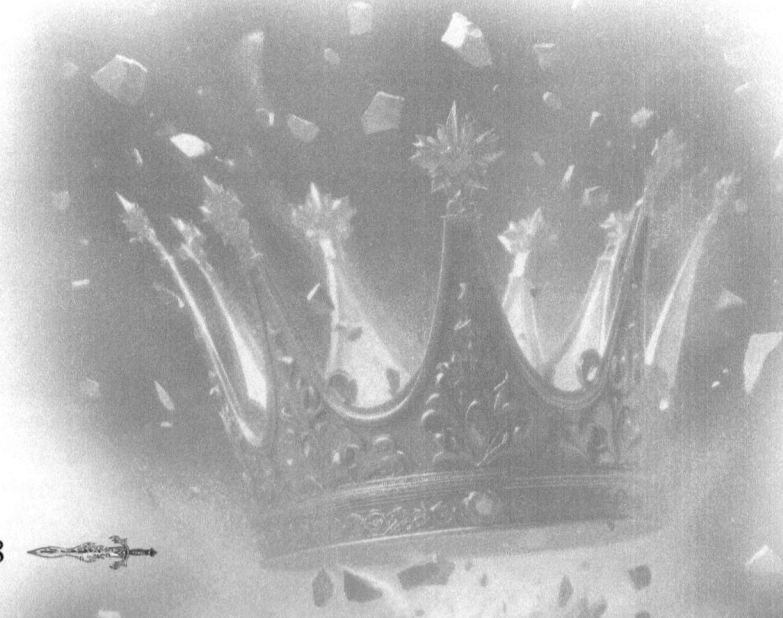

**Discover more at
4HorsemenPublications.com**

10% off using HORSEMEN10

www.ingramcontent.com/pod-product-compliance
Lightning Source LLC
Chambersburg PA
CBHW030239120726
47903CB00005B/1552